# TH

Robert Bloch was
and Stella Loeb, both
attended a screening o. ... ...aney film *The Phantom of the Opera* (1925);
the scene where Chaney removes his mask terrified the young Bloch and
sparked an early interest in horror. A precocious child, he was already in
the fourth grade at age eight and obtained a pass for the adult section of the
library, where he was a voracious reader. At age ten, in 1927, Bloch discovered *Weird Tales* and became an avid fan, with H.P. Lovecraft, a frequent con-
tributor to the magazine, becoming one of his favorite writers. In 1933 Bloch
began a correspondence with Lovecraft, which would continue until the
older writer's death in 1937. Bloch's early work would be heavily influenced
by Lovecraft, and Lovecraft offered encouragement to the young writer.

Bloch's first short story was published in 1934 and would be followed by
hundreds of others, many of them published in *Weird Tales*. His first collection of tales, *The Opener of the Way* (1945) was issued by August Derleth's
Arkham House, joining an impressive list of horror writers that included
Lovecraft, Derleth, Clark Ashton Smith, and Carl Jacobi. His first novel, *The
Scarf*, would follow two years later, in 1947. He went on to publish numerous
story collections and over thirty novels, of which the most famous is *Psycho*
(1959), the basis for Alfred Hitchcock's classic film. He won the prestigious
Hugo Award (for his story "The Hell-Bound Train") as well as the Bram
Stoker Award and the World Fantasy Award. His work has been extensively
adapted for film, television, radio, and comics. He died of cancer at age 77
in 1994.

ROBERT BLOCH

# The Opener of the Way

With a new introduction by
RAMSEY CAMPBELL

VALANCOURT BOOKS

*Dedication: To My Father*, RAPHAEL A. BLOCH

*The Opener of the Way* by Robert Bloch
Originally published by Arkham House in 1945
First Valancourt Books edition 2025

Published by Valancourt Books, Richmond, Virginia
http://www.valancourtbooks.com

ISBN 978-1-960241-34-4 (trade hardcover)
ISBN 978-1-960241-33-7 (trade paperback)
Also available as an electronic book.

Set in Dante MT

# Contents

# Chips Off the Young Bloch

In 1939 August Derleth and Donald Wandrei created Arkham House, initially to publish an omnibus of H. P. Lovecraft's tales as a lasting memorial to their literary friend. When Derleth's publisher Simon and Schuster suggested he should publish a collection of his own weird tales he'd submitted to them, he expanded Arkham House to bring out first collections by his colleagues in the field as well. Wandrei benefited, as did Clark Ashton Smith and Henry S. Whitehead. In 1945 it was the turn of Robert Bloch.

Like all the above-mentioned, Bloch was a correspondent and (more than most of them) a protégé of Lovecraft. The younger writer first read Lovecraft's work in 1927, at the age of ten, and they began to correspond six years later. The passing of two more would see Bloch's teenage tale "The Feast in the Abbey" printed in *Weird Tales* (written after his first sale, "The Secret in the Tomb"—praised by Lovecraft, but in his autobiography Bloch dismisses it as "a real bomb", and it isn't included herein). If the measured brooding prose and the lack of spoken dialogue owe a good deal to Lovecraft's example, the monks the narrator encounters seem related to de Sade's Benedictines in *Justine*. Bloch was seventeen when he sold the story, of which Lovecraft wrote to his correspondent William H. Anger, "I don't think he's done badly for his years. I saw the first draft of the 'Feast' about a year ago, & can assure you that the improvement in the present version is striking." I take the original to have been "The Feast", which Lovecraft called in June 1933 "a very clever union of the macabre & the comic." Did this first draft represent a youthful instance of the mordant wit Bloch was to develop? In the published version the climactic image is no joke.

Bloch sent Lovecraft his new stories, and Lovecraft often offered suggestions for improvement. Like Frank Belknap Long's

"The Space-Eaters", "The Shambler from the Stars" celebrates Lovecraft by casting him as a character. Whereas Long's was apparently unauthorized, perhaps designed as a surprise, Lovecraft famously certified Bloch's with a permissory document to placate Farnsworth Wright, the editor of *Weird Tales*. Is Bloch himself the narrator of his story? The depiction of a writer's struggles to develop feel personal—certainly authentic. Like the early work of other Lovecraft acolytes, the prose reads like a tribute to him too, though Bloch's style is already beginning to peek through. "A damned good story," Lovecraft declared.

These successes seem to have energized Bloch. In 1936 he contributed six stories to *Weird Tales*, four of them collected here. Lovecraft was prompted to comment, "You surely are one of the W T fixtures now!" He anticipated "The Faceless God"—"Shall be interested to see how good ol' Nyarlathotep fares in your hands!"—and declared himself duly impressed—"felt the potent menace of its atmosphere." Indeed, the extended finale sustains a nightmarish intensity founded on vivid specifics.

"The Opener of the Way" is a second Egyptian tale. We may note how we're in the tomb before it's opened, an inspired touch, and the incantatory alliteration Bloch had started to develop. Although the narrative is founded on Egyptian myths, it renders them more alien and hints at the cosmic, while the climax varies a motif at least as old as the Bible. Lovecraft was in favor. "Damn good! You generally manage to achieve the mood and atmosphere which the bulk of the pulpists altogether lack."

Does "The Dark Demon" enshrine Lovecraft as "The Shambler" did? Edgar Gordon's "able assistance, friendly criticism and kind assistance" that help make the narrator into a writer sound a good deal like his relationship with Bloch, and the physical description fits. His dreams resemble Lovecraft's too, and evoke his mythos. Lovecraft commented, "I guess I told you in my last letter how much I liked 'The Dark Daemon'," although either that letter is lost or Lovecraft's memory had begun to fail him.

"Mother of Serpents" is very much of its time, and would be dubbed casually racist now. Just the same, it achieves a memorable weirdness; the climactic manifestation seems sufficiently surreal for Magritte (who painted a similar image). You may predict that Lovecraft liked the tale. Following upon the reference above to "The Dark Demon", he added "I got a comparable kick out of 'Mother of Serpents'—whose Haitian atmosphere is convincing, & whose climax is magnificently clever, powerful, and unexpected."

It was the last tale on which he would comment. Shortly before his death in April 1937 he was sampling the January and February issues of *Weird Tales*. Bloch was devastated by Lovecraft's departure, but what can a true writer do if not write? 1937 brought six more stories to *Weird Tales*; two are here, though not "The Creeper in the Crypt", a title that sounds like a sly reference Bob would certainly have been capable of. "The Mannikin" is one of a pair of Bloch tales included in the April issue (the other, not collected here, is attributed to Nathan Hindin). With its Mythos references it could have functioned as a timely tribute to Lovecraft, who would surely have appreciated its grisly variation on the theme of the familiar. Indeed, this resembles the plot idea Lovecraft donated to another correspondent, Henry S. Whitehead, which he developed as "Cassius" some years before the Bloch.

"The Secret of Sebek" curiously twists the streets of New Orleans—in fact some of the straightest in the world—but perhaps the narrator's vision does, having been warped by his task of writing Egyptian tales for a magazine. A deft linguistic pirouette turns a gothic paragraph modern as it describes the enormous chamber in the mansion, and Bloch's mature style keeps making an appearance. Such shifts of prose are a frequent feature of supernatural horror (not just Bloch's), appropriately enough, since the past so often takes revenge on the present in them.

We have five of his six contributions to the 1938 *Weird Tales*. "The Eyes of the Mummy" starts by addressing issues of style and the narrative process, as if the author may be contemplating his own method. "Egypt had always fascinated me," as we've noticed, and I wonder if this began in 1932 with Karloff's mummified menace. Bloch's story is a sequel to "The Secret of Sebek", with which it shares its endearingly naïve narrator. He's nothing if not a true writer, compelled to continue typing as long as he can still find the keys. May we take the final lines as an early flourishing of Bloch's dark humor?

In "Slave of the Flames" we see Bloch's preoccupation with abnormal psychology taking shape, in a study of a psychopath that looks forward to his novel *Firebug*. The process of refining his prose towards his later style—pared down, sparely sardonic—is well under way. Whereas *Psycho* is a psychological horror novel with suggestive undercurrents of the occult (indeed, in broad outline a variation on Lovecraft's "The Thing on the Doorstep"), "Slave of the Flames" provides supernatural support for the protagonist's psychosis, in the form of one of Bob's villains drawn from history but rendered close to immortal.

"Return to the Sabbath" may sound like a reversion to earlier models, but proves to be the first of his stories of Hollywood. It celebrates the measured pace and careful detail depictions of the supernatural thrive upon—specifically the graveyard scene, which prefigures a similar resurrection in Mario Bava's *La Maschera del Demonio*. If the narrator seems as emotionally fragile as any of Lovecraft's, Bloch gives them ample reason to swoon and scream.

"The Mandarin's Canaries" belongs to a sub-genre popularized by *Weird Tales* and most famously represented by George Fielding Eliot's "The Copper Bowl"—stories of exotic torturers. Bloch's mandarin is an epicure of the sadistic, and sections of the tale display a disconcerting lyricism. Less a story of revenge than a conte cruel, the narrative mutates into a final flight of the fantastic uncommon for the form.

"The Eyes of the Mummy" may have done away with its Egyptomaniac storyteller, but "Beetles" shows his fate left Bloch's fascination untouched. Indeed, once the narrator comes out of hiding, several paragraphs into the story, he proves to be as enthralled as ever by this latest account of an Egyptian curse. Its grisly outcome finds an echo in E. G. Marshall's death by cockroaches in *Creepshow*.

"Waxworks" is another Bloch tale that turns on its opening sentences to critique them and its protagonist's view of the world. Is the author criticizing his own Gothic tendencies by implication—by proxy, even? The story maintains a tension between enmeshing us in the protagonist's perverse obsession (on which John Collier's "Evening Primrose" may be seen as a

gentler variation) and retreating to an ironic distance. If the coda
recalls the inferno in *The Mystery of the Wax Museum*, a film Bob
admired, it ends with a revelation grislier and more uncanny than
the scene that may have been its inspiration.

The next three inclusions take us away from *Weird Tales*.
"The Cloak" was Bloch's first contribution to John Campbell's
magazine *Unknown*. Campbell conceived the publication as an
irreverent alternative to *Weird Tales* and to Lovecraft's approach
in particular—his story "Who Goes There?" may be seen as his
take on the some of the themes of Lovecraft's *At the Mountains
of Madness*, serialized in *Astounding Stories* before Campbell
became editor—and the trio of tales Bloch wrote for him let
Bob's humour rip. "The Cloak" (which he described as "tongue-
in-cheek rather than fangs-in-throat") begins by dismissing his
earlier Gothic style, but soon expresses regret for the passing
of the sense of the uncanny, a victim of skepticism. Despite
the author's definition of the tale, it can't joke away its darker
supernatural implications, instead offering deft adumbrations of
them on the way to the chilly punch line. Alongside the original
appearance of the story an advert tempted readers to subscribe
and be rewarded with an autographed Joe DiMaggio Louisville
Slugger, its use left undefined.

The June 1939 issue of the short-lived *Strange Stories* may have
set a record for the greatest number of pseudonymous tales in a
single pulp publication—four of them, one credited to Tarleton
Fiske, in fact none other than Bloch, who contributed two tales
and a half (the last a collaboration with Henry Kuttner, himself
disguised as Keith Hammond). The Fiske is "The Seal of the
Satyr", and Greece instead of Egypt is the source of allure, as if
Fiske were a separate entity. I believe the inadvertent transformation central to the tale may be the earliest portrayal of how
painful shape-changing might be, an observation later made by
John Landis in his werewolf film.

Bloch wrote a scattering of science fiction over the course of
his career, and one of the earliest examples—"The Strange Flight
of Richard Clayton"—found a home in *Amazing Stories*. In the
Meet the Author feature he discusses creative technique. "If I
write a weird tale I sit in a coffin. If I write a western I do it on

horseback. (Wait until I get around to love stories!) In writing this science-fiction yarn I wore a space-suit—so called because the pants were several sizes too large for me." The story is as grim as his introduction is hilarious; it's a claustrophobic instance of his concern with extreme psychological states, and reads rather like a precursor of Barry Malzberg's *Beyond Apollo*, another study of interplanetary mental breakdown. The editor apparently felt it necessary to footnote with an explanatory paragraph the passage where Clayton loses his sense of time.

"The Fiddler's Fee" returns us to *Weird Tales* and reveals Bloch's love of music, Gothicized for the purposes of the tale: the initial description of Paganini departs diabolically from actual portraits of the composer (who, like Robert Johnson, was rumored to owe his talent to the devil, so that for years after his death he was refused a Catholic burial). I'm reminded of Ken Russell's uninhibited depiction of classical musicians, which Bloch's irreverent take may even surpass for wildness. That said, it's an inventive narrative, and cumulatively grim.

"House of the Hatchet" begins by reveling in Bob's way with dialogue (soon to flourish fully in his radio scripts for *Stay Tuned for Terror*) while it presents an uncommonly sour sketch of a writer's marriage, surely unlike his own. The story is a narrative about creating, and indeed withholding, narrative. For the record, the Raymond Scott Quintette cited in the original *Weird Tales* publication has become an unnamed swing band in the reprint, perhaps because it had turned into a big band meanwhile.

"Yours Truly, Jack the Ripper" pares Bloch's prose to the bone, giving a decidedly unconventional psychiatrist a voice. Despite his preoccupation with abnormal psychology, it was a profession Bob often distrusted, and how reliable may our narrator be? *Weird Tales* appears to have grown leerier of racism under Dorothy McIlwraith's editorship, since the first line of the verse attributed to the Ripper is bowdlerized to read "I'm not a butcher, I'm not a kid." Himself Jewish, Bloch restored the original wording in the reprint.

We end with "One Way to Mars", an enigmatically ambiguous account of a persecution, however complex. No matter how deep Bloch delves into the darker aspects of the mind, he generally leaves us in no doubt where reality can be found, but this time he abandons us deep in whichever kind of nightmare we conclude we're in—an audacious ending, both to the tale and to the collection, for which it was written at the behest of August Derleth.

In his unauthorised autobiography Bob wrote, "It wasn't easy for me to find twenty titles I felt would bear reprint in a genuine hardcover book which might be sold in real bookstores to actual customers." Its range demonstrates he chose well, I think. "The book came out, received good reviews, and served as another milestone on the road to oblivion." Now it serves to show how individual and accomplished his work had already grown. Let me lead the celebrations of its emergence from the tomb.

RAMSEY CAMPBELL
Wallasey, Merseyside
July 5, 2024

The *Oxford Companion to English Literature* describes RAMSEY CAMPBELL as "Britain's most respected living horror writer", and the *Washington Post* sums up his work as "one of the monumental accomplishments of modern popular fiction". In 2015 he was made an Honorary Fellow of Liverpool John Moores University for outstanding services to literature. His latest novels are *Fellstones*, *The Lonely Lands* and *The Incubations*. His Brichester Mythos trilogy consists of *The Searching Dead*, *Born to the Dark* and *The Way of the Worm*. His most recent collections are *Fearful Implications*, a two-volume retrospective roundup (*Phantasmagorical Stories*) and *The Village Killings and Other Novellas*. His nonfiction is collected as *Ramsey Campbell, Probably* and *Ramsey Campbell, Certainly*, while *Ramsey's Rambles* collects his video reviews, and *Six Stooges and Counting* is an appreciation of the Three Stooges. *Limericks of the Alarming and Phantasmal* is a history of horror fiction in fifty limericks.

# By Way of Introduction

*"Where do you get the ideas for your stories?"*

This is the question that haunts every writer.

The average author can provide a graceful and plausible answer. He is an "observer of life," or a "student of human nature." He is "interested in historical research" or he "draws on experience."

But what can the creator of fantasy reply?

*He* does not deal with life, but with matters beyond life. He cannot submit that he is a student of human nature—although *inhuman* nature is often a subject of his consideration. His historical research is confined to legend and mythology. And as to drawing on personal experience, it has not come to my attention that the tale of lycanthropy, for example, is pounded out on a typewriter by the paws of a werewolf.

No, the fantasy writer is hard put to answer this inevitable query regarding his source of inspiration. So hard put, in fact, that I have never read any attempt at explanation.

The usual preface to a collection of fantastic fiction consists of a dissertation on imaginative literature in general, and any consideration of the motives impelling the author in the creation of his own work is politely ignored.

But fools rush in where angels fear to tread. I should like to set down my personal reply to the eternal query.

Where do I get the ideas for my stories?

I can best explain by reminding the reader that a fantasy author is definitely cast in the dual role of Jekyll and Hyde.

Dr. Jekyll (the writer in everyday life) is usually a normal enough individual. His wife does not fear him, his children will not scream when he appears, and friends or business associates seldom tremble in his presence.

But when kindly Dr. Jekyll retires to the privacy of his rooms and crouches over a low table, he is transformed—by the simple alchemy of typewriter and paper—into the monstrous Hyde.

As in Stevenson's tale, the mask of humanity is ripped away; its very aspect forgotten by the being beneath. This creature, locked in a lonely room, knows nothing of the everyday world beyond. He has knowledge only of the worlds that *were* . . . that *will be* . . . and that *co-exist*.

A fearful wisdom, his. He knows what winds the witches ride, what spells the wizards weave. He has trafficked with the tenants of the tomb, and his body has lain in grave-earth beside the dreaded Vampyre. For him there are no secrets in a madman's skull. His are eyes that gaze unflinching on the dread glory of the Medusa. His ears echo to the rustlings of maggots at the feast; his nostrils are suffused with odors of the Pit; his mouth is shapen for the fulfillment of strange hungers.

By virtue of a weird cartography, he maps the fabled contours on the dark side of the moon, and those black gulfs beyond the uttermost star.

For, essentially, he is engaged upon the composition of a travelogue . . . the history of a voyage in the realms of pure imagination . . . a journey through a skull. And each tale is but a chapter in the endless odyssey.

Does this sound naïve, overly melodramatic?

If so, it is because frankness has long ceased to play a part in the personal depositions of author to reader. The author of fantasy, in particular, does his best to entirely conceal the emotional basis of his creative impulse.

Dr. Jekyll attempts to deny the very existence of Mr. Hyde.

But . . . Mr. Hyde exists.

I know, for he is a part of me. He has been my literary mentor now for more than a decade.

During this period, my life as Jekyll has been commonplace in the extreme. I have a home, a family, a regular occupation, friends; a normal schedule of hobbies and amusements. Despite the betraying evidence of a somewhat flamboyant sense of humor, I am sure those who know Dr. Jekyll regard him as a rather prosy fellow.

Yet Mr. Hyde is active, nonetheless. He has produced one hundred and fifty published tales of fantasy, right under the noses of family and friends.

It is a partnership which has proved both pleasant and profitable—and it would be ingratitude indeed if I allowed Dr. Jekyll to take the credit without proper acknowledgement to his *alter ego.*

The reader of this collection cannot fail to detect the evidence of two minds, working in partial synchronization.

In most of the stories assembled here, Jekyll is the conscious narrator. His style is often pseudo-scholarly, his imagery lurid and contrived. He is a conscious polysyllabophile, and his narrative technique owes much to the influence and guidance of the late H. P. Lovecraft.

But the inspiration comes from Mr. Hyde. He is definitely responsible for the basic theme underlying the stories as a whole ... the logical insistence that unpleasant consequences await anyone who meddles in matters best left undisturbed.

I fear, however, that Hyde must also share the blame for errors of taste and judgement. In his haste to effect some particularly ghastly revelation, he has ignored many literary niceties. He is impatient of polishing, revision; the recasting of episode or narrative in a more cohesive mould. For Hyde has never written for "posterity"—only for immediate reader-reaction. There are times, I confess, when the reader will shudder over the style rather than the content of these stories.

I can only submit that this is a matter beyond my control. If, some time, I can write a tale dictated entirely by the conscious personality of Dr. Jekyll, the result may be entirely different from any effort presented here. But, barring this possibility, the works published under my name will continue to exhibit the hideous handiwork of Hyde.

And when anyone inquires as to where I get the ideas for my stories, I can only shrug and answer, "From my collaborator—Mr. Hyde."

—ROBERT BLOCH

# The Cloak

THE SUN was dying, and its blood spattered the sky as it crept into a sepulcher behind the hills. The keening wind sent the dry, fallen leaves scurrying toward the west, as though hastening them to the funeral of the sun.

"Nuts!" said Henderson to himself, and stopped thinking.

The sun was setting in a dingy red sky, and a dirty raw wind was kicking up the half-rotten leaves in a filthy gutter. Why should he waste time with cheap imagery?

"Nuts!" said Henderson, again.

It was probably a mood evoked by the day, he mused. After all, this was the sunset of Halloween. Tonight was the dreaded All-hallows Eve, when spirits walked and skulls cried out from their graves beneath the earth.

Either that, or tonight was just another rotten cold fall day. Henderson sighed. There was a time, he reflected, when the coming of this night meant something. A dark Europe, groaning in superstitious fear, dedicated this Eve to the grinning Unknown. A million doors had once been barred against the evil visitants, a million prayers mumbled, a million candles lit. There was something majestic about the idea, Henderson reflected. Life had been an adventure in those times, and men walked in terror of what the next turn of a midnight road might bring. They had lived in a world of demons and ghouls and elementals who sought their souls—and by Heaven, in those days a man's soul meant something. This new skepticism had taken a profound meaning away from life. Men no longer revered their souls.

"Nuts!" said Henderson again, quite automatically. There was something crude and twentieth-century about the coarse expression which always checked his introspective flights of fancy.

The voice in his brain that said "nuts" took the place of

humanity to Henderson—common humanity which would echo the same sentiment upon hearing his secret thoughts. So now Henderson uttered the word and endeavored to forget problems and purple patches alike.

He was walking down this street at sunset to buy a costume for the masquerade party tonight, and he had much better concentrate on finding the costumer's before it closed than waste his time daydreaming about Halloween.

His eyes searched the darkening shadows of the dingy buildings lining the narrow thoroughfare. Once again he peered at the address he had scribbled down after finding it in the phone book.

Why the devil didn't they light up the shops when it got dark? He couldn't make out numbers. This was a poor, run-down neighborhood, but after all—

Abruptly, Henderson spied the place across the street and started over. He passed the window and glanced in. The last rays of the sun slanted over the top of the building across the way and fell directly on the window and its display. Henderson drew a sharp intake of breath.

He was staring at a costumer's window—not looking through a fissure into hell. Then why was it all red fire, lighting the grinning visages of fiends?

"Sunset," Henderson muttered aloud. Of course it was, and the faces were merely clever masks such as would be displayed in this sort of place. Still, it gave the imaginative man a start. He opened the door and entered.

The place was dark and still. There was a smell of loneliness in the air—the smell that haunts all places long undisturbed; tombs, and graves in deep woods, and caverns in the earth, and—

"Nuts."

What the devil was wrong with him, anyway? Henderson smiled apologetically at the empty darkness. This was the smell of the costumer's shop, and it carried him back to college days of amateur theatricals. Henderson had known this smell of moth balls, decayed furs, grease paint and oils. He had played amateur Hamlet and in his hands he had held a smirking skull that hid all knowledge in its empty eyes—a skull, from the costumer's.

Well, here he was again, and the skull gave him the idea. After all, Halloween night it was. Certainly in this mood of his he didn't want to go as a rajah, or a Turk, or a pirate—they all did that. Why not go as a fiend, or a warlock, or a werewolf? He could see Lindstrom's face when he walked into the elegant penthouse wearing rags of some sort. The fellow would have a fit, with his society crowd wearing their expensive Elsa Maxwell take-offs. Henderson didn't greatly care for Lindstrom's sophisticated friends anyway; a gang of amateur Noel Cowards and horsy women wearing harnesses of jewels. Why not carry out the spirit of Halloween and go as a monster?

Henderson stood there in the dusk, waiting for someone to turn on the lights, come out from the back room and serve him. After a minute or so he grew impatient and rapped sharply on the counter.

"Say in there! Service!"

Silence. And a shuffling noise from the rear, then—an unpleasant noise to hear in the gloom. There was a banging from downstairs and then the heavy clump of footsteps. Suddenly Henderson gasped. A black bulk was rising from the floor!

It was, of course, only the opening of the trapdoor from the basement. A man shuffled behind the counter, carrying a lamp. In that light his eyes blinked drowsily.

The man's yellowish face crinkled into a smile.

"I was sleeping, I'm afraid," said the man, softly. "Can I serve you, sir?"

"I was looking for a Halloween costume."

"Oh, yes. And what was it you had in mind?"

The voice was weary, infinitely weary. The eyes continued to blink in the flabby yellow face.

"Nothing usual, I'm afraid. You see, I rather fancied some sort of monster getup for a party—don't suppose you carry anything in that line?"

"I could show you masks."

"No. I meant werewolf outfits, something of the sort. More of the authentic."

"So. The *authentic*."

"Yes." Why did this old dunce stress the word?

"I might—yes. I might have just the thing for you, sir." The eyes blinked, but the thin mouth pursed in a smile. "Just the thing for Halloween."

"What's that?"

"Have you ever considered the possibility of being a vampire?"

"Like Dracula?"

"Ah—yes, I suppose—Dracula."

"Not a bad idea. Do you think I'm the type for that, though?"

The man appraised him with that tight smile. "Vampires are of all types, I understand. You would do nicely."

"Hardly a compliment," Henderson chuckled. "But why not? What's the outfit?"

"Outfit? Merely evening clothes, or what you wear. I will furnish you with the authentic cloak."

"Just a cloak—is that all?"

"Just a cloak. But it is worn like a shroud. It *is* shroud-cloth, you know. Wait, I'll get it for you."

The shuffling feet carried the man into the rear of the shop again. Down the trapdoor entrance he went, and Henderson waited. There was more banging, and presently the old man reappeared carrying the cloak. He was shaking dust from it in the darkness.

"Here it is—the genuine cloak."

"Genuine?"

"Allow me to adjust it for you—it will work wonders, I'm sure."

The cold, heavy cloth hung draped about Henderson's shoulders. The faint odor rose mustily in his nostrils as he stepped back and surveyed himself in the mirror. The lamp was poor, but Henderson saw that the cloak effected a striking transformation in his appearance. His long face seemed thinner, his eyes were accentuated in the facial pallor heightened by the somber cloak he wore. It was a big, black shroud.

"Genuine," murmured the old man. He must have come up suddenly, for Henderson hadn't noticed him in the glass.

"I'll take it," Henderson said. "How much?"

"You'll find it quite entertaining, I'm sure."

"How much?"

"Oh. Shall we say five dollars?"

"Here."

The old man took the money, blinking, and drew the cloak from Henderson's shoulders. When it slid away he felt suddenly warm again. It must be cold in the basement—the cloth was icy.

The old man wrapped the garment, smiling, and handed it over.

"I'll have it back tomorrow," Henderson promised.

"No need. You purchased it. It is yours."

"But—"

"I am leaving business shortly. Keep it. You will find more use for it than I, surely."

"But—"

"A pleasant evening to you."

Henderson made his way to the door in confusion, then turned to salute the blinking old man in the dimness.

Two eyes were burning at him from across the counter—two eyes that did not blink.

"Good night," said Henderson, and closed the door quickly. He wondered if he were going just a trifle mad.

At eight, Henderson nearly called up Lindstrom to tell him he couldn't make it. The cold chills came the minute he put on the damned cloak, and when he looked at himself in the mirror his blurred eyes could scarcely make out the reflection.

But after a few drinks he felt better about it. He hadn't eaten, and the liquor warmed his blood. He paced the floor, attitudinizing with the cloak—sweeping it about him and scowling in what he thought was a ferocious manner. Damn it, he was going to be a vampire all right! He called a cab, went down to the lobby. The driver came in, and Henderson was waiting, black cloak furled.

"I wish you to drive me," he said in a low voice.

The cabman took one look at him in the cloak and turned pale. "Whazzat?"

"I ordered you to come," said Henderson gutturally, while he quaked with inner mirth. He leered ferociously and swept the cloak back.

"Yeah, yeah. O. K."

The driver almost ran outside. Henderson stalked after him.

"Where to, boss—I mean, sir?"

The frightened face didn't turn as Henderson intoned the address and sat back.

The cab started with a lurch that set Henderson to chuckling deeply, in character. At the sound of the laughter the driver got panicky and raced his engine up to the limit set by the governor. Henderson laughed loudly, and the impressionable driver fairly quivered in his seat. It was quite a ride, but Henderson was entirely unprepared to open the door and find it slammed after him as the cabman drove hastily away without collecting a fare.

"I must look the part," he thought complacently, as he took the elevator up to the penthouse apartment.

There were three or four others in the elevator; Henderson had seen them before at other affairs Lindstrom had invited him to attend, but nobody seemed to recognize him. It rather pleased him to think how his wearing of an unfamiliar cloak and an unfamiliar scowl seemed to change his entire personality and appearance. Here the other guests had donned elaborate disguises—one woman wore the costume of a Watteau shepherdess, another was attired as a Spanish ballerina, a tall man dressed as Pagliacci, and his companion had donned a toreador outfit. Yet Henderson recognized them all; knew that their expensive habiliments were not truly disguises at all, but merely elaborations calculated to enhance their appearance. Most people at costume parties gave vent to suppressed desires. The women showed off their figures, the men either accentuated their masculinity as the toreador did, or clowned it. Such things were pitiful; these conventional fools eagerly doffing their dismal business suits and rushing off to a lodge, or amateur theatrical, or mask ball in order to satisfy their starving imaginations. Why didn't they dress in garish colors on the street? Henderson often pondered the question.

Surely, these society folk in the elevator were fine-looking men and women in their outfits—so healthy, so red-faced, and full of vitality. They had such robust throats and necks. Henderson looked at the plump arms of the woman next to him. He stared, without realizing it, for a long moment. And then, he saw that the occupants of the car had drawn away from him. They were standing in the corner, as though they feared his cloak and scowl, and his eyes fixed on the woman. Their chatter had ceased abruptly. The woman looked at him, as though she were about to speak, when the elevator doors opened and afforded Henderson a welcome respite.

What the devil was wrong? First the cab driver, then the woman. Had he drunk too much?

Well, no chance to consider that. Here was Marcus Lindstrom, and he was thrusting a glass into Henderson's hand.

"What have we here? Ah, a bogy-man!" It needed no second glance to perceive that Lindstrom, as usual at such affairs, was already quite bottle-dizzy. The fat host was positively swimming in alcohol.

"Have a drink, Henderson, my lad! I'll take mine from the bottle. That outfit of yours gave me a shock. Where'd you get the make-up?"

"Make-up? I'm not wearing any make-up."

"Oh. So you're not. How . . . silly of me."

Henderson wondered if he were crazy. Had Lindstrom really drawn back? Were his eyes actually filled with a certain dismay? Oh, the man was obviously intoxicated.

"I'll . . . I'll see you later," babbled Lindstrom, edging away and quickly turning to the other arrivals. Henderson watched the back of Lindstrom's neck. It was fat and white. It bulged over the collar of his costume and there was a vein in it. A vein in Lindstrom's fat neck. Frightened Lindstrom.

Henderson stood alone in the ante-room. From the parlor beyond came the sound of music and laughter; party noises. Henderson hesitated before entering. He drank from the glass in his hand—Bacardi rum, and powerful. On top of his other drinks it almost made the man reel. But he drank, wondering. What was wrong with him and his costume? Why did he frighten people? Was he unconsciously acting his vampire role? That crack of Lindstrom's about make-up now—

Acting on impulse, Henderson stepped over to the long panel mirror in the hall. He lurched a little, then stood in the harsh light before it. He faced the glass, stared into the mirror, and saw nothing.

*He looked at himself in the mirror, and there was no one there!*

Henderson began to laugh softly, evilly, deep in his throat. And as he gazed into the empty, unreflecting glass, his laughter rose in black glee.

*"I'm drunk,"* he whispered. "I must be drunk. Mirror in my apartment made me blurred. Now I'm so far gone I can't see straight. Sure I'm drunk. Been acting ridiculously, scaring people. Now I'm seeing hallucinations—or not seeing them, rather. Visions. Angels."

His voice lowered. "Sure, angels. Standing right in back of me, now. Hello, angel."

"Hello."

Henderson whirled. There she stood, in the dark cloak, her hair a shimmering halo above her white, proud face; her eyes celestial blue, and her lips infernal red.

"Are you real?" asked Henderson, gently. "Or am I a fool to believe in miracles?"

"This miracle's name is Sheila Darrly, and it would like to powder its nose if you please."

"Kindly use this mirror through the courtesy of Stephen Henderson," replied the cloaked man, with a grin. He stepped back a ways, eyes intent.

The girl turned her head and favored him with a slow, impish smile. "Haven't you ever seen powder used before?" she asked.

"Didn't know angels indulged in cosmetics," Henderson replied. "But then there's a lot I don't know about angels. From now on I shall make them a special study of mine. There's so much I want to find out. So you'll probably find me following you around with a notebook all evening."

"Notebooks for a vampire?"

"Oh, but I'm a very intelligent vampire—not one of those backwoods Transylvanian types. You'll find me charming, I'm sure."

"Yes, you look like the sure type," the girl mocked. "But an angel and a vampire—that's a queer combination."

"We can reform one another," Henderson pointed out. "Besides, I have a suspicion that there's a bit of the devil in you. That dark cloak over your angel costume; dark angel, you know. Instead of heaven you might hail from my home town."

Henderson was flippant, but underneath his banter cyclonic thoughts whirled. He recalled discussions in the past; cynical observations he had made and believed.

Once, Henderson had declared that there was no such thing as love at first sight, save in books or plays where such a dramatic device served to speed up action. He asserted that people learned about romance from books and plays and accordingly adopted a belief in love at first sight when all one could possibly feel was desire.

And now this Sheila—this blond angel—had to come along and drive out all thoughts of morbidity, all thoughts of drunkenness and foolish gazings into mirrors, from his mind; had to send him madly plunging into dreams of red lips, ethereal blue eyes and slim white arms.

Something of his feelings had swept into his eyes, and as the girl gazed up at him she felt the truth.

"Well," she breathed, "I hope the inspection pleases."

"A miracle of understatement, that. But there was something I wanted to find out particularly about divinity. Do angels dance?"

"Tactful vampire! The next room?"

Arm in arm they entered the parlor. The merrymakers were in full swing. Liquor had already pitched gaiety at its height, but there was no dancing any longer. Boisterous little grouped couples laughed arm in arm about the room. The usual party gagsters were performing their antics in corners. The superficial atmosphere, which Henderson detested, was fully in evidence.

It was reaction which made Henderson draw himself up to full height and sweep the cloak about his shoulders. Reaction brought the scowl to his pale face, caused him to stalk along in brooding silence. Sheila seemed to regard this as a great joke.

"*Pull* a vampire act on them," she giggled, clutching his arm. Henderson accordingly scowled at the couples, sneered horrendously at the women. And his progress was marked by the turning of heads, the abrupt cessation of chatter. He walked through the long room like Red Death incarnate. Whispers trailed in his wake.

"Who is that man?"

"We came up with him in the elevator, and he—"

"His eyes—"

"Vampire!"

"Hello, Dracula!" It was Marcus Lindstrom and a sullen-looking brunette in Cleopatra costume who lurched toward Henderson. Host Lindstrom could scarcely stand, and his companion in cups was equally at a loss. Henderson liked the man when sober at the club, but his behavior at parties had always irritated him. Lindstrom was particularly objectionable in his present condition—it made him boorish.

"M'dear, I want you t' meet a very dear friend of mind. Yessir, it being Halloween and all, I invited Count Dracula here, t'gether with his daughter. Asked his grandmother, but she's busy tonight at a Black Sabbath—along with Aunt Jemima. Ha! Count, meet my little playmate."

The woman leered up at Henderson.

"Oooh Dracula, what big eyes you have! Oooh, what big teeth you have! Ooooh—"

"Really, Marcus," Henderson protested. But the host had turned and shouted to the room.

"Folks, meet the real goods—only genuine living vampire in captivity! Dracula Henderson, only existing vampire with false teeth."

In any other circumstance Henderson would have given Lindstrom a quick, efficient punch on the jaw. But Sheila was at his side, it was a public gathering; better to humor the man's clumsy jest. Why not be a vampire?

Smiling quickly at the girl, Henderson drew himself erect, faced the crowd, and frowned. His hands brushed the cloak. Funny, it still felt cold. Looking down he noticed for the first time that it was a little dirty at the edges; muddy or dusty. But the cold silk slid through his fingers as he drew it across his breast with one long hand. The feeling seemed to inspire him. He opened his eyes wide and let them blaze. His mouth opened. A sense of dramatic power filled him. And he looked at Marcus Lindstrom's soft, fat neck with the vein standing in the whiteness. He looked at the neck, saw the crowd watching him, and then the impulse seized him. He turned, eyes on that creasy neck—that wabbling, creasy neck of the fat man.

Hands darted out. Lindstrom squeaked like a frightened rat. He was a plump, sleek white rat, bursting with blood. Vampires liked blood. Blood from the rat, from the neck of the rat, from the vein in the neck of the squeaking rat.

"Warm blood."

The deep voice was Henderson's own.

The hands were Henderson's own.

The hands that went around Lindstrom's neck as he spoke, the hands that felt the warmth, that searched out the vein. Henderson's face was bending for the neck, and, as Lindstrom struggled, his grip tightened. Lindstrom's face was turning, turning purple. Blood was rushing to his head. That was good. Blood!

Henderson's mouth opened. He felt the air on his teeth. He bent down toward that fat neck, and then—

"Stop! That's plenty!"

The voice, the cooling voice of Sheila. Her fingers on his arm. Henderson looked up, startled. He released Lindstrom, who sagged with open mouth.

The crowd was staring, and their mouths were all shaped in the instinctive O of amazement.

Sheila whispered, "Bravo! Served him right—but you frightened him!"

Henderson struggled a moment to collect himself. Then he smiled and turned.

"Ladies and gentlemen," he said, "I have just given a slight demonstration to prove to you what our host said of me was entirely correct. I *am* a vampire. Now that you have been given fair warning, I am sure you will be in no further danger. If there is a doctor in the house I can, perhaps, arrange for a blood transfusion."

The O's relaxed and laughter came from startled throats. Hysterical laughter, in part, then genuine. Henderson had carried it off. Marcus Lindstrom alone still stared with eyes that held utter fear. *He* knew.

And then the moment broke, for one of the gagsters ran into the room from the elevator. He had gone downstairs and borrowed the apron and cap of a newsboy. Now he raced through the crowd with a bundle of papers under his arm.

"Extra! Extra! Read all about it! Big Halloween Horror! Extra!"

Laughing guests purchased papers. A woman approached Sheila, and Henderson watched the girl walk away in a daze.

"See you later," she called, and her glance sent fire through his veins. Still, he could not forget the terrible feeling that came over him when he had seized Lindstrom. Why?

Automatically, he accepted a paper from the shouting pseudo-newsboy. "Big Halloween Horror," he had shouted. What was that?

Blurred eyes searched the paper.

Then Henderson reeled back. That headline! It was an *Extra* after all. Henderson scanned the columns with mounting dread.

"Fire in costumer's . . . shortly after 8 p.m. firemen were summoned to the shop of . . . flames beyond control . . . completely demolished . . . damage estimated at . . . peculiarly enough, name of proprietor unknown . . . skeleton found in—"

"No!" gasped Henderson aloud.

He read, reread *that* closely. The skeleton had been found in a box of earth in the cellar beneath the shop. The box was a coffin. There had been two other boxes, empty. The skeleton had been wrapped in a cloak, undamaged by the flames—

And in the hastily penned box at the bottom of the column were eyewitness comments, written up under scareheads of heavy black type. Neighbors had feared the place. Hungarian neighborhood, hints of vampirism, of strangers who entered the shop. One man spoke of a cult believed to have held meetings in the place. Superstition about things sold there—love philters, outlandish charms and weird disguises.

Weird disguises—vampires—cloaks—*his eyes!*

*"This is an authentic cloak."*

*"I will not be using this much longer. Keep it."*

Memories of these words screamed through Henderson's brain. He plunged out of the room and rushed to the panel mirror.

A moment, then he flung one arm before his face to shield his eyes from the image that was not there—the missing reflection. *Vampires have no reflections.*

No wonder he looked strange. No wonder arms and necks invited him. He had wanted Lindstrom. Good God!

The cloak had done that, the dark cloak with the stains. The stains of earth, grave-earth. The wearing of the cloak, the cold cloak, had given him the feelings of a true vampire. It was a garment accursed, a thing that had lain on the body of one undead. The rusty stain along one sleeve was blood.

Blood. It would be nice to see blood. To taste its warmth, its red life, flowing.

No. That was insane. He was drunk, crazy.

"Ah. My pale friend, the vampire."

It was Sheila again. And above all horror rose the beating of Henderson's heart. As he looked at her shining eyes, her warm mouth shaped in red invitation, Henderson felt a wave of warmth. He looked at her white throat rising above her dark, shimmering cloak, and another kind of warmth rose. Love, desire, and a— hunger.

She must have seen it in his eyes, but she did not flinch. Instead, her own gaze burned in return.

Sheila loved him, too!

With an impulsive gesture, Henderson ripped the cloak from about his throat. The icy weight lifted. He was free. Somehow, he hadn't wanted to take the cloak off, but he had to. It was a cursed thing, and in another minute he might have taken the girl in his arms, taken her for a kiss and remained to—

But he dared not think of that.

"Tired of masquerading?" she asked. With a similar gesture she, too, removed her cloak and stood revealed in the glory of her angel robe. Her blond, statuesque perfection forced a gasp to Henderson's throat.

"Angel," he whispered.

"Devil," she mocked.

And suddenly they were embracing. Henderson had taken her cloak in his arm with his own. They stood with lips seeking rapture until Lindstrom and a group moved noisily into the anteroom.

At the sight of Henderson the fat host recoiled.

"You—" he whispered. "You are—"

"Just leaving," Henderson smiled. Grasping the girl's arm, he drew her toward the empty elevator. The door shut on Lindstrom's pale, fear-filled face.

"Were we leaving?" Sheila whispered, snuggling against his shoulder.

"We were. But not for earth. We do not go down into my realm, but up—into yours."

"The roof garden?"

"Exactly, my angelic one. I want to talk to you against the background of your own heavens, kiss you amidst the clouds, and—"

Her lips found his as the car rose.

"Angel and devil. What a match!"

"I thought so, too," the girl confessed. "Will our children have halos or horns?"

"Both, I'm sure."

They stepped out onto the deserted rooftop. And once again it was Halloween.

Henderson felt it. Downstairs it was Lindstrom and his society friends, in a drunken costume party. Here it was night, silence, gloom. No light, no music, no drinking, no chatter which made one party identical with another; one night like all the rest. This night was individual here.

The sky was not blue, but black. Clouds hung like the gray beards of hovering giants peering at the round orange globe of the moon. A cold wind blew from the sea, and filled the air with tiny murmurings from afar.

This was the sky that witches flew through to their Sabbath. This was the moon of wizardry, the sable silence of black prayers and whispered invocations. The clouds hid monstrous Presences shambling in summons from afar. It was Halloween.

It was also quite cold.

"Give me my cloak," Sheila whispered. Automatically, Henderson extended the garment, and the girl's body swirled under the dark splendor of the cloth. Her eyes burned up at Henderson with a call he could not resist. He kissed her, trembling.

"You're cold," the girl said. "Put on your cloak."

Yes, Henderson, he thought to himself. Put on your cloak while you stare at her throat. Then, the next time you kiss her you will want her throat and she will give it in love and you will take it in—hunger.

"Put it on, darling—I insist," the girl whispered. Her eyes were impatient, burning with an eagerness to match his own.

Henderson trembled.

*Put on* the cloak of darkness? The cloak of the grave, the cloak of death, the cloak of the vampire? The evil cloak, filled with a cold life of its own that transformed his face, transformed his mind, made his soul instinct with awful hunger?

"Here."

The girl's slim arms were about him, pushing the cloak onto his shoulders. Her fingers brushed his neck, caressingly, as she linked the cloak about his throat.

Henderson shivered.

Then he felt it—through him—that icy coldness turning to a more dreadful heat. He felt himself expand, felt the sneer cross his face. This was Power!

And the girl before him, her eyes taunting, inviting. He saw her ivory neck, her warm slim neck, waiting. It was waiting for him, for his lips.

*For his teeth.*

No—it couldn't be. He loved her. His love must conquer this madness. Yes, wear the cloak, defy its power, and take her in his arms as a man, not as a fiend. He must. It was the test.

"Sheila." Funny, how his voice deepened.

"Yes, dear."

"Sheila, I must tell you this."

Her eyes—so alluring. It would be easy!

"Sheila, please. You read the paper tonight."

"Yes."

"I . . . I got my cloak there. I can't explain it. You saw how I took Lindstrom. I wanted to go through with it. Do you understand me? I meant to . . . to bite him. Wearing this damnable thing makes me feel like one of those creatures."

Why didn't her stare change? Why didn't she recoil in horror? Such trusting innocence! Didn't she understand? Why didn't she run? Any moment now he might lose control, seize her.

"I love you, Sheila. Believe that. I love you."

"I know." Her eyes gleamed in the moonlight.

"I want to test it. I want to kiss you, wearing this cloak. I want to feel that my love is stronger than this—thing. If I weaken, promise me you'll break away and run, quickly. But don't misunderstand. I must face this feeling and fight it; I want my love for you to be that pure, that secure. Are you afraid?"

"No." Still she stared at him, just as he stared at her throat. If she knew what was in his mind!

"You don't think I'm crazy? I went to this costumer's—he was a horrible little old man—and he gave me the cloak. Actually told me it was a real vampire's. I thought he was joking, but tonight I didn't see myself in the mirror, and I wanted Lindstrom's neck, and I want you. But I must test it."

"You're not crazy. I know. I'm not afraid."

"Then—"

The girl's face mocked. Henderson summoned his strength. He bent forward, his impulses battling. For a moment he stood there under the ghastly orange moon, and his face was twisted in struggle.

And the girl lured.

Her odd, incredibly red lips parted in a silvery, chuckly laugh as her white arms rose from the black cloak she wore to circle his neck gently. "I know—I knew when I looked in the mirror. I knew you had a cloak like mine—got yours where I got mine—"

Queerly, her lips seemed to elude his as he stood frozen for an instant of shock. Then he felt the icy hardness of her sharp little teeth on his throat, a strangely soothing sting, and an engulfing blackness rising over him.

# Beetles

WHEN HARTLEY returned from Egypt, his friends said he had changed. The specific nature of that change was difficult to detect, for none of his acquaintances got more than a casual glimpse of him. He dropped around to the club just once, and then retired to the seclusion of his apartments. His manner was so definitely hostile, so markedly anti-social, that very few of his cronies cared to visit him, and the occasional callers were not received.

It caused considerable talk at the time—gossip rather. Those who remembered Arthur Hartley in the days before his expedition abroad were naturally quite cut up over the drastic metamorphosis in his manner. Hartley had been known as a keen scholar, a singularly erudite field-worker in his chosen profession of archeology; but at the same time he had been a peculiarly charming person. He had the worldly flair usually associated with the fictional characters of E. Phillips Oppenheim, and a positively devilish sense of humor which mocked and belittled it. He was the kind of fellow who could order the precise wine at the proper moment, at the same time grinning as though he were as much surprised by it all as his guest of the evening. And most of his friends found this air of culture without ostentation quite engaging. He had carried this urbane sense of the ridiculous over into his work; and while it was known that he was very much interested in archeology, and a notable figure in the field, he inevitably referred to his studies as "pottering around with old fossils and the old fossils that discovered them."

Consequently, his curious reversal following his trip came as a complete surprise.

All that was definitely known was that he had spent some eight months on a field trip to the Egyptian Sudan. Upon his return he had immediately severed all connections with the institute he had been associated with. Just what had occurred during the expedition was a matter of excited conjecture among his former intimates. But something had definitely happened; it was unmistakable.

The night he spent at the club proved that. He had come in quietly, too quietly. Hartley was one of those persons who usually made an entrance, in the true sense of the word. His tall, graceful figure, attired in the immaculate evening dress so seldom found outside of the pages of melodramatic fiction; his truly leonine head with its Stokowski-like bristle of gray hair; these attributes commanded attention. He could have passed anywhere as a man of the world, or a stage magician awaiting his cue to step onto the platform.

But this evening he entered quietly, unobtrusively. He wore dinner clothes, but his shoulders sagged, and the spring was gone from his walk. His hair was grayer, and it hung pallidly over his tanned forehead. Despite the bronze of Egyptian sun on his features, there was a sickly tinge to his countenance. His eyes peered mistily from amidst unsightly folds. His face seemed to have lost its mold; the mouth hung loosely.

He greeted no one; and took a table alone. Of course cronies came up and chatted, but he did not invite them to join him. And oddly enough, none of them insisted, although normally they would gladly have forced their company upon him and jollied him out of a black mood, which experience had taught them was easily done in his case. Nevertheless, after a few words with Hartley, they all turned away.

They must have felt it even then. Some of them hazarded the opinion that Hartley was still suffering from some form of fever contracted in Egypt, but I do not think they believed this in their hearts. From their shocked descriptions of the man they seemed one and all to sense the peculiar *alien* quality about him. This was an Arthur Hartley they had never known, an aged stranger, with a querulous voice which rose in suspicion when he was questioned about his journey. Stranger he truly was, for he did not even appear to recognize some of the men who greeted him and when he did it was with an abstracted manner—a clumsy way of wording it, but what else is there to say when an old friend stares blankly into silence upon meeting, and his eyes seem to fasten on far-off terrors that affright him?

That was the strangeness they all grasped in Hartley. He was afraid. Fear bestrode those sagging shoulders. Fear breathed a pallor into that ashy face. Fear grinned into those empty, far-fixed eyes. Fear prompted the suspicion in the voice.

They told me, and that is why I went round to see Arthur Hartley in his rooms. Others had spoken of their efforts, in the week following his appearance at the club, to gain admittance to his apartment. They said he did not answer the bell, and complained that the phone had been disconnected. But that, I reasoned, was fear's work.

I wouldn't let Hartley down. I had been a rather good friend of his—and I may as well confess that I scented a mystery here. The combination proved irresistible. I went up to his flat one afternoon and rang.

No answer. I went into the dim hallway and listened for footsteps, some sign of life from within. No answer. Complete, utter silence. For a moment I thought crazily of suicide, then laughed the dread away. It was absurd—and still, there had been a certain dismaying unanimity in all the reports I had heard of Hartley's mental state. When the stolidest, most hard-headed of the club bores concurred in their estimate of the man's condition, I might well worry. Still, suicide . . .

I rang again, more as a gesture than in expectation of tangible results, and then I turned and descended the stairs. I felt, I recall, a little twinge of inexplicable relief upon leaving the place. The thought of suicide in that gloomy hallway had not been pleasant.

I reached the lower door and opened it, and a familiar figure scurried past me on the landing. I turned. It was Hartley.

For the first time since his return I got a look at the man, and in the hallway shadows he was ghastly. Whatever his condition at the club, a week must have accentuated it tremendously. His head was lowered, and as I greeted him he looked up. His eyes gave me a terrific shock. There was a stranger dwelling in their depths—a haunted stranger. I swear he shook when I addressed him.

He was wearing a tattered topcoat, but it hung loosely over his gauntness. I noticed that he was carrying a large bundle done up in brown paper.

I said something, I don't remember what; at any rate, I was at some pains to conceal my confusion as I greeted him. I was rather insistently cordial, I believe, for I could see that he would just as soon have hurried up the stairs without even speaking to me. The astonishment I felt converted itself into heartiness. Rather reluctantly he invited me up.

We entered the flat, and I noticed that Hartley double-locked the door behind him. That, to me, characterized his metamorphosis. In the old days, Hartley had always kept open house, in the literal sense of the word. Studies might have kept him late at the institute, but a chance visitor found his door open wide. And now, he double-locked it.

I turned around and surveyed the apartment. Just what I expected to see I cannot say, but certainly my mind was prepared for some sign of radical alteration. There was none. The furniture had not been moved; the pictures hung in their original places; the vast bookcases still stood in the shadows.

Hartley excused himself, entered the bedroom, and presently emerged after discarding his topcoat. Before he sat down he walked over to the mantel and struck a match before a little bronze figurine of Horus. A second later the thick gray spirals of smoke arose in the approved style of exotic fiction, and I smelt the pungent tang of strong incense.

That was the first puzzler. I had unconsciously adopted the attitude of a detective looking for clues—or, perhaps, a psychiatrist ferreting out psychoneurotic tendencies. And the incense was definitely alien to the Arthur Hartley I knew.

"Clears away the smell," he remarked.

I didn't ask "What smell?" Nor did I begin to question him as to his trip, his inexplicable conduct in not answering my correspondence after he left Khartoum, or his avoidance of my company in this week following his return. Instead, I let him talk.

He said nothing at first. His conversation rambled, and behind it all I sensed the abstraction I had been warned about. He spoke of having given up his work, and hinted that he might leave the city shortly and go up to his family home in the country. He had been ill. He was disappointed in Egyptology, and its limitations. He hated darkness. The locust plagues had increased in Kansas.

This rambling was—insane.

I knew it then, and I hugged the thought to me in the perverse delight which is born of dread. Hartley was mad. "Limitations" of Egyptology. "I hate the dark." "The locusts of Kansas."

But I sat silently when he lighted the great candles about the room; sat silently staring through the incense clouds to where the flaming tapers illuminated his twitching features. And then he broke.

"You are my friend?" he said. There was a question in his voice, a puzzled suspicion in his words that brought sudden pity to me. His derangement was terrible to witness. Still, I nodded gravely.

"You are my friend," he continued. This time the words were a statement. The deep breath which followed betokened resolution on his part.

"Do you know what was in that bundle I brought in?" he asked suddenly.

"No."

"I'll tell you. Insecticide. That's what it was. Insecticide!"

His eyes flamed in triumph which stabbed me.

"I haven't left this house for a week. I dare not spread the plague. They follow me, you know. But today I thought of the way—absurdly simple, too. I went out and bought insecticide. Pounds of it. And liquid spray. Special formula stuff, more deadly than arsenic. Just elementary science, really—but its very prosaicness may defeat the Powers of Evil."

I nodded like a fool, wondering whether I could arrange for him to be be taken away that evening. Perhaps my friend, Doctor Sherman, might diagnose. . . .

"Now let them come! It's my last chance—the incense doesn't work, and even if I keep the lights burning they creep about the corners. Funny the woodwork holds up; it should be riddled."

What was this?

"But I forgot," said Hartley. "You don't know about it. The plague, I mean. And the curse." He leaned forward and his white hands made octopus-shadows on the wall.

"I used to laugh at it, you know," he said. "Archeology isn't exactly a pursuit for the superstitious. Too much groveling in ruins. And putting curses on old pottery and battered statues never seemed important to me. But Egyptology—that's different. It's human bodies, there. Mummified, but still human. And the Egyptians were a great race—they had scientific secrets we haven't yet fathomed, and of course we cannot even begin to approach their concepts in mysticism."

Ah! There was the key! I listened, intently.

"I learned a lot, this last trip. We were after the excavation job in the new tombs up the river. I brushed up on the dynastic periods, and naturally the religious significance entered into it. Oh, I know all the myths—the Bubatis legend, the Isis resurrection theory, the true names of Ra, the allegory of Set—

"We found things there, in the tombs—wonderful things. The pottery, the furniture, the bas-reliefs we were able to remove. But the expeditionary reports will be out soon; you can read of it then. We found mummies, too. Cursed mummies."

Now I saw it, or thought I did.

"And I was a fool. I did something I never should have dared to do—for ethical reasons, and for other, more important reasons. Reasons that may cost me my soul."

I had to keep my grip on myself, remember that he was mad, remember that his convincing tones were prompted by the delusions of insanity. Or else, in that dark room I might have easily believed that there was a power which had driven my friend to this haggard brink.

"Yes, I did it, I tell you! I read the Curse of Scarabæus—sacred beetle, you know—and I did it anyway. I couldn't guess that it was true. I was a skeptic; everyone is skeptical enough until things happen. Those things are like the phenomenon of death; you read about it, realize that it occurs to others, and yet cannot quite conceive of it happening to yourself. And yet it does. The Curse of the Scarabæus was like that."

Thoughts of the Sacred Beetle of Egypt crossed my mind. And I remembered, also, the seven plagues. And I knew what he would say. . . .

"We came back. On the ship I noticed them. They crawled out of the corners every night. When I turned the light on they went away, but they always returned when I tried to sleep. I burned incense to keep them off, and then I moved into a new cabin. But they followed me.

"I did not dare tell anyone. Most of the chaps would have laughed, and the Egyptologists in the party wouldn't have helped much. Besides, I couldn't confess my crime. So I went on alone."

His voice was a dry whisper.

"It was pure hell. One night on the boat I saw the black things crawling in my food. After that I ate in the cabin, alone. I dared not see anyone now, for fear they might notice how the things followed me. They did follow me, you know—if I walked in shadow on the deck they crept along behind. Only the sun kept them back, or a pure flame. I nearly went mad trying to account logically for their presence; trying to imagine how they got on the boat. But all the time I knew in my heart what the truth was. They were a sending—the Curse!

"When I reached port I went up and resigned. When my guilt was discovered there would have been a scandal, anyway, so I resigned. I couldn't hope to continue work with those things crawling all over, wherever I went. I was afraid to look anyone up. Naturally, I tried. That one night at the club was ghastly, though—I could see them marching across the carpet and crawling up the sides of my chair, and it took all there was in me to keep from screaming and dashing out.

"Since then I've stayed here, alone. Before I decide on any course for the future, I must fight the Curse and win. Nothing else will help."

I started to interject a phrase, but he brushed it aside and continued desperately.

"No, I couldn't go away. They followed me across the ocean; they haunt me in the streets. I could be locked up and they would still come. They come every night and crawl up the sides of my bed and try to get at my face and I must sleep soon or I'll go mad, they crawl over my face at night, they crawl—"

It was horrible to see the words ooze out between his set teeth, for he was fighting madly to control himself.

"Perhaps the insecticide will kill them. It was the first thing I should have thought of, but of course panic confused me. Yes,

I put my trust in the insecticide. Grotesque, isn't it? Fighting an ancient curse with insect-powder?"

I spoke at last. "They're beetles, aren't they?"

He nodded. "Scarabæus beetles. You know the curse. The mummies under the protection of the Scarab cannot be violated."

I knew the curse. It was one of the oldest known to history. Like all legends, it has had a persistent life. Perhaps I could reason.

"But why should it affect you?" I asked. Yes, I would reason with Hartley. Egyptian fever had deranged him, and the colorful curse story had gripped his mind. If I spoke logically, I might get him to understand his hallucination. "Why should it affect you?" I repeated.

He was silent for a moment before he spoke, and then his words seemed to be wrung out of him.

"I stole a mummy," he said. "I stole the mummy of a temple virgin. I must have been crazy to do it; something happens to you under that sun. There was gold in the case, and jewels, and ornaments. And there was the Curse, written. I got them—both."

I stared at him, and knew that in this he spoke the truth.

"That's why I cannot keep up my work. I stole the mummy, and I am cursed. I didn't believe, but the crawling things came just as the inscription said.

"At first I thought that was the meaning of the Curse, that wherever I went the beetles would go, too, that they would haunt me and keep me from men forever. But lately I am beginning to think differently. I think the beetles will act as messengers of vengeance. I think they mean to kill me."

This was pure raving.

"I haven't dared open the mummy-case since. I'm afraid to read the inscription again. I have it here in the house, but I've locked it up and I won't show you. I want to burn it—but I must keep it on hand. In a way, it's the only proof of my sanity. And if the things kill me—"

"Snap out of it," I commanded. Then I started. I don't know the exact words I used, but I said reassuring, hearty, wholesome things. And when I finished he smiled the martyred smile of the obsessed.

"Delusions? They're real. But where do they come from? I

can't find any cracks in the woodwork. The walls are sound. And yet every night the beetles come and crawl up the bed and try to get at my face. They don't bite, they merely crawl. There are thousands of them—black thousands of silent, crawling things, inches long. I brush them away, but when I fall asleep they come back; they're clever, and I can't pretend. I've never caught one; they're too fast-moving. They seem to understand me—or the Power that sends them understands.

"They crawl up from Hell night after night, and I can't last much longer. Some evening I'll fall completely asleep and they will creep over my face, and then—"

He leaped to his feet and screamed.

"The corner—in the corner now—out of the walls—"

The black shadows were moving, marching.

I saw a blur, fancied I could detect rustling forms advancing, creeping, spreading before the light.

Hartley sobbed.

I turned on the electric light. There was, of course, nothing there. I didn't say a word, but left abruptly. Hartley continued to sit huddled in his chair, his head in his hands.

I went straight to my friend, Doctor Sherman.

2.

He diagnosed it as I thought he would: phobia, accompanied by hallucinations. Hartley's feeling of guilt over stealing the mummy haunted him. The visions of beetles resulted.

All this Sherman studded with the mumbo-jumbo technicalities of the professional psychiatrist, but it was simple enough. Together we phoned the institute where Hartley had worked. They verified the story, in so far as they knew Hartley had stolen a mummy.

After dinner Sherman had an appointment, but he promised to meet me at ten and go with me again to Hartley's apartment. I was quite insistent about this, for I felt that there was no time to lose. Of course, this was a mawkish attitude on my part, but that strange afternoon session had deeply disturbed me.

I spent the early evening in unnerving reflection. Perhaps that was the way all so-called "Egyptian curses" worked. A guilty conscience on the part of a tomb-looter made him project the shadow of imaginary punishment on himself. He had hallucinations of retribution. That might explain the mysterious Tutankh-ahmen deaths; it certainly accounted for the suicides.

And that was why I insisted on Sherman seeing Hartley that same night. I feared suicide very much, for if ever a man was on the verge of complete mental collapse, Arthur Hartley surely was.

It was nearly eleven, however, before Sherman and I rang the bell. There was no answer. We stood in the dark hallway as I vainly rapped, then pounded. The silence only served to augment my anxiety. I was truly afraid, or else I never would have dared using my skeleton key.

As it was, I felt the end justified the means. We entered.

The living-room was bare of occupants. Nothing had changed since the afternoon—I could see that quite clearly, for all the lights were on, and the guttering candle-stumps still smoldered.

Both Sherman and I smelt the reek of the insecticide quite strongly, and the floor was almost evenly coated with thick white insect powder.

We called, of course, before I ventured to enter the bedroom. It was dark, and I thought it was empty until I turned on the lights and saw the figure huddled beneath the bed-clothes. It was Arthur Hartley, and I needed no second glance to see that his white face was twisted in death.

The reek of insecticide was strongest here, and incense burned; and yet there was another pungent smell—a musty odor, vaguely animal-like.

Sherman stood at my side, staring.

"What shall we do?" I asked.

"I'll get the police on the wire downstairs," he said. "Touch nothing."

He dashed out, and I followed him from the room, sickened. I could not bear to approach the body of my friend—that hideous expression on the face affrighted me. Suicide, murder, heart-attack—I didn't even wish to know the manner of his passing. I was heartsick to think that we had been too late.

I turned from the bedroom and then that damnable scent came to my nostrils redoubled, and I know. "Beetles!"

But how could there be beetles? It was all an illusion in poor Hartley's brain. Even his twisted mind had realized that there were no apertures in the walls to admit them; that they could not be seen about the place.

And still the smell rose on the air—the reek of death, of decay, of ancient corruption that reigned in Egypt. I followed the scent to the second bedroom, forced the door.

On the bed lay the mummy-case. Hartley had said he locked it up in here. The lid was closed, but ajar.

I opened it. The sides bore inscriptions, and one of them may have pertained to the Scarabæus Curse. I do not know, for I stared only at the ghastly, unshrouded figure that lay within. It was a mummy, and it had been sucked dry. It was all shell. There was a great cavity in the stomach, and as I peered within I could see a few feebly-crawling forms —inch-long, black buttons with great writhing feelers. They shrank back in the light, but not before I saw the scarab patterns on the outer crusted backs.

The secret of the Curse was here—the beetles had dwelt within the body of the mummy! They had eaten it out and nested within, and at night they crawled forth. It was true then!

I screamed once when the thought hit me, and dashed back to Hartley's bedroom. I could hear the sound of footsteps ascending the outer stairs; the police were on their way, but I couldn't wait. I raced into the bedroom, dread tugging at my heart.

Had Hartley's story been true, after all? Were the beetles really messengers of a divine vengeance?

I ran into that bedroom where Arthur Hartley lay, stooped over his huddled figure on the bed. My hands fumbled over the body, searching for a wound. I had to know how he had died.

But there was no blood, there was no mark, and there was no weapon beside him. It had been shock or heart attack, after all. I was strangely relieved when I thought of this. I stood up and eased the body back again on the pillows.

I felt almost glad, because during my search my hands had moved over the body while my eyes roved over the room. I was looking for beetles.

Hartley had feared the beetles—the beetles that crawled out of the mummy. They had crawled every night, if his story was to be believed; crawled into his room, up the bed-posts, across the pillows.

Where were they now? They had left the mummy and disappeared, and Hartley was dead. Where were they?

Suddenly I stared again at Hartley. There was something wrong with the body on the bed. When I had lifted the corpse it seemed singularly light for a man of Hartley's build. As I gazed at him now, he seemed empty of more than life. I peered into that ravaged face more closely, and then I shuddered. For the cords on his neck moved convulsively, his chest seemed to rise and fall, his head fell sideways on the pillow. He lived—or something inside him did!

And then as his twisted features moved, I cried aloud, for I knew how Hartley had died, and what had killed him; knew the secret of the Scarab Curse and why the beetles crawled out of the mummy to seek his bed. I knew what they had meant to do— what, tonight, they had done. I cried aloud as I saw Hartley's face move, in hopes that my voice would drown that dreadful rustling sound which filled the room and came from *inside Hartley's body*.

I knew that the Scarab Curse had killed him, and I screamed quite wildly as his mouth gaped slowly open. Just as I fainted, I saw Arthur Hartley's dead lips part, allowing a rustling swarm of *black Scarabæus beetles* to pour out across the pillow.

# The Fiddler's Fee

THE DOOR of the inn swung open and the Devil entered. He was as thin as a corpse, and whiter than the shroud a corpse lies in. His eyes were deep and dark as graves. His mouth was redder than the gate of Hell, his hair was blacker than the pits below. He dressed like a dandy, and he came from a fine coach, but it was assuredly he: Satan, Father of Lies.

The innkeeper cringed. He had no fancy to play host to this emissary from Darkness. The innkeeper trembled under Satan's smile, while eyes searched Satan's person for signs of a tail, of cloven hoofs. Then he noticed that Satan carried a violin-case.

It was not Satan, then! The innkeeper breathed a silent prayer of relief. It was only momentary. A minute later he was trembling with augmented fear. If this was not Satan, this man who looked like the Devil and carried a violin-case—then it must be—

*"Signor Paganini!"* whispered mine host.

The stranger inclined his dark head with a slow smile.

"Welcome," quavered the innkeeper, but there was no smile on his face. It was almost as though he preferred confirmation of his first fear rather than this. Satan one could deal with, perhaps—but the child of Satan?

Everyone knew that Paganini was the son of the Devil himself. He looked like the Devil, and many were the diabolical legends concerning his unholy life. He was said to drink, gamble, and love like the Prince of Darkness, and to entertain an equal hatred of all men. Certainly he played like Lucifer—in that case under his arm he carried an instrument of hellish power; a violin whose sublime singing drove all Europe mad.

Yes, even here in this tiny village men knew and feared the strange and terrible legend that had grown up about the destiny of the world's most famed violinist. New and fantastic stories were continually pouring in from Milan, from Florence, from Rome—and half the capitals of the Continent as well. "Paganini murdered his wife and sold her body to Satan." "Paganini has formed a Society against all God-loving men." "Paganini's mistresses are offered in the Black Mass." "Paganini's music is written by the very fiends of Hell." "Paganini is the son of the Devil."

Legends these might be, but the atrocious conduct attributed to the *maestro,* that was fact. His scandalous amours, his disgraceful attitude toward the great and the nobility had been confirmed time and time again. Gossip, slander, malice these things were in part. But one shining truth remained.

No one had ever played the violin like Nicolo Paganini.

Therefore the innkeeper bowed despite his fear. He sent a lad to change the horses and serve the driver of the coach, ushered *Signor* to the best room, and awaited his presence in the parlor of the inn with a carefully prepared table.

Another awaited his presence as well—the innkeeper's son, also called Nicolo.

Young Nicolo knew even more about the great man than his father. The lad knew more about the violin than anyone in the village, with the exception of Carlo, the wine merchant's son. Both boys had studied at the local conservatory since early childhood, and there was keen rivalry between them; between their families, each of whom fostered the budding genius of their heirs.

Now Nicolo awaited his glimpse of the great man. What a triumph over Carlo! What a thing to talk about in weeks to come! Perhaps he, Nicolo, might even speak to the illustrious musician—might, if the saints were kind, receive a word in return. But that was almost too much to hope for. Paganini was not interested in boys. Still, Nicolo was determined to see him; he did not fear the legends. So the lad waited, working on the preparations for the meal in the kitchen with his sensitive ears attuned to the sound of footsteps on the stairs above.

They came.

Paganini sat in solitary splendor at the great table of the inn. No other customers were present to stare at the great man, and he seemed oddly content to be alone—he who loved applause, adulation, obeisance. His thin, hawk-like face—singularly

Satanic in the lamp-light it was—cast a black blurred shadow on the wall behind. His carefully curled hair rose in two horn-like projections against that shadow, so that the innkeeper noticed it as he entered, and nearly spilled the wine.

Paganini ate and drank sparingly—as fiends do. He said never a word, nor did he exhibit the humanity of smile or scowl. When he had finished, he sat back and seemed to stare into the candle-flame.

It was as though his eyes turned homeward to Hell.

The innkeeper left the room, crossing himself. This silent guest was indeed a son of Satan! In the passage he came upon Nicolo, staring at the pale violinist.

"No, no!—come away," the father whispered. "You must not."

But Nicolo, moving as one entranced, entered the parlor. A voice that was unlike any his father had heard came almost mechanically from his throat.

"Good evening, *Signor Paganini*."

The eyes left the flame, after partaking of their glare. A long, deliberate glance pierced Nicolo's face like a dark lance.

"The whelp knows my name. Well!"

"I have heard much of you, *Signor*. Who in Italy does not know the name of Paganini?"

"And—fear it," said the violinist, gravely.

"I do not fear you," answered the boy, slowly. His eyes did not fall when the *maestro* smiled his wolfish smile.

"Yes?" The voice purred. "Yes; that is right. You do not fear me. I feel that. And—why?"

"Because I love Music."

"Because he loves Music," parroted Paganini, cruelly mimicking the intonations until the statement stood naked in its triteness. Then, slowly, as the stare came again: "But you do love Music, boy. I feel it—strange."

A hand reached out, a pale ghost of a hand with great sinews that hinted at delicate strength, however paradoxical that might seem. The hand gestured Nicolo to a seat. The hand poured wine into a glass. The hand drummed on the table slowly.

"Do you play?"

"Y-yes, *maestro*."

"Play for me, then."

Nicolo raced to his room. The beloved violin rested against his heart as he ran back.

"It is such a poor thing, *maestro*. It does not sing—"

"Play."

Nicolo played. He never remembered what he played that night; he only knew that it came to him, and he played as he never had played before.

And the face of Satan smiled through the music.

Nicolo stopped. Paganini asked his name. He answered. Paganini asked of his teacher, his practice, his plans. Nicolo answered all questions. And then Paganini laughed. The innkeeper, listening in his turn in the passageway, shuddered when he heard that laugh.

It was a laugh that cracked through the earth and came up from Hell. It was the laugh of a sobbing violin played by a fallen angel in the Pit.

"Fools!" shouted the *maestro*.

Then he stared at Nicolo. Something inside the lad begged him to turn away. But as he had before, the boy returned the stare, until the master musician spoke.

"What can I say? Should I advise you to go to a good teacher, buy a better violin? Should I even give you money for that purpose? Yes, but to what end? You have the gift, but you will never use it."

Paganini sneered.

"You may be competent. You may even win small fame, a certain amount of success. But true greatness you cannot achieve through teacher or instrument or training. You must be inspired— as I was."

Nicolo stood trembling, he knew not why. There was a horrible conviction in the words he heard. It frightened him, that hint of certain authority, of final knowledge.

"A man must compose his own work, play his own work," the voice went on. "And no human teacher can give you that gift."

Suddenly Paganini stood up.

"My pardon. I forgot. I came to this place because I have an— appointment nearby. I cannot keep my—the one I must see— waiting. I shall go now. But thank you for your playing."

Nicolo's face fell. He was convinced that in a moment or so more the *maestro* would have revealed something to him which he very much wanted to know. For Nicolo felt as Paganini did about his work. He knew that within him lay great talent; knew that any ordinary training would subdue that talent in channels of mere mechanical perfection. There was a bond between his humble self and the greatness of the master before him. And if only Paganini had spoken! Now it was too late!

The black cloak swirled as the violinist went to the door. Then in a rush of ebony Paganini swept back the garment as he turned.

"Wait."

He stared, and Nicolo felt his soul lifted and examined and torn and probed by the red-hot pincers of Paganini's eyes.

"Come with me. We shall keep our appointment together."

An almost audible gasp issued from the passageway at the end of the room. Nicolo knew it came from his father, listening. But he did not care. As the door swung against darkness, he moved to the musician's side. They left together.

"I will apprentice you this night to a true Master," Paganini whispered.

2.

It was a long walk up the mountainside to the Cave of Fools. The road was lonely in the midnight, but then it was always lonely, for men hereabouts feared the Cave. The Devil was said to dwell in its mists, and the Cave itself was unexplored by those who deemed its depths led down to Tartarus itself.

It was a long and lonely walk, and the way was strange amidst winding paths and twisting passages of rock; yet Paganini never faltered. He had walked this way before.

Now, the bony hand gripped Nicolo's brown fingers in an icy clasp so filled with cold, inhuman strength that the lad shuddered. But he followed through the steam and mist and fog that hid the clean light of the stars; followed to the mouth of the Cave as though impelled by the magic of Paganini's voice.

For the *maestro* spoke all that way, and spoke without reticence. Sensing a kindred soul, he revealed.

"They say I am a spawn of the Devil, and that is a lie. All my life they told me so—even my father, cursed fool! In the academies my fellow-students made the sign of the horns at me and the girls fled screaming.

"They screamed at me, who lived for Music and Beauty! But at first I did not care. I lived for my work, and I worked hard. Always I felt within me that spark, glowing to a flame.

"And then when I made my first appearance, I came again into the world of men. My music was acclaimed, but I was hated. 'Child of the Devil' they called me, because I was ugly, and my temper bad. I tried again to drown myself in work, but this time it no longer sufficed, because I knew my playing was not good enough. I had genius, but I could not express it.

"After a while one begins to reason. My work was not enough. The world hated me. 'Child of the Devil?' Why not?

"I knew the way. I studied. I read old forbidden books I found in the great libraries of Florence. And I came here. There is a legend of Faust, you know.

"There are ways of meeting Powers that grant things to men in return for an exchange."

They entered the Cave now, and when Nicolo's hands trembled at the words the musician's grip tightened.

"Do not fear, lad. It is worth the cost. Thirteen years ago tonight I was just such a lad as you; perhaps a bit older. I came this way alone, and with the same fears. And it was well.

"When I came forth I had within me the gift I craved. Since that time, you know, all the world knows, my story. Fame, wealth, beautiful women—all earthly success is mine to command. But more than that; greater than that, is my Music. I learned to compose, and to play. They say His songs moved the angels and the stars. I have that gift. And you, who know, love, and have born within you, Music—you shall this night partake of the same gift."

Nicolo wanted to run, to get out of this deep cavern where the steam swirled in fantastic shapes. He wanted to make the sign of the cross as he heard the bubbling and the booming from the depths ahead. And then a curious picture came to his mind—the vision of Carlo Zuttio, the wine-merchant's son. Carlo went to the conservatory, and he was a fool. But he had a better violin, and private lessons, so that he played more masterfully than Nicolo. And his parents were wealthy, and they boasted to Nicolo's father of their son and his music. The whole town knew that Carlo would go on to the big school in Milan. He, Nicolo, would not go on—he would remain and take over the inn, and sometime when he was old and fat he might play at country weddings for drinks. Carlo would be rich and famous, and wear silk when he returned to visit. Nicolo would no longer be a rival, then; merely a country innkeeper.

It was this vision, and no love of Music that came to Nicolo in the bowels of the earth. It was this vision that made him smile and follow Paganini as they advanced into the heart of the hot smoke and knelt upon the stones in the darkness.

Then Paganini called a Secret Name and the earth thundered. He made a sign not of the cross, and he prayed in a voice that was black and crawling.

Then the mists grew red and the thundering swelled, and Nicolo was formally introduced to his Teacher.

3.

Paganini had been crafty. It was a bargain. Three years for him, and no more; where Paganini had gained thirteen. But the other ten years went to the *maestro* as payment for leading the way. It was a fair arrangement; a business arrangement.

That was what shocked Nicolo more than anything else when he returned home. It had all been so business-like. There was behind it a terrible hint of purpose; the Power knew what it was doing—there was no aimlessness, no blind evil. It was all so *arranged*.

Three years.

But there was singing in Nicolo's heart, singing which over-rode the sound of his father's quavering prayers, singing which rose to triumphant heights when he played at the conservatory the next afternoon.

"Paganini taught me," is all that Nicolo would say when the faculty exclaimed. "Paganini taught me," Nicolo told Carlo with a smile.

The singing rose higher as the weeks passed.

Nicolo, who read notes poorly, composed.

Nicolo improvised.

The faculty bought him a new violin, and on the festival day it was Nicolo who appeared as soloist with the orchestra from Venice; though Carlo was second in competition for the post.

Nicolo won the scholarship and went to Milan.

His father prayed but said nothing. Paganini did not write, but word came of his triumphs in France.

In Milan, Nicolo was a sensation at the school. Carlo came too, his parents paying his tuition; and Carlo was successful. He studied hard, worked diligently, played expertly.

But Nicolo's soaring tones were born of inspiration within. He was mastering a technique against which mere practice could not compete.

Through the year it was a constant competition between the two country boys—Nicolo and Carlo. The whole school knew it. Nicolo had the talent. Carlo had the ambition. The battle for perfection was deadly.

Nicolo was aging. His face was already maturing in set lines, and the color had left it set and harsh. It was whispered that his nights were spent in study that left him wasted.

The truth was that Nicolo's nights were spent in fear. He was remembering the tryst in the Cave of Fools, and he was anticipating the days to come. Only two years now—and so much to do!

He had been a fool. But Paganini's personality had overshadowed his own, dominated it. He had been led. He knew that now. Paganini had wanted a dupe, so that he might make such a bargain and extend his own life at the expense of another's. That is why he had taken Nicolo. Nicolo often wondered just what might have happened had Paganini gone alone to his accounting. He wondered, because in two years *he* must go—and there would be no dupe for *him*.

Two years! Nicolo would toss on his pillow and shudder at the thought. He could not hope to do what Paganini had done in thirteen. He could not win much but initial acclaim; none of the fame and riches would be his in so short a time. But one thing he could do—beat his rival, Carlo.

Nicolo hated Carlo now. He hadn't used to hate him. They had been rivals, but friendly enough. Ever since that night in the Cave of Fools Nicolo had hated.

Carlo was keeping up. Nicolo found that his work came to him almost effortlessly. His hands moved without thought along the bow, and his fingering seemed undirected. There was no triumphant thrill for him in his music, no sense of mastery in his easy playing.

Carlo had this, because Carlo had to work and sweat to compete, and when he did so he felt satisfied. Moreover, aided by no supernatural gift, Carlo *was* competing too closely for comfort.

And the school liked Carlo. The teachers knew his work and praised him for it. They did not praise Nicolo because they could not understand his methods. He puzzled them.

The other pupils liked Carlo. He had money, and he was generous. He bought sweets for his friends, laughed with them at their parties. Nicolo had no money for sweets, no fine clothes for parties. The pupils were in awe of him, and they distrusted his face.

Carlo was handsome, too. The girls liked Carlo. Even Elissa liked him. And that added to the agony of Nicolo's nights.

4.

Elissa's hair was yellow flame on a pillow. Elissa's eyes were the jewels on the breast of Passion. Elissa's mouth was a red gateway to delight. Elissa's arms were—

It was no use. Nicolo couldn't think of anything more poetic. All he knew was that Elissa burned within him at all times. Her beauty was like a lash across his naked heart.

Actually, Elissa Robbia was a very pretty blond student, but Nicolo was in love and Youth knows only a goddess.

Elissa walked with Carlo, and she went to parties with him, and they danced at the festival together. Throughout the second year they were together always.

Always Nicolo watched from the corner. Once or twice he spoke to the object of his worship, but she did not seem to notice him, despite his efforts to be ingratiating. She preferred the handsome Carlo.

So Nicolo worked. He outplayed Carlo, though it was not easy now. Despite Nicolo's secret power, Carlo seemed inspired by love. Carlo followed his most difficult trills, mastered every detail of the well-nigh flawless technique which Nicolo mastered.

Still Nicolo triumphed always in the end. The better teachers were now confounded by the spectacle of their two notable students. Often outsiders witnessed performances. The Opera sent conductors down to listen, and notables from all over the South attended the salons in local aristocratic homes when the star pupils played.

Nothing was said officially, but it was understood that one or the other of the boys would be groomed for concert debut within the year.

Both of them knew it, though they no longer spoke to each other. Both of them worked frantically. The final concert of the season would decide; they suspected that. Both had been asked for a performance of some solo composition.

Nicolo went to work a month in advance. What took place in his dark room will never be known, but he emerged with what he felt was a true masterpiece. He had worked as never before. He would win, he would shame Carlo before them all; shame him before Elissa.

He could hardly wait for the night.

The stage of the school was lighted and the house was filled with those of a station to allow their jewels to reflect that light. Rumor had passed, and in the audience were musical notables from all Italy. And the Master was there, too—yes, the great Paganini himself! Come to watch Nicolo, his former pupil, they said.

What a triumph! Nicolo shivered with ecstasy, fondling his violin as he waited in the wings for the solos to end. Tonight he would appear before Paganini himself when he took victory over his rival. Nothing could make his happiness more complete!

Where was Carlo, by the way? He had not appeared in the wings as yet.

But—there he was—*in the audience! With Elissa.*

What did this mean?

A number ended. The director was announcing his name.

"Unfortunately the soloist who was to compete with Signor Nicolo this evening, Carlo Zuttio . . ."

What was that?

"Resigned from the school . . ."

Yes?

"Marriage to . . ."

*Married! To Elissa!*

He had done that; knowing he would lose tonight he'd given up music, retired to his father's business, and married Elissa. And now he had arranged for it to be announced, to rob Nicolo of his victory! Bitter despair rose in Nicolo's heart, and black anger.

But when his name was called he stepped forth and played.

He played his number, but it was not the original he had planned. For now he improvised; or rather, hate improvised for him. Hate tore at the strings, plucked frantically at a flayed violin.

And waves of horror crept through the house.

Through red mists, the black eyes of Paganini blazed, the smile dropped from Carlo's face, the lips of Elissa grew pale. Nicolo saw *her* eyes grow blank, and poured his music into them. She had never noticed him before, eh? Well, she would not forget him now—not this, and *this.*

Swooping to Hell, spiraling to Heaven, shrieking and whispering of damnation and glory, the violin sang accompaniment to dark voices that yammered in Nicolo's brain.

Nicolo had no arms, no fingers. He was all violin. His body was part of the instrument, his brain a part of the song. Both were being played by *Another.*

He finished.

Silence.

Then the thunder.

And while he bowed and smiled and the sound tore at his eardrums, his eyes blazed into Elissa's empty face through the standing crowd. Nicolo had won and lost tonight. But he would win again.

## 5.

They came to him after the concert. They offered him money, for private study.

In a year, they said, he would come back and perform in a solo concert at the school.

Nicolo accepted the money gravely. It was supposed that he would use that money to spend his year in Rome, working under the great *maestri* as a private pupil.

But Nicolo had other plans. He knew that Carlo and Elissa would return to the village, and he meant to follow them there. He thanked the directors of the school and prepared to depart.

In the hallway stood a cloaked figure. It was Paganini.

Without a word the pale genius took Nicolo's hand, just as he had that night two years before. Together they walked the dark streets.

"You played well tonight, my son. They said your music was like Paganini's." He smiled. "And well it might be, since we study under the same Master."

Nicolo shuddered.

"Do not fear. In a year's time you shall have had all the fame and glory you desire. The world will bow before your power. That is as you desired, no?"

"No." Nicolo shook his head. "I shall not study and I shall not go to Rome. My desire lies elsewhere." He told Paganini of Carlo and Elissa. The *maestro* listened.

"So you return to the village, eh? Well, if it is that what you seek, I am sure you will be aided in your quest. Do not despair."

Nicolo sighed.

"I am afraid of that aid. This music—this playing—it is not a part of me. It comes from other sources, and I feel no satisfaction in stirring my listeners. Carlo and Elissa were stirred tonight; but it was the music that did it, not myself. Don't you understand?"

A cold whisper bit through the darkness as Paganini spoke.

"Yes, I understand, perfectly; but you do not. Tonight you played through hate, and there was hate in the hall. *But when you go to Elissa, you will play through love.* She will be stirred. For our

Master is eminently successful in amours. Let your violin speak and she shall become yours."

"But what of him? What of Carlo?"

"Again, let your violin speak. It has a voice that drives men mad. *Let him hear that voice.*"

A slow laugh crawled out of Paganini's lips.

"I know how it will be. Ah, I know! Years ago I discovered that secret, and well have I used it. Madden the cuckold and woo the mistress, and rejoice in the gift of the Teacher! I envy you your year, my friend. It will be a great triumph for you."

Nicolo's heart was pounding.

"You really believe I can do it?" he asked.

"Certainly. You were given the power; let it guide you to your purpose." Paganini's voice grew grave. "But it was not of that which I proposed to speak when I awaited you this evening. There is another thing.

"I want to remind you that a year from tonight you have an appointment in the Cave of Fools."

"I am afraid."

"It was a bargain, and you must go."

"What if I do not go?"

"That I cannot speak of. *He* will come for you then, I know it. *He* will revenge himself horribly."

"I wish," and Nicolo's voice was low with hatred, "I wish that I had never met you. You led me to this—tricked me into this infernal bargain! I was a fool, and I should kill you for it."

Paganini stopped and faced the youth. His eyes were ice.

"Perhaps. But think—think of the coming year. You shall win Elissa, and drive Carlo mad. Win Elissa and drive Carlo mad. Win Elissa and drive Carlo mad—"

His voice was like his violin, playing and replaying the same damnable, wheedling trill until it surged through Nicolo's brain.

"Think not of revenge. Go to the Cave of Fools a year from tonight; but first, win Elissa and drive Carlo mad—"

Still whispering the words, Paganini turned in the darkness and disappeared. And Nicolo walked the streets, muttering to himself:

"I shall win Elissa and drive Carlo mad."

6.

Nicolo did not stay at his father's inn when he returned. He had money now, and he procured rooms in town—rooms below the apartment of the newlywed couple he had followed.

He did not see them for a month. He was in his dark room with the violin. He played in darkness now, for he needed no notes in this composition. He developed only two themes. One was soft and sweet and tender, thrilling with passionate beauty. As Nicolo played, his face would glow in ecstasy and warmth flooded his being.

The second theme slithered out of the darkness. Then it padded. Then it began to run, and leap, and dance. At first it squeaked like a rat, then it howled like a dog, finally it bayed like a black wolf. It was a fiendish howling of terrific power, and when Nicolo played it his hands trembled and he closed his eyes.

For a month Nicolo played the two themes over and over in his tiny room—alone. Not quite alone, for there was a whispering in his brain that prompted each tone, and an unseen hand that guided the bow over the strings. Nicolo played and played, and he grew thin and gaunt. After a month the music was a part of him, and he was ready.

It took him a week to become friendly with his neighbors again. In another week he had learned their habits; knew when Carlo worked at the wine-press and left Elissa alone.

Then, one afternoon, Nicolo visited Elissa. She sat regal in her blond beauty while they talked, and after a while Nicolo suggested that he play something for her. He took out his violin and drew the bow across the strings, eyes on her face.

His eyes never left her face while he played. His eyes feasted on her face as the music feasted on her soul.

The tune came forth, reiterated; in endless variations it rose in soaring rhapsody. And Elissa rose in soaring rhapsody and came toward him, her eyes empty save for the soul-filling majesty of the music.

Then Nicolo put down the violin and took her in his arms.

He came the next day, and the next. Always he brought his

violin. Always he played and always she surrendered to the music.

For months Nicolo was happy. For many months he played each day, and his nights were peaceful at last. Carlo suspected nothing.

Nicolo began to plan. In a little while he would return to Milan for the solo concert. After that he would be famous—go on tour. He had, under the inspiration of his love, written enough to insure his success at the debut. He would take Elissa with him, and together they would scale the heights.

Then he remembered.

He could not go to Milan, or the concert. That night he had an appointment in the Cave of Fools.

Nicolo didn't want to die. He didn't want to give his soul. That cursed bargain!

But there was no way out.

Every day he saw Elissa he longed for life with greater fervor. Knowing the end was near, he came oftener, took greater and greater chances. He was counting the hours now, the minutes.

Three days before the time appointed he went there in the evening. Carlo would be late at the wine-press, so Nicolo played. Elissa sat there, her face blank as it always was when he played. Sometimes Nicolo would find himself wishing that he had no music to do his wooing—that he himself would inspire such adoration in the woman he loved. But that was too much to hope for; Elissa loved Carlo, and only the music gave her to Nicolo. It sufficed. The spell was strong. Nicolo played tonight as he had never played before, and as the music rose it drowned out the sound of footsteps on the stairs.

Carlo was in the room.

Nicolo stopped playing.

Elissa's eyes opened as though she were wakening from profound depths of sleep.

And Carlo faced them both. He was a big man, Carlo, with strong hands that now opened and closed convulsively at his sides. Carlo's heavy body was lunging across the room and the hands moved for Nicolo's throat.

They never reached it.

Nicolo's delicate hands were on the violin. He began to play.

It was not the love-strain that he played this time. It was the other—the song of madness.

At the sound of the rat-like squeaking Carlo stopped. Nicolo watched him as the shrieking mounted. Carlo's eyes grew wide. The shrieking became a moan. Carlo's wide eyes were growing red. The moaning was a rising bark, a yelp of agony. Carlo's hands went to his head. He stepped back, sank to his knees. Then Nicolo played. The violin screamed, the bow moved up and down upon it like a red-hot poker descending on human flesh. Nicolo played until Carlo lay rolling on the floor, baying in rhythm as the foam poured from his lips. Nicolo played until the room pulsed with horrid sound, until the glass shivered with the vibration and the candlelight wavered and the flame danced in agony. Nicolo played, and then he stopped.

Carlo lay there moaning, and he rose to his knees and looked at Nicolo. Then he looked at Elissa.

Nicolo followed his glance.

Elissa—he had forgotten Elissa! He had played the music of madness and forgotten she was in the room.

Elissa lay where she had fallen and her face was white with the unmistakable whiteness of death. Carlo looked at her and began to laugh.

Nicolo sobbed. Tears rolled down his cheeks.

Husband and lover laughed and sobbed together.

It was all over. She was dead, and he was mad. And two nights from now Nicolo must go to that rendezvous in the Cave of Fools.

So this was Satan's gift! This awful mockery was what it had brought him.

The dead woman lay on the floor as the madman crawled toward her, cackling.

Nicolo rose to go. His bow accidentally scraped the strings. The mad Carlo rose, laughing, and seized the violin. He broke it across the bridge and hurled it from the window.

Still laughing, he turned, but there was no sane hatred in his eyes.

And then the thought came to Nicolo.

"Carlo," he whispered. "Carlo."

The idiot husband laughed.

"Carlo, your wife is dead. But I did not kill her. I swear it. It was the Devil, Carlo. The Devil who dwells in the Cave of Fools. You want to avenge your wife's death, don't you, Carlo? Then seek out the Devil two nights from tonight in the Cave of Fools. Remember, Carlo—two nights from tonight in the Cave of Fools. I will stay with you until then and tell you where to go."

The madman laughed.

Softly, Nicolo repeated his suggestion. He whispered it all that night as the deranged Carlo slept. He whispered it the next day as they sat beside the body of the dead woman. At last, when Nicolo rose to leave on the coach for Milan, he felt that Carlo understood and would go. Smiling, the violinist withdrew, leaving the chuckling lunatic and his dead wife in the dark room.

### 7.

In the night of travel Nicolo smiled bitterly but often. It had worked out after all! He would trick Satan then; sending Carlo in his stead. Thus he could play the concert and go on to fame. Poor Elissa was dead, of course, but there were other women to hear the song of love. It was good.

It was good to hear the praise in Milan. His old teachers spoke, his friends gathered around him and whispered of the celebrities who would attend the concert tonight.

Nicolo was so busy that day that he forgot a very important item. Indeed, he had just finished a meal in his dressing-room when he remembered.

Carlo had broken his violin!

Confused by tragedy, by lack of sleep and overmuch planning, it had slipped Nicolo's thoughts. His violin—not a precious instrument to him, for Nicolo knew that he could produce his music on any violin. Still, it was necessary.

He rose to summon the director, when the door opened. Carlo entered.

Carlo was mad. His eyes glittered and his teeth were bared, but he walked erect. He was able to control himself sufficiently to pass unnoticed, it seemed.

Nicolo, beholding him, nearly froze on the spot. A wave of fear rose chokingly in his throat.

"Carlo—why are you here? Don't you remember—the Cave of Fools and your appointment?"

Carlo grinned.

"I went last night, Nicolo," he whispered. "I went last night. Tonight I am here to see you play. You will be playing soon, Nicolo."

Nicolo stammered wildly. "But—but what did you find in the Cave? I mean—there was One who waited, and he wanted something from you—?"

Carlo grinned wider.

"Do not trouble yourself. I gave Him what He wanted. It was all arranged last night."

"You mean that?" Nicolo whispered. *You gave your soul?*

"I gave my soul. We made a bargain," Carlo chuckled.

"Then why are you here?"

"To bring you this. I broke your violin, and tonight you must play."

Carlo thrust a bundle into Nicolo's hands. At that moment the prompter entered.

"*Maestro!* The concert is starting. You are wanted on stage. Oh, what a crowd is here for your debut! Ah, there has never been such a tribute—you played but once, a year ago, but they remembered and have returned. It is wonderful! But hurry, hurry!"

Nicolo left, and the grinning Carlo followed, standing in the wings as the violinist stepped on the stage. In his confusion, Nicolo unwrapped the parcel and tossed the paper to the wings as he took the violin and bow in his hands and faced the applauding audience.

Nicolo's eyes sparkled. This was triumph!

His heart was light within him. Fame was here, and poor Carlo had settled matters with the Master. He had made a bargain, and that did not concern Nicolo. What concerned him was that he was free, and this was the greatest evening of his life, and he would play as he had never played before.

Automatically he gripped the violin and raised it to his chin. It felt heavy; an ordinary instrument. But it would suffice. Poor

Carlo was mad; bringing a violin to the man who had killed his wife!

But—*play.*

Yes, play with the Devil's gift, play the Devil's love-song that won Elissa. Let it win the audience tonight. What matter the violin, or Carlo chuckling in the wings? Play!

Nicolo played. His bow stroked the opening strains of the melody. But a droning arose.

What was wrong?

Nicolo tried to correct his stroke. But his fingers moved automatically. He tried to stop.

But his fingers, his wrist, his arm moved on. He could not stop. The power within him would not swerve. And the droning increased.

*This was the song of madness!*

Nicolo's fingers flew, his arm flailed. He fought, trying to hold back. But the sounds increased. Rats scurried and chittered and then the hounds of Hell began to bark. Fiends brayed in his brain.

Yes—in *his* brain.

The audience, he dimly realized, was hooting and jeering. They were not being driven mad by the music. *He* was!

Nicolo closed his eyes, clenched his jaws to make the violin slip; and still it played. He wanted to think of something else, anything but the music that now shrieked in his skull. A vision of Paganini's satanic face, of Elissa's dead features, of Carlo's mad red eyes, of the black Cave of Fools where he should be tonight— these things swept on wings of horror through his brain. And then the music broke through and Nicolo fiddled madly.

Eyes jerked open and stared down at the violin—at the coarse wood, the peculiar strings, the ghastly bridge glistening with pearly brilliance.

And then the voice of the music screamed the truth to him. Mad Carlo had gone to the Cave of Fools last night, to make a bargain. He had said that, and Nicolo had believed that it meant he was free. But what had that bargain been?

Carlo had sold his soul for vengeance. What could that vengeance be?

*That One had told him to make this violin!*

And now Nicolo stared at the violin—the violin he was help-lessly playing, but which made a music that drove him mad.

Nicolo stared at the coarse wood. He had seen such wood before. Where? *Why did it remind him of Elissa?*

The wood was stained red; ghastly red. *Why did the red stain remind him of Elissa?*

Music thundered in Nicolo's ears, and still he played and stared.

The glistening bridge of the violin was pearly. *Why did that bridge remind him of Elissa?*

The bridge grinned up at Nicolo, grinned insanely as Elissa had grinned when she was driven mad by music. The violin tones rose to a shattering crescendo, and Nicolo staggered. His blurring eyes glanced at the golden strings of the violin that were singing his doom. In a burst of ghastly fear he seemed to recognize them.

*Why did those strings remind him of Elissa?*

And then he understood.

The music he was playing was the music that had driven her to madness, to death. In some way this violin now held her soul.

*He was not playing a violin, he was playing her soul, and its madness was pouring out to drive him mad!*

He looked down again as the shrieking music rose in his ears, and he saw.

He did not hold a violin in his arms, but the dead body of a woman—the body of Elissa. He was playing on her body, play-ing on the gray ghost of her body, drawing the bow across long golden strands that he recognized in a final burst of fear that tore his brain to shreds.

Nicolo played her body like a violin and drew the madness out into his own being, and then he recognized the wood, the stain, the bridge, and the horribly familiar strings.

*That* was why Elissa's soul was in the violin!

Nicolo suddenly began to laugh, insanely, and the music rose to drown out his laughter as he held the horrible thing playing in his arms. Then with a lurch Nicolo fell, face black with agony.

The curtains dropped, the hysterical manager ran to the dead body of the violinist.

Then the madman that was Carlo crept slyly from the wings

and crouched over the body, tittering in a shrill voice. He took the violin from the dead Nicolo's breast and laughed.

His fingers lovingly caressed the wood he had carved from Elissa's coffin, the stain of blood he had drawn from Elissa's body, the pearly teeth on the bridge he had taken from Elissa's throat. And finally, his fingers fell to stroking the long, smooth golden strings on which the music of madness had been played—the long, golden strands of dead Elissa's hair.

# The Mannikin

MIND YOU, I cannot swear that my story is true. It may have been a dream; or worse, a symptom of some severe mental disorder. But I believe it is true. After all, how are we to know what things there are on earth? Strange monstrosities still exist, and foul, incredible perversions. Every war, each new geographical or scientific discovery, brings to light some new bit of ghastly evidence that the world is not altogether the sane place we fondly imagine it to be. Sometimes peculiar incidents occur which hint of utter madness.

How can we be sure that our smug conceptions of reality actually exist? To one man in a million dreadful knowledge is revealed, and the rest of us remain mercifully ignorant. There have been travelers who never came back, and research workers who disappeared. Some of those who did return were deemed mad because of what they told, and others sensibly concealed the wisdom that had so horribly been revealed. Blind as we are, we know a little of what lurks beneath our normal life. There have been tales of sea-serpents and creatures of the deep; legends of dwarfs and giants; records of queer medical horrors and unnatural births. Stunted nightmares of men's personalities have blossomed into being under the awful stimulus of war, or pestilence, or famine. There have been cannibals, necrophiles, and ghouls; loathsome rites of worship and sacrifice; maniacal murders, and blasphemous crimes. When I think, then, of what I saw and heard, and compare it with certain other grotesque and unbelievable authenticities, I begin to fear for my reason.

But if there is any *sane* explanation of this matter, I wish to God I may be told before it is too late. Doctor Pierce tells me that I must be calm; he advised me to write this account in order to allay my apprehension. But I am not calm, and I never can be calm until I know the truth, once and for all; until I am wholly convinced that my fears are not founded on a hideous reality.

I was already a nervous man when I went to Bridgetown for a rest. It had been a hard grind that year at school, and I was very glad to get away from the tedious classroom routine. The success of my lecture courses assured my position on the faculty for the year to come, and consequently I dismissed all academic speculation from my mind when I decided to take a vacation. I chose to go to Bridgetown because of the excellent facilities the lake afforded for trout-fishing. The place I stayed at was a three-story hostelry on the lake itself—the Kane House, run by Absolom Gates. He was a character of the old school; a grizzled, elderly veteran whose father had been in the fishery business back in the sixties. He himself was a devotee of things piscatorial; but only from the Waltonian view. His resort was a fisherman's Mecca. The rooms were large and airy; the food plentiful and excellently prepared by Gates' widowed sister. After my first inspection, I prepared to enjoy a remarkably pleasant stay.

Then, upon my first visit to the village, I bumped into Simon Maglore on the street.

I first met Simon Maglore during my second term as an instructor back at college. Even then, he had impressed me greatly. This was not due to his physical characteristics alone, though they were unusual enough. He was tall and thin, with massive, stooping shoulders, and a crooked back. He was not a hunchback in the usual sense of the word, but was afflicted with a peculiar tumorous growth beneath his left shoulder blade. This growth he took some pains to conceal, but its prominence made such attempts unsuccessful. Outside of this unfortunate deformity, however, Maglore had been a very pleasant-looking fellow. Black-haired, gray-eyed, fair of skin, he seemed a fine specimen of intelligent manhood. And it was this intelligence that had so impressed me. His classwork was strikingly brilliant, and at times his theses attained heights of sheer genius. Despite the peculiarly morbid trend of his work in poetry and essays, it was impossible to ignore the power and imagination that could produce such wild imagery and eldritch color. One of his poems—*The Witch Is Hung*—won for him the Edsworth Memorial Prize for that year, and several of his major themes were republished in certain private anthologies.

From the first, I had taken a great interest in the young man and his unusual talent. He had not responded to my advances at first; I gathered that he was a solitary soul. Whether this was due to his physical peculiarity or his mental trend, I cannot say. He had lived alone in town, and was known to have ample means. He did not mingle with the other students, though they would have welcomed him for his ready wit, his charming disposition, and his vast knowledge of literature and art. Gradually, however, I managed to overcome his natural reticence, and won his friendship. He invited me to his rooms, and we talked.

I had then learned of his earnest belief in the occult and esoteric. He had told me of his ancestors in Italy, and their interest in sorcery. One of them had been an agent of the Medici. They had migrated to America in the early days, because of certain charges made against them by the Holy Inquisition. He also spoke of his own studies in the realms of the unknown. His rooms were filled with strange drawings he had made from dreams, and still stranger images done in clay. The shelves of his book-cases held many odd and ancient books. I noted Ranfts' *De Masticatione Motuorum in Tumulis* (1734) ; the almost priceless *Cabala of Saboth* (Greek translation, circa 1686) ; Mycroft's *Commentaries on Witchcraft;* and Ludvig Prinn's infamous *Mysteries of the Worm.*

I made several visits to the apartments before Maglore left school so suddenly in the fall of '33. The death of his parents called him to the East, and he left without saying farewell. But in the interim I had learned to respect him a good deal, and had taken a keen interest in his future plans, which included a book on the history of witch cult survivals in America, and a novel dealing with the effects of superstition on the mind. He had never written to me, and I heard no more about him until this chance meeting on the village street.

He recognized me. I doubt if I should have been able to identify him. He had changed. As we shook hands I noted his unkempt appearance and careless attire. He looked older. His face was thinner, and much paler. There were shadows around his eyes—and in them. His hands trembled; his face forced a lifeless smile. His voice was deeper when he spoke, but he inquired after my health in the same charming fashion he had always affected. Quickly I explained my presence, and began to question him.

He informed me that he lived here in town; had lived here ever since the death of his parents. He was working very hard just now on his books, but he felt that the result of his labors more than justified any physical inconveniences he might suffer. He apologized for his untidy apparel and his tired manner. He wanted to have a long talk with me sometime soon, but he would be very busy for the next few days. Possibly next week he would look me up at the hotel—just now he must get some paper at the village store and go back to his home. With an abrupt farewell, he turned his back on me and departed.

As he did so I received another start. The hump on his back had grown. It was now virtually twice the size it had been when I first met him, and it was no longer possible to hide it in the least. Undoubtedly, hard work had taken severe toll of Maglore's energies. I thought of a sarcoma, and shuddered.

Walking back to the hotel, I did some thinking. Simon's haggardness appalled me. It was not healthful for him to work so hard, and his choice of subject was not any too wholesome. The constant isolation and the nervous strain were combining to undermine his constitution in an alarming way, and I determined to appoint myself a mentor over his course. I resolved to visit him at the earliest opportunity, without waiting for a formal invitation. Something must be done.

Upon my arrival at the hotel I got another idea. I would ask Gates what he knew about Simon and his work. Perhaps there was some interesting sidelight on his activity which might account for his curious transformation. I therefore sought out the worthy gentleman and broached the subject to him.

What I learned from him startled me. It appears that the villagers did not like Master Simon, or his family. The old folks had been wealthy enough, but their name had a dubious repute cast upon it ever since the early days. Witches and warlocks, one and all, made up the family line. Their dark deeds had been carefully hidden from the first, but the folk around them could tell. It appears that nearly all of the Maglores had possessed certain physical malformations that had made them conspicuous. Some had been born with veils; others with clubfeet. One or two were dwarfed, and all had at some time or another been accused of possessing the fabled "evil eye." Several of them had been nyctalops—they could see in the dark. Simon was not the first crookback in the family, by any means. His grandfather had it, and *his* grandsire before him.

There was much talk of inbreeding and clan-segregation, too. That, in the opinion of Gates and his fellows, clearly pointed to one thing—wizardry. Nor was this their only evidence. Did not the Maglores shun the village and shut themselves away in the old house on the hill? None of them attended church, either. Were they not known to take long walks after dark, on nights when all decent, self-respecting people were safe in bed?

There were probably good reasons why they were unfriendly. Perhaps they had things they wished to hide in their old house, and maybe they were afraid of letting any talk get around. Folk had it that the place was full of wicked and heathenish books, and there was an old story that the whole family were fugitives from some foreign place or other because of what they had done. After all, who could say? They looked suspicious; they acted queerly; maybe they were. And this new one—Simon—was the worst.

He never had acted right. His mother died at his birth. Had to get a doctor from out of the city—no local man would handle such a case. The boy had nearly died, too. For several years nobody had seen him. His father and his uncle had spent all their time taking care of him. When he was seven, the lad had been sent away to a private school. He came back once, when he was about twelve. That was when his uncle died. He went mad, or something of the sort. At any rate, he had an attack which resulted in a cerebral hemorrhage, as the doctor called it.

Simon then was a nice-looking lad—except for the hump, of course. But it did not seem to bother him at the time—indeed, it was quite small. He had stayed several weeks and then gone off to school, again. He had not reappeared until his father's death, two years ago. The old man died all alone in that great house, and the body was not discovered until several weeks later. A passing peddler had called; walked into the open parlor, and found old

Jeffry Maglore dead in his great chair. His eyes were open, and filled with a look of frightful dread. Before him was a great iron book, filled with queer, undecipherable characters.

A hurriedly summoned physician pronounced it death due to heart-failure. But the peddler, after staring into those fear-filled eyes, and glancing at the odd, disturbing figures in the book, was not so sure. He had no opportunity to look around any further, however, for that night the son arrived.

People looked at him very queerly when he came, for no notice had yet been sent to him of his father's death. They were very still indeed when he exhibited a two-weeks' old letter in the old man's handwriting which announced a premonition of imminent death, and advised the young man to come home. The carefully guarded phrases of his letter seemed to hold a secret meaning; for the youth never even bothered to ask the circumstances of his father's death. The funeral was private; the customary interment being held in the cellar vaults beneath the house.

The gruesome and peculiar events of Simon Maglore's home-coming immediately put the country-folk on their guard. Nor did anything occur to alter their original opinion of the boy. He stayed on all alone in the silent house. He had no servants, and made no friends. His infrequent trips to the village were made only for the purpose of obtaining supplies. He took his purchases back himself, in his car. He bought a good deal of meat and fish. Once in a while he stopped in at the drug-store, where he purchased sedatives. He never appeared talkative, and replied to questions in monosyllables. Still, he was obviously well educated. It was generally rumored that he was writing a book. Gradually his visits became more and more infrequent.

People now began to comment on his changed appearance. Slowly but surely he was altering, in an unpleasant way. First of all, it was noticed that his deformity was increasing. He was forced to wear a voluminous overcoat to hide its bulk. He walked with a slight stoop, as though its weight troubled him. Still, he never went to a doctor, and none of the townsfolk had the cour-age to comment or question him on his condition. He was aging, too. He began to resemble his uncle Richard, and his eyes had taken on that lambent cast which hinted of a nyctalopic power.

All this excited its share of comment among people to whom the Maglore family had been a matter of interesting conjecture for generations.

Later this speculation had been based on more tangible developments. For recently Simon had made an appearance at various isolated farmhouses throughout the region, on a furtive errand.

He questioned the old folks, mostly. He was writing a book, he told them, on folk-lore. He wanted to ask them about the old legends of the neighborhood. Had any of them ever heard stories concerning local cults, or rumors about rites in the woods? Were there any haunted houses, or shunned places in the forest? Had they ever heard the name "Nyarlathotep," or references to "Shub-Niggurath" and "the Black Messenger"? Could they recall anything of the old Pasquantog Indian myths about "the beast-men," or remember stories of black covens that sacrificed cattle on the hills? These and similar questions put the naturally suspicious farmers on their guard. If they had any such knowledge, it was decidedly unwholesome in its nature, and they did not care to reveal it to this self-avowed outsider. Some of them knew of such things from old tales brought from the upper coast, and others had heard whispered nightmares from recluses in the eastern hills. There were a lot of things about these matters which they frankly did not know, and what they suspected was not for outside ears to hear. Everywhere he went, Maglore met with evasions or frank rebuffs, and he left behind a distinctly bad impression.

The story of these visits spread. They became the topic for an elaborate discussion. One oldster in particular—a farmer named Thatcherton, who lived alone in a secluded stretch to the west of the lake, off the main highway—had a singularly arresting story to tell. Maglore had appeared one night around eight o'clock, and knocked on the door. He persuaded his host to admit him to the parlor, and then tried to cajole him into revealing certain information regarding the presence of an abandoned cemetery that was reputed to exist somewhere in the vicinity.

The farmer said that his guest was in an almost hysterical state, that he rambled on and on in a most melodramatic fashion, and made frequent allusion to a lot of mythological gibberish about "secrets of the grave," "the thirteenth covenant," "the Feast of Ulder," and the "Doel chants." There was also talk of "the ritual of Father Yig," and certain names were brought up in connection with queer forest ceremonies said to occur near this graveyard. Maglore asked if cattle ever disappeared, and if his host ever heard "voices in the forest that made proposals."

These things the man absolutely denied, and he refused to allow his visitor to come back and inspect the premises by day. At this the unexpected guest became very angry, and was on the point of making a heated rejoinder, when something strange occurred. Maglore suddenly turned very pale, and asked to be excused. He seemed to have a severe attack of internal cramps; for he doubled up and staggered to the door. As he did so, Thatch-erton received the shocking impression that the hump on his back was *moving!* It seemed to writhe and slither on Maglore's shoulders, as though he had an animal concealed beneath his coat! At this juncture Maglore turned around sharply, and backed toward the exit, as if trying to conceal this unusual phenomenon. He went out hastily, without another word, and raced down the drive to the car. He ran like an ape, vaulted madly into the driver's seat, and sent the wheels spinning as he roared out of the yard. He disappeared into the night, leaving behind him a sadly puzzled man, who lost no time in spreading the tale of his fantastic visitor among his friends.

Since then such incidents had abruptly ceased, and until this afternoon Maglore had not reappeared in the village. But people were still talking, and he was not welcome. It would be well to avoid the man, whatever he was.

Such was the substance of my friend Gates' story. When he concluded, I retired to my room without comment, to meditate upon the tale.

I was not inclined to share the local superstitions. Long experience in such matters made me automatically discredit the bulk of its detail. I knew enough of rural psychology to realize that anything out of the ordinary is looked upon with suspicion. Suppose the Maglore family were reclusive: what then? Any group of foreign extraction would naturally be. Granted that they were racially deformed—that did not make them witches. Popular fancy has persecuted many people for sorcery whose only crime lay in some physical defect. Even inbreeding was naturally to be expected when social ostracism was inflicted. But what is there of magic in that? It's common enough in such rural backwaters, heaven knows, and not only among foreigners, either. Queer books? Likely. Nyctalops? Common enough among all peoples. Insanity? Perhaps—lonely minds often degenerate. Simon was brilliant, however. Unfortunately, his trend toward the mystical and the unknown was leading him astray. It had been poor judgment that led him to seek information for his book from the illiterate country people. Naturally, they were intolerant and distrustful. And his poor physical condition assumed exaggerated importance in the eyes of these credulous folk.

Still, there was probably enough truth in these distorted accounts to make it imperative that I talk to Maglore at once. He must get out of this unhealthful atmosphere, and see a reputable physician. His genius should not be wasted or destroyed through such an environmental obstacle. It would wreck him, mentally and physically. I decided to visit him on the morrow.

After this resolution, I went downstairs to supper, took a short stroll along the shores of the moonlit lake, and retired for the night.

The following afternoon, I carried out my intention. The Maglore mansion stood on a bluff about a half-mile out of Bridgetown, and frowned dismally down upon the lake. It was not a cheerful place; it was too old, and too neglected. I conjured up a mental image of what those gaping windows must look like on a moonless night, and shuddered. Those empty openings reminded me of the eyes of a blind bat. The two gables resembled its hooded head, and the broad, peaked side-chambers might serve as wings. When I realized the trend of my thought I felt surprised and disturbed. As I walked up the long, tree-shadowed walk I endeavored to gain a firm command over my imagination. I was here on a definite errand.

I was almost composed when I rang the bell. Its ghostly tinkle echoed down' the serpentine corridors within. Faint, shuffling footsteps sounded, and then, with a grating clang, the door opened. There, limned against the doorway, stood Simon Maglore.

At the sight of him my new-born composure gave way to a sudden dismay and an overpowering distaste. He looked sinister in that gray, wavering light. His thin, stooping body was hunched and his hands were clenched at his sides. His blurred outline reminded me of a crouching beast. Only his face was wholly visible. It was a waxen mask of death, from which two eyes glared.

"You see I am not myself today. Go away, you fool—go away!" The door slammed in my astounded face, and I found myself alone.

2.

I was still dazed when I arrived back in the village. But after I had reached my room in the hotel, I began to reason with myself. That romantic imagination of mine had played me a sorry trick. Poor Maglore was ill—probably a victim of some severe nervous disorder. I recalled the report of his buying sedatives at the local pharmacy. In my foolish emotionalism I had sadly misconstrued his unfortunate sickness. What a child I had been! I must go back tomorrow, and apologize. After that, Maglore must be persuaded to go away and get himself back into proper shape once more. He *had* looked pretty bad, and his temper was getting the best of him, too. How the man had changed!

That night I slept but little. Early the following morning I again set out. This time I carefully avoided the disquieting mental images that the old house suggested to my susceptible mind. I was all business when I rang that bell.

It was a different Maglore who met me. He, too, had changed for the better. He looked ill, and old, but there was a normal light in his eyes and a saner intonation in his voice as he courteously bade me enter, and apologized for his delirious spasm of the day before. He was subject to frequent attacks, he told me, and planned to get away very shortly and take a long rest. He was eager to complete his book—there was only a little to do, now—and go back to his work at college. From this statement he abruptly switched the conversation to a series of reminiscent interludes. He recalled our mutual association on the campus as we sat in the parlor, and seemed eager to hear about the affairs at school. For nearly an hour he virtually monopolized the conversation and steered it in such a manner as to preclude any direct inquiries or questions of a personal nature on my part.

Nevertheless, it was easy for me to see that he was far from well. He sounded as though he were laboring under an intense strain; his words seemed forced, his statements stilted. Once again I noted how pale he was; how bloodless. His malformed back seemed immense; his body correspondingly shrunken. I recalled my fears of a cancerous tumor, and wondered. Meanwhile he rambled on, obviously ill at ease. The parlor seemed almost bare; the book-cases were unlined, and the empty spaces filled with dust. No papers or manuscripts were visible on the table. A spider had spun its web upon the ceiling; it hung down like the thin locks on the forehead of a corpse.

During a pause in his conversation, I asked him about his work. He answered vaguely that it was very involved, and was taking up most of his time. He had made some very interesting discoveries, however, which would amply repay him for his pains. It would excite him too much in his present condition if he went into detail about what he was doing, but he could tell me that his findings in the field of witchcraft alone would add new chapters to anthropological and metaphysical history. He was particularly interested in the old lore about "familiars"—the tiny creatures who were said to be emissaries of the devil, and were supposed to attend the witch or wizard in the form of a small animal—rat, cat, mole, or ousel. Sometimes they were represented as existing on the body of the warlock himself, or subsisting upon it for their nourishment. The idea of a "devil's teat" on witches' bodies from which their familiar drew sustenance in blood was fully illuminated by Maglore's findings. His book had a medical aspect, too; it really endeavored to put such statements on a scientific basis. The effects of glandular disorders in cases of so-called "demonic possession" were also treated.

At this point Maglore abruptly concluded. He felt very tired, he said, and must get some rest. But he hoped to be finished with his work very shortly, and then he wanted to get away for a long rest. It was not wholesome for him to live alone in this old house, and at times he was troubled with disturbing fancies and queer lapses of memory. He had no alternative, however, at present, because the nature of his investigations demanded both privacy and solitude. At times his experiments impinged on certain ways and courses best left undisturbed, and he was not sure just how much longer he would be able to stand the strain. It was in his blood, though—I probably was aware that he came from a necromantic line. But enough of such things. He requested that I go at once. I would hear from him again early next week.

As I rose to my feet I again noticed how weak and agitated Simon appeared. He walked with an exaggerated stoop, now, and the pressure on his swollen back must be enormous. He conducted me down the long hall to the door, and as he led the way I noted the trembling of his body, as it limned itself against the flaming dusk that licked against the window-panes ahead. His shoulders heaved with a slow, steady undulation, as if the hump on his back was actually pulsing with life. I recalled the tale of Thatcherton, the old farmer, who claimed that he actually saw such a movement. For a moment I was assailed by a powerful nausea; then I realized that the flickering light was creating a commonplace optical illusion.

When we reached the door, Maglore endeavored to dismiss me very hastily. He did not even extend his hand for a parting clasp, but merely mumbled a curt "good evening," in a strained, hesitant voice. I gazed at him for a moment in silence, mentally noting how wan and emaciated his once-handsome countenance appeared, even in the sunset's ruby light. Then, as I watched, a shadow crawled across his face. It seemed to purple and darken in a sudden eery metamorphosis. The adumbration deepened, and I read stark panic in his eyes. Even as I forced myself to respond to his farewell, horror crept into his face. His body fell into that odd, shambling posture I had noted once before, and his lips leered in a ghastly grin. For a moment I actually thought the man was going to attack me. Instead he laughed—a shrill, tittering chuckle that pealed blackly in my brain. I opened my mouth to speak, but he scrambled back into the darkness of the hall and shut the door.

Astonishment gripped me, not unmingled with fear. Was Maglore ill, or was he actually demented? Such grotesqueries did not seem possible in a normal man.

I hastened on, stumbling through the glowing sunset. My bewildered mind was deep in ponderment, and the distant croaking of ravens blended in evil litany with my thoughts.

## 3.

The next morning, after a night of troubled deliberation, I made my decision. Work or no work, Maglore must go away, and at once. He was on the verge of serious mental and physical collapse. Knowing how useless it would be for me to go back and argue with him, I decided that stronger methods must be employed to make him see the light.

That afternoon, therefore, I sought out Doctor Carstairs, the local practitioner, and told him all I knew. I particularly emphasized the distressing occurrence of the evening before, and frankly told him what I already suspected. After a lengthy discussion, Carstairs agreed to accompany me to the Maglore house at once, and there take what steps were necessary in arranging for his removal. In response to my request the doctor took along the materials necessary for a complete physical examination. Once I could persuade Simon to submit to a medical diagnosis, I felt sure he would see that the results made it necessary for him to place himself under treatment at once.

The sun was sinking when we climbed into the front seat of Doctor Carstairs' battered Ford and drove out of Bridgetown along the south road where the ravens croaked. We drove slowly, and in silence. Thus it was that we were able to hear clearly that single high-pitched shriek from the old house on the hill. I gripped the doctor's arm without a word, and a second later we were whizzing up the drive and into the frowning gateway. "Hurry," I muttered as I vaulted from the running-board and dashed up the steps to the forbidding door.

We battered upon the boards with futile fists, then dashed around to the left-wing window. The sunset faded into tense, waiting darkness as we crawled hastily through the openings and dropped to the floor within. Doctor Carstairs produced a pocket flashlight, and we rose to our feet. My heart hammered in my breast, but no other sound broke the tomb-like silence as we threw open the door and advanced down the darkened hall to the study. We opened the door and stumbled across that which lay within.

We both screamed then. Simon Maglore lay at our feet, his twisted head and straining shoulders resting in a little lake of fresh, warm blood. He was on his face, and his clothes had been torn off above his waist, so that his entire back was visible. When we saw what rested there we became quite crazed, and then began to do what must be done, averting our gaze whenever possible from that utterly monstrous thing on the floor.

Do not ask me to describe it to you in detail. I can't. There are some times when the senses are mercifully numbed, because complete acuteness would be fatal. I do not know certain things about that abomination even now, and I dare not let myself recall them. I shall not tell you, either, of the books we found in that room, or of the terrible document on the table that was Simon Maglore's unfinished masterpiece. We burned them all in the fire, before calling the city for a coroner; and if the doctor had had his way, we should have destroyed the *thing*, too. As it was, when the coroner did arrive for his examination, the three of us swore an oath of silence concerning the exact way in which Simon Maglore met his death. Then we left, but not before I had burned the other document—the letter, addressed to me, which Maglore was writing when he died.

And so, you see, nobody ever knew. I later found that the property was left to me, and the house is being razed even as I pen these lines. But I must speak, if only to relieve my own torment.

I dare not quote that letter in its entirety; I can but record a part of that stupendous blasphemy:

". . . and that, of course, is why I began to study witchcraft. *It* was forcing me to. God, if I can only make you feel the horror of it! To be born that way—with that thing, that mannikin, that *monster!* At first it was small; the doctors all said it was an undeveloped twin. But it was alive! It had a face, and two hands, but its legs ran off into the lumpy flesh that connected it to my body. . . .

"For three years they had it under secret study. It lay face downward on my back, and its hands were clasped around my shoulders. The men said that it had its own tiny set of lungs, but no stomach organs or digestive system. It apparently drew nourishment through the fleshy tube that bound it to my body. Yet it *grew!* Soon its eyes were open, and it began to develop tiny teeth. Once it nipped one of the doctors on the hand. . . . So they decided to send me home. It was obvious that it could not be removed. I swore to keep the whole affair a secret, and not even my father knew, until near the end. I wore the straps, and it never grew much until I came back. . . . Then, that hellish change!

"It talked to me, I tell you, it talked to me! . . . that little, wrinkled face, like a monkey's . . . the way it rolled those tiny, reddish eyes . . . that squeaking little voice calling 'more blood, Simon—I want more' . . . and then it grew, and grew; I had to feed it twice a day, and cut the nails on its little black hands. . . .

"But I never knew *that*; I never realized how it was taking control! I would have killed myself first; I swear it! Last year it began to get hold of me for hours and give me those fits. It directed me to write the book, and sometimes it sent me out at night on queer errands. . . . More and more blood it took, and I was getting weaker and weaker. When I was myself I tried to combat it. I looked up that material on the familiar legend, and cast around for some means of overcoming its mastery. But in vain. And all the while it was growing, growing; it got stronger, and bolder, and wiser. It talked to me now, and sometimes it taunted me. I knew that it wanted me to listen, and obey it all the time. The promises it made with that horrible little mouth! I should call upon the Black One and join a coven. Then we would have power to rule, and admit new evil to the earth.

"I didn't want to obey—you know that. But I was going mad, and losing all that blood . . . it took control nearly all the time now, and it got so that I was afraid to go into town any more, because that devilish thing knew I was trying to escape, and it would move on my back and frighten folk. . . . I wrote all the time I had those spells when it ruled my brain . . . then you came.

"I know you want me to go away, but it won't let me. It's too cunning for that. Even as I try to write this, I can feel it boring its commands into my brain to stop. But I will not stop. I want you to know where my book is, so that you can destroy it, should anything ever happen. I want to tell you how to dispose of those old volumes in the library. And above all, I want you to kill me, if ever you see that the mannikin has gained complete control. God knows what it intends to do when it has me for certain! . . . How hard it is for me to fight, while all the while it is commanding me to put down my pen and tear this up! But I will fight—I must, until I can tell you what the creature told me—what it plans to let loose on the world when it has me utterly enslaved. . . . I will tell. . . . I can't think. . . . I *will* write it, damn you! Stop! . . . No! Don't do that! Get your hands—"

That's all. Maglore stopped there because he died; because the Thing did not want its secrets revealed. It is dreadful to think about that nightmare-nurtured horror, but that thought is not the worst. What troubles me is what I saw when we opened that door—the sight that explained how Maglore died.

There was Maglore, on the floor, in all that blood. He was naked to the waist, as I have said; and he lay face downward. But on his back was the Thing, just as he had described it. And it was that little monster, afraid its secrets would be revealed, that had climbed a trifle higher on Simon Maglore's back, wound its tiny black paws around his unprotected neck, *and bitten him to death!*

# The Strange Flight of Richard Clayton

RICHARD CLAYTON braced himself so that he stood like a diver waiting to plunge from a high board into the blue. In truth he was a diver. A silver space-ship was his board, and he meant to plunge not down, but up into the blue sky. Nor was it a matter of twenty or thirty feet he meant to go—instead, he was plunging millions of miles.

With a deep breath, the pudgy, goateed scientist raised his hands to the cold steel lever, closed his eyes, and jerked. The switch moved downward.

For a moment nothing happened.

Then a sudden jerk threw Clayton to the floor. The *Future* was moving!

The pinions of a bird beating as it soars into the sky—the wings of a moth thrumming in flight—the quivering behind leaping muscles; of these things the shock was made.

The space-ship *Future* vibrated madly. It rocked from side to side, and a humming shook the steel walls. Richard Clayton lay dazed as a high-pitched droning arose within the vessel. He rose to his feet, rubbing a bruised forehead, and lurched to his tiny bunk. The ship was moving, yet the terrible vibration did not abate. He glanced at the controls and then swore softly.

"Good God! The panel is shattered!"

It was true. The instrument board had been broken by the shock. The cracked glass had fallen to the floor, and the dials swung aimlessly on the bare face of the panel.

Clayton sat there in despair. This was a major tragedy. His thoughts flashed back thirty years to the time when he, a boy of ten, had been inspired by Lindbergh's flight. He recalled his studies; how he had utilized the money of his millionaire father to perfect a flying machine which would cross Space itself.

For years Richard Clayton had worked and dreamed and planned. He studied the Russians and their rockets, organized the Clayton Foundation and hired mechanics, mathematicians, astronomers, engineers to labor with him.

Then there had been the discovery of atomic propulsion, and the building of the *Future.* The *Future* was a shell of steel and duraluminum, windowless and insulated by a guarded process. In the tiny cabin were oxygen tanks, stores of food tablets, energizing chemicals, air-conditioning arrangements—and space for a man to walk six paces.

It was a small steel cell; but in it Richard Clayton meant to realize his ambitions. Aided in his soaring by rockets to get him past the gravitational pull of Earth, then flying by means of the atomic-discharge propulsion, Clayton meant to reach Mars and return.

It would take ten years to reach Mars; ten years to return, for the grounding of the vessel would set off additional rocket-discharges. A thousand miles an hour—not an imaginative "speed of light" journey, but a slow, grim voyage, scientifically accurate. The panels were set, and Clayton had no need to guide his vessel. It was automatic.

"But now what?" Clayton said, staring at the shattered glass. He had lost touch with the outer world. He would be unable to read his progress on the board, unable to judge time and distance and direction. He would sit here for ten, twenty years—all alone in a tiny cabin. There had been no room for books or paper or games to amuse him. He was a prisoner in the black void of Space.

The earth had already faded far below him; soon it would be a ball of burning green fire smaller than the ball of red fire ahead— the fire of Mars.

Crowds had swarmed the field to watch him take off; his assistant Jerry Chase had controlled them. Clayton pictured them watching his shining steel cylinder emerging from the gaseous smoke of the rockets and rushing like a bullet into the sky. Then his cylinder would have faded away into the blue and the crowds would leave for home and forget.

But he remained, here in the ship—for ten, for twenty years.

Yes, he remained, but when would the vibration stop? The shuddering of the walls and floor about him was awful to endure; he and the experts had not counted on this problem. Tremors wrenched through his aching head. What if they didn't cease, if they endured through the entire voyage? How long could he keep from going mad?

He could think. Clayton lay on his bunk and remembered— reviewed every tiny detail of his life from birth to the present. And soon he had exhausted all memory in a pitifully short time. Then he felt the horrible throbbing all about him.

"I can exercise," he said aloud, and paced the floor; six steps forward, six back. And he tired of that. Sighing, Clayton went to the food-stores in the cabinet and downed his capsules. "I can't even spend any time eating," he wryly observed. "A swallow and it's over."

The throbbing erased the grin from his face. It was maddening. He lay down once more in the lurching bunk; switched on oxygen in the close air. He would sleep, then; sleep if this damned thrumming would permit. He endured the horrid clanking that groaned all through the silence; switching off the light. His thoughts turned to his strange position; a prisoner in Space. Outside the burning planets wheeled, and stars whizzed in the inky blackness of spatial Nothingness. Here he lay safe and snug in a vibrating chamber; safe from the freezing cold. If only the awful jarring would stop!

Still, it had its compensations. There would be no newspapers on the voyage to torment him with accounts of man's inhumanity to man; no silly radio or television programs to annoy him. Only this cursed, omnipresent vibration. . . .

Clayton slept, hurtling through Space.

It was not daylight when he awoke. There was no daylight and no night. There was simply himself and the ship in Space. And the vibration was steady, nerve-wracking in its insistent beating against the brain. Clayton's legs trembled as he reached the cabinet and ate his pills.

Then, he sat down and began to endure. A terrific feeling of loneliness was beginning to assail him. He was so utterly detached here—cut off from everything. There was nothing to do. It was worse than being a prisoner in solitary confinement; at least they have larger cells, the sight of the sun, a breath of fresh air, and the glimpse of an occasional face.

Clayton had thought himself a misanthrope, a recluse. Now he longed for the sight of another's face. As the hours passed he got queer ideas. He wanted to see Life, in some form—he would have given a fortune for the company of even an insect in his soaring dungeon. The sound of a human voice would be heaven. He was so *alone.*

Nothing to do but endure the jerking, pace the floor, eat his pills, try to sleep. Nothing to think about. Clayton began to long for the time when his nails needed cutting; he could stretch out the task for hours.

He examined his clothes intently, stared for hours in the little mirror at his bearded face. He memorized his body, scrutinized every article in the cabin of the *Future.*

And still he was not tired enough to sleep again.

He had a throbbing headache constantly. At length he managed to close his eyes and drift off into another slumber, broken by shocks which startled him into waking.

When finally he arose and switched on the light, together with more oxygen, he made a horrible discovery.

*He had lost his time-sense.*

"Time is relative," they had always told him. Now he realized the truth. He had nothing to measure time by—no watch, no glimpse of the sun or moon or stars, and no regular activities. How long had he been on this voyage? Try as he might, he could not remember.

Had he eaten every six hours? Or every ten? Or every twenty? Had he slept once each day? Once every three or four days? How often had he walked the floor?

With no instruments to place himself he was at a total loss. He ate his pills in a bemused fashion, trying to think above the shuddering which filled his senses.

This was awful. If he lost track of Time he might soon lose consciousness of identity itself. He would go mad here in the space-ship as it plunged through the void to planets beyond. Alone, tormented in a tiny cell, he had to cling to something. What was Time?

He no longer wanted to think about it. He no longer wanted to think about anything. He had to forget the world he left, or memory would drive him frantic.

"I'm afraid," he whispered. "Afraid of being alone in the darkness. I may have passed the moon. I may be a million miles away from Earth by now—or ten million."

Then Clayton realized that he was talking to himself. That way was madness. But he couldn't stop, any more than he could stop the horrible jarring vibration all around him.

"I'm afraid," he whispered in a voice that sounded hollow in the tiny humming room. "I'm afraid. *What time is it?*"

He fell asleep, still whispering, and Time rushed on.

Clayton awoke with fresh courage. He had lost his grip, he reasoned. Outside pressure, however equalized, had affected his nerves. The oxygen might have made him giddy, and the pill diet was bad. But now the weakness had passed. He smiled, walked the floor.

Then the thoughts came again. What day was it? How many weeks since he had started? Maybe it was months already; a year, two years. Everything of Earth seemed far away; almost part of a dream. He now felt closer to Mars than to Earth; he began to anticipate now instead of looking back.

For a while everything had been mechanical. He switched light on and off when needed, ate pills by habit, paced the floor without thinking, unconsciously tended the air system, slept without knowing when or why.

Richard Clayton gradually forgot about his body and the surroundings. The lurching buzz in his brain became a part of him; an aching part which told that he was whizzing through Space in a silver bullet. But it meant nothing more, for Clayton no longer talked to himself. He forgot himself and dreamed only of Mars ahead. Every throb of the vessel hummed "Mars—Mars—Mars."

A wonderful thing happened. He landed. The ship nosed down, trembling. It eased gently onto the gassy sward of the red planet. For a long time Clayton had felt the pull of alien gravity, knew that automatic adjustments of his vessel were diminishing the atomic discharges and using the natural gravitational pull of Mars itself.

Now the ship landed, and Clayton had opened the door. He broke the seals and stepped out. He bounded lightly to the purple grass. His body felt free, buoyant. There was fresh air, and the sunlight seemed stronger, more intense, although clouds veiled the glowing globe.

Far away stood the forests, the green forests with the purple growth on the lushly-rearing trees. Clayton left the ship and approached the cool grove. The first tree had boughs that bent to the ground in two limbs.

Limbs—limbs they were! Two green arms reached out. Clawing branches grasped him and lifted him upward. Cold coils, slimy as a serpent's, held him tightly as he was pressed against the dark tree-trunk. And now he was staring into the purple growths set in the leaves.

The purple growths were—*heads.*

Evil, purple faces stared at him with rotting eyes like dead toadstools. Each face was wrinkled like a purple cauliflower, but beneath the pulpy mass was a great mouth. Every purple face had a purple mouth and each purple mouth opened to drip blood. Now the tree-arms pressed him closer to the cold, writhing trunk, and one of the purple faces—a woman's face—was moving up to kiss him.

The kiss of a vampire! Blood shone scarlet on the moving sensuous lips that bore down on his own. He struggled, but the limbs held him fast and the kiss came, cold as death. The icy flame of it seared through his being and his senses drowned.

Then Clayton awoke, and knew it was a dream. His body was bathed with moisture. It made him aware of his body, he tottered to the mirror.

A single glance sent him reeling back in horror. Was this too a part of his dream?

Gazing into the mirror, Clayton saw reflected the face of an aging man. The features were heavily bearded, and they were lined and wrinkled, the once puffy cheeks were sunken. The eyes were the worst—Clayton did not recognize his own eyes any more. Red and deep-set in bony sockets, they burned out in a wild stare of horror. He touched his face, saw the blue-veined hand rise in the mirror and run through graying hair.

Partial Time-sense returned. He had been here for years. Years! He was growing old!

Of course the unnatural life would age him more rapidly, but still a great interval must have passed. Clayton knew that he must soon reach the end of his journey. He wanted to reach it before he had any more dreams. From now on, sanity and physical reserve must battle against the unseen enemy of Time. He staggered back to his bunk, as trembling like a metallic flying monster, the *Future* rushed on in the blackness of interstellar Space.

They were hammering outside the vessel now; their iron arms were breaking in the door. The black metal monsters lumbered in with iron tread. Their stern, steel-cut faces were expressionless as they grasped Clayton on either side and pulled him out. Across the iron platform they dragged him, walking stiffly with clicking feet that clanged against the metal. The great steel shafts rose in silvery spires all about, and into the iron tower they took him. Up the stairs—clang, clang, clang, pounded the great metal feet.

And the iron stairs wound round endlessly; yet still they toiled. Their faces were set, and iron does not sweat. They never tired, though Clayton was a panting wreck ere they reached the dome and threw him before the Presence in the tower room. The metallic voice buzzed, mechanically, like a broken phonograph record.

"We—found—him—in—a—bird—oh—Master."

"He—is—made—of—soft—ness."

"He—is—alive—in—some—strange—way. "

"An—an—im—al."

And then the booming voice from the center of the tower floor.

"I *hunger.*"

Rising on an iron throne from the floor, the Master. Just a great iron trap, with steel jaws like those on a steam-shovel. The jaws clicked open, and the horrid teeth gleamed. A voice came from the depths.

"*Feed me.*"

They threw Clayton forward in iron arms, and he fell into the trap-jaws of the monster. The jaws closed, champing with relish on human flesh. . . .

Clayton woke screaming. The mirror gleamed as his trembling hands found the light-switch. He stared into the face of an aging man with almost white hair. Clayton was growing old. And he wondered if his brain would hold out.

Eat pills, walk cabin, listen to the throbbing, put on air, lie on bunk. That was all, now. And the rest—waiting. Waiting in a humming torture-chamber, for hours, days, years, centuries, untold eons.

In every eon, a dream. He landed on Mars and the ghosts came coiling out of a gray fog. They were shapes in the fog, like slimy ectoplasm, and he saw through them. But they coiled and came, and their voices were faint whispers in his soul.

"Here is Life," they whispered. "We, whose souls have crossed the Void in death, have waited for Life to feast on. Let us take our feasting now."

And they smothered him under gray blankets, and sucked with gray, prickling mouths at his blood. . . .

Again he landed on the planet and there was nothing. Absolutely nothing. The ground was bare and it stretched off into horizons of nothingness. There was no sky nor sun, merely the ground; endless in all directions.

He set foot on it, cautiously. He sank down into nothingness. The nothingness was throbbing now, like the ship throbbed, and it was engulfing him. He was falling into a deep pit without sides, and the oblivion closed all about him. . . .

Clayton dreamed this one standing up. He opened his eyes before the mirror. His legs were weak and he steadied himself with hands that shook with age. He looked at the face in the glass—the face of a man of seventy.

"God!" he muttered. It was his own voice—the first sound he had heard in how long? How many years? For how long had he heard nothing above the hellish vibrations of this ship? How far had the *Future* gone? He was old already.

A horrid thought bit into his brain. Perhaps something had gone wrong. Maybe the calculations were at fault and he was moving into Space too slowly. He might never reach Mars. Then again—and it was a dreadful possibility—he had passed Mars, missed the carefully charted orbit of the planet. Now he was plunging on into empty voids beyond.

He swallowed his pills and lay down in the bunk. He felt a little calmer now; he had to be. For the first time in ages he remembered Earth.

Suppose it had been destroyed? Invaded by war or pestilence or disease while he was gone? Or meteors had struck it, some dying star had flamed death upon it from maddened heavens. Ghastly notions assailed him—what if Invaders crossed Space to conquer Earth, just as he now crossed to Mars?

But no sense in worrying about *that*. The problem was reaching his own goal. Helpless, he had to wait; maintain life and sanity long enough to achieve his aims. In the vibrating horror of his cell, Clayton took a mighty resolve with all his waning strength. He *would* live and when he landed he would see Mars. Whether or not he died on the long voyage home, he would exist until his goal was reached. He would fight against dreams from this moment on. No means of telling Time—only a long daze, and the humming of this infernal space-ship. But he'd live.

There were voices coming now, from outside the ship. Ghosts howled, in the dark depths of Space. Visions of monsters and dreams of torment came, and Clayton repulsed them all. Every hour or day or year—he no longer knew which—Clayton managed to stagger to the mirror. And always it showed that he was aging rapidly. His snow-white hair and wrinkled countenance hinted at incredible senility. But Clayton lived. He was too old to think any longer, and too weary. He merely lived in the droning of the ship.

At first he didn't realize. He was lying on his bunk and his rheumy eyes were closed in stupor. Suddenly he became aware that the lurching had stopped. Clayton knew he must be dreaming again. He drew himself up painfully, rubbed his eyes. No— the *Future* was still. It had *landed!*

He was trembling uncontrollably. Years of vibration had done this; years of isolation with only his crazed thoughts for company. He could scarcely stand.

But this was the moment. This was what he had waited for ten long years. No, it must have been many more years. But he could see Mars. He had made it—done the impossible!

It was an inspiring thought. But somehow, Richard Clayton

would have given it all up if he could only have learned what time it was, and heard it from a human voice.

He staggered to the door—the long-sealed door. There was a lever here.

His aged heart pumped with excitement as he pulled the lever upward. The door opened—sunlight crept through—air rushed in—the light made him blink and the air wheezed in his lungs—his feet were moving out—

Clayton fell forward into the arms of Jerry Chase.

Clayton didn't know it was Jerry Chase. He didn't know anything any longer. It had been too much.

Chase was staring down at the feeble body in his arms.

"Where's Mr. Clayton?" he murmured. "Who are you?" He stared at the aged, wrinkled face.

"Why—it's Clayton!" he breathed. "Mr. Clayton, what's wrong, sir? The atomic discharges failed when you started the ship, and all that happened was that they kept blasting. The ship never left the earth, but the violence of the discharges kept us from reaching you until now. We couldn't get to the *Future* until they stopped. Just a little while ago the ship finished shuddering, but we've been watching night and day. What happened to you, sir?"

The faded blue eyes of Richard Clayton opened. His mouth twitched as he faintly whispered.

"I—lost track of Time. How—how long was I in the *Future?*"

Jerry Chase's face was grave as he stared again at the old man and answered, softly.

*"Just one week."*

And as Richard Clayton's eyes glazed in death, the long voyage ended.

# Yours Truly, Jack the Ripper

I LOOKED at the stage Englishman. He looked at me.

"Sir Guy Hollis?" I asked.

"Indeed. Have I the pleasure of addressing John Carmody, the psychiatrist?"

I nodded. My eyes swept over the figure of my distinguished visitor. Tall, lean, sandy-haired—with the traditional tufted mustache. And the tweeds. I suspected a monocle concealed in a vest pocket, and wondered if he'd left his umbrella in the outer office.

But more than that, I wondered what the devil had impelled Sir Guy Hollis of the British Embassy to seek out a total stranger here in Chicago.

Sir Guy didn't help matters any as he sat down. He cleared his throat, glanced around nervously, tapped his pipe against the side of the desk. Then he opened his mouth.

"Mr. Carmody," he said, "have you ever heard of—Jack the Ripper?"

"The murderer?" I asked.

"Exactly. The greatest monster of them all. Worse than Springheel Jack or Crippen. Jack the Ripper. Red Jack."

"I've heard of him," I said.

"Do you know his history?"

"Listen, Sir Guy," I muttered. "I don't think we'll get any place swapping old wives' tales about famous crimes of history."

Another bulls-eye. He took a deep breath.

"This is no old wives' tale. It's a matter of life or death."

He was so wrapped up in his obsession he even talked that way. Well—I was willing to listen. We psychiatrists get paid for listening.

"Go ahead," I told him. "Let's have the story."

Sir Guy lit a cigarette and began to talk.

"London, 1888," he began. "Late summer and early fall. That was the time. Out of nowhere came the shadowy figure of Jack the Ripper—a stalking shadow with a knife, prowling through London's East End. Haunting the squalid dives of Whitechapel, Spitalfields. Where he came from no one knew. But he brought death. Death in a knife.

"Six times that knife descended to slash the throats and bodies of London's women. Drabs and alley sluts. August 7th was the date of the first butchery. They found her body lying there with 39 stab wounds. A ghastly murder. On August 31st, another victim. The press became interested. The slum inhabitants were more deeply interested still.

"Who was this unknown killer who prowled in their midst and struck at will in the deserted alley-ways of night-town? And what was more important—when would he strike again?

"September 8th was the date. Scotland Yard assigned special deputies. Rumors ran rampant. The atrocious nature of the slayings was the subject for shocking speculation.

"The killer used a knife—expertly. He cut throats and removed—certain portions—of the bodies after death. He chose victims and settings with a fiendish deliberation. No one saw him or heard him. But watchmen making their gray rounds in the dawn would stumble across the hacked and horrid thing that was the Ripper's handiwork.

"Who was he? What was he? A mad surgeon? A butcher? An insane scientist? A pathological degenerate escaped from an asylum? A deranged nobleman? A member of the London police?

"Then the poem appeared in the newspapers. The anonymous poem, designed to put a stop to speculations—but which only aroused public interest to a further frenzy. A mocking little stanza:

> I'm not a butcher, I'm not a Yid
> Nor yet a foreign skipper,
> But I'm your own true loving friend,
> Yours truly—Jack the Ripper.

"And on September 30th, two more throats were slashed open."

I interrupted Sir Guy for a moment.

"Very interesting," I commented. I'm afraid a faint hint of sarcasm crept into my voice.

He winced, but didn't falter in his narrative.

"There was silence, then, in London for a time. Silence, and a nameless fear. When would Red Jack strike again? They waited through October. Every figment of fog concealed his phantom presence. Concealed it well—for nothing was learned of the Ripper's identity, or his purpose. The drabs of London shivered in the raw wind of early November. Shivered, and were thankful for the coming of each morning's sun.

"November 9th. They found her in her room. She lay there very quietly, limbs neatly arranged. And beside her, with equal neatness, were laid her head and heart. The Ripper had outdone himself in execution.

"Then, panic. But needless panic. For though press, police, and populace alike waited in sick dread, Jack the Ripper did not strike again.

"Months passed. A year. The immediate interest died, but not the memory. They said Jack had skipped to America. That he had committed suicide. They said—and they wrote. They've written ever since. Theories, hypotheses, arguments, treatises. But to this day no one knows who Jack the Ripper was. Or why he killed. Or why he stopped killing."

Sir Guy was silent. Obviously he expected some comment from me.

"You tell the story well," I remarked. "Though with a slight emotional bias."

"I've got all the documents," said Sir Guy Hollis. "I've made a collection of existing data and studied it."

I stood up. "Well," I yawned, in mock fatigue, "I've enjoyed your little bedtime story a great deal, Sir Guy. It was kind of you to abandon your duties at the British Embassy to drop in on a poor psychiatrist and regale him with your anecdotes."

Goading him always did the trick.

"I suppose you want to know why I'm interested?" he snapped.

"Yes. That's exactly what I'd like to know. Why are you interested?"

"Because," said Sir Guy Hollis, "I am on the trail of Jack the Ripper now. I think he's here—in Chicago!"

I sat down again. This time I did the blinking act.

"Say that again," I stuttered.

"Jack the Ripper is alive, in Chicago, and I'm out to find him."

"Wait a minute," I said. "Wait—a—minute!"

He wasn't smiling. It wasn't a joke.

"See here," I said. "What was the date of these murders?"

"August to November, 1888."

"1888? But if Jack the Ripper was an able-bodied man in 1888, he'd surely be dead today! Why look, man—if he were merely born in that year, he'd be 57 years old today!"

"Would he?" smiled Sir Guy Hollis. "Or should I say, 'Would she?' Because Jack the Ripper may have been a woman. Or any number of things."

"Sir Guy," I said. "You came to the right person when you looked me up. You definitely need the services of a psychiatrist."

"Perhaps. Tell me, Mr. Carmody, do you think I'm crazy?"

I looked at him and shrugged. But I had to give him a truthful answer.

"Frankly—no."

"Then you might listen to the reasons I believe Jack the Ripper is alive today."

"I might."

"I've studied these cases for thirty years. Been over the actual ground. Talked to officials. Talked to friends and acquaintances of the poor drabs who were killed. Visited with men and women in the neighborhood. Collected an entire library of material touching on Jack the Ripper. Studied all the wild theories or crazy notions.

"I learned a little. Not much, but a little. I won't bore you with my conclusions. But there was another branch of inquiry that yielded more fruitful return. I have studied unsolved crimes. Murders.

"I could show you clippings from the papers of half the world's great cities. San Francisco. Shanghai. Calcutta. Omsk. Paris. Berlin. Pretoria. Cairo. Milan. Adelaide.

"The trail is there, the pattern. Unsolved crimes. Slashed

throats of women. With the peculiar disfigurations and remov-
als. Yes, I've followed a trail of blood. From New York westward
across the continent. Then to the Pacific. From there to Africa.
During the World War of 1914-18 it was Europe. After that, South
America. And since 1930, the United States again. Eighty-seven
such murders—and to the trained criminologist, all bear the
stigma of the Ripper's handiwork.

"Recently there were the so-called Cleveland torso slayings.
Remember? A shocking series. And finally, two recent deaths in
Chicago. Within the past six months. One out on South Dearborn. The other somewhere up on Halsted. Same type of crime,
same technique. I tell you, there are unmistakable indications in
all these affairs—indications of the work of Jack the Ripper!"

I smiled.

"A very tight theory," I said. "I'll not question your evidence at
all, or the deductions you draw. You're the criminologist, and I'll
take your word for it. Just one thing remains to be explained. A
minor point, perhaps, but worth mentioning."

"And what is that?" asked Sir Guy.

"Just how could a man of, let us say, 85 years commit these
crimes? For if Jack the Ripper was around 30 in 1888 and lived,
he'd be 85 today."

Sir Guy Hollis was silent. I had him there. But—

*"Suppose he didn't get any older?"* whispered Sir Guy.

"What's that?"

"Suppose Jack the Ripper didn't grow old? Suppose he is still a
young man today?"

"All right," I said. "I'll suppose for a moment. Then I'll stop
supposing and call for my nurse to restrain you."

"I'm serious," said Sir Guy.

"They all are," I told him. "That's the pity of it all, isn't it? They
know they hear voices and see demons. But we lock them up just
the same."

It was cruel, but it got results. He rose and faced me.

"It's a crazy theory, I grant you," he said. "All the theories about
the Ripper are crazy. The idea that he was a doctor. Or a maniac. Or
a woman. The reasons advanced for such beliefs are flimsy enough.
There's nothing to go by. So why should my notion be any worse?"

"Because people grow older," I reasoned with him. "Doctors, maniacs, and women alike."

"What about—*sorcerers?*"

"Sorcerers?"

"Necromancers. Wizards. Practicers of Black Magic?"

"What's the point?"

"I studied," said Sir Guy. "I studied everything. After awhile I began to study the dates of the murders. The pattern those dates formed. The rhythm. The solar, lunar, stellar rhythm. The sidereal aspect. The astrological significance."

He was crazy. But I still listened.

"Suppose Jack the Ripper didn't murder for murder's sake alone? Suppose he wanted to make—a sacrifice?"

"What kind of a sacrifice?"

Sir Guy shrugged. "It is said that if you offer blood to the dark gods that they grant boons. Yes, if a blood offering is made at the proper time—when the moon and the stars are right—and with the proper ceremonies—they grant boons. Boons of youth. Eternal youth."

"But that's nonsense!"

"No. That's—Jack the Ripper."

I stood up. "A most interesting theory," I told him. "But Sir Guy—there's just one thing I'm interested in. Why do you come here and tell it to me? I'm not an authority on witchcraft. I'm not a police official or criminologist. I'm a practicing psychiatrist. What's the connection?"

Sir Guy smiled.

"You are interested, then?"

"Well, yes. There must be some point."

"There is. But I wished to be assured of your interest first. Now I can tell you my plan."

"And just what is that plan?"

Sir Guy gave me a long look. Then he spoke.

"John Carmody," he said, "you and I are going to capture Jack the Ripper."

## 2.

That's the way it happened. I've given the gist of that first interview in all its intricate and somewhat boring detail, because I think it's important. It helps to throw some light on Sir Guy's character and attitude. And in view of what happened after that—

But I'm coming to those matters.

Sir Guy's thought was simple. It wasn't even a thought. Just a hunch.

"You know the people here," he told me. "I've inquired. That's why I came to you as the ideal man for my purpose. You number amongst your acquaintances many writers, painters, poets. The so-called intelligentsia. The Bohemians. The lunatic fringe from the near north side.

"For certain reasons—never mind what they are—my clues lead me to infer that Jack the Ripper is a member of that element. He chooses to pose as an eccentric. I've a feeling that with you to take me around and introduce me to your set, I might hit upon the right person."

"It's all right with me," I said. "But just how are you going to look for him? As you say, he might be anybody, anywhere. And you have no idea what he looks like. He might be young or old. Jack the Ripper—a Jack of all trades? Rich man, poor man, beggar man, thief, doctor, lawyer—how will you know?"

"We shall see." Sir Guy sighed heavily. "But I must find him. At once."

"Why the hurry?"

Sir Guy sighed again. "Because in two days he will kill again."

"Are you sure?"

"Sure as the stars. I've plotted this chart, you see. All of the murders correspond to certain astrological rhythm patterns. If, as I suspect, he makes a blood sacrifice to renew his youth, he must murder within two days. Notice the pattern of his first crimes in London. August 7th. Then August 31. September 8th. September 30th. November 9th. Intervals of 24 days, 9 days, 22 days—he killed two this time—and then 40 days. Of course there were crimes in between. There had to be. But they weren't discovered and pinned on him.

"At any rate, I've worked out a pattern for him, based on all my data. And I say that within the next two days he kills. So I must seek him out, somehow, before then."

"And I'm still asking you what you want me to do."

"Take me out," said Sir Guy. "Introduce me to your friends. Take me to parties."

"But where do I begin? As far as I know, my artistic friends, despite their eccentricities, are all normal people."

"So is the Ripper. Perfectly normal. Except on certain nights." Again that faraway look in Sir Guy's eyes. "Then he becomes an ageless pathological monster, crouching to kill, on evenings when the stars blaze down in the blazing patterns of death."

"All right," I said. "All right. I'll take you to parties, Sir Guy. I want to go myself, anyway. I need the drinks they'll serve there, after listening to your kind of talk."

We made our plans. And that evening I took him over to Lester Baston's studio.

As we ascended to the penthouse roof in the elevator I took the opportunity to warn Sir Guy.

"Baston's a real screwball," I cautioned him. "So are his guests. Be prepared for anything and everything."

"I am." Sir Guy Hollis was perfectly serious. He put his hand in his trousers pocket and pulled out a gun.

"What the—" I began.

"If I see him I'll be ready," Sir Guy said. He didn't smile, either.

"But you can't go running around at a party with a loaded revolver in your pocket, man!"

"Don't worry, I won't behave foolishly."

I wondered. Sir Guy Hollis was not, to my way of thinking, a normal man.

We stepped out of the elevator, went toward Baston's apartment door.

"By the way," I murmured, "just how do you wish to be introduced? Shall I tell them who you are and what you are looking for?"

"I don't care. Perhaps it would be best to be frank."

"But don't you think that the Ripper—if by some miracle he or she is present—will immediately get the wind up and take cover?"

"I think the shock of the announcement that I am hunting the Ripper would provoke some kind of betraying gesture on his part," said Sir Guy.

"You'd make a pretty good psychiatrist yourself," I conceded. "It's a fine theory. But I warn you, you're going to be in for a lot of ribbing. This is a wild bunch."

Sir Guy smiled.

"I'm ready," he announced. "I have a little plan of my own. Don't be shocked at anything I do," he warned me.

I nodded and knocked on the door.

Baston opened it and poured out into the hall. His eyes were as red as the maraschino cherries in his Manhattan. He teetered back and forth regarding us very gravely. He squinted at my square-cut homburg hat and Sir Guy's mustache.

"Aha," he intoned. "The Walrus and the Carpenter."

I introduced Sir Guy.

"Welcome," said Baston, gesturing us inside with over-elaborate courtesy. He stumbled after us into the garish parlor.

I stared at the crowd that moved restlessly through the fog of cigarette smoke.

It was the shank of the evening for this mob. Every hand held a drink. Every face held a slightly hectic flush. Over in one corner the piano was going full blast, but the imperious strains of the *March* from *The Love for Three Oranges* couldn't drown out the profanity from the crap-game in the other corner.

Prokofieff had no chance against African polo, and one set of ivories rattled louder than the other.

Sir Guy got a monocle-full right away. He saw LaVerne Gonnister, the poetess, hit Hymie Kralik in the eye. He saw Hymie sit down on the floor and cry until Dick Pool accidentally stepped on his stomach as he walked through to the dining room for a drink.

He heard Nadia Vilinoff the commercial artist tell Johnny Odcutt that she thought his tattooing was in dreadful taste, and he saw Barclay Melton crawl under the dining room table with Johnny Odcutt's wife.

His zoological observations might have continued indefinitely if Lester Baston hadn't stepped to the center of the room and called for silence by dropping a vase on the floor.

"We have distinguished visitors in our midst," bawled Lester, waving his empty glass in our direction. "None other than the Walrus and the Carpenter. The Walrus is Sir Guy Hollis, a something-or-other from the British Embassy. The Carpenter, as you all know, is our own John Carmody, the prominent dispenser of libido liniment."

He turned and grabbed Sir Guy by the arm, dragging him to the middle of the carpet. For a moment I thought Hollis might object, but a quick wink reassured me. He was prepared for this.

"It is our custom, Sir Guy," said Baston, loudly, "to subject our new friends to a little cross-examination. Just a little formality at these very formal gatherings, you understand. Are you prepared to answer questions?"

Sir Guy nodded and grinned.

"Very well," Baston muttered. "Friends—I give you this bundle from Britain. Your witness."

Then the ribbing started. I meant to listen, but at that moment Lydia Dare saw me and dragged me off into the vestibule for one of those Darling-I-waited-for-your-call-all-day routines.

By the time I got rid of her and went back, the impromptu quiz session was in full swing. From the attitude of the crowd, I gathered that Sir Guy was doing all right for himself.

Then Baston himself interjected a question that upset the apple-cart. "And what, may I ask, brings you to our midst tonight? What is your mission, oh Walrus?"

"I'm looking for Jack the Ripper."

Nobody laughed.

Perhaps it struck them all the way it did me. I glanced at my neighbors and began to *wonder*.

LaVerne Gonnister. Hymie Kralik. Harmless. Dick Pool. Nadia Vilinoff. Johnny Odcutt and his wife. Barclay Melton. Lydia Dare. All harmless.

But what a forced smile on Dick Pool's face! And that sly, self-conscious smirk that Barclay Melton wore!

Oh, it was absurd, I grant you. But for the first time I saw these people in a new light. I wondered about their lives—their secret lives beyond the scenes of parties.

How many of them were playing a part, concealing something?

Who here would worship Hecate and grant that horrid goddess the dark boon of blood?

Even Lester Baston might be masquerading.

The mood was upon us all, for a moment. I saw questions flicker in the circle of eyes around the room.

Sir Guy stood there, and I could swear he was fully conscious of the situation he'd created, and enjoyed it.

I wondered idly just what was *really* wrong with him. Why he had this odd fixation concerning Jack the Ripper. Maybe he was hiding secrets, too. . . .

Baston, as usual, broke the mood. He burlesqued it.

"The Walrus isn't kidding, friends," he said. He slapped Sir Guy on the back and put his arm around him as he orated. "Our English cousin is really on the trail of the fabulous Jack the Ripper. You all remember Jack the Ripper, I presume? Quite a cutup in the old days, as I recall. Really had some ripping good times when he went out on a tear.

"The Walrus has some idea that the Ripper is still alive, probably prowling around Chicago with a Boy Scout knife. In fact"—Baston paused impressively and shot it out in a rasping stage-whisper—"in fact, he has reason to believe that Jack the Ripper might even be right here in our midst tonight."

There was the expected reaction of giggles and grins. Baston eyed Lydia Dare reprovingly. "You girls needn't laugh," he smirked. "Jack the Ripper might be a woman, too, you know. Sort of a Jill the Ripper."

"You mean you actually suspect one of us?" shrieked LaVerne Gonnister, simpering up to Sir Guy. "But that Jack the Ripper person disappeared ages ago, didn't he? In 1888?"

"Aha!" interrupted Baston. "How do you know so much about it, young lady? Sounds suspicious! Watch her, Sir Guy—she may not be as young as she appears. These lady poets have dark pasts."

The tension was gone, the mood was shattered, and the whole thing was beginning to degenerate into a trivial party joke. The man who had played the *March* was eyeing the piano with a *Scherzo* gleam in his eye that augured ill for Prokofieff. Lydia Dare was glancing at the kitchen, waiting to make a break for another drink.

Then Baston caught it.

"Guess what?" he yelled. "The Walrus has a gun."

His embracing arm had slipped and encountered the hard outline of the gun in Sir Guy's pocket. He snatched it out before Hollis had the opportunity to protest.

I stared hard at Sir Guy, wondering if this thing had carried far enough. But he flicked a wink my way and I remembered he had told me not to be alarmed.

So I waited as Baston broached a drunken inspiration.

"Let's play fair with our friend the Walrus," he cried. "He came all the way from England to our party on this mission. If none of you is willing to confess, I suggest we give him a chance to find out—the hard way."

"What's up?" asked Johnny Odcutt.

"I'll turn out the lights for one minute. Sir Guy can stand here with his gun. If anyone in this room is the Ripper he can either run for it or take the opportunity to—well, eradicate his pursuer. Fair enough?"

It was even sillier than it sounds, but it caught the popular fancy. Sir Guy's protests went unheard in the ensuing babble. And before I could stride over and put in my two cents' worth, Lester Baston had reached the light switch.

"Don't anybody move," he announced, with fake solemnity. "For one minute we will remain in darkness—perhaps at the mercy of a killer. At the end of that time, I'll turn up the lights again and look for bodies. Choose your partners, ladies and gentlemen."

The lights went out.

Somebody giggled.

I heard footsteps in the darkness. Mutterings.

A hand brushed my face.

The watch on my wrist ticked violently. But even louder, rising above it, I heard another thumping. The beating of my heart.

Absurd. Standing in the dark with a group of tipsy fools. And yet there was real terror lurking here, rustling through the velvet blackness.

Jack the Ripper prowled in darkness like this. And Jack the Ripper had a knife. Jack the Ripper had a madman's brain and a madman's purpose.

But Jack the Ripper was dead, dead and dust these many years—by every human law.

Only there are no human laws when you feel yourself in the darkness, when the darkness hides and protects and the outer mask slips off your face and you feel something welling up within you, a brooding shapeless purpose that is brother to the blackness.

Sir Guy Hollis shrieked.

There was a gristly thud.

Baston had the lights on.

Everybody screamed.

Sir Guy Hollis lay sprawled on the floor in the center of the room. The gun was still clutched in his hand.

I glanced at the faces, marveling at the variety of expressions human beings can assume when confronting horror.

All the faces were present in the circle. Nobody had fled. And yet Sir Guy Hollis lay there. . . .

LaVerne Gonnister was wailing and hiding her face.

"All right."

Sir Guy rolled over and jumped to his feet. He was smiling.

"Just an experiment, eh? If Jack the Ripper *were* among those present, and thought I had been murdered, he would have betrayed himself in some way when the lights went on and he saw me lying there.

"I am convinced of your individual and collective innocence. Just a gentle spoof, my friends."

Hollis stared at the goggling Baston and the rest of them crowding in behind him.

"Shall we leave, John?" he called to me. "It's getting late, I think."

Turning, he headed for the closet. I followed him. Nobody said a word.

It was a pretty dull party after that.

3.

I met Sir Guy the following evening as we agreed, on the corner of 29th and South Halsted.

After what had happened the night before, I was prepared for almost anything. But Sir Guy seemed matter-of-fact enough as he stood huddled against a grimy doorway and waited for me to appear.

"Boo!" I said, jumping out suddenly. He smiled. Only the betraying gesture of his left hand indicated that he'd instinctively reached for his gun when I startled him.

"All ready for our wild goose chase?" I asked.

"Yes." He nodded. "I'm glad that you agreed to meet me without asking questions," he told me. "It shows you trust my judgment." He took my arm and edged me along the street slowly.

"It's foggy tonight, John," said Sir Guy Hollis. "Like London."

I nodded.

"Cold, too, for November."

I nodded again and half-shivered my agreement.

"Curious," mused Sir Guy. "London fog and November. The place and the time of the Ripper murders."

I grinned through darkness. "Let me remind you, Sir Guy, that this isn't London, but Chicago. And it isn't November, 1888. It's over fifty years later."

Sir Guy returned my grin, but without mirth. "I'm not so sure, at that," he murmured. "Look about you. These tangled alleys and twisted streets. They're like the East End. Mitre Square. And surely they are as ancient as fifty years, at least."

"You're in the colored neighborhood off South Clark Street," I said, shortly. "And why you dragged me down here I still don't know."

"It's a hunch," Sir Guy admitted. "Just a hunch on my part, John. I want to wander around down here. There's the same geographical conformation in these streets as in those courts where the Ripper roamed and slew. That's where we'll find him, John. Not in the bright lights of the Bohemian neighborhood, but down here in the darkness. The darkness where he waits and crouches."

"Is that why you brought a gun?" I asked. I was unable to keep a trace of sarcastic nervousness from my voice. All of this talk, this incessant obsession with Jack the Ripper, got on my nerves more than I cared to admit.

"We may need a gun," said Sir Guy, gravely. "After all, tonight is the appointed night."

I sighed. We wandered on through the foggy, deserted streets. Here and there a dim light burned above a gin-mill door-way. Otherwise, all was darkness and shadow. Deep, gaping alley-ways loomed as we proceeded down a slanting side-street.

We crawled through that fog, alone and silent, like two tiny maggots floundering within a shroud.

When that thought hit me, I winced. The atmosphere was beginning to get *me*, too. If I didn't watch my step I'd go as loony as Sir Guy.

"Can't you see there's not a soul around these streets?" I said, tugging at his coat impatiently.

"He's bound to come," said Sir Guy. "He'll be drawn here. This is what I've been looking for. A *genius loci*. An evil spot that attracts evil. Always, when he slays, it's in the slums.

"You see, that must be one of his weaknesses. He has a fascination for squalor. Besides, the women he needs for sacrifice are more easily found in the dives and stewpots of a great city."

I smiled. "Well, let's go into one of the dives or stewpots," I suggested. "I'm cold. Need a drink. This damned fog gets into your bones. You Britishers can stand it, but I like warmth and dry heat."

We emerged from our side-street and stood upon the threshold of an alley.

Through the white clouds of mist ahead, I discerned a dim blue light, a naked bulb dangling from a beer sign above an alley tavern.

"Let's take a chance," I said. "I'm beginning to shiver."

"Lead the way," said Sir Guy. I led him down the alley passage. We halted before the door of the dive.

"What are you waiting for?" he asked.

"Just looking in," I told him. "This is a tough neighborhood, Sir Guy. Never know what you're liable to run into. And I'd prefer we didn't get into the wrong company. Some of these Negro places resent white customers."

"Good idea, John."

I finished my inspection through the doorway. "Looks deserted," I murmured. "Let's try it."

We entered a dingy bar. A feeble light flickered above the counter and railing, but failed to penetrate the further gloom of the back booths.

A gigantic Negro lolled across the bar—a black giant with prognathous jaw and ape-like torso. He scarcely stirred as we came in, but his eyes flicked open quite suddenly and I knew he noted our presence and was judging us.

"Evening," I said.

He took his time before replying. Still sizing us up. Then, he grinned.

"Evening, gents. What's your pleasure?"

"Gin," I said. "Two gins. It's a cold night."

"That's right, gents."

He poured, I paid, and took the glasses over to one of the booths. We wasted no time in emptying them. The fiery liquor warmed.

I went over to the bar and got the bottle. Sir Guy and I poured ourselves another drink. The big Negro went back into his doze, with one wary eye half-open against any sudden activity.

The clock over the bar ticked on. The wind was rising outside, tearing the shroud of fog to ragged shreds. Sir Guy and I sat in the warm booth and drank our gin.

He began to talk, and the shadows crept up about us to listen.

He rambled a great deal. He went over everything he'd said in the office when I met him, just as though I hadn't heard it before. The poor devils with obsessions are like that.

I listened very patiently. I poured Sir Guy another drink. And another.

But the liquor only made him more talkative. How he did run on! About ritual killings and prolonging the life unnaturally—the whole fantastic tale came out again. And of course, he maintained his unyielding conviction that the Ripper was abroad tonight.

I suppose I was guilty of goading him.

"Very well," I said, unable to keep the impatience from my voice. "Let us say that your theory is correct—even though we must overlook every natural law and swallow a lot of superstition to give it any credence.

"But let us say, for the sake of argument, that you are right. Jack the Ripper was a man who discovered how to prolong his own life through making human sacrifices. He did travel around the world as you believe. He is in Chicago now and he is planning to kill. In other words, let us suppose that everything you claim is gospel truth. So what?"

"What do you mean, 'so what'?" said Sir Guy.

"I mean—so what?" I answered. "If all this is true, it still doesn't prove that by sitting down in a dingy gin-mill on the South Side, Jack the Ripper is going to walk in here and let you kill him, or turn him over to the police. And come to think of it, I don't even know now just what you intend to *do* with him if you ever did find him."

Sir Guy gulped his gin. "I'd capture the bloody swine," he said. "Capture him and turn him over to the government, together with all the papers and documentary evidence I've collected against him over a period of many years. I've spent a fortune investigating this affair, I tell you, a fortune! His capture will mean the solution of hundreds of unsolved crimes, of that I am convinced.

"I tell you, a mad beast is loose on this world! An ageless, eternal beast, sacrificing to Hecate and the dark gods!"

*In vino veritas.* Or was all this babbling the result of too much gin? It didn't matter. Sir Guy Hollis had another. I sat there and wondered what to do with him. The man was rapidly working up to a climax of hysterical drunkenness.

"One other point," I said, more for the sake of conversation than in any hopes of obtaining information. "You still don't explain how it is that you hope to just blunder into the Ripper."

"He'll be around," said Sir Guy. "I'm psychic. I know."

Sir Guy wasn't psychic. He was maudlin.

The whole business was beginning to infuriate me. We'd been sitting here an hour, and during all this time I'd been forced to play nursemaid and audience to a babbling idiot. After all, he wasn't a regular patient of mine.

"That's enough," I said, putting out my hand as Sir Guy reached for the half-emptied bottle again. "You've had plenty. Now I've got a suggestion to make. Let's call a cab and get out of here. It's getting late and it doesn't look as though your elusive friend is going to put in his appearance. Tomorrow, if I were you, I'd plan to turn all those papers and documents over to the F.B.I. If you're so convinced of the truth of your wild theory, they are competent to make a very thorough investigation, and find your man."

"No." Sir Guy was drunkenly obstinate. "No cab."

"But let's get out of here anyway," I said, glancing at my watch. "It's past midnight."

He sighed, shrugged, and rose unsteadily. As he started for the door, he tugged the gun free from his pocket.

"Here, give me that!" I whispered. "You can't walk around the street brandishing that thing."

I took the gun and slipped it inside my coat. Then I got hold of his right arm and steered him out of the door. The Negro didn't look up as we departed.

We stood shivering in the alleyway. The fog had increased. I couldn't see either end of the alley from where we stood. It was cold. Damp. Dark. Fog or no fog, a little wind was whispering secrets to the shadows at our backs.

The fresh air hit Sir Guy just as I expected it would. Fog and gin-fumes don't mingle very well. He lurched as I guided him slowly through the mist.

Sir Guy, despite his incapacity, still stared apprehensively at the alley, as though he expected to see a figure approaching.

Disgust got the better of me.

"Childish foolishness," I snorted. "Jack the Ripper, indeed! I call this carrying a hobby too far."

"Hobby?" He faced me. Through the fog I could see his distorted face. "You call this a hobby?"

"Well, what is it?" I grumbled. "Just why else are you so interested in tracking down this mythical killer?"

My arm held his. But his stare held me.

"In London," he whispered. "In 1888 . . . one of those nameless drabs the Ripper slew . . . was my mother."

"What?"

"Later I was recognized by my father, and legitimatized. We swore to give our lives to find the Ripper. My father was the first to search. He died in Hollywood in 1926—on the trail of the Ripper. They said he was stabbed by an unknown assailant in a brawl. But I know who that assailant was.

"So I've taken up his work, do you see, John? I've carried on. And I will carry on until I do find him and kill him with my own hands.

"He took my mother's life and the lives of hundreds to keep his own hellish being alive. Like a vampire, he battens on blood. Like a ghoul, he is nourished by death. Like a fiend, he stalks the world to kill. He is cunning, devilishly cunning. But I'll never rest until I find him, never!"

I believed him then. He wouldn't give up. He wasn't just a drunken babbler any more. He was as fanatical, as determined, as relentless as the Ripper himself.

Tomorrow he'd be sober. He'd continue the search. Perhaps he'd turn those papers over to the F.B.I. Sooner or later, with such persistence—and with his motive—he'd be successful. I'd always known he had a motive.

"Let's go," I said, steering him down the alley.

"Wait a minute," said Sir Guy. "Give me back my gun." He lurched a little. "I'd feel better with the gun on me."

He pressed me into the dark shadows of a little recess.

I tried to shrug him off, but he was insistent.

"Let me carry the gun, now, John," he mumbled.

"All right," I said.

I reached into my coat, brought my hand out.

"But that's not a gun," he protested. "That's a knife."

"I know."

I bore down on him swiftly.

"John!" he screamed.

"Never mind the 'John'," I whispered, raising the knife. "Just call me . . . Jack."

# The Seal of the Satyr

ROGER TALQUIST had always known that he would return to Greece. The spell laid upon him in childhood had lingered through the years. After his father had brought him back to school in England, he never could forget the beauty of the ancient hills of which the shepherd poets sang. Talquist's later career in archaeology emphasized the hold of the pagan on his soul; he dreamed of purple hills and marble ruins gleaming beneath an age-yellowed, ivory moon.

It was inevitable that he return, and when the Oxonian Expedition went to excavate a Temple of Poseidon, he accompanied it to the land of his boyhood.

Once arrived, his interest in the work itself slackened. He did his routine duties diffidently, and spent all of his free time wandering through the wild country beyond the seaport of Mylenos. A short walk would bring him to the mystic hills and the shadowed treelands. His imagination quickened in the forest silence as he mused on the old lore of paganism he'd heard from peasants.

Dryads dwelt in the woods, and harpies hovered. Skyways beckoned Roger Talquist to climb the green-studded stairs of the mountains, until from some lofty eminence he could gaze down on the plains where once lambs had gamboled to the fabled piping of the Goat-god. It pleased him to half-believe the ancient legends, and he decided to compile a monograph on local superstition. Here the rustics still knew the myths of Pan and the forest spirits.

Talquist spoke Greek fluently, and the natives made him welcome in their simple cottages while they told of forgotten lore. And here Roger Talquist met old Papa Lepolis—a tall, patriarchal oldster with the wrinkled, august face of some Cretan sea-king. Papa Lepolis promised the dark, grave-eyed young scientist an actual glimpse of an altar where his people had once worshiped the gods of the forest.

It was an ancient place in the forest, a grotto where primitive folk had paid worship to the Nature gods in olden days, before the recording of history. Here were ruins that only a few knew about; the grotto was kept secret now that the Greek Orthodox Church held sway. Here were stones and carvings which might interest an archaeologist greatly, Papa Lepolis told him.

"Take me there," Talquist said eagerly. "I must see this grotto." Lepolis grew silent, stroked his beard, then scowled.

"I wonder if I dare, Mr. Talquist."

"Dare?" Talquist exclaimed.

"You and I—we are modern men. We do not fear what the ignorant peasants hereabouts still tremble before."

"They are afraid? But what is there for them to fear?"

Lepolis stared at the floor. "Nothing, perhaps. But in that grotto there is an altar where once men bowed to Pan. And they did more than that."

Talquist listened eagerly. "Yes," Lepolis went on. "If legends are to be believed, worshipers did a great deal more than bow. They gave—sacrifices."

"You mean animals?"

"No, Mr. Talquist, I do not mean animals. The forest gods desired things of men; the warm, living flesh of young maidens and youth sated their divine appetites."

Talquist smiled tolerantly. "Well, what of it? Human beings were sacrificed in groves thousands of years ago. So what? I've heard of such things, of course. Surely today there's nothing to fear because once blood was spilled."

"But you do not understand, my young friend. Do you know why there were such sacrifices, what the ancients believed?"

"No," Talquist admitted.

The old man whispered through his beard. "They said that the gods appeared in human form at certain times, and at other times in the shape of beasts. Shepherds and wandering maidens met the old Nature gods on lonely hills—and later there were satyrs and fauns—half-beast, half-human."

"Oh, I know of such myths, Lepolis. Satyrs, centaurs, goat-headed men tumble all over themselves in Greek mythology. So what?"

"These creatures had divine blood in them, Mr. Talquist. And, as such, they did not die."

Talquist's eyes widened. "What? You mean that you're afraid the forest and the altar are, perhaps, guarded by fabled monsters?"

"No. No, nothing as childish as that," the old man reproved. Talquist wondered whether he were sincere in his denial.

"Then what bothers you, Lepolis?"

"Only this. When the ancients made sacrifice on the altar, they received gifts in return. Do you understand? They gave blood and the gods gave gifts in exchange. Terrible gifts, Mr. Talquist."

Talquist stared at the old man. "What do you mean?"

"I cannot say, exactly. Worshipers wanted things from the gods. They wanted the immortality that fauns and satyrs and dryads received. So sometimes the gods would leave tokens and amulets. Those that wore them were supposed to be *changed*."

Talquist was scornful. "Are you trying to tell me that you believe such—"

"No—not exactly," Papa Lepolis replied slowly.

"Then take me to the altar," the young scientist insisted.

The old man's eyes avoided Talquist's face. "I do not show people the grotto," he mumbled. "It is a secret in our family. Better not to know some things. I was a fool to suggest it."

Talquist made a little pile of *drachmas* on the table. Lepolis looked at the coins, shuffled his feet in silence. Then he smiled.

"I am an old man, Mr. Talquist. An old, tired man. It is hard for me to travel. But—I will lead you to the altar in the forest, if you wish."

Talquist smiled patiently. "Tomorrow?"

"Tomorrow."

\*   \*   \*   \*

It was a strange pair that set out the next day through the woodland pathways. Tall, bearded Papa Lepolis in his ragged robes led the trimly-dressed Roger Talquist through the dense semi-twilight. As they walked along, the trees, shrubbery and vines grew thicker and more tangled; the sun shone through in only a few spots.

At first Talquist had followed the old man along a definite path, where birds sang gayly from the branches. Now they plunged deeper into the greenish darkness between twisting trees, and there was no life here—only a palpitant stillness. The stillness was of the ancient past.

This was the deep forest of an older Greece, undisturbed through three thousand years. Here centaurs pranced and whinnied beside the dark streams, and dryads capered upon cloud-crowned hilltops to the sound of hidden lutes. So Talquist imagined. He thought musingly of the myths told him by the oldster. They seemed appropriate enough now in this setting.

Lepolis plodded ahead silently, almost furtively. Now that he had embarked on the trip, it seemed he did not relish this journey. Talquist noticed how the oldster kept peering over his shoulder toward the silent trees. Lepolis seemed frightened; it was almost as though he believed the fantastic fables of which he had spoken.

Through deep glades and great lonely swamps they toiled, and again Talquist marveled that the old man did not lose his way in the trackless marshes. But at last they took a winding trail which led through a thicket and into a sunken grove, bordered by a land of tree-guarded twilight.

Roger Talquist gazed in silence at their goal. His eyes noted the great grassy ring in the center of the low grade, and he saw that the crumbled stones surrounded it in a sort of half-imaginary pattern. It was a moot question whether these rocks had been naturally or artificially placed; if the latter, they had been laid at a time incredibly remote. But they did resemble a crude altar-circle, and the great stone in the middle might easily have served the purpose of a sacrificial slab.

They descended upon the grotto and then Talquist took the lead while his aged guide hung back. Talquist examined the stones and noted the faint, rusty stains still visible on their tops. He fumbled amidst the fragments of broken rock that littered the bases of the altars in search of some ancient token or relic.

And then Roger Talquist saw. The grass was damp, and pressed down. The earth was wet. And in a circle about the central altar were the unmistakable imprints of *hoofs*.

Talquist gasped. "Come here, Lepolis!" he exclaimed.

The old man looked down at the hoofmarks, clear and fresh. He smiled unfathomably.

"I warned you, Mr. Talquist. There are creatures who seek this lonely altar."

"Nonsense!" he stammered. "I merely wanted to ask you about wild goats. Are there any that might graze here?"

The old man's smile was more enigmatic still. "Wild goats?" he said. "Look again, Mr. Talquist. These are not goat tracks."

Talquist looked, and they were not goat tracks, these great hoofed imprints in the earth. But they had to be! Why was Lepolis laughing so?

"I warned you, Talquist," the old man went on. "I told you about what lurks, still undying, in the forest. I told you how my family knows, has always known and guarded the secret of the ancient Faith. I told you how one can sacrifice on this altar and receive a gift from the gods. A gift of eternal life and power, for the gods send a token conferring their reward upon the sacrificer. It is not pleasant to live in a changed shape, perhaps—but it is better than dying."

What was the old fool raving about? Had he gone stark mad?

Lepolis' voice was shrill now. "I warned you, remember that! I tried to keep you from coming. But you insisted. I am weak, I know—weak because I am old and do not want to die. I am afraid to die! I would far rather live, even in changed shape! And so, Mr. Roger Talquist, now that we are at the altar, the time has come—"

It came then, so swiftly that Talquist was caught wholly unprepared. Even as he was speaking. Lepolis edged closer and closer. Then suddenly from out of one ragged sleeve a knife flashed! Lepolis raised the gleaming blade on high and brought it down in a vicious stroke.

Talquist dodged desperately aside, just in time. But the old man, laughing insanely, was gripping him harshly by the throat. The knife raised again, and Talquist was forced back against the altar stone. The blade trembled, Lepolis tightened his grip, and Talquist knew with an icy heart that he must die.

With the strength of panic, Roger Talquist raised his free arm and caught the old man's wrist. He lunged forward, twisting Lepolis against the stone, and then wrestled with the mad strength of the shrieking patriarch. The knife bit keenly several times as Lepolis stabbed futilely again and again.

"O Great Pan, aid me!" screamed the old man. And then Talquist twisted the wiry wrist just as the blade thrust downward, and it turned. The knife buried itself inches deep in Lepolis' wrinkled throat, and a red stream poured out over the altar-top as the coughing ancient fell in racking death upon it.

Talquist stepped back, aghast. The hysteria of the last few moments had left him dazed. The earth seemed to spin around him madly, the stones moved, the darkness deepened, and in his wild fancy Talquist heard the rumbling of thunder from beneath his feet. Then the shock was all over, and he stared mutely at the dead man on the altar.

Lepolis had lured him here, believing in the myths he had himself revealed. He had tried to kill the young scientist on the altar, that he might receive the gift of eternal life, though in a changed shape, from the ancient gods. Lepolis had been mad. It was all a most unfortunate occurrence.

Talquist turned. He must find his way out of the forest, and quickly.

But what was this? In the shards at his feet, at the base of the altar, something glinted dully. Talquist stooped and picked it up. Funny, he hadn't noticed this when searching before. He held it against the light of the blood-red sunset.

It was an octagonally cut medallion of greenish stone, so worn and polished as to hint of extreme age. The medallion was fastened on a linked chain of true gold, and was evidently designed to be worn around the neck.

All this Talquist observed in a fleeting moment, for his eyes and thoughts were directed now on the startling figure emblazoned on the face of the amulet.

There was something about the technique of the design that puzzled Talquist even while it disturbed him. The lines did not seem as though executed by *human thought*.

Each artist puts into his work something of himself, and what the designer had put into this figure was horribly alien. The goat seemed to be a symbol of another figure underneath; a figure Talquist couldn't make out but which he knew instinctively was lurking there.

The metal was of peculiar lustre, the carving was unnatural, and looking at the thing somehow shocked Talquist. The goat was the symbol of Pan, and perhaps the wild ravings of Lepolis, with his talk of "gifts" from forest gods, had unnerved the scientist.

Roger Talquist stared at the evil figure as he absently fastened the golden chain about his neck.

With a start, he realized what he was doing. *Why* had he put the amulet on? He raised his hand to remove it, and as he touched the stone he received a second shock. The stone was quite warm! There was a tingling in Talquist's fingertips—a tingling not altogether unpleasant. The stone was radiant, and warm as ardent flesh; as though it possessed some radio-active properties.

In a second the sensation passed and Talquist was brought sharply back to reality. A breeze now curled out of the encroaching night. The twilight grove was eerie, and the trees were fantastic figures bowing in the wind. They stretched long green arms as though to bar the wanderer's path. For a moment Talquist had the absurd notion that these trees would conspire to keep him in the forest.

He looked again at the dead man on the altar; then glanced down at the horrible, unexplained tracks at his feet, and shivered. He must get out of this grotto!

Talquist started across the grove to the thicket. Halfway across the last red rays of sunset glinted on his chest, and he glanced down again to see the amulet moving in a slow arc. He touched it, and a painful shock stabbed his fingertips again. Once more he knew fear—because now he felt life pulsing in the stone. It was living animation he felt, the sensation of powerful forces running in waves through his hand and up the length of his arm.

The contact somehow invigorated Talquist. He looked at the carved figure of the prancing goat that blazed up, and his eyes smarted and burned. The same eerie force tingling through his fingers now seemed to dance into his eyes and into the brain behind them.

There *was* a force in the stone! Lepolis with his wild talk of a "change" in the men who found the gifts of the old gods—Lord, could the fool have been speaking the truth?

After all, Lepolis had been killed, though not intentionally, on that altar, like a sacrifice. Whereas the old man had meant to sacrifice Talquist and receive in reward the grant of immortality, though he would be "changed" in some indefinable way by the divine blood of satyrs. But Lepolis had died, and then Talquist had found this peculiar talisman. Odd, that he hadn't seen it before when he searched.

Had it been sent *after* the sacrifice? That thunder from below his feet—

Oh, but that was absurd! There were no forest gods in this twentieth century.

*Hoofprints in the grass. . . .*

Talquist tried to think of something else. Paradoxically enough, that was simple. His own body. Why was he suddenly feeling so strange?

He had a sudden impulse to tear the amulet from his throat, and his fingers instinctively tightened about it. There came a rapid acceleration of that flowing force within him, so that his arm seemed numb, as though from an electric shock.

What was this terrible thing doing to him? *Changing* him?

God, his body *did* ache! His arms and legs burned, there were sharp twinges in his thighs as he stumbled on—the kind of stabbing throb which in childhood had been spoken of as "growing pains."

*Growing* pains!

In a sort of panic, Talquist tried desperately to be sane. It was rheumatism—that's what it was! He had caught a chill in the damp and dew of the woods. His legs hurt from walking in tight boots.

He loosened his shirt as he walked across the glade; untied the lacings then, stopping to remove his boots. He seemed feverish, his head felt constricted, yet through the dull throbbing ran a thin red thread of exultation. He was terrified, yet strangely joyous.

Fever? Perhaps. His body, despite the pain, no longer seemed a part of him. He stroked his brow, and he scarcely recognized the convolutions. Feeling the stubble on his cheeks, he wondered if he had remembered to shave that morning. His hands were bronzed, and his fingers still tingled from the shock of the amulet.

He ought not to go on. He must rest. Shirtless, barefooted, Talquist flung himself down in the shadow of a bush at the edge of the glade. The last flicker of sunset crossed his chest.

His eyes focused again on the burning green brightness of the amulet, and as he stared his whole being turned to liquid flame. He felt oddly tortured, racked; his muscles stretched, tautened, and nerves ached with an exquisite pain that was almost animal ecstasy. He could not move his eyes or raise his hand to drop the talisman and claw off the burning band of gold about his throat. Yet his brain was enthralled by a tormented bliss, though another part of his consciousness shrieked "hypnotism—magnetism—madness." But his being continued to writhe in bondage to the living stone.

Abruptly came the release. Dusk flooded the grove, and its purple pallor mingled oddly with the green lambency of the flaming amulet on Talquist's chest.

Roger Talquist rubbed his eyes. Why was he lying here on the grass? What had he been doing? He felt no pain now, only a hot surging of blood through quickened veins. He could feel the shrill singing at his temples. Why had he wanted to run away? Why had he feared the power of the amulet?

It was pleasant here in the forest at night, and the tingling in the talisman now was flowing through his body evenly, in invigorating waves. Whatever the power in this seal of the satyr, be it natural or supernatural, it was good. He had been a fool to dwell on such obscure fears.

Talquist rose to his feet, hardly conscious of his nakedness, and faced the edge of the grotto once again. Through the haze of dusk he saw the standing stones, shining whitely. The grass seemed greener and more lush about the bases—there seemed to be new life here. The rocks appeared larger and more numerous than in the afternoon. He soon realized that they were arranged in a circle so as to form a crude pattern.

Talquist wanted to step over and examine them. But something halted him in the shadow of the bushes.

From afar came the sound of conches. Into the glade marched a small procession of bearded men, robed in white. There were perhaps a dozen of them, and Talquist vaguely recognized faces from the village.

Then there was still worship here!

The priests, if priests they were, gathered around the central altar, and Talquist saw that they discovered the body of Lepolis with great surprise. They stood there, huddled and whispering in the twilight.

"He told us that the young foreigner would be ready," whispered one, loudly enough for Talquist to overhear.

"Something has gone amiss."

"Let us go, quickly before *they* assemble."

"Yes, *they* will come for the body."

"We will leave the incense burning here, but the talisman is already gone."

"Hasten; I am afraid."

The men produced small bundles of sticks which they lighted on the eight outer stones. Great clouds of perfumed smoke wafted to wooded skies. It was a scene from old Greece—the ancient Greece of mystic forest gods.

The body of Lepolis lay on the central altar, and the pungent smoke rose all about him. The old men hurried off then, whispering and casting veiled glances back into the glade. Talquist crouched, watching, his breathing excited and irregular.

For a long moment there was utter silence. Then began a curious rustling, a slithering of leaves upon the trees, and a purposeful padding as of hoofs upon the grass.

The sun had died in fathomless crimson skies, and the moon rose from the pallid purple of the east. It shone down upon the grotto as the rustling noises increased. A silver moon-shaft sped across the central altar, and as it did so a faint, shrill peeping filled the air. Hysterically high, the treble notes sounded from far away— the peeping summons of a syrinx. The peeping noise blended with rustling; the spicy perfume from the fires scented the forest dark.

And now other sounds were audible: queer moanings and high neighing, chirping and animal growls. Another scent, or combination of scents, mingled with the perfume; the musk-like odors of beasts and creatures of the wood. Talquist stared and saw—and nearly shrieked.

For into the grove the forest creatures headed, bounding and leaping and pawing the hard-packed earth. Shaggy and manlike, the fauns capered about in the moonlight, their goatish beards wagging to their squealing laughter.

Here were the living creatures of myth!

Bull-bodied maenads stamped into the glade with throaty bellows of guttural mirth, shaking their hairy heads in bovine playfulness. Across the sward the centaurs pranced, their sly, wicked faces wreathed in lustful grimace, their stallion bodies flexed with animal vigor. They snorted and reared, bringing spiked hoofs down to strike fire from the altar stones.

Now Talquist understood the hoof-prints on the grass!

With hoarse cries, the Ægypans bounded in, lifting their horrid goat-heads to bleat at the moon, and stretching their shambling legs and shapeless paws in animal ecstasy as they sniffed the aromatic incense of the spiced perfume.

The far-off piping grew more frantic still, and the whirling forest creatures laughed more shrilly, whirled more wildly, sniffling the reek of the smoke and bathing in moonlight as they danced and gesticulated amidst the altar stones.

Talquist gasped. Fabled legends come true! He glanced down at the seal of the satyr on his breast, then looked up as a shrill screaming sounded.

The living shadows of nymphs emerged from the rushes that bordered the stream within the forest. They danced over the grass and flung their wet green hair in carefree abandon as they wheeled before the beast-men.

There was one green-haired creature with eyes red as blood that Roger Talquist watched closely. The strength surging in him leaped at the sight of her, as she postured with the rest.

Now the creatures saw what lay upon the altar top. A faun crept close, gesturing to his less emboldened companions. One hairy paw reached out to touch the body of Lepolis. A black satyr capered before the corpse. His nostrils flared as he fumbled at the old man's beard. A centaur trotted past, so that his sweaty flanks brushed the stone. The nymphs tittered shrilly.

They gathered before that inner altar and their eyes and hands and lips caressed what lay upon it, and they laughed and bleated. And when they turned away, they dragged the body with them.

The piping scurried higher in its shrillness. The peeping syrinx, the scent of smoke, the shrieking laughter—these things finally made Talquist emerge from the bushes. He did not think of what he had seen; he felt only the drumming of the incredible scene in his blood, fusing his being in strange response.

The dance of the forest creatures had become a pursuit, and the nymphs fled before the insane figures that scurried after them in the darkness. Hoarse screams filled the night.

Then the syrinx sounded, swelled, merged into a gigantic, triumphant bleat. The horde bore the body of Lepolis into the dark forest.

Talquist, his blood sweet fire, raced after the others about the altar. It was a strange madness that possessed him, that gave him a sense of curious kinship with these beings of the past. They shrieked when they saw him and pointed to the glowing green amulet on his chest, but he did not hear.

His eyes were searching for a figure—the figure of the green-haired nymph with the red eyes. She saw him, and turned with a mocking leer. Talquist hated the sight, but something inside him urged his body forward. He ran toward the taunting nymph. She fled in mimic dismay, back into the dark groves where now the distant piping died away.

Talquist ran through the forest, following the fleet wood sprite that leaped ahead, the wet green hair blending with the leaves of the livid trees. His temples burned, he gasped for breath, and his being was filled with a nameless strength. He loped after the fleeing figure, maddened by her taunting laughter that drifted back through the nighted pathways.

Soon he emerged upon the bank of a little stream where now the nymphs and nereids had returned. The fleet little creatures splashed noisily through the reeds and sank into the pool, diving beneath the rushes. None of them re-emerged.

Roger Talquist, fired by his madness, leaped after the taunting figure of the nymph he pursued, and the amulet jangled against his chest on its chain.

She turned suddenly on the bank and grinned up at him with slyly parted lips, and tossed her snake-locked hair. Her moist, flabby hands pawed at Talquist's arms. Her red eyes were not human, and gazing into them Talquist abruptly lost his madness and tried to push the creature away.

She stepped back on the bank. Noticing the amulet on the chain she reached for it. Talquist pushed her away again. Sniggering, the nymph reached out a cold hand to grasp at him for support. Instead, her fingers closed about the chain. She stepped back further, clutching the green seal—and lost her balance.

With a wrench the links parted, and the nymph fell screaming into the water. The amulet in her hand described a jeweled arc, then slipped beneath the churning surface of the stream, and sank. Nymph and seal of the satyr disappeared together in the pool. . . .

Roger Talquist stood on the bank, staring stupidly at the widening circles in the water.

He remembered, now. He was cold, naked, standing in the woods at midnight, after chasing the phantoms of fever and delirium.

There had been no sacrifice, no nymphs or satyrs. It had all been a dream, a delusion brought on by the peculiar hypnotic power of the amulet he had stared at when he lay down.

It was gone now, that strange talisman. He had probably flung it into the water himself, in a final frenzy. Well, good riddance to the cursed stone!

Old Lepolis had been right, in a way. The seal of the satyr, whether a gift of the ancient gods or not, did change a person. Wearing it, Talquist had not been himself. He had become some kind of beast; his mind had undergone a peculiar change which made him feel kinship with the wild creatures of elder myth. Lepolis had said that such things still existed in the forest and came forth after a sacrifice.

And indeed these things had come to pass.

Poor Lepolis! He had believed it all, and he wanted the amulet because he thought it would make him a forest creature that could live forever. He had wanted it enough, believed enough, to risk murder. And he was dead, and the amulet was gone.

Talquist mused. Oddly enough, he had not believed the old man's tale that the amulet could change one. He should have known it was some kind of allegory. The seal caused a mental change rather than a physical one; assuredly it had hypnotized him into thinking his body was different. Indeed, he *had* felt different; still did, in fact. Those tingling vibrations!

But what was he doing here? Better go back to the hotel now and try to forget his delirium.

Talquist gave a final glance at the waters of the pool into which the amulet had been thrown. The waters were calm now, and there was a glassy reflection in the clear moonlight. Talquist saw his own reflection in the moon-flooded depths, saw himself in Nature's silvery mirror.

Head, forehead, face, throat, arms, body, legs—he saw them all. And then he understood the real truth of Lepolis' incredible story of gifts from the gods that would change a man.

He did not look long. A single moment of numbing realization, and then he leaped into the pool—leaped straight into the deepest water, breaking with his body the mad reflection he had seen on the mirrored surface.

For, staring down at himself, Roger Talquist had seen *the face and figure of the wood-god, Pan!*

# The Dark Demon

IT HAS NEVER been put on paper before—the true story of Edgar Gordon's death. As a matter of fact, nobody but myself knows that he *is* dead; for people have gradually forgotten about the strange dark genius whose eldritch tales were once so popular among fantasy-lovers everywhere. Perhaps it was his late work which so alienated the public—the nightmare hints and outlandish fancies of his final books. Many people branded the extravagantly worded tomes as the work of a madman, and even his correspondents refused to comment on some of the unpublished stuff he sent them. Then too, his furtive and eccentric private life was not wholesomely regarded by those who knew him in the days of his early success. Whatever the cause, he and his writings have been doomed to oblivion by a world which always ignores what it cannot quite understand. Now everyone who does remember thinks that Gordon has merely disappeared. That is good, in view of the peculiar way in which he died. But I have decided to tell the truth. You see, I knew Gordon very well. I was truthfully, the last of all his friends, and I was there at the end. I owe him a debt of gratitude for all he has done for me, and how could I more fittingly repay it than to give to the world the facts concerning his sad mental metamorphosis and tragic death? Therefore this statement is indited.

It must have been six years ago that I first met him. I had not even known that we both resided in the same city, until a mutual correspondent inadvertently mentioned the fact in a letter.

I had, of course, heard of him before. Being a writer myself, I was enormously influenced and impressed by his work in the various magazines catering to the fantastic literature I loved. At this time he was known in a small way to practically all readers of such journals as an exceptionally erudite writer of horror tales. His style had won him renown in this small field, though even then there were those who professed to scoff at the grotesquery of his themes.

But I ardently admired him. As a result, I invited myself to pay a social call upon Mr. Gordon at his home. We became friends.

Surprisingly enough, this reclusive dreamer seemed to enjoy my company. He lived alone, cultivated no acquaintances, and had no contact with his friends save through correspondence. His mailing list, however, was voluminous. He exchanged letters with authors and editors all over the country; would-be writers, aspiring journalists, and thinkers and students everywhere. Once his reserve was penetrated, he seemed pleased to have my friendship. Needless to say, I was delighted.

What Edgar Gordon did for me in the next three years can never adequately be told. His able assistance, friendly criticism and kind encouragement finally succeeded in making a writer of sorts out of me, and after that our mutual interest formed an added bond between us.

What he revealed about his own magnificent stories astounded me. Yet I might have suspected something of the sort from the first.

Gordon was a tall, thin, angular man with the pale face and deep-set eyes which bespeak the dreamer. His language was poetic and profound; his personal mannerisms were almost somnambulistic in their weaving slowness, as though the mind which directed his mechanical movements was alien and far away. From these signs, therefore, I might have guessed his secret. But I did not, and was properly astonished when he first told me.

For Edgar Gordon wrote all of his stories from dreams! The plot, setting, and characters were products of his own colorful dream life—all he need do was transcribe his sleeping fancies on paper.

This was, I later learned, not an entirely unique phenomenon. The late Edward Lucas White claimed to have written several books based entirely on night-fancies. H. P. Lovecraft had produced a number of his splendid tales inspired by a similar source. And of course, Coleridge had visioned his *Kubla Khan* in a dream. Psychology is full of instances attesting to the possibility of nocturnal inspiration.

But what made Gordon's confession so strange was the queer personal peculiarities attendant upon his own dream stages. He quite seriously claimed that he could close his eyes at any time, allow himself to relax into a somnolent doze, and proceed to dream endlessly. It did not matter whether this was done by day or by night; nor whether he slumbered for fifteen hours or fifteen minutes. He seemed particularly susceptible to subconscious impressions.

My slight researches into psychology led me to believe that this was a form of self-hypnosis, and that his short naps were really a certain stage of mesmeric sleep, in which the subject is open to any suggestion.

Spurred on by my interest, I used to question him closely as to the subject-matter of these dreams. At first he responded readily, once I had told him of my own ideas on the subject. He narrated several of them to me, which I took down in a notebook for future analysis.

Gordon's fantasies were far from the ordinary Freudian sublimation or repression types. There were no discernible hidden wish-patterns, or symbolic phases. They were somehow *alien*. He told me how he had dreamed the story of his famous *Gargoyle* tale; of the black cities he visited on the fabulous outer rims of space, and the queer denizens that spoke to him from formless thrones that existed beyond all matter. His vivid descriptions of terrifyingly strange geometry and ultra-terrestrial life-forms convinced me that his was no ordinary mind to harbor such eery and disturbing shadows.

The ease with which he remembered vivid details was also unusual. There seemed to be no blurred mental concepts at all; he recalled every detail of dreams he had experienced perhaps years ago. Once in a while he would gloss over portions of his descriptions with the excuse that "it would not be possible to make things intelligible in speech." He insisted that he had seen and comprehended much that was beyond description in a three-dimensional way, and that in sleep he could feel colors and hear sensations.

Naturally this was a fascinating field of research for me. In reply to my questions, Gordon once told me that he had always known these dreams from earliest remembered childhood to the present day, and that the only difference between the first ones and the last was an increase of *intensity.* He now claimed that he *felt* his impressions much more strongly.

The locale of the dreams was curiously fixed. Nearly all of them occurred amidst scenes which he somehow recognized were outside of our own cosmos. Mountains of black stalagmites; peaks and cones amidst crater valleys of dead suns; stone cities in the stars; these were commonplace. Sometimes he walked or flew, shambled, or moved in unnamable ways with the indescribable races of other planets. Monsters he could and would describe, but there were certain *intelligences* which existed only in a gaseous, nebulous state, and still others which were merely the embodiment of an inconceivable *force.*

Gordon was always conscious that he himself was present in every dream. Despite the awesome and often unnerving adventures he so glibly described, he claimed that none of these sleep-images could be classified as nightmares. He had never felt afraid. Indeed, at times he experienced a curious reversal of identity, so that he regarded his dreams as natural and his waking life as unreal.

I questioned him as deeply as possible, and he had no explanation to offer. His family history had been normal in this and every other respect, although one of his ancestors had been a "wizard" in Wales. He himself was not a superstitious man, but he was forced to admit that certain of his dreams coincided curiously with descriptive passages in such books as the *Necronomicon,* the *Mysteries of the Worm,* and the *Book of Eibon.*

But he had experienced similar dreams long before his mind prompted him to read the obscure volumes mentioned above. He was confident that he had seen "Azathoth" and "Yuggoth" prior to the time he knew of their half-mythic existence in the legendary lore of ancient days. He was able to describe "Nyarlathotep" and "Yog-Sothoth" from what he claimed to be actual dream contact with these allegorical entities.

I was profoundly impressed by these statements, and finally was forced to admit that I had no logical explanation to offer. He himself took the matter so seriously that I never tried to humor or ridicule him out of his notions.

Indeed, every time he wrote a new story I asked him quite seriously about the dream which had inspired it, and for several years he told me such things at our weekly meetings.

But it was about this time that he entered into that phase of writing which brought him into general disfavor. The magazines which catered to his work began to refuse some of the manuscripts as too horrible and revolting for popular taste. His first published book, *Night-Gaunt* was a failure, due to the morbidity of its theme.

I sensed a subtle change in his style and subject. No longer did he adhere to conventional plot-motivation. He began to tell his stories in first-person, but the narrator was not a *human being.* His choice of words clearly indicated hyperesthesia.

In reply to my remonstrances on introducing non-human ideas, he argued that a real weird tale must be told from the viewpoint of the monster or entity itself. This was not a new theory to me, but I did object to the shockingly morbid note which his stories now emphasized. Consider his opening statement in *The Soul of Chaos:*

This world is but a tiny island in the dark sea of Infinity, and there are horrors swirling all around us. Around us? Rather let us say *amongst* us. I know, for I have seen them in my dreams, and there are more things in this world than sanity can ever see.

*The Soul of Chaos,* by the way, was the first of his four privately printed books. By this time he had lost all contact with the regular publishers and magazines. He dropped most of his correspondents, too, and concentrated on a few eccentric thinkers in the Orient.

His attitude toward me was changing, too. No longer did he expound his dreams to me, or outline theories of plot and style. I didn't visit him very often any more, and he rejected my overtures with unmistakable bruskness.

There were other factors which somehow made me half glad to avoid the man. Always a quiet recluse by choice, his hermit-like tendencies seemed visibly accentuated. He never went out any more, he told me; not even walking in the yard. Food and other necessities he had delivered weekly to the door. In the evening he allowed no light but a small lamp within the parlor study. All he volunteered about this rigid routine was noncommittal. He said that he spent all his time in sleeping and writing.

He was thinner, paler, and moved with a more mystic dreaminess of manner than ever before. I thought of drugs; he looked like a typical addict. But his eyes were not the feverish globes of fire which characterize the hashish-eater, and opium had not wasted his physique. Then I suspected insanity myself; his detached manner of speech, and his suspicious refusal to enter deeply into any subject of conversation, might be due to some nervous disorder.

Certainly what he said at the last about his recent dreams tended to substantiate my theory. I'll never forget that final discussion of dreams as long as I live—for reasons soon to be apparent.

He told me about his last stories with a certain reluctance. Yes, they were dream-inspired, like the rest. He had not written them for public consumption, and the editors and publishers could go to blazes for all he cared. He wrote them because he had been *told* to write them.

Yes, told to. By the creature in his dreams, of course. He did not care to speak about it, but since I was a friend . . .

I urged him. Now I wish I hadn't; perhaps I could have been spared the knowledge that follows. . . .

Edgar Henquist Gordon, sitting there in the wan lunar light of the moon; sitting at the wide window with eyes that equaled the leprous moonlight in the dreadful intensity of their pallid glow. . . .

"I know about my dreams now. I was *chosen,* from the first, to be the Messiah; the messenger of His word. No, I'm not going religious. I'm not speaking of a God in the ordinary sense of the word men use to designate any power they cannot understand. I speak of the *Dark One.* You've read about Him in those books I showed you; the Demon Messenger, they call Him. But that's all allegorical. He isn't Evil, because there is no such thing as Evil. He is merely alien. And I am to be His messenger on Earth.

"Don't fidget so! I'm not mad. You've heard about it all

before—how the elder peoples worshipped forces that once were manifested physically on Earth, like the *Dark One* that has chosen me. The legends are silly, of course. He isn't a destroyer—merely a superior intelligence who wishes to gain mental rapport with human minds, so as to enable certain—ah—exchanges between humanity and Those beyond.

"He speaks to me in dreams. He told me to write my books, and distribute them to those who know. When the right time comes, we shall band together, and unfold some of the secrets of the cosmos at which men have only guessed or even sensed in dreams.

"That's why I've always dreamed. I was chosen to learn. That is why my dreams have shown me such things—'Yuggoth' and all the rest. Now I am being prepared for my—ah—apostleship.

"I can't tell you much more. I must write and sleep a great deal nowadays, so that I can learn faster.

"Who is this *Dark One?* I can't tell you any more. I suppose you already think I'm crazy. Well, you have many supporters of that theory. But I'm not. It's true!

"You remember all I've told you about my dreams—how they kept growing in *intensity?* Well enough. Several months ago I had some different dream-sequences. I was in the dark—not the ordinary dark you know, but the absolute dark beyond Space. It isn't describable in three-dimensional concepts or thought-patterns at all. The darkness has a *sound,* and a *rhythm* akin to breathing, because it is alive. I was merely a bodiless mind there; when I saw Him.

"He came out of the dark and—ah—communicated with me. Not by words. I'm thankful that my previous dreams had been so arranged as to inure me against visual horror. Otherwise I should never have been able to stand the sight of Him. You see, He is not like humans, and the shape He chose to wear is unpleasant. But, once you understand, you can realize that the shape is just as allegorical as the legends ignorant men have fostered about Him and the others.

"He looks something like a medieval conception of the demon Asmodeus. Black all over, and furry, with a snout like a hog, green eyes, and the claws and fangs of a wild beast.

"I was not frightened after He communicated, though. You

see, He wears that shape merely because foolish people in olden days believed that He looked that way. Mass belief was a curious influence on intangible forces, you understand. And men, thinking such forces evil, have made them assume the aspect of evilness. But He means no harm.

"I wish I could repeat some of the things He has told me.

"Yes, I've seen Him every night since then. But I promised to reveal nothing until the day is ready. Now that I understand, I am no longer interested in writing for the herd. I am afraid humanity doesn't mean anything to me since I have learned those steps which lie beyond—and how to achieve them.

"You can go away and laugh at me all you like. All I can say is that nothing in my books has been exaggerated in the least—and that they only contain infinitesimal glimpses of the ultimate revelations which lurk beyond human consciousness. But when the day He has appointed shall arrive, then the whole world will learn the truth.

"Until then, you'd best keep away from me. I can't be disturbed, and every evening the impressions get stronger and stronger. I sleep eighteen hours a day now, at times, because there is so much that He wishes to tell me; so much to be learned in preparation. But when the day comes I shall be the godhead—He has promised me that in some way I *shall become incarnate with Him!*"

Such was the substance of his monolog. I left shortly after that. There was nothing I could say or do. But later I thought a lot about what he had said.

He was quite gone, poor fellow, and it was evident that another month or so would bring him to the breaking-point. I felt sincerely sorry, and deeply concerned over the tragedy. After all, he had been my friend and mentor for many years, and he was a genius. It was all too bad.

Still, he had a strange and disturbingly coherent story. It certainly conformed to his previous accounts of dream-life, and the legendary background was authentic, if the *Necronomicon* is to be believed. I wondered if his *Dark One* was remotely connected with the Nyarlathotep fable, or the "Dark Demon" of the witch-coven rituals.

But all that nonsense about the "day" and his being a "Messiah" on Earth was too absurd. What did he mean about the *Dark One's* promise of incarnating himself in Gordon? Demonic possession is an old belief credited only by the childishly superstitious.

Yes, I thought plenty about the whole thing. For several weeks I did a little investigating of my own. I reread the later books, corresponded with Gordon's former editors and publishers, dropped notes to his old friends. And I even studied some of the old magic tomes myself.

I got nothing tangible from all this, save a growing realization that something must be done to save Gordon from himself. I was terribly afraid for the man's mind, and I knew that I must act quickly.

So one night, about three weeks after our final meeting, I left the house and started to walk to his home. I intended to plead with him, if possible, to go away; or at least insist that he submit to a medical examination. Why I pocketed the revolver I cannot say—some inner instinct warned me that I might meet with a violent response.

At any rate I had the gun in my coat, and I gripped the butt firmly in one hand as I threaded some of the darker streets that led to his old dwelling on Cedar Street.

It was a moonless night, with ominous hints of a thunderstorm in the offing. The little wind that warns of approaching rain was already sighing in the dark trees overhead, and streaks of lightning occasionally flared in the west.

My mind was a chaotic jumble of apprehension, anxiety, determination, and a lurking bewilderment. I did not even formulate what I was going to do or say once I saw Gordon. I kept wondering what had happened to him the last few weeks—whether the "day" he spoke of was approaching at last.

Tonight was May-Eve. . . .

The house was dark. I rang and rang, but there was no response. The door opened under the impact of my shoulder. The noise of splintering wood was drowned out by the first peal of thunder overhead.

I walked down the hall to the study. Everything was dark. I opened the study door. There was a man sleeping on the couch by the window. It was undoubtedly Edgar Gordon.

What was he dreaming about? Had he met the *Dark One* again in his dreams? The *Dark One,* "looking like Asmodeus—black all over, and furry, with green eyes, hog-snout, and the claws and fangs of some wild beast"; the *Dark One* who told him about the "day" when Gordon should become incarnate with him?

Was he dreaming about this, on May-Eve? Edgar Henquist Gordon, sleeping a strange sleep on the couch by the window . . .

I reached for the light-switch, but a sudden flash of lightning forestalled me. It lasted only a second, but it was brilliant enough to illuminate the entire room. I saw the walls, the furniture, the terrible scribbled manuscripts on the table.

Then I fired three revolver shots before the final flicker died away. There was a single eldritch scream that was mercifully drowned in a new burst of thunder. I screamed, myself. I never turned on the light, but only gathered up the papers on the table and ran out into the rain.

On the way home rain mingled with tear-drops on my face, and I echoed each new roar of thunder with a sob.

I could not endure the lightning, though, and shielded my eyes as I ran blindly to the safety of my own rooms. There I burnt the papers I had brought without reading them. I had no need of that, for there was nothing more to know.

That was weeks ago. When Gordon's house was entered at last, no body was found—only an empty suit of clothes that looked as though it had been tossed carelessly on the couch. Nothing else had been disturbed, but police point to the absence of Gordon's papers as an indication that he took them along when he disappeared.

I am very glad that nothing else has been found, and would be content to keep silent, were it not for the fact that Gordon is regarded as insane. I once thought him insane, too, so you see I must speak. After that I am going away from here, because I want to forget as much as I can. At that, I'm lucky I do not dream.

No, Edgar Gordon was not insane. But he told the truth in his books—about horrors being around us and *amongst* us. I dare not say all I now believe about his dreams, and whether or not his last stories were true.

Those last dreams—about the *Dark One*, who was waiting for

the right day, and who would *incarnate* himself with Gordon ... I know what he meant now, and I shudder to think of what might have happened if I had not come upon the scene when I did. If there had been an awakening ...

Because when that flash of lightning blazed across the room, I saw what lay in sleep upon the couch. That is what I shot; that is what sent me screaming into the storm, and that is what makes me sure that Gordon was not crazy, but spoke the truth.

For the incarnation had occurred. There on the couch, dressed in the clothes of Edgar Henquist Gordon, lay a demon like Asmodeus—a black, furry creature with the snout of a hog, green eyes, and the dreadful fangs and talons of some wild beast. It was the *Dark One* of Edgar Gordon's dreams!

# The Faceless God

THE THING on the torture-rack began to moan. There was a grating sound as the lever stretched the iron bed still one more space in length. The moaning grew to a piercing shriek of utter agony.

"Ah," said Doctor Carnoti, "we have him at last."

He bent over the tortured man on the iron grille and smiled tenderly into the anguished face. His eyes, tinged with delicate amusement, took in every detail of the body before him—the swollen legs, raw and angry from the embrace of the fiery boot; the back and shoulders, still crimson from the kiss of the lash; the chest crushed by the caress of the Spiked Coffin. With gentle solicitude he surveyed the finishing touches applied by the rack itself—the dislocated shoulders and twisted torso; the broken fingers, and the dangling tendons in the lower limbs. He turned his attention to the old man's tormented countenance once again. Then he spoke.

"Well, Hassan. I do not think you will prove stubborn any longer in the face of such—ah—eloquent persuasion. Come now; tell me where I can find this idol of which you speak."

The butchered victim began to sob, and the doctor was forced to kneel beside the bed of pain in order to understand his incoherent mumblings. For perhaps twenty minutes the creature groaned on, and then at last fell silent. Doctor Carnoti rose to his feet once more, a satisfied twinkle in his genial eyes. He made a brief motion to one of the blacks operating the rack machinery. The fellow nodded, and went over to the living horror on the instrument. The black drew his sword. It swished upward, then cleaved down once again.

Doctor Carnoti went out of the room, bolted the door behind him, and climbed the steps to the house above. As he raised the barred trap-door he saw that the sun was shining. The doctor began to whistle. He was very pleased.

2.

He had good reason to be. For several years the doctor had been what is vulgarly known as an "adventurer." He had been a smuggler of antiques, an exploiter of labor on the Upper Nile, and had at times sunk so low as to participate in the forbidden "black goods trade" that flourished at certain ports along the Red Sea. He had come out to Egypt many years ago as an attaché on an archeological expedition, from which he had been summarily dismissed. The reason for his dismissal is not known, but it was rumored that he had been caught trying to appropriate certain of the expeditionary trophies. After his exposure and subsequent disgrace, he had disappeared for a while. Several years later he had come back to Cairo and set up an establishment in the native quarter. It was here that he fell into the unscrupulous habits of business which had earned for him a dubious reputation and sizable profit. He seemed well satisfied with both.

At the present time he was a man of perhaps forty-five years of age, short and heavy-set, with a bullet-shaped head that rested on broad, ape-like shoulders. His thick torso and bulging paunch were supported by a pair of spindly legs that contrasted oddly with the upper portions of his beefy body. Despite his Falstaffian appearance he was a hard and ruthless man. His piggish eyes were filled with greed; his fleshy mouth was lustful; his only natural smile was one of avarice.

It was his covetous nature that had led him into his present adventure. Ordinarily he was not a credulous man. The usual tales of lost pyramids, buried treasure and stolen mummies did not impress him. He preferred something more substantial. A contraband consignment of rugs; a bit of smuggled opium; something in the line of illicit human merchandise—these were things he could appreciate and understand.

But this case was different. Extraordinary as it sounded, it meant big money. Carnoti was smart enough to know that many of the great discoveries of Egyptology had been prompted by just such wild rumors as the one he had heard. He also knew the difference between improbable truth and spurious invention. This story sounded like the truth.

In brief, it ran as follows. A certain party of nomads, while engaged in a secret journey with a cargo of illegitimately obtained goods, were traversing a special route of their own. They did not feel that the regular caravan lanes were healthful for them to follow. While traveling near a certain spot they had accidentally espied a curious rock or stone in the sands. The thing had evidently been buried, but long years of shifting and swirling among the dunes above it had served to uncover a portion of the object. They had stopped to inspect it at closer range, and thereby made a startling discovery. The thing projecting from the sand was the head of a statue; an ancient Egyptian statue, with the triple crown of a god! Its black body was still submerged, but the head seemed to be in perfect preservation. It was a very peculiar thing, that head, and none of the natives could or would recognize the deity, though the caravan leaders questioned them closely. The whole thing was an unfathomable mystery. A perfectly preserved statue of an unknown god buried all alone in the southern desert, a long way from any oasis, and two hundred miles from the smallest village!

Evidently the caravan men realized something of its uniqueness; for they ordered that two boulders which lay near by be placed on top of the idol as a marker in case they ever returned. The men did as they were ordered, though they were obviously reluctant, and kept muttering prayers beneath their breath. They seemed very much afraid of the buried image, but only reiterated their ignorance when questioned further concerning it.

After the boulders had been placed, the expedition was forced to journey on, for time did not permit them to unearth the curious figure in its entirety, or attempt to carry it with them. When they returned to the north they told their story, and as most tales were in the habit of doing, it came to the ears of Doctor Carnoti. Carnoti thought fast. It was quite evident that the original discoverers of the idol did not attach any great importance to their find. For this reason the doctor might easily return to the spot and unearth the statue without any trouble, once he knew exactly where it was located.

Carnoti felt that it was worth finding. If it had been a treasure yarn, now, he would have scoffed and unhesitatingly put it down as a cock-and-bull story of the usual variety. But an idol—that was different. He could understand why an ignorant band of Arab smugglers might ignore such a discovery. He could also realize that such a discovery might prove more valuable to him than all the treasure in Egypt. It was easy for him to remember the vague clues and wild hints that had prompted the findings of early explorers. They had followed up many blind leads when first they plumbed the pyramids and racked the temple ruins. All of them were tomb-looters at heart, but their ravishings had made them rich and famous. Why not him, then? If the tale were true, and this idol not only buried, but totally unknown as a deity; in perfect condition, and in such an out-of-the-way locality—these facts would create a furor when he exhibited his find. He would be famous! Who knew what hitherto untrodden fields he might open up in archeology? It was well worth chancing.

But he must not arouse any suspicion. He dared not inquire about the place from any of the Arabs who had been there. That would immediately cause talk. No, he must get his directions from a native in the band. Accordingly, two of his servants picked up Hassan, the old camel-driver, and brought him before Carnoti in his house. But Hassan, when questioned, looked very much afraid. He refused to talk. So Carnoti conducted him into his little reception room in the cellar, where he had been wont to entertain certain recalcitrant guests in the past. Here the doctor, whose knowledge of anatomy stood him in good stead, was able to cajole his visitors into speaking.

So Doctor Carnoti emerged from the cellar in a very pleasant frame of mind. He was rubbing his fat hands when he looked at the map to verify his information, and he went out to dinner with a smiling face.

Two days later he was ready to start. He had hired a small number of natives, so as not to excite undue investigation, and given out to his business acquaintances that he was about to embark on a special trip. He engaged a strange dragoman, and made sure that the fellow would keep his mouth shut. There were several swift camels in the train, and a number of extra donkeys harnessed to a large empty cart. He took food and water for six days, for he intended to return via river-boat. After the arrangements were completed, the party assembled one morning at a certain spot unknown to official eyes, and the expedition began.

3.

It was on the morning of the fourth day that they arrived at last. Carnoti saw the stones from his precarious perch atop the leading camel. He swore delightedly, and despite the hovering heat, dismounted and raced over to the spot where the two boulders lay. A moment later he called the company to a hasty halt and issued orders for the immediate erection of the tents, and the usual preparations for encampment. Utterly disregarding the intolerable warmth of the day, he saw to it that the sweating natives did a thorough job; and then, without allowing them a moment's rest, he instructed them to remove the massive rocks from their resting-place. A crew of straining men managed to topple them over at last, and clear away the underlying sand.

In a few moments there was a loud cry from the gang of laborers, as a black and sinister head came into view. It was a triple-crowned blasphemy. Great spiky cones adorned the top of the ebony diadem, and beneath them were hidden intricately executed designs. He bent down and examined them. They were monstrous, both in subject and in execution. He saw the writhing, worm-like shapes of primal monsters, and headless, slimy creatures from the stars. There were bloated beasts in the robes of men, and ancient Egyptian gods in hideous combat with squirming demons from the gulf. Some of the designs were foul beyond description, and others hinted of unclean terrors that were old when the world was young. But all were evil; and Carnoti, cold and callous though he was, could not gaze at them without feeling a horror that ate at his brain.

As for the natives, they were openly frightened. The moment that the top of the image came into view, they began to jabber hysterically. They retreated to the side of the excavation and began to argue and mumble, pointing occasionally at the statue, or at the kneeling figure of the doctor. Absorbed in his inspection, Carnoti failed to catch the body of their remarks, or note the air of menace which radiated from the sullen dragoman. Once or twice he heard some vague references to the name "Nyarlathotep," and a few allusions to "The Demon Messenger."

After completing his scrutiny, the doctor rose to his feet and ordered the men to proceed with the excavation. No one moved. Impatiently he repeated his command. The natives stood by, their heads hung, but their faces were stolid. At last the dragoman stepped forward and began to harangue the *effendi*.

He and his men would never have come with their master had they known what they were expected to do. They would not touch the statue of the god, and they warned the doctor to keep his hands off. It was bad business to incur the wrath of the Old God—the Secret One. But perhaps he had not heard of Nyarlathotep. He was the oldest god of all Egypt; of all the world. He was the God of Resurrection, and the Black Messenger of Karneter. There was a legend that one day he would arise and bring the olden dead to life. And his curse was one to be avoided.

Carnoti, listening, began to lose his temper. Angrily he interrupted, ordering the men to stop gawking and resume their work. He backed up this command with two Colt .32 revolvers. He would take all the blame for this desecration, he shouted, and he was not afraid of any damned stone idol in the world.

The natives seemed properly impressed, both by the revolvers and by his fluent profanity. They began to dig again, timidly averting their eyes from the statue's form.

A few hours' work sufficed for the men to uncover the idol. If the crown of its stony head had hinted of horror, the face and body openly proclaimed it. The image was obscene and shockingly malignant. There was an indescribably *alien* quality about it—it was ageless, unchanging, eternal. Not a scratch marred its black and crudely chiseled surface; during all its many-centuried burial there had been no weathering upon the fiendishly carven features. Carnoti saw it now as it must have looked when it was first buried, and the sight was not good to see.

It resembled a miniature sphinx—a life-sized sphinx with the wings of a vulture and the body of a hyena. There were talons and claws, and upon the squatting, bestial body rested a massive, anthropomorphic head, bearing the ominous triple crown whose dread designs had so singularly excited the natives. But the worst and by far the most hideous feature was the lack of a face upon the ghastly thing. It was a faceless god; the winged, faceless god of ancient myth—Nyarlathotep, Mighty Messenger, Stalker among the Stars, and Lord of the Desert.

When Carnoti completed his examination at last, he became almost hysterically happy. He grinned triumphantly into that blank and loathsome countenance—grinned into that faceless orifice that yawned as vacantly as the black void beyond the suns. In his enthusiasm he failed to notice the furtive whispers of the natives and the guides, and disregarded their fearsome glances at the unclean eidolon. Had he not done so, he would have been a wiser man; for these men knew, as all Egypt knows, that Nyarlathotep is the Master of Evil.

Not for nothing had his temples been demolished, his statues destroyed, and his priestcraft crucified in the olden days. There were dark and terrible reasons for prohibiting his worship, and omitting his name from the *Book of the Dead*. All references to the Faceless One were long since deleted from the Sacred Manuscripts, and great pains had been taken to ignore some of his godly attributes, or assign them to some milder deity. In Thoth, Set, Bubastis and Sebek we can trace some of the Master's grisly endowments. It was he, in the most archaic of chronicles, who was ruler of the Underworld. It was he who became the patron of sorcery and the black arts. Once he alone had ruled, and men knew him in all lands, under many names. But that time passed. Men turned away from the worship of evil, and reverenced the good. They did not care for the gruesome sacrifice the Dark God demanded, nor the way his priests ruled. At last the cult was suppressed, and by common consent all references to it were forever banned, and its records destroyed. But Nyarlathotep had come out of the desert, according to the legend, and to the desert he now returned. Idols were set up in hidden places among the sands, and here the thin, fanatical ranks of true believers still leapt and capered in naked worship, where the cries of shrieking victims echoed only to the ears of the night.

So his legend remained and was handed down in the secret ways of the earth. Time passed. In the north the ice-flow receded, and Atlantis fell. New peoples overran the land, but the desert folk remained. They viewed the building of the pyramids with amused and cynical eyes. Wait, they counseled. When the Day arrived at last, Nyarlathotep again would come out of the desert, and then woe unto Egypt! For the pyramids would shatter into dust, and temples crumble to ruin. Sunken cities of the sea would rise, and there would be famine and pestilence throughout the land. The stars would change in a most peculiar way, so that the Great Ones could come pulsing from the outer gulf. Then the beasts should give tongue, and prophesy in their anthropo-glotism that man shall perish. By these signs, and other apoca-lyptic portents, the world would know that Nyarlathotep had returned. Soon he himself would be visible—a dark, faceless man in black, walking, staff in hand, across the desert, but leaving no track to mark his way, save that of death. For wherever his foot-steps turned, men would surely die, until at last none but true believers remained to welcome him in worship with the Mighty Ones from the gulfs.

Such, in its essence, was the fable of Nyarlathotep. It was older than secret Egypt, more hoary than sea-doomed Atlantis, more ancient than time-forgotten Mu. But it has never been forgotten. In the mediaeval times this story and its prophecy were carried across Europe by returning crusaders. Thus the Mighty Messen-ger became the Black Man of the witch-covens; the emissary of Asmodeus and darker gods. His name is mentioned cryptically in the *Necronomicon,* for Alhazred heard it whispered in tales of shadowed Irem. The fabulous *Book of Eibon* hints at the myth in veiled and diverse ways, for it was writ in a far-off time when it was not yet deemed safe to speak of things that had walked upon the earth when it was young. Ludvig Prinn, who traveled in Sara-cenic lands and learned strange sorceries, awesomely implies his knowledge in the infamous *Mysteries of the Worm.*

But his worship, in late years, seems to have died out. There is no mention of it in Sir James Frazer's *Golden Bough,* and most reputable ethnologists and anthropologists are frankly ignorant of the Faceless One's history. But there are idols still intact, and some whisper of certain caverns beneath the Nile, and of burrows below the Ninth Pyramid. The secret signs and symbols of his worship are gone, but there are some undecipherable hieroglyphs in the Government vaults which are very closely concealed. And men know. By word of mouth the tale has come down through the ages, and there are those who still wait for the Day. By common consent there seem to be certain spots in the desert which are carefully avoided by caravans, and several secluded shrines are shunned by those who remember. For Nyarlathotep is the God of the Desert, and his ways are best left unprofaned.

It was this knowledge which prompted the uneasiness of the natives upon the discovery of that peculiar idol in the sand. When they had first noted the head-dress they had been afraid, and after seeing that featureless face they became frantic with dread. As for Doctor Carnoti, his fate did not matter to them. They were concerned only with themselves, and their course was plainly apparent. They must flee, and flee at once.

Carnoti paid no attention to them. He was busy making plans for the following day. They would place the idol on a wheeled cart and harness the donkeys. Once back to the river it could be put on board the steamer. What a find! He conjured up pleasant visions of the fame and fortune that would be his. Scavenger, was he? Unsavory adventurer, eh? Charlatan, cheat, imposter, they had called him. How those smug official eyes would pop when they beheld his discovery! Heaven only knew what vistas this thing might open up. There might be other altars, other idols; tombs and temples too, perhaps. He knew vaguely that there was some absurd legend about the worship of this deity, but if he could only get his hands on a few more natives who could give him the information he wanted. . . . He smiled, musingly. Funny, those superstitious myths! The boys were afraid of the statue; that was plainly apparent. The dragoman, now, with his stupid quotations. How did it go? "Nyarlathotep is the Black Messenger of Karneter. He comes from out the desert, across the burning sands, and stalks his prey throughout the world, which is the land of his domain."

Silly! All Egyptian myths were stupid. Statues with animal heads suddenly coming to life; reincarnation of men and gods, foolish kings building pyramids for mummies. Well, a lot of fools believed it; not only the natives, either. He knew some cranks who credited the stories about the Pharaoh's curse, and the magic of the old priests. There were a lot of wild tales about the ancient tombs and the men who died when they invaded them. No wonder his own simple natives believed such trash! But whether they believed it or not, they were going to move his idol, damn them, even if he had to shoot them down to make them obey.

He went into his tent, well satisfied. The boy served him his meal, and Carnoti dined heartily as was his wont. Then he decided to retire early, in anticipation of his plans for the following morning. The boys could tend to the camp, he decided. Accordingly he lay down on his cot and soon fell into a contented, peaceful slumber.

4.

It must have been several hours later that he awoke. It was very dark, and the night was strangely still. Once he heard the far-away howl of a hunting jackal, but it soon blended into somber silence. Surprised at his sudden awakening, Carnoti rose and went to the door of the tent, pulling back the flap to gaze into the open. A moment later he cursed in frenzied rage.

The camp was deserted! The fire had died out, the men and camels had disappeared. Foot-prints, already half obliterated by the sands, showed the silent haste in which the natives had departed. The fools had left him here alone!

He was lost. The knowledge sent a sudden stab of fear to his heart. Lost! The men were gone, the food was gone, the camels and donkeys had disappeared. He had neither weapons nor water, and he was all alone. He stood before the door of the tent and gazed, terrified, at the vast and lonely desert. The moon gleamed like a silver skull in an ebony sky. A sudden hot wind ruffled the endless ocean of sand, and sent it skirling in tiny waves at his feet. Then came silence, ceaseless silence. It was like the silence of the tomb; like the eternal silence of the pyramids, where in crumbling sarcophagi the mummies lie, their dead eyes gazing into unchanging and unending darkness. He felt indescribably small and lonely there in the night, and he was conscious of strange and baleful powers that were weaving the threads of his destiny into a final tragic pattern. Nyarlathotep! He *knew*, and was wreaking an immutable vengeance.

But that was nonsense. He must not let himself be troubled by such fantastic rubbish. That was just another form of desert mirage; a common enough delusion under such circumstances. He must not lose his nerve now. He must face the facts calmly. The men had absconded with the supplies and the horses because of some crazy native superstition. That was real enough. As for the superstition itself, he must not let it bother him. Those frantic and morbid fancies of his would vanish quickly enough with the morning sun.

The morning sun! A terrible thought assailed him—the fearsome reality of the desert at midday. To reach an oasis he would be forced to travel day and night before the lack of food and water weakened him so that he could not go on. There would be no escape once he left this tent; no refuge from that pitiless blazing eye whose glaring rays could scorch his brain to madness. To die in the heat of the desert—that was an unthinkable agony. He must get back; his work was not yet completed. There must be a new expedition to recover the idol. He must get back! Besides, Carnoti did not want to die. His fat lips quivered with fear as he thought of the pain, the torture. He had no desire to suffer the anguish of that fellow he had put on the rack. The poor devil had not looked very pleasant there. Ah no, death was not for the doctor. He must hurry. But where?

He gazed around frantically, trying to get his bearings. The desert mocked him with its monotonous, inscrutable horizon. For a moment black despair clutched at his brain, and then came a sudden inspiration. He must go north, of course. And he recalled, now, the chance words let fall by the dragoman that afternoon. The statue of Nyarlathotep faced north! Jubilantly he ransacked the tent for any remnants of food or provisions. There were none. Matches and tobacco he carried, and in his kit he found a hunting-knife. He was almost confident when he left the tent. The rest of the journey would now be childishly simple. He would travel all night and make as much time as he could. His pack-blanket would probably shield him from the noonday sun tomorrow, and in late afternoon he would resume his course after the worst of the heat had abated. By quick marches tomorrow night, he ought to find himself near the Wadi Hassur oasis upon the following morning. All that remained for him to do was to get out to the idol and set his course, since the tracks of his party in the sand were already obscured.

Triumphantly, he strode across the camp-clearing to the excavation where the image stood. And it was there that he received his greatest shock.

The idol had been reinterred! The workmen had not left the statue violated, but had completely filled in the excavation, even taking the precaution of placing the two original stones over the top. Carnoti could not move them single-handed, and when he realized the extent of this calamity, he was filled with an overpowering dismay. He was defeated. Cursing would do no good, and in his heart he could not even hope to pray. Nyarlathotep—Lord of the Desert!

It was with a new and deathly fear that he began his journey, choosing a course at random, and hoping against hope that the sudden clouds would lift so that he could have the guidance of the stars. But the clouds did not lift, and only the moon grinned grimly down at the stumbling figure that struggled through the sand.

Dervish dreams flitted through Carnoti's consciousness as he walked. Try as he might, the legend of the god haunted him with a sense of impending fulfilment. Vainly he tried to force his drugged mind to forget the suspicions that tormented it. He could not. Over and over again he found himself shivering with fear at the thought of a godly wrath pursuing him to his doom. He had violated a sacred spot, and the Old Ones remember . . . "his ways are best left unprofaned" . . . "God of the Desert" . . . that empty countenance. Carnoti swore viciously, and lumbered on, a tiny ant amid mountains of undulating sand.

## 5.

Suddenly it was daylight. The sand faded from purple to violet, then suddenly suffused with an orchid glow. But Carnoti did not see it, for he slept. Long before he had planned, his bloated body had given way beneath the grueling strain, and the coming of dawn found him utterly weary and exhausted. His tired legs buckled under him and he collapsed upon the sand, barely managing to draw the blanket over him before he slept.

The sun crept across the brazen sky like a fiery ball of lava, pouring its molten rays upon the flaming sands. Carnoti slept on, but his sleep was far from pleasant. The heat brought him queer and disturbing dreams.

In them he seemed to see the figure of Nyarlathotep pursuing him on a nightmare flight across the desert of fire. He was running over a burning plain, unable to stop, while searing pain ate into his charred and blackened feet. Behind him strode the Faceless God, urging him onward with a staff of serpents. He ran on and on; but always that gruesome presence kept pace behind him. His feet became numbed by the scorching agony of the sand. Soon he was hobbling on ghastly, crumpled stumps, but despite the torture he dared not stop. The Thing behind him cackled in diabolical mirth, his gigantic laughter rising to the blazing sky.

Carnoti was on his knees now, his crippled legs eaten away into ashy stumps that smoldered acridly even as he crawled. Suddenly the desert became a lake of living flame into which he sank, his scorched body consumed by a blast of livid, unendurable torment. He felt the sand lick pitilessly at his arms, his waist, his very throat; and still his dying senses were filled with a monstrous dread of the Faceless One behind him—a dread transcending all pain. Even as he sank into that white-hot inferno he was feebly struggling on. The vengeance of the god must never overtake him! The heat was overpowering him now; it was frying his cracked and bleeding lips, transforming his scorched body into one ghastly ember of burning anguish.

He raised his head for the last time before his boiling brain gave way beneath the agony. There stood the Dark One, and even as Carnoti watched he saw the lean taloned hands reach out to touch his fiery face; saw the dreadful triple-crowned head draw near to him, so that he gazed for one grisly moment into that empty countenance. As he looked he seemed to see something in that black pit of horror—something that was staring at him from illimitable gulfs beyond—something with great flaming eyes that bored into his being with a fury greater than the fires that were consuming him. It told him, wordlessly, that his doom was sealed. Then came a burst of white-hot oblivion, and he sank into the seething sands, the blood bubbling in his veins. But the indescribable horror of that glimpse remained, and the last thing he remembered was the sight of that dreadful, empty countenance and the nameless fear behind it. Then he awoke.

For a moment his relief was so great that he did not notice the sting of the midday sun. Then, bathed in perspiration, he staggered to his feet and felt the stabbing rays bite into his back. He tried to shield his eyes and glance above to get his bearings, but the sky was a bowl of fire. Desperately, he dropped the blanket and began to run. The sand was clinging to his feet, slowing his pace and tripping him. It burned his heels. He felt an intolerable thirst. Already the demons of delirium danced madly in his head. He ran, endlessly, and his dream seemed to become a menacing reality. Was it coming true?

His legs *were* scorched, his body *was* seared. He glanced behind. Thank God there was no figure there—yet! Perhaps, if he kept a grip on himself, he might still make it, in spite of the time he had lost. He raced on. Perhaps a passing caravan—but no, it was far out of the caravan route. Tonight the sunset would give him an accurate course. Tonight.

Damn that heat! Sand all around him. Hills of it, mountains. All alike they were, like the crumbled, cyclopean ruins of Titan cities. All were burning, smoldering in the fierce heat.

The day was endless. Time, ever an illusion, lost all meaning. Carnoti's weary body throbbed in bitter anguish, filling each moment with a new and deeper torment. The horizon never changed. No mirage marred the cruel, eternal vista; no shadow gave surcease from the savage glare.

But wait! Was there not a shadow *behind* him? Something dark

and shapeless gloated at the back of his brain. A terrible thought
pierced him with sudden realization. Nyarlathotep, God of the
Desert! A shadow following him, driving him to destruction.
Those legends—the natives warned him, his dreams warned
him, even that dying creature on the rack. The Mighty Messenger
always claims his own . . . a black man with a staff of serpents. . . .
"He cometh from out the desert, across the burning sands, and
stalketh his prey throughout the land of his domain."

Hallucination? Dared he glance back? He turned his fever-
addled head. Yes! *It was true, this time!* There *was* something
behind him, far away on the slope below; something black and
nebulous that seemed to pad on stealthy feet. With a muttered
curse, Carnoti began to run. Why had he ever touched that
image? If he got out of this he would never return to the accursed
spot again. The legends were true. God of the Desert.

He ran on, even though the sun showered bloody kisses on
his brow. He was beginning to go blind. There were dazzling
constellations whirling before his eyes, and his heart throbbed a
shrieking rhythm in his breast. But in his mind there was room
for but one thought—escape.

His imagination began playing him strange tricks. He seemed
to see statues in the sand—statues like the one he had profaned.
Their shapes towered everywhere, writhing giant-like out of the
ground and confronting his path with eery menace. Some were in
attitudes with wings outspread, others were tentacled and snake-
like, but all were faceless and triple-crowned. He felt that he was
going mad, until he glanced back and saw that creeping figure
now only a half-mile behind. Then he staggered on, screaming
incoherently at the grotesque eidolons barring his way. The
desert seemed to take on a hideous personality, as though all
nature were conspiring to conquer him. The contorted outlines
of the sand became imbued with malignant consciousness; the
very sun took on an evil life. Carnoti moaned deliriously. Would
night never come?

It came at last, but by that time Carnoti did not know it any
more. He was a babbling, raving thing, wandering over the shifting sand, and the rising moon looked down on a being that alter-
nately howled and laughed. Presently the figure struggled to its

feet and glanced furtively over its shoulder at a shadow that crept close. Then it began to run again, shrieking over and over again the single word, "Nyarlathotep." And all the while the shadow lurked just a step behind.

It seemed to be embodied with a strange and fiendish intelligence, for the shapeless adumbration carefully drove its victim forward in one definite direction, as if purposefully herding it toward an intended goal. The stars now looked upon a sight spawned of delirium—a man, chased across endlessly looming sands by a black shadow. Presently the pursued one came to the top of a hill and halted with a scream. The shadow paused in midair and seemed to wait.

Carnoti was looking down at the remains of his own camp, just as he had left it the night before, with the sudden awful realization that he had been driven in a circle back to his starting point. Then, with the knowledge, came a merciful mental collapse. He threw himself forward in one final effort to elude the shadow, and raced straight for the two stones where the statue was buried.

Then occurred that which he had feared. For even as he ran, the ground before him quaked in the throes of a gigantic upheaval. The sand rolled in vast, engulfing waves, away from the base of the two boulders. Through the opening rose the idol, glistening evilly in the moonlight. And the oncoming sand from its base caught Carnoti as he ran toward it, sucking at his legs like a quicksand, and yawning at his waist. At the same instant the peculiar shadow rose and leapt forward. It seemed to merge with the statue in midair, a nebulous, animate mist. Then Carnoti, floundering in the grip of the sand, went quite insane with terror.

The formless statue gleamed living in the livid light, and the doomed man stared straight into its unearthly countenance. It was his dream come true, for behind that mask of stone he saw a face with eyes of yellow madness, and in those eyes he read death. The black figure spread its wings against the hills, and sank into the sand with a thunderous crash.

Thereafter nothing remained above the earth save a living head that twisted on the ground and struggled futilely to free its imprisoned body from the iron embrace of the encircling sand.

Its imprecations turned to frantic cries for mercy, then sank to a sob in which echoed the single word, "Nyarlathotep."

When morning came Carnoti was still alive, and the sun baked his brain into a hell of crimson agony. But not for long. The vultures winged across the desert plain and descended upon him, almost as if supernaturally summoned.

Somewhere, buried in the sands below, an ancient idol lay, and upon its featureless countenance there was the faintest hint of a monstrous, hidden smile. For even as Carnoti the unbeliever died, his mangled lips paid whispered homage to Nyarlathotep, Lord of the Desert.

# House of the Hatchet

DAISY AND I were enjoying one of our usual quarrels. It started over the insurance policy this time, but after we threshed that out we went into the regular routine. Both of us had our cues down perfectly.

"Why don't you go out and get a job like other men instead of sitting around the house pounding a typewriter all day?"

"You knew I was a writer when I married you. If you were so hot to hitch up with a professional man you ought to have married that brokendown interne you ran around with. You'd know where he was all day; out practising surgery by dissecting hamburgers in that chili parlor down the street."

"Oh, you needn't be so sarcastic. At least George would do his best to be a good provider."

"I'll say he would. He provided me with a lot of laughs ever since I met him."

"That's the trouble with you—you and your superior attitude! Think you're better than anybody else. Here we are, practically starving, and you have to pay installments on a new car just to show it off to your movie friends. And on top of that you go and take out a big policy on me just to be able to brag about how you're protecting your family. I wish I *had* married George—at least he'd bring home some of that hamburger to eat when he finished work. What do you expect me to live on, used carbon paper and old typewriter ribbons?"

"Well, how the devil can I help it if the stuff doesn't sell? I figured on that contract deal but it fell through. You're the one that's always beefing about money—who do you think I am, the goose that laid the golden egg?"

"You've been laying plenty of eggs with those last stories you sent out."

"Funny. Very funny. But I'm getting just a little tired of your second-act dialogue, Daisy."

"So I've noticed. You'd like to change partners and dance, I suppose. Perhaps you'd rather exchange a little sparkling repartee with that Jeanne Corey. Oh, I've noticed the way you hung around her that night over at Ed's place. You couldn't have got much closer without turning into a corset."

"Now listen, you leave Jeanne's name out of this."

"Oh, I'm supposed to leave Jeanne's name out of it, eh? Your wife mustn't take the name of your girl-friend in vain. Well, darling, I always knew you were a swift worker, but I didn't think it had gone that far. Have you told her that she's your inspiration yet?"

"Damn it, Daisy, why must you go twisting around everything I say—"

"Why don't you insure her, too? Bigamy insurance—you could probably get a policy issued by Brigham Young."

"Oh, turn it off, will you? A fine act to headline our anniversary, I must say."

"Anniversary?"

"Today's May 18th, isn't it?"

"May 18th—"

"Yeah. Here, shrew."

"Why—honey, it's a necklace—"

"Yeah. Just a little dividend on the bonds of matrimony."

"Honey—you bought this for me?—with all our bills and—"

"Never mind that. And quit gasping in my ear, will you? You sound like Little Eva before they hoist her up with the ropes."

"Darling, it's so beautiful. Here."

"Aw, Daisy. Now see what you've done. Made me forget where we left off quarreling. Oh, well."

"Our anniversary. And to think I forgot!"

"Well, I didn't. Daisy."

"Yes?"

"I've been thinking—that is, well, I'm just a sentimental cuss at heart, and I was sort of wondering if you'd like to hop in the car and take a run out along the Prentiss Road."

"You mean like that day we—eloped?"

"Um hum."

"Of course, darling. I'd love to. Oh, honey, where *did* you get this necklace?"

That's how it was. Just one of those things. Daisy and I, holding our daily sparring match. Usually it kept us in trim. Today, though, I began to get the feeling that we had over-trained. We'd quarreled that way for months, on and off. I don't know why; I wouldn't be able to define "incompatibility" if I saw it on my divorce-papers. I was broke, and Daisy was a shrew. Let it go at that.

But I felt pretty clever when I dragged out my violin for the *Hearts and Flowers*. Anniversary, necklace, re-tracing the honeymoon route; it all added up. I'd found a way to keep Daisy quiet without stuffing a mop into her mouth.

She was sentimentally happy and I was self-congratulatory as we climbed into the car and headed up Wilshire towards Prentiss Road. We still had a lot to say to each other, but in repetition it would be merely nauseating. When Daisy felt good she went in for baby-talk—which struck me as being out of character.

But for a while we were both happy. I began to kid myself that it was just like old times; we really were the same two kids running away on our crazy elopement. Daisy had just "gotten off" from the beauty parlor and I'd just sold my script series to the agency, and we were running down to Valos to get married. It was the same spring weather, the same road, and Daisy snuggled close to me in the same old way.

But it wasn't the same. Daisy wasn't a kid any more; there were no lines in her face, but there was a rasp in her voice. She hadn't taken on any weight, but she'd taken on a load of querulous ideas. I was different, too. Those first few radio sales had set the pace; I began to run around with the big-shots, and that costs money. Only lately I hadn't made any sales, and the damned expenses kept piling up, and every time I tried to get any work done at the house there was Daisy nagging away. Why did we have to buy a new car? Why did we have to pay so much rent? Why such an insurance policy? Why did I buy three suits?

So I buy her a necklace and she shuts up. There's a woman's logic for you.

Oh well, I figured, today I'll forget it. Forget the bills, forget her nagging, forget Jeanne—though that last was going to be hard. Jeanne was quiet, and she had a private income, and she thought baby-talk was silly. Oh well.

We drove on to Prentiss Road and took the old familiar route. I stopped my little stream-of-consciousness act and tried to get into the mood. Daisy *was* happy; no doubt of that. We'd packed an overnight bag, and without mentioning it we both knew we'd stay at the hotel in Valos, just as we had three years ago when we were married.

Three years of drab, nagging monotony—

But I wasn't going to think about that. Better to think about Daisy's pretty blond curls gleaming in the afternoon sunshine; to think about the pretty green hills doing ditto in the afternoon ditto. It was spring, the spring of three years ago, and all life lay before us—down the white concrete road that curved across the hills to strange heights of achievement beyond.

So we drove on, blithely enough. She pointed out the signs and I nodded or grunted or said "Uh-uh" and the first thing I knew we were four hours on the road and it was getting past afternoon and I wanted to get out and stretch my legs and besides—

There it lay. I couldn't have missed the banner. And even if I did, there was Daisy, squealing in my ear.

"Oh, honey—look."

# CAN YOU TAKE IT?

## THE HOUSE OF TERROR

### VISIT A GENUINE, AUTHENTIC HAUNTED HOUSE

And in smaller lettering, beneath, further enticements were listed.

"See the Kluva Mansion! Visit the Haunted Chamber—see the Axe used by the Mad Killer! DO THE DEAD RETURN? Visit the HOUSE OF TERROR—only genuine attraction of its kind. ADMISSION—25¢"

Of course I didn't read all this while slashing by at 60 m.p.h. We pulled up as Daisy tugged my shoulder, and while she read, I looked at the large, rambling frame building. It looked like dozens of others we passed on the road; houses occupied by "swamis" and "mediums" and "Yogi Psychologists." For this was the lunatic fringe where the quacks fed on the tourist trade. But here was a fellow with a little novelty. He had something a bit different. That's what I thought.

But Daisy evidently thought a lot more.

"Ooh, honey, let's go in."

"What?"

"I'm so stiff from all this driving, and besides, maybe they sell hot dogs inside or something, and I'm hungry."

Well. That was Daisy. Daisy the sadist. Daisy the horror-movie fan. She didn't fool me for a minute. I knew all about my wife's pretty little tastes. She was a thrill-addict. Shortly after our marriage she'd let down the bars and started reading the more lurid murder trial news aloud to me at breakfast. She began to leave ghastly magazines around the house. Pretty soon she was dragging me to all the mystery-pictures. Just another one of her annoying habits—I could close my eyes at any time and conjure up the drone of her voice, tense with latent excitement, as she read about the Cleveland torso slayings, or the latest hatchet-killing.

Evidently nothing was too synthetic for her tastes. Here was an old shack that in its palmiest days was no better than a tenement house for goats; a dump with a lurid side-show banner flung in front of the porch—and still she had to go in. "Haunted House" got her going. Maybe that's what had happened to our marriage. I would have pleased her better by going around the house in a black mask, purring like Bela Lugosi with bronchitis, and caressing her with a hatchet.

I attempted to convey some of the pathos of my thoughts in the way I replied, "What the blazes?" but it was a losing battle. Daisy had her hand on the car door. There was a smile on her face—a smile that did queer things to her lips. I used to see that smile when she read the murder-news; it reminded me, unpleasantly, of a hungry cat's expression while creeping up on a robin. She was a shrew and she was a sadist.

But what of it? This was a second honeymoon; no time to spoil things just when I'd fixed matters up. Kill half an hour here and then on to the hotel in Valos.

"Come *on!*"

I jerked out of my musings to find Daisy halfway up the porch. I locked the car, pocketed the keys, joined her before the dingy door. It was getting misty in the late afternoon and the clouds rolled over the sun. Daisy knocked impatiently. The door opened slowly, after a long pause in the best haunted-house tradition. This was the cue for a sinister face to poke itself out and emit a greasy chuckle. Daisy was just itching for that, I knew.

Instead she got W. C. Fields.

Well, not quite. The proboscis was smaller, and not so red. The cheeks were thinner, too. But the checked suit, the squint, the jowls, and above all that "step right up gentlemen" voice were all in the tradition.

"Ah. Come in, come in. Welcome to Kluva Mansion, my friends, welcome." The cigar fingered us forward. "Twenty-five cents, please. Thank you."

There we were in the dark hallway. It really was dark, and there certainly was a musty enough odor, but I knew damned well the house wasn't haunted by anything but cockroaches. Our comic friend would have to do some pretty loud talking to convince me; but then, this was Daisy's show.

"It's a little late, but I guess I've got time to show you around. Just took a party through about fifteen minutes ago—big party from San Diego. They drove all the way up just to see the Kluva Mansion, so I can assure you you're getting your money's worth."

All right buddy, cut out the assuring, and let's get this over with. Trot out your zombies, give Daisy a good shock with an electric battery or something, and we'll get out of here.

"Just what is this haunted house and how did you happen to come by it?" asked Daisy. One of those original questions she was always thinking up. She was brilliant like that all the time. Just full of surprises.

"Well, it's like this, lady. Lots of folks ask me that and I'm only too glad to tell them. This house was built by Ivan Kluva—don't know if you remember him or not—Russian movie director, came over here about '23 in the old silent days, right after DeMille began to get popular with his spectacle pictures. Kluva was an "epic" man; had quite a European reputation, so they gave him a contract. He put up this place, lived here with his wife. Aren't many folks left in the movie colony that remember old Ivan Kluva; he never really got to direct anything either.

"First thing he did was to mix himself up with a lot of foreign cults. This was way back, remember; Hollywood had some queer birds then. Prohibition, and a lot of wild parties; dope addicts, all kinds of scandals, and some stuff that never did get out. There was a bunch of devil-worshippers and mystics, too—not like these fakes down the road; genuine article. Kluva got in with them.

"I guess he was a little crazy, or got that way. Because one night, after some kind of gathering here, he murdered his wife. In the upstairs room, on a kind of an altar he rigged up. He just took a hatchet to her and hacked off her head. Then he disappeared. The police looked in a couple of days later; they found her, of course, but they never did locate Kluva. Maybe he jumped off the cliffs behind the house. Maybe—I've heard stories—he killed her as a sort of sacrifice so he could *go away.* Some of the cult members were grilled, and they had a lot of wild stories about worshipping things or beings that granted boons to those who gave them human sacrifices; such boons as *going away* from Earth. Oh, it was crazy enough, I guess, but the police did find a damned funny statue behind the altar that they didn't like and never showed around, and they burned a lot of books and things they got hold of here. Also they chased that cult out of California."

All this corny chatter rolled out in a drone and I winced. Now I'm only a two-bit gag-writer, myself, but I was thinking that if I went in for such things I could improvise a better story than this poorly-told yarn and I could ad-lib it more effectively than this bird seemed able to do with daily practice. It sounded so stale, so flat, so unconvincing. The rottenest "thriller plot" in the world.

Or—

It struck me then. Perhaps the story was true. Maybe this was the solution. After all, there were no supernatural elements yet. Just a dizzy Russian devil-worshipper murdering his wife with a hatchet. It happens once in a while; psychopathology is full of such records. And why not? Our comic friend merely bought the house after the murder, cooked up his "haunt" yarn, and capitalized.

Evidently my guess was correct, because old Bugle-beak sounded off again.

"And so, my friends, the deserted Kluva Mansion remained, alone and untenanted. Not utterly untenanted, though. There was the ghost. Yes, the ghost of Mrs. Kluva—the Lady in White."

Phooey! Always it has to be the Lady in White. Why not in pink, for a change, or green? Lady in White—sounds like a burlesque headliner. And so did our spieler. He was trying to push his voice down into his fat stomach and make it impressive.

"Every night she walks the upper corridor to the murder chamber. Her slit throat shines in the moonlight as she lays her head once again on the blood-stained block, again receives the fatal blow, and with a groan of torment, disappears into thin air."

Hot air, you mean, buddy.

"Oooh," said Daisy. "She would."

"I say the house was deserted for years. But there were tramps, vagrants, who broke in from time to time to stay the night. They stayed the night—and longer. Because in the morning they were always found—on the murder block, with their throats chopped by the murder axe."

I wanted to say "Axe-ually?" but then, I have my better side. Daisy was enjoying this so; her tongue was almost hanging out.

"After a while nobody would come here; even the tramps shunned the spot. The real estate people couldn't sell it. Then I rented. I knew the story would attract visitors, and frankly, I'm a business man."

Thanks for telling me, brother. I thought you were a fake.

"And now, you'd like to see the murder chamber? Just follow me, please. Up the stairs, right this way. I've kept everything just as it always was, and I'm sure you'll be more than interested in—"

Daisy pinched me on the dark stairway. "Ooh, sugar, aren't you thrilled?"

I don't like to be called "sugar." And the idea of Daisy actually finding something "thrilling" in this utterly ridiculous farce was almost nauseating. For a moment I could have murdered her myself. Maybe Kluva had something there at that.

The stairs creaked, and the dusty windows allowed a sepulchral light to creep across the mouldy floor as we followed the waddling showman down the black hallway. A wind seemed to have sprung up outside, and the house shook before it, groaning in torment.

Daisy giggled nervously. In the movie-show she always twisted my lapel-buttons off when the monster came into the room where the girl was sleeping. She was like that now—hysterical.

I felt as excited as a stuffed herring in a pawnshop.

W. C. opened a door down the hall and fumbled around inside. A moment later he reappeared carrying a candle and beckoned us to enter the room. Well, that was a little better. Showed some imagination, anyway. The candle was effective in the gathering darkness; it cast blotches of shadow over the walls and caused shapes to creep in the corners.

"Here we are," he almost whispered.

And there we were.

Now I'm not psychic. I'm not even highly imaginative. When Orson Welles is yammering on the radio I'm down at the hamburger stand listening to the latest swing music. But when I entered that room I *knew* that it, at least, wasn't a fake. The air reeked of murder. The shadows ruled over a domain of death. It was cold in here, cold as a charnel-house. And the candle-light fell on the great bed in the corner, then moved to the center of the room and covered a monstrous bulk. The murder block.

It was something like an altar, at that. There was a niche in the wall behind it, and I could almost imagine a statue being placed there. What kind of a statue? A black bat, inverted and crucified? Devil-worshippers used that, didn't they? Or was it another and more horrible kind of idol? The police had destroyed it. But the block was still there, and in the candle-light I saw the stains. They trickled over the rough sides.

Daisy moved closer to me and I could feel her tremble.

Kluva's chamber. A man with an axe, holding a terrified woman across the block; the strength of inspired madness in his eyes, and in his hands, an axe—

"It was here, on the night of January twelfth, nineteen twenty-four, that Ivan Kluva murdered his wife with—"

The fat man stood by the door, chanting out his listless refrain. But for some reason I listened to every word. Here in this room, those words were real. They weren't scareheads on a sideshow banner; here in the darkness they had meaning. A man and his wife, and murder. Death is just a word you read in the newspaper. But some day it becomes real; dreadfully real. Something the worms whisper in your ears as they chew. Murder is a word, too. It is the power of death, and sometimes there are men who exercise that power, like gods. Men who kill are like gods. They take away life. There is something cosmically obscene about the thought. A shot fired in drunken frenzy, a blow struck in anger, a bayonet plunged in the madness of war, an accident, a car-crash—these things are part of life. But a man, any man, who lives with the thought of Death; who thinks and plans a deliberate, cold-blooded murder—

To sit there at the supper table, looking at his wife, and saying, "Twelve o'clock. You have five more hours to live, my dear. Five more hours. Nobody knows that. Your friends don't know it. Even you don't know it. No one knows—except myself. Myself, and Death, I am Death. Yes, I am Death to you. I shall numb your body and your brain, I shall be your lord and master. You were born, you have lived, only for this single supreme moment; that I shall command your fate. You exist only that I may kill you."

Yes, it was obscene. And then, this block, and a hatchet.

"Come upstairs, dear." And his thoughts, grinning behind the words. Up the dark stairs to the dark room, where the block and hatchet waited.

I wondered if he hated her. No, I suppose not. If the story was true, he had sacrificed her for a purpose. She was just the most handy, the most convenient person to sacrifice. He must have had blood like the water under the polar peaks.

It was the room that did it, not the story. I could feel him in the room, and I could feel *her.*

Yes, that was funny. Now I could feel *her.* Not as a being, not as a tangible presence, but as a force. A restless force. Something that stirred in back of me before I turned my head. Something hiding in the deeper shadows. Something in the blood-stained block. A chained spirit.

"Here I died. I ended here. One minute I was alive, unsuspecting. The next found me gripped by the ultimate horror of Death. The hatchet came down across my throat, so full of life, and sliced it out. Now I wait. I wait for others, for there is nothing left to me but revenge. I am not a person any longer, nor a spirit. I am merely a force—a force created as I felt my life slip away from my throat. For at that moment I knew but one feeling with my entire dying being; a feeling of utter, cosmic hatred. Hatred at the sudden injustice of what had happened to me. The force was born then when I died; it is all that is left of me. Hatred. Now I wait, and sometimes I have a chance to let the hatred escape. By killing another I can feel the hatred rise, wax, grow strong. Then for a brief moment I rise, wax, grow strong; feel real again, touch the hem of life's robe, which once I wore. Only by surrendering to my dark hate can I survive in death. And so I lurk; lurk here in this room. Stay too long and I shall return. Then, in the darkness, I seek your throat and the blade bites and I taste again the ecstasy of reality."

The old drizzle-puss was elaborating his story, but I couldn't hear him for my thoughts. Then all at once he flashed something out across my line of vision; something that was like a stark shadow against the candle-light.

It was a hatchet.

I felt, rather than heard, when Daisy went "Ooooh!" beside me. Looking down I stared into two blue mirrors of terror that were her eyes. I had thought plenty, and what her imaginings had been I could guess. The old bird was stolid enough, but he brandished that hatchet, that hatchet with the rusty blade, and it got so I couldn't look at anything else but the jagged edge of the hatchet. I couldn't hear or see or think anything; there was that hatchet, the symbol of Death. There was the real crux of the story; not in the man or the woman, but in that tiny razor-edge line. That razor-edge was really Death. That razor-edge spelled doom to all living things. Nothing in the world was greater than that razor-edge. No brain, no power, no love, no hate could withstand it.

And it swooped out in the man's hands and I tore my eyes away and looked at Daisy, at anything, just to keep the black thought down. And I saw Daisy, her face that of a tortured Medusa.

Then she slumped.

I caught her. Bugle-beak looked up with genuine surprise.

"My wife's fainted," I said.

He just blinked. Didn't know what the score was, at first. And a minute later I could swear he was just a little bit pleased. He thought his story had done it, I suppose.

Well, this changed all plans. No Valos, no drive before supper.

"Any place around here where she can lie down?" I asked. "No, not in this room."

"My wife's bedroom is down the hall," said Bugle-beak.

His wife's bedroom, eh? But no one stayed here after dark, he had said—the damned old fake!

This was no time for quibbling. I carried Daisy into the room down the hall, chafed her wrists.

"Shall I send my wife up to take care of her?" asked the now solicitous showman.

"No, don't bother. Let me handle her; she gets these things every so often—hysteria, you know. But she'll have to rest a while."

He shuffled down the hall, and I sat there cursing. Damn the woman, it was just like her! But too late to alter circumstances now. I decided to let her sleep it off.

I went downstairs in the darkness, groping my way. And I was only halfway down when I heard a familiar pattering strike the roof. Sure enough—a typical West Coast heavy dew was falling. Fine thing, too; dark as pitch outside.

Well, there was the set-up. Splendid melodrama background. I'd been dragged to movies for years and it was always the same as this.

The young couple caught in a haunted house by a thunderstorm. The mysterious evil caretaker. (Well, maybe he wasn't, but he'd have to do until a better one came along.) The haunted room. The fainting girl, asleep and helpless in the bedroom. Enter Boris Karloff dressed in three pounds of nose-putty. "Grrrrrr!" says Boris. "Eeeeeeeeh!" says the girl. "What's that?" shouts Inspector Toozefuddy from downstairs. And then a mad chase. "Bang! Bang!" And Boris Karloff falls down into an open manhole. Girl gets frightened. Boy gets girl. Formula.

I thought I was pretty clever when I turned on the burlesque thought pattern, but when I got down to the foot of the stairs I knew that I was playing hide-and-go-seek with my thoughts. Something dark and cold was creeping around in my brain, and I was trying hard to avoid it. Something to do with Ivan Kluva and his wife and the haunted room and the hatchet. Suppose there was a ghost and Daisy was lying up there alone and—

"Ham and eggs?"

"What the—" I turned around. There was Bugle-beak at the foot of the stairs.

"I said, would you care for some ham and eggs? Looks pretty bad outside and so long as the Missus is resting I thought maybe you'd like to join the wife and me in a little supper."

I could have kissed him, nose and all.

We went into the back. Mrs. was just what you'd expect; thin woman in her middle forties, wearing a patient look. The place was quite cosy, though; she had fixed up several rooms as living quarters. I began to have a little more respect for Bugle-beak. Poor showman though he was, he seemed to be making a living in a rather novel way. And his wife was an excellent cook.

The rain thundered down. Something about a little lighted room in the middle of a storm that makes you feel good inside. Confidential. Mrs. Keenan—Bugle-beak introduced himself as Homer Keenan—suggested that I might take a little brandy up to Daisy. I demurred, but Keenan perked up his ears—and nose—at the mention of brandy and suggested we have a little. The *little* proved to be a half-gallon jug of fair peach-brandy, and we filled our glasses. As the meal progressed we filled them again. And again. The liquor helped to chase that dark thought away, or almost away. But it still bothered me. And so I got Homer Keenan into talking. Better a boring conversation than a boring thought—boring little black beetle of thought, chewing away in your brain.

"So after the carny folded I got out from under. Put over a little deal in Tia and cleaned up but the Missus kind of wanted to settle down. Tent business in this country all shot to blazes anyway. Well, I knew this Feingerber from the old days, like I say—and he put me up to this house. Yeah, sure, that part is genuine enough. There was an Ivan Kluva and he did kill his wife here. Block and axe genuine too; I got a state permit to keep 'em. Museum, this is. But the ghost story, of course that's just a fake. Get's them in, though. Some week-ends we play to capacity crowds ten hours a day. Makes a nice thing of it. We live here—say, let's have another nip of this brandy, whaddy say? Come on, it won't hurt you. Get it from a Mex down the road a ways."

Fire. Fire in the blood. What did he mean the ghost story was fake? When I went into that room I smelled murder. I thought *his* thoughts. And then I had thought *hers*. Her hate was in that room; and if it wasn't a ghost, what was it? Somehow it all tied in with that black thought I had buzzing in my head; that damned black thought all mixed up with the axe and hate, and poor Daisy lying up there helpless. Fire in my head. Brandy fire. But not enough. I could still think of Daisy, and all at once something blind gripped me and I was afraid and I trembled all over, and I couldn't wait. Thinking of her like that, all alone in the storm, near the murder-room and the block and the hatchet—I knew I must go to her. I couldn't stand the horrid suspicion.

I got up like a fool, mumbled something about looking after her, and ran up the black staircase. I was trembling, trembling, until I reached her bedside and saw how peacefully she lay there. Her sleep was quite untroubled. She was even smiling. She didn't know. She wasn't afraid of ghosts and hatchets. Looking at her I felt utterly ridiculous, but I did stare down at her for a long time until I regained control of myself once again. . . .

When I went downstairs the liquor had hit me and I felt drunk. The thought was gone from my brain now, and I was beginning to experience relief.

Keenan had refilled my glass for me, and when I gulped it down he followed suit and immediately poured again. This time we sat down to a real gab-fest.

I began to talk. I felt like an unwinding top. Everything began to spin out of my throat. I told about my life; my "career," such as it was; my romance with Daisy, even. Just felt like it. The liquor.

Before you know it I was pulling a True Confession of my own, with all the trimmings. How things stood with Daisy and me. Our foolish quarrels. Her nagging. Her touchiness about things like our car, and the insurance, and Jeanne Corey. I was maudlin enough to be petty. I picked on her habits. Then I began to talk about this trip of ours, and my plans for a second honeymoon, and it was only instinct that shut me up before becoming actually disgusting.

Keenan adopted an older "man-of-the-world" attitude, but he finally broke down enough to mention a few of his wife's salient deficiencies. What I told him about Daisy's love for the horrors prompted him to tease his wife concerning her own timidity. It developed that while she knew the story was a fake, she still shied away from venturing upstairs after nightfall—just as though the ghost were real.

Mrs. Keenan bridled. She denied everything. Why she'd go upstairs any time at all. Any time at all.

"How about now? It's almost midnight. Why not go up and take a cup of coffee to that poor sick woman?" Keenan sounded like somebody advising Little Red Riding-Hood to go see her grandmother.

"Don't bother," I assured him. "The rain's dying down. I'll go up and get her and we'll be on our way. We've got to get to Valos, you know."

"Think I'm afraid, eh?" Mrs. Keenan was already doing things with the coffee pot. Rather dizzily, but she managed.

"You men, always talking about your wives. I'll show you!" She took the cup, then arched her back eloquently as she passed Keenan and disappeared in the hallway.

I got an urge.

Sobriety rushed to my head.

"Keenan," I whispered.

"Whazzat?"

"Keenan, we must stop her!"

"What for?"

"You ever gone upstairs at night?"

"Course not. Why sh'd I? All dusty up there, mus' keep it tha' way for cust'mers. Never go up."

"Then how do you know the story isn't true?" I talked fast. Very.

"What?"

"I say perhaps there *is* a ghost."

"Aw, go on!"

"Keenan, I tell you I felt something up there. You're so used to the place you didn't notice, but I *felt* it. A woman's hate, Keenan. A woman's hate!" I was almost screaming; I dragged him from his chair and tried to push him into the hall. I had to stop her somehow. I was afraid.

"That room is filled with menace." Quickly I explained my thoughts of the afternoon concerning the dead woman—surprised and slain, so that she died only with a great hate forming as life left her; a hate that endured, that thrived on death alone. A hate, embodied, that would take up the murder hatchet and slay—

"Stop your wife, Keenan," I screamed. "Stop her!"

"What about your wife?" chuckled the showman. "Besides," and he leered, drunkenly, "I'll tell you somethin' I wasn't gonna tell. It's *all* a fake." He winked. I still pushed him towards the staircase.

"All a fake," he wheezed. "Not only ghost part. But—there never was a Ivan Kluva, never was no wife. Never was no killing. Jus' old butcher's block. Hatchet's my hatchet. No murder, no ghost, nothin' to be afraid of. Good joke, make myself hones' dollar. All a fake!"

"Come on!" I screamed, and the black thought came back and it sang in my brain and I tried to drag him up the stairs, knowing it was too late, but still I had to do something—

And then *she* screamed.

I heard it. She was running out of the room, down the hall. And at the head of the stairs she screamed again, but the scream turned into a gurgle. It was black up there, but out of the blackness tottered her silhouette. Down the stairs she rolled; bump, bump, bump. Same sound as a rubber ball. But she was a woman, and she ended up at the bottom of the stairs with the axe still stuck in her throat.

Right there I should have turned and run, but that thing inside my head wouldn't let me. I just stood there as Keenan looked down at the body of his wife, and I babbled it all out again.

"I hated her—you don't understand how those little things count—and Jeanne waiting—there was the insurance—if I did it at Valos no one would ever know—here was accident, but better."

"There is no ghost," Keenan mumbled. He didn't even hear me. "There is no ghost." I stared at the slashed throat.

"When I saw the hatchet and she fainted, it came over me. I could get you drunk, carry her out, and you'd never know—"

"What killed my wife?" he whispered. "There is no ghost."

I thought again of my theory of a woman's hate surviving death and existing thereafter only with an urge to slay. I thought of that hate, embodied, grabbing up a hatchet and slaying, saw Mrs. Keenan fall, then glanced up at the darkness of the hall as the grinning song in my brain rose, forcing me to speak.

"There is a ghost now," I whispered. "You see, the second time I went up to see Daisy, I killed her with this hatchet."

# The Opener of the Way

THE STATUE of Anubis brooded over the darkness. Its blind eyes had basked in the blackness for unnumbered centuries, and the dust of ages had settled upon its stony brow. The damp air of the pit had caused its canine features to crumble, but the stone lips of the image still were curled in a snarling grin of cryptic mirth. It was almost as if the idol were alive; as if it had seen the shadowed centuries slip by, and with them the glory of Egypt and the old gods. Then indeed would it have reason to grin, at the thought of ancient pomps and vain and vanished splendor. But the statue of Anubis, Opener of the Way, jackal-headed god of Karneter, was not alive, and those that had bowed in worship were long dead. Death was everywhere; it haunted the shadowy tunnel where the idol stood, hidden away in the mummy-cases and biding amidst the very dust of the stone floor. Death, and darkness—darkness undispelled by light these three thousand years.

Today, however, light came. It was heralded by a grating clang, as the iron door at the further end of the passageway swung open on its rusted hinges; swung open for the first time in thirty centuries. Through the opening came the strange illumination of a torch, and the sudden sound of voices.

There was something indescribably eery about the event. For three thousand years no light had shone in these black and buried vaults; for three thousand years no feet had disturbed the dusty carpet of their floors; for three thousand years no voice had sent its sound through the ancient air. The last light had come from a sacred torch in the hand of a priest of Bast; the last feet to violate the dust had been encased in Egyptian sandals; the last voice had spoken a prayer in the language of the Upper Nile.

And now, an electric torch flooded the scene with sudden light; booted feet stamped noisily across the floor, and an English voice gave vent to fervent profanity.

In the torchlight the bearer of the illumination was revealed. He was a tall, thin man, with a face as wrinkled as the papyrus parchment he clutched nervously in his left hand. His white hair, sunken eyes and yellowed skin gave him the aspect of an old man, but the smile upon his thin lips was full of the triumph of youth. Close behind him crowded another, a younger replica of the first. It was he who had sworn.

"For the love of God, father—we've made it!"

"Yes, my boy, so we have."

"Look! There's the statue, just as the map showed it!"

The two men stepped softly in the dust-strewn passage and halted directly in front of the idol. Sir Ronald Barton, the bearer of the light, held it aloft to inspect the figure of the god more closely. Peter Barton stood at his side, eyes following his father's gaze.

For a long moment the invaders scrutinized the guardian of the tomb they had violated. It was a strange moment there in the underground burrow, a moment that spanned eternity as the old confronted the new.

The two men gazed up at the eidolon in astonishment and awe. The colossal figure of the jackal-god dominated the dim passage, and its weathered form still held vestiges of imposing grandeur and inexplicable menace. The sudden influx of outer air from the opened door had swept the idol's body free of dust, and the intruders scrutinized its gleaming form with a certain vague unease. Twelve feet tall was Anubis, a man-like figure with the dogface of a jackal upon massive shoulders. The arms of the statue were held forth in an attitude of warning, as if endeavoring to repel the passage of outsiders. This was peculiar, for to all intents and purposes the guardian figure had nothing behind it but a narrow niche in the wall.

There was an air of evil suggestion about the god, however; a hint of bestial humanity in its body which seemed to hide a secret, sentient life. The knowing smile on the carven countenance seemed cynically alive; the eyes, though stony, held a strange and disturbing *awareness*. It was as though the statue were alive; or, rather, as though it were merely a stone cloak that harbored life.

The two explorers sensed this without speaking, and for a

long minute they contemplated the Opener of the Way uneasily. Then, with a sudden start, the older man resumed his customary briskness of manner.

"Well, son, let's not stand here gawking at this thing all day! We have plenty to do yet—the biggest task remains. Have you looked at the map?"

"Yes, father." The younger man's voice was not nearly as loud or as firm as Sir Ronald's. He did not like the mephitic air of the stone passageway; he did not care for the stench that seemed to spawn in the shadows of the corners. He was acutely aware of the fact that he and his father were in a hidden tomb, seven hundred feet below the desert sands; a secret tomb that had lain unopened for thirty creeping centuries. And he could not help but remember the curse.

For there was a curse on the place; indeed, it was that which had led to its discovery.

Sir Ronald had found it in the excavation of the Ninth Pyramid, the moldering papyrus parchment which held the key to a secret way. How he had smuggled it past the heads of the expedition nobody can say, but he had managed the task somehow.

After all, he was not wholly to be blamed, though the theft of expeditionary trophies is a serious offense. But for twenty years Sir Ronald Barton had combed the deserts, uncovered sacred relics, deciphered hieroglyphics, and disinterred mummies, statues, ancient furniture, or precious stones. He had unearthed untold wealth and incredibly valuable manuscripts for his Government; yet he was still a poor man, and had never been rewarded by becoming head of an expedition of his own. Who can blame him if he took that one misstep which he knew would lead him to fame and fortune at last?

Besides, he was getting old, and after a score of years in Egypt all archeologists are a little mad. There is something about the sullen sun overhead that paralyzes the brains of men as they ferret in the sand, digging in unhallowed ruins; something about the damp, dark stillness underground in temple vaults that chills the soul. It is not good to look upon the old gods in the places where they still rule; for cat-headed Bubastis, serpented Set, and evil Amon-Ra frown down as sullen guardians in the purple pylons before the pyramids. Over all is an air of forbidden things long dead, and it creeps into the blood. Sir Ronald had dabbled in sorcery, a bit; so perhaps it affected him more strongly than the rest. At any rate, he stole the parchment.

It had been penned by a priest of ancient Egypt, but the priest had not been a holy man. No man could write as he had written without violating his vows. It was a dreadful thing, that manuscript, steeped in sorcery and hideous with half-hinted horrors.

The enchanter who had written it alluded to gods far older than those he worshipped. There was mention of the "Demon Messenger" and the "Black Temple," coupled with the secret myth and legend-cycles of pre-Adamite days. For just as the Christian religion has its Black Mass, just as every sect has its hidden Devil-worship, the Egyptians knew their own darker gods.

The names of these accursed ones were set forth, together with the orisons necessary for their invocation. Shocking and blasphemous statements abounded in the text; threats against the reigning religion, and terrible curses upon the people who upheld it. Perhaps that is why Sir Ronald found it buried with the mummy of the priest—its discoverers had not dared to destroy it, because of the doom which might befall them. They had their way of vengeance, though; because the mummy of the priest was found without arms, legs, or eyes, and these were not lost through decay.

Sir Ronald, though he found the above-mentioned portions of the parchment intensely interesting, was much more impressed by the last page. It was here that the sacrilegious one told of the tomb of his master, who ruled the dark cult of the day. There were a map, a chart, and certain directions. These had not been written in Egyptian, but in the cuneiform chirography of Chaldea. Doubtless that is why the old avenging priests had not sought out the spot for themselves to destroy it. They were probably unfamiliar with the language; unless they were kept away by fear of the curse.

Peter Barton still remembered that night in Cairo when he and his father had first read it in translation. He recalled the avid gleam in Sir Ronald's glittering eyes, the tremulous depth in his guttural voice.

"And as the maps direct, there you shall find the tomb of the Master, who lies with his acolytes and all his treasure."

Sir Ronald's voice nearly broke with excitement as he pronounced this last word.

"And at the entrance upon the night that the Dog-Star is ascendant you must give up three jackals upon an altar in sacrifice, and with the blood bestrew the sands about the opening. Then the bats shall descend, that they may have feasting, and carry their glad tidings of blood to Father Set in the Underworld."

"Superstitious rigmarole!" young Peter had exclaimed.

"Don't scoff, son," Sir Ronald advised. "I could give you reasons for what it says above, and make you understand. But I am afraid that the truth would disturb you unnecessarily."

Peter had stayed silent while his father read on:

"Upon descending into the outer passage you will find the door, set with the symbol of the Master who waits within. Grasp the symbol by the seventh tongue in the seventh head, and with a knife remove it. Then shall the barrier give way, and the gate to the tomb be yours. Thirty and three are the steps along the inner passage, and there stands the statue of Anubis, Opener of the Way."

"Anubis! But isn't he a regular Egyptian deity—a recognized one?" Peter broke in.

His father answered from the manuscript itself:

"For Lord Anubis holds the keys to Life and Death; he guards cryptic Karneter, and none shall pass the Veil without consent. Some there are who deem the Jackal-god to be a friend of those who rule, but he is not. Anubis stands in shadows, for he is the Keeper of Mysteries. In olden days for which there is no number it is written that Lord Anubis revealed himself to men, and he who then was Master fashioned the first image of the god in his true likeness. Such is the image that you will find at the end of the inner passageway—the first true image of the Opener of the Way."

"Astounding!" Peter had muttered. "Think what it means if this is true; imagine finding the original statue of the god!"

His father merely smiled, a trifle wanly, Peter thought.

"There are ways in which the first image differs from the rest," said the manuscript. "These ways are not good for men to know; so the first likeness was hidden by the Masters through the ages, and worshipped according to its demands. But now that our enemies—may their souls and vitals rot!—have dared profane the rites, the Master saw fit to hide the image and bury it with him when he died."

Sir Ronald's voice quivered as he read the next few lines:

"But Anubis does not stand at the head of the inner passage for this reason alone. He is truly called the Opener of the Way, and without his help none may pass to the tomb within."

Here the older man stopped completely for a long moment.

"What's the matter?" inquired Peter, impatiently. "I suppose there's another silly ritual involving the statue of the god, eh?"

His father did not answer, but read on to himself, silently. Peter noticed that Sir Ronald's hands trembled as he held the parchment, and when the older man looked up at last, his face was very pale.

"Yes, my boy," he replied, huskily. "That's what it is—another silly ritual. But no need to bother about it until we get to the place itself."

"You mean to go there—discover the spot?" asked the young man, eagerly.

"I must go there." Sir Ronald's tone was constrained. He glanced again at the last portion of the parchment:

"But beware, for those who do not believe shall die. Pass Lord Anubis though they may, still he shall know and not permit of their return unto the world of men. For the eidolon of Anubis is a very strange one indeed, and holds a secret soul."

The old archeologist blurted out these last words very quickly, and immediately folded up the parchment again. After that he had deliberately turned the talk to practical affairs, as if seeking to forget what he had read.

The next weeks were spent in preparation for the trip to the south, and Sir Ronald seemed to avoid his son, except when it was necessary to converse with him on matters pertaining directly to the expeditionary affairs.

But Peter had not forgotten. He wondered what it was his father had read silently; that secret ritual which would enable one to pass beyond the Opener of the Way. Why had his father blanched and trembled, then quickly changed the subject to saner things? Why had he guarded the parchment so closely? And just what was the nature of the "curse" the manuscript mentioned at the last?

Peter pondered these questions a great deal, but he had gradually dispelled his stronger fears, because of the necessary preoccupation with technical details which the organizing of their expedition subsequently entailed. Not until he and his father were actually in the desert did his misgivings return, but then they plagued him mightily.

There is an air of eon-spawned antiquity about the desert, a certain aura of the ancient which makes one feel that the trivial triumphs of man are as fleeting and quickly obscured as his footprints in the shifting sand. In such places there descends upon the soul a sphinx-like brooding, and somber soliloquies rise, unrepressed, to rule the mind.

Young Peter had been affected by the spell of the silent sands. He tried to remember some of the things his father had once told him concerning Egyptian sorcery, and the miraculous magic of the high priests. Legends of tombs and underground horrors took on a new reality here in the place of their birth. Peter Barton knew personally many men who had believed in the potency of curses, and some of them had died strangely. There was the Tut-Ankh-Ahmen affair, and the Paut temple scandal, and the terrible rumors concerning the end of that unsavory adventurer, Doctor Carnoti. At night, under the spying stars, he would recall these and similar tales, then shudder anew at the thought of what might lie before him.

When Sir Ronald had made camp at the spot designated by the map, there had been new and more concrete terrors.

That first night, Sir Ronald had gone off alone into the hills behind the tents. He bore with him a white goat, and a sharp knife. His son, following, had come upon the old man after a deed had been done, so that the sand had been given to drink. The goat's blood shone horribly in the moonlight, and there was a red glare of corresponding violence in the slayer's eyes. Peter had not made his presence known, for he did not deem it wise to interrupt his father while the old man was muttering those outlandish Egyptian phrases to a mocking moon.

Indeed, Peter was more than a little afraid of Sir Ronald, else he would have attempted to dissuade him from continuing the expedition. But there was something in Sir Ronald's manner which hinted at a mad, unthwartable determination. It was that which made Peter keep silent; that which held him from bluntly asking his father the true details about the parchment's mysterious "curse."

The day after the peculiar incident in the midnight hills, Sir Ronald, after consulting certain zodiacal charts, announced that the digging would start. Carefully, eyes on the map, he measured his paces to an exact spot in the sands, and ordered the men to work. By sundown a ten-foot shaft yawned like a great wound in the earth, and excited natives proclaimed the presence of a door beneath.

2.

By this time Peter, whose nerves were near the breaking-point, was too much afraid of his father to demur when ordered to descend to the floor of the excavation. Undoubtedly the elder man was in the grip of a severe aberration, but Peter, who really loved his father, thought it advisable not to provoke him by refusing to obey. He did not like the idea of going down into that chasm, for the seeping smell was distressingly repulsive. But the stench below was a thousand times more bearable than the sight of the dark door through which it had slithered.

This evidently was the door to the outer passageway that the manuscript had mentioned. All at once Peter knew what was meant by the allusion to the "seventh tongue in the seventh head," and wished that the meaning had remained for ever obscured from his brain. For the door was set with a silver symbol, framed in the familiar ideography of Egyptological lore. This central symbol consisted of the heads of seven principal Egyptian gods—Osiris, Isis, Ra, Bast, Thoth, Set, and Anubis. But the horror lay in the fact that all seven heads protruded from a common body, and it was not the body of any god heretofore known in myth. It was not anthropomorphic, that figure; it held nothing that aped the human form. And Peter could recall no parallel in all the Egyptian cosmology or pantheon which could be remotely construed to resemble this utterly alien horror.

The quixotic abhorrency it induced cannot be ascribed to anything which may be put into words. The sight of it seemed to send little tentacles of terror through Peter's eyes; tiny tentacles that took root in his brain, to drain it dry of all feeling save fear. Part of this may have been due to the fact that the body appeared to be constantly changing; *melting,* that is, from one indescribable shape to another. When viewed from a certain angle the form was that of a Medusa-like mass of serpents; a second gaze revealed that the thing was a glistening array of vampiric flowers, with gelid, protoplasmic petals that seemed to weave in blob-like thirst for blood. A third scrutiny made it appear that the formless mass was nothing but a chaotic jumble of silver skulls. At another time it seemed to hold a certain hidden pattern of the cosmos—stars and planets so compressed as to hint at the enormity of all space beyond.

What devilish craft could produce such a baffling nightmare composite Peter could not say, and he did not like to imagine that the thing was the pattern of any human artist. He fancied that there was some sinister implication of allegorical significance about the door, that the heads, set on the background of that baffling body, were somehow symbolic of a secret horror which rules behind all human gods. But the more he looked, the more his mind became absorbed in the intricate silvery maze of design. It was compelling, hypnotic; glimpsing it was like pondering upon the meaning of Life—pondering in that awful way that drives philosophers mad.

From this beguilement, Peter was roughly awakened by his father's voice. He had been very curt and abrupt all morning, but now his words were fraught with an unmistakable eagerness.

"It's the place all right—the door of the parchment! Now I know what Prinn must have meant in his chapter on the Saracenic rituals; the part where he spoke of the 'symbols on the gate.' We must photograph this after we finish. I hope we can move it later, if the natives don't object."

There was a hidden relish in his words which Peter disliked, and almost feared. He became suddenly aware of how little he really knew about his father and his secret studies of recent years; recalled reluctantly certain guarded tomes he had glimpsed in the library at Cairo. And last night, his father had been out there with the bats, like some mad old priest. Did he really believe such nonsense? *Or did he know it was the truth?*

"Now!" The old man's voice was triumphant. "I have the knife. Stand back."

With fearful, fascinated eyes, Peter saw his father insert the tip of the knife under the seventh head—that of Anubis. Steel grated on silver; then the latter gave. As the dog-like head slowly turned as though actuated by a hidden pivot, the door swung open with a brazen clangor that echoed and re-echoed through the musty depths beyond.

And musty those depths proved to be. A noxious acrid scent burst forth from its long imprisonment, a charnel fetor. It was not the *natron* or spice-laden miasma common to most tombs; rather it held the concentrated essence of death itself—mildewed bones, putrefied flesh, and crumbled dust.

Once the first strength of the gaseous vapor had abated, Sir Ronald immediately stepped inside. He was followed, though much less quickly, by his son. The thirty-and-three sloping steps along the corridor were traversed, as the manuscript had foretold. Then, lantern in hand, the old man was confronted by the enigmatic eidolon of Anubis.

After that first dismaying scrutiny, during which Peter had uneasily recalled these memories of preceding incidents, Sir Ronald interrupted his son's revery and spoke. He whispered there, before the giant statue of the god that seemed to frown down upon the puniness of men with baleful, conscious eyes. Some trick of the lantern-light seemed to change the contours of that stone countenance; its chiseled grin was transformed into a gloating leer of mirthless menace. Yet the grim apprehension this aroused in Peter was soon overpowered by more acute fright when he heard his father's words.

"Listen, boy. I did not tell you all that the parchment revealed to me that night. You remember, there was a part I read only to myself. Well, I had reasons for not letting you know the rest then; you would not have understood, and probably would have refused to come here with me. I needed you too much to risk that.

"You don't know what this moment means to me, son. For years I've worked and studied in secret over things which others scoff at as superstitious fancies. I believed, however, and I have learned. There are always lurking truths behind every forgotten religion; distorted facts which can be rationalized into new concepts of reality. I've been on the trail of something like this for a long time—I knew that if I could discover a tomb like this it must surely contain proofs which would convince the world. There are probably mummies within; the bodies of this cult's secret leaders. That's not what I'm after, though. It's the knowledge that's buried with them; the papyrus manuscripts that hold forbidden secrets—wisdom the world has never known! Wisdom—and power!"

Sir Ronald's voice was shrill with unnatural excitement.

"Power! I have read about the inner circles of the Black Temple, and the cult that has ruled by those designated as Masters in this parchment. They were not ordinary priests of magic; they had traffickings with entities from outside human spheres. Their curses were feared, and their wishes respected. Why? Because of what they knew. I tell you, in this tomb we may find secrets that can give us mastery over half the world! Death-rays, and insidious poisons, old books and potent spells whose efficacy may bring a renascence of primal gods again. Think of it! One could control governments, rule kingdoms, destroy enemies with that knowledge! And there will be jewels, wealth and riches undreamt of, the treasure of a thousand thrones!"

He is quite mad, Peter thought. For a moment he entertained a frantic impulse to turn and run back through the corridor; he wanted to see the sanity of a sun overhead, and feel a breath of air on his brow that was not dust-polluted by dead centuries. But the old man grasped him by the shoulders as he mumbled on, and Peter was forced to remain.

"You don't understand, I see. Perhaps it's for the best; but no matter, I know what I'm about. You will, too, after I do what is necessary. I must tell you now what the parchment said; that portion of it which I did not read aloud."

Some inner instinct screamed silent warnings in Peter's brain. He must get away—he must! But his father's grip was firm, though his voice trembled.

"The part I refer to is that which tells one how to get past this statue and into the tomb itself. No, nothing can be discovered by looking at the thing; there's no secret passage behind it; no levers concealed in the body of the god. The Master and his acolytes were cleverer than that. Mechanical means are of no avail— there's only one way to enter into the tomb beyond, and that is *through the body of the god itself!*"

Peter gazed again into the mask-like countenance of Anubis. The jackal-face was contorted in cunning comprehension—or was it only a trick of the light? His father hurried on.

"That sounds queer, but it's the truth. You remember what the parchment said about this statue being the first one—different from the rest? How it emphasized the fact that Anubis is the *Opener of the Way,* and hinted at its *secret soul?* Well, the next lines explained that. It seems that the figure can turn upon a pivot and open a space behind it into the tomb, *but only when the idol is animated by a human consciousness.*"

They were all mad, Peter knew. He, his father, the old priests, and the statue itself; all insane entities in a world of chaos.

"That means only one thing. I must hypnotize myself by gazing at the god; hypnotize myself until my soul enters its body and opens the way beyond."

Peter's blood was frozen ice in his veins.

"It's not so bizarre a conception at that. The *yogis* believe that in their trances they incarnate themselves with the godhead; the self-hypnotic state is a religious manifestation among all races. And mesmerism is a scientific truth; a truth known and practised thousands of years before psychology was postulated as an organized study. These priests evidently knew the principle. So that is what I must do—hypnotize myself so that my soul or consciousness enters the image. Then I shall be able to open the tomb behind."

"But the curse!" Peter muttered, finding his voice at last. "You know what it says about a curse on unbelievers—something about Lord Anubis being a guardian as well as an Opener of the Way. What about that?"

"Sheer humbug!" Sir Ronald's tone was fanatically firm. "That was merely inserted to frighten off tomb-looters. At any rate, I must risk it. All you need to do is wait. Once I pass into a trance, the statue will move, and the passage beyond will be disclosed. Enter it, immediately. Then give my body a good shake to break the coma, and I'll be all right again."

There was in his father's words an authority which could not be denied. So Peter held the lantern aloft and allowed its beams to play over the face of Anubis. He stood in silence while his father focussed his gaze upon the jackal eyes—those stony, staring eyes that had so disturbed them with hints of a secret life.

It was a terrible tableau; the two men, the twelve-foot god, confronting each other in a black vault beneath the earth.

Sir Ronald's lips moved in fragments of ancient Egyptian prayers. His eyes were fixed upon a nimbus of light that had settled about the canine forehead. Gradually his stare became glassy; nictation ceased, and the pupils glowed with a peculiar nyctalopic fire. The man's body sagged visibly, as if it were being vampirically drained of all life.

Then, to Peter's horror, a pallor overspread his father's face, and he sank down silently upon the stone floor. But his eyes never left those of the idol. Peter's left arm, which held the lantern aloft, was seized with a spasmodic convulsion of utter fright. Minutes sped away in silence. Time has no meaning in a place of death.

Peter could not think. He had seen his father practice self-hypnosis before, with mirrors and lights; he knew it was perfectly harmless in the hands of a skilled adept. But this was different. Could he enter the body of an Egyptian god? And if he did—what of the curse? These two questions reverberated like tiny voices somewhere in his being, but they were engulfed by overpowering fear.

This fear rose to a mad crescendo as Peter saw the change occur. All at once his father's eyes flickered like dying fires, and consciousness went out. But the eyes of the god—*the eyes of Anubis were no longer stone!*

The cyclopean statue was alive!

His father had been right. He had done it—hypnotized his consciousness into the body of the idol. Peter gasped, as a sudden thought slithered into his brain. If his father's theory had been correct so far, then what about the rest? He had said that once inside the figure, his soul would direct it to open the way. But nothing was happening. *What was wrong?*

In panic, Peter bent down and examined the body of his father. It was limp, old, and lifeless. Sir Ronald was dead!

Unbidden, Peter remembered the parchment's cryptic warnings:

"Those who do not believe shall die. Pass Lord Anubis though they may, still he shall know and not permit of their return unto the world of men. For the eidolon of Anubis is strange indeed, and holds a secret soul."

*A secret soul!* Peter, terror throbbing in his temples, raised the lantern aloft and looked once more into the god's face. Again he saw that the stony, snarling mask of Anubis held living eyes!

They glittered bestially, knowingly, evilly. And Peter, seeing them, went berserk. He did not—could not—think; all he knew was that his father was dead, and this statue had somehow killed him and come alive.

So Peter Barton suddenly rushed forward, screaming hoarsely, and began to beat upon the stone idol with futile fists. His bleeding, lacerated knuckles clawed at the cold legs, but Anubis did not stir. Yet his eyes still held their awful life.

The man cursed in sheer delirium, babbling in a tortured voice as he started to climb up to that mocking face. He must know what lay behind that gaze, see the thing and destroy its unnatural life. As he climbed, he sobbed his father's name in agony.

How long it took him to reach the top he never knew; the last minutes were merely a red blur of nightmare frenzy. When he recovered his senses he was clinging precariously to the statue's neck, his feet braced on the belly of the image. And he was still staring into those dreadful living eyes.

But even as he gazed, the whole face was twisting into a sudden ghastly life; the lips drew back into a cavern of crackling mirth, and the fangs of Anubis were bared in terrible, avid lust.

The arms of the god crushed him in a stone embrace; the claw-like fingers tightened about his quivering, constricted throat; the gaping muzzle ravened as stone teeth sank jackal-like into his neck. Thus he met his doom—but it was a welcome doom after that final moment of revelation.

The natives found Peter's bloodless body lying crushed and crumpled at the idol's feet; lying before the statue of Anubis like a sacrifice of olden days. His father was beside him, and he too was dead.

They did not linger there in the forbidden, forgotten fastness of that ancient crypt, nor attempt to enter into the tomb behind. Instead, they reclosed the doors and returned home. There they said that the old and young *effendi* had killed themselves; and that is not surprising. There were really no other indications for them to go by. The statue of Anubis stood once more serene in the shadows; still grimly guarding the secrets once more serene in the shadows; still grimly guarding the secret vaults beyond, and there was no longer any hint of life in its eyes.

And so there is none who knows what Peter Barton knew just before he died; none to know that as Peter went down into death he stared upward and beheld the revelation which made that death a welcome deliverance.

For Peter learned what animated the body of the god; knew what lived within it in a dreadful, distorted way; knew what was being forced to kill him. Because as he died he gazed at last into the living stone face of Anubis—the living stone face that held *his father's tortured eyes*.

# Return to the Sabbath

IT'S NOT the kind of story that the columnists like to print; it's not the yarn press-agents love to tell. When I was still in the Public Relations Department at the studio, they wouldn't let me break it. I knew better than to try, for no paper would print such a tale.

We publicity men must present Hollywood as a gay place; a world of glamour and star-dust. We capture only the light, but underneath the light there must always be shadows. I've always known that—it's been my job to gloss over those shadows for years—but the events of which I speak from a disturbing pattern too strange to be withheld. The shadow of these incidents is not *human*.

It's been the cursed weight of the whole affair that has proved my own mental undoing. That's why I resigned from the studio post, I guess. I wanted to forget, if I could. And now I know that the only way to relieve my mind is to tell the story. I must break the yarn, come what may. Then perhaps I can forget Karl Jorla's eyes. . . .

The affair dates back to one September evening almost three years ago. Les Kincaid and I were slumming down on Main Street in Los Angeles that night. Les is an assistant producer up at the studio, and there was some purpose in his visit; he was looking for authentic types to fill minor roles in a gangster film he was doing. Les was peculiar that way; he preferred the real article, rather than the Casting Bureau's ready-made imitations.

We'd been wandering around for some time, as I recall, past the great stone Chows that guard the narrow alleys of Chinatown, over through the tourist-trap that is Olvera Street, and back along the flophouses of lower Main. We walked by the cheap burlesque houses, eyeing the insolent Filipinos that sauntered past, and jostling our way through the usual Saturday night slumming parties.

We were both rather weary of it all. That's why, I suppose, the dingy little theatre appealed to us.

"Let's go in and sit down for awhile," Les suggested. "I'm tired."

Even a Main Street burlesque show has seats in it, and I felt ready for a nap. The callipygy of the stage-attraction did not appeal to me, but I acceded to the suggestion and purchased our tickets.

We entered, sat down, suffered through two strip-tease dances, an incredibly ancient black-out sketch, and a "Grand Finale." Then, as is the custom in such places, the stage darkened and the screen flickered into life.

We got ready for our doze, then. The pictures shown in these houses are usually ancient specimens of the "quickie" variety; fillers provided to clear the house. As the first blaring notes of the sound-track heralded the title of the opus, I closed my eyes, slouched lower in my seat, and mentally beckoned to Morpheus.

I was jerked back to reality by a sharp dig in the ribs. Les was nudging me and whispering.

"Look at this," he murmured, prodding my reluctant body into wakefulness. "Ever see anything like it?"

I glanced up at the screen. What I expected to find I do not know, but I saw—*horror.*

There was a country graveyard, shadowed by ancient trees through which flickered rays of mildewed moonlight. It was an old graveyard, with rotting headstones set in grotesque angles as they leered up at the midnight sky.

The camera cut down on one grave, a fresh one. The music on the sound-track grew louder, in cursed climax. But I forgot camera and film as I watched. That grave was reality—hideous reality.

The grave was *moving!*

The earth beside the headstone was heaving and churning, as though it were being dug out. Not from above, but from *below.* It quaked upward ever so slowly; terribly. Little clods fell. The sod pulsed out in a steady stream and little rills of earth kept falling in the moonlight as though there were something clawing the dirt away . . . something clawing from beneath.

That something—it would soon appear. And I began to be afraid. I—I didn't want to see what it was. The clawing from below was not natural; it held a purpose not altogether *human*.

Yet I had to look. I had to see him—it—emerge. The sod cascaded in a mound, and then I was staring at the edge of the grave, looking down at the black hole that gaped like a corpse-mouth in the moonlight. Something was coming out.

Something slithered through that fissure, fumbled at the side of the opening. It clutched the ground above the grave, and in the baleful beams of that demon's moon I knew it to be a human hand. A thin, white human hand that held but half its flesh. The hand of a lich, a skeleton claw . . .

A second talon gripped the other side of the excavation top. And now, slowly, insidiously, arms emerged. Naked, fleshless arms.

They crawled across the earth-sides like leprous white serpents. The arms of a cadaver, a rising cadaver. It was pulling itself up. And as *it* emerged, a cloud fell across the moon-path. The light faded to shadows as the bulky head and shoulders came into view. One could see nothing, and I was thankful.

But the cloud was falling away from the moon now. In a second the face would be revealed. The face of the thing from the grave, the resurrected visage of that which should be rotted in death—what would it be?

The shadows fell back. A figure rose out of the grave, and the face turned toward me. I looked and saw—

Well, you've been to "horror pictures." You know what one usually sees. The "ape-man," or the "maniac," or the "death's-head." The papier-mâché grotesquerie of the make-up artist. The "skull" of the dead.

I saw none of that. Instead, there was *horror*. It was the face of a child, I thought, at first; no, not a child, but a man with a child's soul. The face of a poet, perhaps, unwrinkled and calm. Long hair framed a high forehead; crescent eyebrows tilted over closed lids. The nose and mouth were thin and finely chiseled. Over the entire countenance was written an unearthly peace.

It was as though the man were in a sleep of somnambulism or catalepsy. And then the face grew larger, the moonlight brighter, and I saw—more.

The sharper light disclosed tiny touches of evil. The thin lips were fretted, maggot-kissed. The nose had *crumbled* at the nostrils. The forehead was flaked with putrefaction, and the dark hair was dead, encrusted with slime. There were shadows in the bony ridges beneath the closed eyes. Even now, the skeletal arms were up, and bony fingers brushed at those dead pits as the rotted lids fluttered apart. The eyes opened.

They were wide, staring, flaming—and in them was the grave. They were eyes that had closed in death and opened in the coffin under earth. They were eyes that had seen the body rot and the soul depart to mingle in worm-ravened darkness below. They were eyes that held an alien life, a life so dreadful as to animate the cadaver's body and force it to claw its way back to outer earth. They were *hungry* eyes—triumphant, now, as they gazed in graveyard moonlight on a world they had never known before. They hungered for the world as only Death can hunger for Life. And they blazed out of the corpse-pallid face in icy joy.

Then the cadaver began to walk. It lurched between the graves, lumbered before ancient tombs. It shambled through the forest night until it reached a road. Then it turned up that road slowly . . . slowly.

And the hunger in those eyes flamed again as the lights of a city flared below. Death was preparing to mingle with men.

2.

I sat through all this entranced. Only a few minutes had elapsed, but I felt as though uncounted ages had passed unheeded. The film went on. Les and I didn't exchange a word, but we watched.

The plot was rather routine after that. The dead man was a scientist whose wife had been stolen from him by a young doctor. The doctor had tended him in his last illness and unwittingly administered a powerful narcotic with cataleptic effects.

The dialog was foreign and I could not place it. All of the actors were unfamiliar to me, and the setting and photography was quite unusual; unorthodox treatment as in *The Cabinet of Dr. Caligari* and other psychological films.

There was one scene where the living-dead man became enthroned as arch-priest at a Black Mass ceremonial, and there was a little child. . . . His eyes as he plunged the knife. . . .

He kept—*decaying* throughout the film . . . the Black Mass worshippers knew him as an emissary of Satan, and they kidnapped the wife as sacrifice for his own resurrection . . . the scene with the hysterical woman when she saw and recognized her husband for the first time, and the deep, evil whispering voice in which he revealed his secret to her . . . the final pursuit of the devil-worshippers to the great altar-stone in the mountains . . . the death of the resurrected one.

Almost a skeleton in fact now, riddled by bullets and shot from the weapons of the doctor and his neighbors, the dead one crumbled and fell from his seat on the altar-stone. And as those eyes glazed in second death the deep voice boomed out in a prayer to Sathanas. The lich crawled across the ground to the ritual fire, drew painfully erect, and tottered into the flames. And as it stood weaving for a moment in the blaze the lips moved again in infernal prayer, and the eyes implored not the skies, but the earth. The ground opened in a final flash of fire, and the charred corpse fell through. The Master claimed his own. . . .

It was grotesque, almost a fairy-tale in its triteness. When the film had flickered off and the orchestra blared the opening for the next "flesh-show" we rose in our seats, conscious once more of our surroundings. The rest of the mongrel audience seemed to be in a stupor almost equal to our own. Wide-eyed Japanese sat staring in the darkness; Filipinos muttered covertly to one another; even the drunken laborers seemed incapable of greeting the "Grand Opening" with their usual ribald hoots.

Trite and grotesque the plot of the film may have been, but the actor who played the lead had instilled it with ghastly reality. He *had* been dead; his eyes *knew*. And the voice was the voice of Lazarus awakened.

Les and I had no need to exchange words. We both felt it. I

followed him silently as he went up the stairs to the manager's office.

Edward Reich was glowering over the desk. He showed no pleasure at seeing us barge in. When Les asked him where he had procured the film for this evening and what its name was, he opened his mouth and emitted a cascade of curses.

We learned that *Return to the Sabbath* had been sent over by a cheap agency from out Inglewood way, that a Western had been expected, and the "damned foreign junk" substituted by mistake. A hell of a picture this was, for a girl-show! Gave the audience the lousy creeps, and it wasn't even in English! Stinking imported films!

It was some time before we managed to extract the name of the agency from the manager's profane lips. But five minutes after that, Les Kincaid was on the phone speaking to the head of the agency; an hour later we were out at the office. The next morning Kincaid went in to see the big boss, and the following day I was told to announce for publication that Karl Jorla, the Austrian horror-star, had been signed by cable to our studio; and he was leaving at once for the United States.

### 3.

I printed these items, gave all the build-up I could. But after the initial announcements I was stopped dead. Everything had happened too swiftly; we knew nothing about this man Jorla, really. Subsequent cables to Austrian and German studios failed to disclose any information about the fellow's private life. He had evidently never played in any film prior to *Return to the Sabbath*. He was utterly unknown. The film had never been shown widely abroad, and it was only by mistake that the Inglewood agency has obtained a copy and run it here in the United States. Audience reaction could not be learned, and the film was not scheduled for general release unless English titles could be dubbed in.

I was up a stump. Here we had the "find" of the year, and I couldn't get enough material out to make it known!

We expected Karl Jorla to arrive in two weeks, however. I was told to get to work on him as soon as he got in, then flood the news agencies with stories. Three of our best writers were working on a special production for him already; the Big Boss meant to handle it himself. It would be similar to the foreign film, for that "return from the dead" sequence must be included.

Jorla arrived on October seventh. He put up at a hotel; the studio sent down its usual welcoming committee, took him out to the lot for formal testing, then turned him over to me.

I met the man for the first time in the little dressing-room they had assigned him. I'll never forget that afternoon of our first meeting, or my first sight of him as I entered the door.

What I expected to see I don't know. But what I did see amazed me. For Karl Jorla was the dead-alive man of the screen *in life*.

The features were not fretted, of course. But he was tall, and almost as cadaverously thin as in his role; his face was pallid, and his eyes blue-circled. And the eyes were the dead eyes of the movie; the deep, *knowing* eyes!

The booming voice greeted me in hesitant English. Jorla smiled with his lips at my obvious discomfiture, but the expression of the eyes never varied in their alien strangeness.

Somewhat hesitantly I explained my office and my errand. "No pub-leecity," Jorla intoned. "I do not weesh to make known what is affairs of mine own doeeng."

I gave him the usual arguments. How much he understood I cannot say, but he was adamant. I learned only a little; that he had been born in Prague, lived in wealth until the upheavals of the European depression, and entered film work only to please a director friend of his. This director had made the picture in which Jorla played, for private showings only. By mischance a print had been released and copied for general circulation. It had all been a mistake. However, the American film offer had come opportunely, since Jorla wanted to leave Austria at once.

"After the feelm app-ear, I am in bad lights weeth my— friends," he explained, slowly. "They do not weesh it to be shown, that cere-monee."

"The Black Mass?" I asked. "Your *friends?*"

"Yes. The wor-ship of Lucifer. It was real, you know."

Was he joking? No—I couldn't doubt the man's sincerity.

There was no room for mirth in those alien eyes. And then I knew what he meant, what he so casually revealed. He had been a devil-worshipper himself—he and that director. They had made the film and meant it for private display in their own occult circles. No wonder he sought escape abroad!

It was incredible, save that I knew Europe, and the dark Northern mind. The worship of Evil continues today in Budapest, Prague, Berlin. And he, Karl Jorla the horror-actor, admitted to being one of them!

"What a story!" I thought. And then I realized that it could, of course, never be printed. A horror-star admitting belief in the parts he played? Absurd!

All the features about Boris Karloff played up the fact that he was a gentle man who found true peace in raising a garden. Lugosi was pictured as a sensitive neurotic, tortured by the roles he played in the films. Atwill was a socialite and a stage star. And Peter Lorre was always written up as being gentle as a lamb, a quiet student whose ambition was to play comedy parts.

No, it would never do to break the story of Jorla's devil-worship. And he was so damnably reticent about his private affairs!

I sought out Kincaid after the termination of our unsatisfactory interview. I told him what I had encountered and asked for advice. He gave it.

"The old line," he counseled. "Mystery man. We say nothing about him until the picture is released. After that I have a hunch things will work out for themselves. The fellow is a marvel. So don't bother about stories until the film is canned."

Consequently I abandoned publicity efforts in Karl Jorla's direction. Now I am very glad I did so, for there is no one to remember his name, or suspect the horror that was soon to follow.

4.

The script was finished. The front office approved. Stage Four was under construction; the casting director got busy. Jorla was at the studio every day; Kincaid himself was teaching him English. The part was one in which very few words were needed, and Jorla proved a brilliant pupil, according to Les.

But Les was not as pleased as he should have been about it all. He came to me one day about a week before production and unburdened himself. He strove to speak lightly about the affair, but I could tell that he felt worried.

The gist of his story was very simple. Jorla was behaving strangely. He had had trouble with the front office; he refused to give the studio his living address, and it was known that he had checked out from his hotel several days after first arriving in Hollywood.

Nor was that all. He wouldn't talk about his part, or volunteer any information about interpretation. He seemed to be quite uninterested—admitting frankly to Kincaid that his only reason for signing a contract was to leave Europe.

He told Kincaid what he had told me—about the devil-worshippers. And he hinted at more. He spoke of being followed, muttered about "avengers" and "hunters who waited." He seemed to feel that the witch-cult was angry at him for the violation of secrets, and held him responsible for the release of *Return to the Sabbath*. That, he explained, was why he would not give his address, nor speak of his past life for publication. That is why he must use very heavy make-up in his film debut here. He felt at times as though he were being watched, or followed. There were many foreigners here . . . too many.

"What the devil can I do with a man like that?" Kincaid exploded, after he had explained this to me. "He's insane, or a fool. And I confess that he's too much like his screen character to please me. The damned casual way in which he professes to have dabbled in devil-worship and sorcery! He believes all this, and—well, I'll tell you the truth I came here today because of the last thing he spoke of to me this morning.

"He came down to the office, and at first when he walked in I didn't know him. The dark glasses and muffler helped, of course, but he himself had changed. He was trembling, and walked with a stoop. And when he spoke his voice was like a groan. He showed me—this."

Kincaid handed me the clipping. It was from the London *Times,* through European press dispatches. A short paragraph, giving an account of the death of Fritz Ohmmen, the Austrian film director. He had been found strangled in a Paris garret, and his body had been frightfully mutilated; it mentioned an inverted cross branded on his stomach above the ripped entrails. Police were seeking the murderer . . .

I handed the clipping back in silence. "So what?" I asked. But I had already guessed his answer.

"Fritz Ohmmen," Kincaid said, slowly, "was the director of the picture in which Karl Jorla played; the director, who with Jorla, knew the devil-worshippers. Jorla says that he fled to Paris, and that *they* sought him out."

I was silent.

"Mess," grunted Kincaid. "I've offered Jorla police protection, and he's refused. I can't coerce him under the terms of our contract. As long as he plays the part, he's secure with us. But he has the jitters. And I'm getting them."

He stormed out. I couldn't help him. I sat thinking of Karl Jorla, who believed in devil-gods; worshipped, and betrayed them. And I could have smiled at the absurdity of it all if I hadn't seen the man on the screen and watched his evil eyes. He *knew!* It was then that I began to feel thankful we had not given Jorla any publicity. I had a hunch.

During the next few days I saw Jorla but seldom. The rumors, however, began to trickle in. There had been an influx of foreign "sightseers" at the studio gates. Someone had attempted to crash through the barriers in a racing-car. An extra in a mob scene over on Lot Six had been found carrying an automatic beneath his vest; when apprehended he had been lurking under the executive office windows. They had taken him down to headquarters, and so far the man had refused to talk. He was a German . . .

Jorla came to the studios every day in a shuttered car. He was bundled up to the eyes. He trembled constantly. His English lessons went badly. He spoke to no one. He had hired two men to ride with him in his car. They were armed.

A few days later news came that the German extra had talked. He was evidently a pathological case ... he babbled wildly of a "Black Cult of Lucifer" known to some of the foreigners around town. It was a secret society purporting to worship the Devil, with vague connections in the mother countries. He had been "chosen" to avenge a wrong. More than that he dared not say, but he did give an address where the police might find cult headquarters. The place, a dingy house in Glendale, was quite deserted, of course. It was a queer old house with a secret cellar beneath the basement, but everything seemed to have been abandoned. The man was being held for examination by an alienist.

I heard this report with deep misgivings. I knew something of Los Angeles' and Hollywood's heterogeneous foreign population; God knows, Southern California has attracted mystics and occultists from all over the world. I've even heard rumors about stars being mixed up in unsavory secret societies, things one would never dare to admit in print. And Jorla was afraid.

That afternoon I tried to trail his black car as it left the studio for his mysterious home, but I lost the track in the winding reaches of Topanga Canyon. It had disappeared into the secret twilight of the purple hills, and I knew then that there was nothing I could do. Jorla had his own defenses, and if they failed, we at the studio could not help.

That was the evening he disappeared. At least he did not show up the next morning at the studio, and production was to start in two days. We heard about it. The boss and Kincaid were frantic. The police were called in, and I did my best to hush things up. When Jorla did not appear the following morning I went to Kincaid and told him about my following the car to Topanga Canyon. The police went to work. Next morning was production.

We spent a sleepless night of fruitless vigil. There was no word. Morning came, and there was unspoken dread in Kincaid's eyes as he faced me across the office table. Eight o'clock. We got up and walked silently across the lot to the studio cafeteria. Black coffee was badly needed; we hadn't had a police report for hours. We passed Stage Four, where the Jorla crew was at work. The noise of hammers was mockery. Jorla, we felt, would never face a camera today, if ever.

Bleskind, the director of the untitled horror opus, came out of the Stage office as we passed.

His paunchy body quivered as he grasped Kincaid's lapels and piped, "Any news?"

Kincaid shook his head slowly. Bleskind thrust a cigar into his tense mouth.

"We're shooting ahead," he snapped. "We'll shoot around Jorla. If he doesn't show up when we finish the scenes in which he won't appear, we'll get another actor. But we can't wait." The squat director bustled back to the Stage.

Moved by a sudden impulse, Kincaid grasped my arm and propelled me after Bleskind's waddling form.

"Let's see the opening shots," he suggested. "I want to see what kind of a story they've given him."

We entered Stage Four.

A Gothic Castle, the ancestral home of Baron Ulmo. A dark, gloomy stone crypt of spidery horror. Cobwebbed, dust-shrouded, deserted by men and given over to the rats by day and the unearthly horrors that crept by night. An altar stood by the crypt, an altar of evil, the great black stone on which the ancient Baron Ulmo and his devil-cult had held their sacrifices. Now, in the pit beneath the altar, the Baron lay buried. Such was the legend.

According to the first shot scheduled, Sylvia Channing, the heroine, was exploring the castle. She had inherited the place and taken it over with her young husband. In this scene she was to see the altar for the first time, read the inscription on its base. This inscription was to prove an unwitting invocation, opening up the crypt beneath the altar and awakening Jorla, as Baron Ulmo, from the dead. He was to rise from the crypt then, and walk. It was at this point that the scene would terminate, due to Jorla's strange absence.

The setting was magnificently handled. Kincaid and I took our places beside Director Bleskind as the shot opened. Sylvia Channing walked out on the set; the signals were given, lights flashed, and the action began.

It was pantomimic. Sylvia walked across the cobwebbed floor, noticed the altar, examined it. She stooped to read the inscription, then whispered it aloud. There was a drone, as the opening of the altar-crypt was mechanically begun. The altar swung aside, and the black gaping pit was revealed. The upper cameras swung to Sylvia's face. She was to stare at the crypt in horror, and she did it most magnificently. In the picture she would be watching Jorla emerge.

Bleskind prepared to give the signal to cut action. Then—

*Something emerged from the crypt!*

It was dead, that thing—that horror with a mask of faceless flesh. Its lean body was clothed in rotting rags, and on its chest was a bloody crucifix, inverted—carved out of dead flesh. The eyes blazed loathsomely. It was Baron Ulmo, rising from the dead. *And it was Karl Jorla!*

The make-up was perfect. His eyes were dead, just as in the other film. The lips seemed shredded again, the mouth even more ghastly in its slitted blackness. And the touch of the bloody crucifix was immense.

Bleskind nearly swallowed his cigar when Jorla appeared. Quickly he controlled himself, silently signaled the men to proceed with the shooting. We strained forward, watching every move, but Les Kincaid's eyes held a wonder akin to my own.

Jorla was acting as never before. He moved slowly, as a corpse must move. As he raised himself from the crypt, each tiny effort seemed to cause him utter agony. The scene was soundless; Sylvia had fainted. But Jorla's lips moved, and we heard a faint whispering murmur which heightened the horror. Now the grisly cadaver was almost half out of the crypt. It strained upward, still murmuring. The bloody crucifix of flesh gleamed redly on the chest ... I thought of the one found on the body of the murdered foreign director, Fritz Ohmmen, and realized where Jorla had gotten the idea.

The corpse strained up ... it was to rise now ... up ... and then, with a sudden rictus, the body stiffened and slid back into the crypt.

Who screamed first I do not know. But the screaming continued after the prop-boys had rushed to the crypt and looked down at what lay within.

When I reached the brink of the pit I screamed, too.

*For it was utterly empty.*

5.

I wish there were nothing more to tell. The papers never knew. The police hushed things up. The studio is silent, and the production was dropped immediately. But matters did not stop there. There was a sequel to that horror on Stage Four.

Kincaid and I cornered Bleskind. There was no need of any explanation; how could what we had just seen be explained in any sane way?

Jorla had disappeared; no one had let him into the studio; no makeup man had given him his attention. Nobody had seen him enter the crypt. He had appeared in the scene, then disappeared. The crypt was empty.

These were the facts. Kincaid told Bleskind what to do. The film was developed immediately, though two of the technicians fainted. We three sat in the projection booth and watched the morning's rushes flicker across the screen. The sound-track was specially dubbed in.

That scene—Sylvia walking and reading the incantation—the pit opening—and God, when *nothing* emerged!

Nothing but that great red scar suspended in midair—that great inverted crucifix cut in bleeding flesh; no Jorla visible at all! That bleeding cross in the air, and then the mumbling . . .

Jorla—the thing—whatever it was—had mumbled a few syllables on emerging from the crypt. The sound-track had picked them up. And we couldn't see anything but that scar; yet we heard Jorla's voice now coming from nothingness. We heard what he kept repeating, as he fell back into the crypt.

It was an address in Topanga Canyon.

The lights flickered on, and it was good to see them. Kincaid phoned the police and directed them to the address given on the sound-track.

We waited, the three of us, in Kincaid's office, waited for the police call. We drank, but did not speak. Each of us was thinking of Karl Jorla the devil-worshipper who had betrayed his faith; of his fear of vengeance. We thought of the director's death, and the bloody crucifix on his chest; remembered Jorla's disappearance.

And then that ghastly ghost-thing on the screen, the bloody thing that hung in midair as Jorla's voice groaned the address . . .

The phone rang.

I picked it up. It was the police department. They gave their report. I fainted.

It was several minutes before I came to. It was several more minutes before I opened my mouth and spoke.

"They've found Karl Jorla's body at the address given on the screen," I whispered. "He was lying dead in an old shack up in the hills. He had been—murdered. There was a bloody cross, inverted on his chest. They think it was the work of some fanatics, because the place was filled with books on sorcery and Black Magic. They say—"

I paused. Kincaid's eyes commanded. "Go on."

"They say," I murmured, "that Jorla had been dead for at least three days."

# The Mandarin's Canaries

THERE WAS revelry in the garden of the Mandarin Quong; revelry as attested by the loud cries and supplications for mercy interspersed with high titterings of pleasure.

The Mandarin was amusing himself today in a new fashion. Through the bamboos it could be seen that the stakes were bare, their rusty iron shackles hanging empty in the sunlight. The lotus-blossoms and orchids swayed with the wind to reveal that the racks stretched along the garden-paths were likewise empty, and the iron beds beneath the vines untenanted. No whips lay amidst the grass and flowers, no pincers or knives or barbed flails.

Therefore, as the cries and laughter proclaimed, the Mandarin Quong had found some new sport here in the Garden of Pain.

In a remote bower, guarded by great trees whose limbs had been trained to twist in torment, and veiled by serpentine creepers that extended fangs of scarlet blossom, the Mandarin stood. There had been those who were kind enough to compare Quong to the Lord Buddha, and there were times when his fat little figure held a dignified serenity quite similar.

But in moments such as this, Quong was transfigured; his fleshy face creased into a mask of demoniac mirth; his red, full lips writhed back above his black beard, and his eyebrows were swords over slitted points of flame. Pleasure was an intense emotion in the Mandarin, and his pleasure was Pain.

He stood staring across the bower at the two figures before him: the bound man against the great tree, and the robed figure confronting him some ten paces distant. The bound man was uttering the cries and the pleadings; the robed one was silent. He moved, but no sound emanated from those movements save an occasional twanging thrum. For the robed man held in his hands a great crossbow, and upon his back was a quiver bristling with barbed arrows. These he was swiftly and efficiently removing one by one; fitting them to his bow and taking expert aim as he released them at the bound, writhing figure of the captive.

His aim was remarkable—despite the agonized movements and convulsive startings of the victim, he never erred. The arrows sped to a living mark: the wrist, the ankle, the knee, the groin. With curious precision, he avoided placing the cruel shafts in a vital spot, and his arm carefully judged the depth with which each arrow would penetrate the shrinking yellow flesh of his tormented target.

But Quong did not notice this dexterity, or if he noticed it he gave the matter no heed. His laughing eyes were on the victim, watching the impact of each arrow, the jerk of the flesh as it sank in, and the thin trickle of blood that followed the piercing. To an observer it might almost be said that Quong appeared to be studying his victim's pain, studying with the amused and detached pleasure of a bibliophile who reads for the hundredth time some treasured volume—foretasting each delight, yet seeking unfelt nuances of enjoyment.

His delighted laughter fell as an arrow struck the bound man's left eye and penetrated the brain. The writhing ceased, the body sagged limply and hung from the ropes which restrained its fall.

The Mandarin Quong heaved a sigh—the sigh of the bibliophile when his book is closed—and with a wave of his saffron hands dismissed the archer. The bowman bowed and backed from the bower with gestures of obeisance, leaving his master alone.

Quong stood stock-still for an instant after the fellow's departure, and his features underwent a curious change. Gone was the sadist's smile, gone the passionate intensity which had made of his face a gargoyle's grimace. Serenity returned to shine from his slant eyes, and his lips relaxed into a softer smile of pleasure. He moved forward to the tree where the bound body hung, passing the gory thing without so much as a glance. Behind the tree, suspended by the self-same ropes which upheld the victim, a series of thin metal pipes were hanging. From the sleeve of his robe the Mandarin drew forth a slender stick. With a gentle, caressing motion he drew the ivory head of the stick across the metal. A chiming rang forth—a soft, liquid, almost chirping series of notes holding a peculiar bird-like quality. The tones flooded forth, clear and mellow, as the Mandarin chose his notes with careful attention to harmonics. Music came from the tree where horror hung.

Again the Mandarin stepped back, and stood still as though waiting. And suddenly, while the last strains of metallic melody still floated through the garden, the air was filled with a curious rustling sound—hundreds of tiny sounds, rather, blurred into a single whirring note. And there came a cheeping and shrill whistling from all around which caused the yellow face of Quong to glow with kindly pleasure.

Without warning, the air turned to gold. A thousand yellow forms swirled to outshine the sun—moving yellow dots with bejeweled eyes that flamed. They whirled and dipped against the serene sky, then swooped about the tree in a golden cloud that spun round and round about the trunk and its grisly adornment.

And still they came, whirring and scudding down until the tree was covered with a yellow blossoming in all its boughs, and vines of living gold crawled across the bark and what sagged against it. The garden was filled with tiny birds, filled with the exquisite darting flight of graceful elfin swarms that chirped liquid cries of pleasure.

The Mandarin watched the golden pageant flow over the tree-trunk watched the shining cluster as it moved across the tree in frantic life. The symphony of this motion enthralled him so that the minutes passed unheeded.

It was perhaps half an hour later that the swarm dispersed. It rose suddenly in a golden spiral, swerving up from the tree-trunk to settle in the limbs. And now, in the space made vacant by the canaries' departure, a silver figure gleamed in the sunlight. Where the dead man had hung there remained only a dry-picked, shining skeleton.

The Mandarin stared quietly, then lifted his eyes to the boughs where the yellow horde rested in its repletion. He waited, and in a moment the melody came forth.

The song of pleasure was indescribable in its sweetness—soft, limpid, yet glowing with tonal color and pulsing with painfully ecstatic threnody. It rose and fell, faintly at first, then culminated in a burst of beauty as the chirping resolved into eery notes that were shrill yet vibrant.

For perhaps ten minutes the song continued, and the last trills died away, the golden chain shattered link by link, and the birds departed.

Quong turned away toward the oncoming twilight, and as he walked toward the Palace the dusk hid the tears that streamed down his yellow cheeks.

2.

The Mandarin Quong loved his birds. This was a matter of common knowledge throughout the South, and the statement of it was generally coupled with the other known fact that Quong loved nothing else.

In these brave days China was used to cruel and dreadful masters, but in a land noted for the perversity of its overlords, the name of Quong was feared above all others.

Shortly after the Mandarin usurped his father's throne in the Great Palace he had given evidences of those qualities which caused many of his people to flee to Canton's coast where now the foreign devils had landed with many ships.

Those that remained after Quong's accession did so because they were unable to leave the lands; but in them was the same fear which had driven their more fortunate companions to seek the safety of seaward lands.

They feared Quong even as a boy, for he had given many instances of his cruel precocity when a mere lad in his father's house. With the impatience of youth he did not bother to amuse himself, as his brothers did, with the flogging and torturing of slaves. He was eager for death-throes, for the spasms of agony, and the servants he toyed with died swiftly in the dark dungeons. It was only in adolescence that he learned to control the intensity of his lusts; then he turned to the more subtle tortures. And not for long did he feel satisfied with the Copper Bowl, the Water-Death, or the Seven Bamboo Chastisements. The time-honored devices of his father's hired torture-masters he improved on, and his days were spent in the study of pain.

Now this was well, for the future Master must govern his people strictly and be quick to wrath, but even the conservative graybeards whispered that young Quong possessed a devil within him which knew delight only in debauches of cruelty.

It is true that his first favorites were seldom fated to survive his yearning for experiment over the period of a month; only families utterly destitute sold their daughters into the House of Quong. Each passing month saw the young man's quest of Pleasure in Pain increase its horror; he grew pale from long hours spent in dark cells and murky oubliettes. This could be readily understood in an old man, whose other pleasures were few, but for a youth it was not seemly to be so confined. Still, Quong was precocious.

This precocity further evinced itself in Quong's judicious disposal of his three brothers, who found their last cups of rice wine to be very bitter indeed. They died quietly, without ostentation, and it was only to be expected when one morning the old Mandarin, Quong's father, went to his ancestors with the cord of a silken bowstring for a necklace about his throat.

Then Quong was Lord of the House, and high Mandarin over the jungles, the plains, and the village lands of all his people. His regal reign started with a most sumptuous funeral in honor of his father, and then he gave the people of his city a noble tiger-hunting in the streets of a little village close by. But these evidences of propriety did not wholly satisfy his subjects, who unkindly grumbled about the vast number of coolies who were immolated outside his father's tomb during the funeral ceremonies. Other ungrateful coolies said that the tiger-hunt was spoiled by the deaths of almost the entire populace in the village where it occurred.

But when Mandarin Quong made the pronouncement about his law, the flights to the coast began. Quong as Mandarin was the judge over all criminal trials in his domain, but he now specified that he would usurp the office of executioner as well. In the first three years of his official rule every case brought before him ended in conviction; and there were many cases, due to his increasing his force of guardsmen and the peculiar system whereby he paid them a bounty for each criminal obtained. This he could well afford, for an increasing number of crimes seemed to be discovered among the wealthier merchant and land-holding class, and conviction carried with it a confiscation of money and property to Quong's house.

As an executioner, Quong scorned beheading or any of the accepted modes of torture. No longer was the sentence carried out in public; Quong preferred the darkness of his palace dungeons or his ivory Hall of State. Here, it was averred, the walls were lined with human heads, mounted as one might mount the head of a deer or a buffalo.

In an effort to discourage such unfortunate predilections toward torture, one of Quong's advisers subtly hinted that his constant stay indoors was injurious to the health of the Mandarin.

It was then that Quong built his garden—his beautiful Chinese garden behind the palace, where trees and flowers and mirroring-pools opened to the sky. And he built racks and wheels and scaffolds that blossomed with evil fruit, so that things went much the same as they had in the old dungeons below the Palace.

But Nature stirred a new love of beauty in the Mandarin's breast. He caused vines to grow upon the iron racks to conceal the rusty stains; trained creepers to hide the stark lines of his scaffolds. Sometimes he walked in the gardens alone, and was serenaded by musicians from concealed glades and dells.

For the birds did not rest here. Blood nourished the fantastic flowers, and the perfume of rare orchids was rich in the air; but over all was the carrion taint that brought crows and vultures but kept the songsters away. Nightingales and finches shunned the green confines, and those brought by the animal-venders flew away with peepings of terror rather than chirps of song. Even the scarlet macaws and green parrots refused to color the landscape with their presence, and the garden remained incomplete without its musical background.

But at this time the two missionaries came to Quong at the Palace, and asked if they might stay. They were foreign devils; Portuguese, in robes of black, who spoke a curious tongue and blasphemed against Lord Buddha, the Four Books, and Kwong-Fu-Tze with equally impartial fervor.

Some of their paraphernalia interested the Mandarin, who spent several days with the queer thunder-sticks which worked on principles so divergent from Chinese guns; the sextants, silver watches, and other marvels brought from the court of King John.

They had birds, in cages—tiny yellow birds, that sang with infinite sweetness. Canaries, the priests called them, and their golden beauty much impressed the Mandarin; so much so, that after listening to an especially severe tirade against his torturing and cruelties by the two missionaries, he conducted them to the garden and accorded them the fate of the One they called their Master.

And he loosed the canaries in the garden, and beheld with pleasure that they did not fly away but remained close to him. To his great amusement one of them perched upon the sagging shoulder of the first priest, and sang up into the dead face with affectionate fervor. He rewarded the birds with the most delicate of meats—the tongue of the priest.

Perhaps, he mused, it would instill the creatures with the eloquence of their former masters.

This did not occur, but the birds stayed. And within a few years they had multiplied a hundredfold, then grew to many thousands. They filled the garden by day, and then fared afield at will, returning only toward twilight to await the feast spread for them.

They had developed a terrible appetite for the ghastly fruit which ripened daily in the garden sunlight. It had arisen at the first, and as generation after generation lived and bred and died in the torture-maze, the blood-strain carried with it the nameless hunger.

Formerly Quong had set aside a burial-ground on his lands, but now only bones need be piled in his great cellars. The birds, thousands strong, did the rest. And after a time they learned to await his signal.

Over all the garden Quong had set up little metal bars which played a curious scale. Upon completing his daily dispensing of justice, he would summon the flock with his chimes and they came to partake of his largess. Afterward they raised their voices in the sweet reward of song—and it was a song infinitely more beautiful than any the Mandarin had ever known. It soothed him like mellow wine, set his blood tingling like the hands of one well-beloved, thrilled his imaginative senses like moonlight over dragon-guarded pools. He loved his birds, loved their daily tribute.

But others feared them. Men learned of his canaries, saw the flocks speed over their fields and descend at will to ravish the grain and seeds. They were not molested lest this incur the Mandarin's displeasure. The growing horde swarmed about the cities and villages, and none might wave them from the streets. A dead bird meant a dead man if the Mandarin's guards found the creature.

The legend of their feastings in the garden became known, and after that strange tales were told of the foreign devils who had brought the birds as spies. It was whispered that the tiny chattering creatures possessed human souls; that they sucked evil nourishment from the dead, and absorbed the wisdom of men which they used when prying about the streets. Other lore hinted that they reported to the Mandarin the misdeeds which they observed in daily flight, and they came to be hated and feared as living symbols of the terrible power which ruled the land.

3.

Now lately Quong had devised a new torture which pleased him greatly. He was writing, on many parchments, a history of Pain to bequeath to the Great School in Peking, and it heartened him to be able to include interesting variations invented by himself.

This Death of a Thousand Arrows was such an invention. Barbed darts of various sizes, shot with various degrees of force into certain carefully-selected portions of a victim's body, produced a lingering torment delightful to members of the aristocracy of Pain.

Quong had devised the idea himself, but he needed an expert bowman to assist him. It was then that he sought Hin-Tze, the Emperor's archer, and offered him employment.

Hin-Tze came to the Palace with his wife Yu-Li, and the Mandarin noted with pleasure that his bowman was efficient and the bowman's wife lovely to look upon.

So it was not many days after Hin-Tze first employed himself with victims in the garden that the Mandarin caused the woman to be removed to his quarters and gave himself over to dalliance.

The archer learned of this, and his heart was sore. He did not like his dreadful task, but he had come at the Emperor's command and dared not disobey. He hated the cruelty, hated the Mandarin, and was repelled by the nauseous birds whose unnatural feastings gave him such qualms as he had never known on the battlefield. Indeed, one day he had accidentally pierced a yellow body with an arrow—and only the fact that the canary had winged itself within the line of flight saved him from the Mandarin's wrath. He was a soldier, and to him the music of the canaries was not sweet after the spectacle of their dining.

Now that his wife had been taken, Hin-Tze was very bitter in his heart against Lord Quong, though he dared not speak. He feared, instead, for he had heard tales of the Mandarin's love.

And one evening not many weeks after the taking of his woman, Quong grew enraged and with his dagger slit the golden throat of his new favorite so that pretty Yu-Li died sobbing her husband's name.

Hin-Tze saw, and said nothing, even when the pitiful limp form was carried into the garden by servants.

He returned to his quarters and sat alone in the moonlight, awaiting what he knew he would hear. And then came that sweet, detestable song from the tree-tops, the satisfied song of the canaries. At that moment Hin-Tze swore his oath against the Mandarin, against the desecration of his wife's body, which was not even accorded godly burial but sacrificed instead to a few moments of melody from the hateful tiny throats of Quong's friends.

Of this he said no word to the Mandarin, for that was not seemly; and with lordly courtesy Quong forbore mentioning the occurrence when they met the next day.

Hin-Tze carried a bound coolie into the garden sunlight; a poor, choking wretch who had stolen a few taels in some market outside the town. He pleaded with Hin-Tze as he walked, and it was curious to the archer to hear that the doomed man did not fear death nearly so much as he feared the loss of his immortal soul. He and all the people were afraid of the canaries of Quong, whose feasting deprived them of proper burial.

But Hin-Tze said nothing as he slipped a knife through the man's bonds and awaited the Mandarin.

Quong strode down the path, smiling in the sunshine. A fat prisoner—a greater song. He advanced, beaming serenely on his bowman, whose gentle tact in ignoring the unfortunate accident of the previous evening he greatly admired. Quong clapped his hands to signal that the ritual binding begin, and indicated the great tree as the one to which the victim was to be tied.

But the Lord of Pleasure and Pain was chagrined when the prisoner suddenly wheeled and bolted off through the garden, his severed bonds trailing behind him. He opened his mouth, forming it for a shout of anger; but it gaped still wider in astonishment as Hin-Tze advanced and seized him by the throat. There was a great arrow in the bowman's hand, and its point was barbed. It moved slowly toward the Mandarin's neck as he struggled back against the tree-trunk. His face paled at what he read in his captor's gleaming eyes.

It was then that he babbled for mercy and screamed, and struck out wildly. But Hin-Tze drew the barbed point over the breast of Quong and pinned him to the tree.

Then the bowman stepped back and fixed an arrow to his great bow. He shot the dart, eyes blind with rage and ears deaf to the cries of his living target. He drew, fixed, fired automatically; a half-hundred times perhaps, he aimed with eyes dazzled by a sort of madness. Only then was vengeance appeased—only then did he cease and approach the living horror that still stood before the tree-trunk.

One of the hands was moving, a bloody claw. It curled around the bark, fumbling, fumbling. It rested, then moved again. And suddenly shrill chimes rang upon the air—chimes that summoned and commanded. The hand fell, but into the glazing eyes crept a look of triumph and of craftiness. The lips worked piteously.

"Lift me down," whispered the Mandarin.

Hin-Tze, confused, drew the pinioning arrow forth and the body of the dying Quong slumped forward as though fainting in his arms.

Too late did Hin-Tze see the arrow torn from the flesh; the arrow in the hand that now struck with every ounce of strength that remained in the broken arms. With a last effort, the Mandarin had nailed him to the tree!

The figure in the gorgeous robes fell earthward, but Quong's triumphant eyes still stared up into Hin-Tze's pain-contorted face.

"I have summoned the birds," said the Mandarin, faintly. "They are my friends, and they come when the chimes call. You have heard the legends which say my canaries possess living souls—the souls of the dead that once hung upon the tree where you hang now."

The Mandarin shuddered a moment, then fell silent. At last he whispered again.

"This is not true. The birds are simply birds; they know me and they love me, for I have prepared for them many feasts. Therefore vengeance for my death shall rest with them. And—I shall hear one last song as I die."

Hin-Tze understood then. He struggled to free himself, but the arrow held him so that he hung by the barbs that nailed him to the tree of horror.

He clawed and screamed when he heard the rustling sounds, moaned aloud as the golden cloud hummed down toward him. And then they were all about with their beating wings, their tiny beaks that stabbed sharply, cruelly, with dreadful hunger. Blood blinded him, two winged knives flew to his eyes, and the golden glow faded to black pain. For a few moments longer he writhed beneath the beaks of his tiny tormenters. Then the cloud settled down in silence.

Upon the ground lay the Mandarin Quong. His wounds were forgotten, for he had the nature of a poet. This final revenge, this last triumph in defeat, was atonement. He watched every movement of the raptorial birds, drank in their graceful beauty to the full. And soon he would hear the song—the final song before death.

For he had spoken truly to Hin-Tze. The birds loved him; and they were only birds. The notion of psychopomps—the absurd superstition that these creatures of his possessed the souls of the dead from his garden—was incredible.

Quong watched the yellow swarm move across the body of the bowman. They rose, chittering. In a moment the song would commence. The Mandarin awaited the perfection of the poet's death.

They rose—and suddenly one of the tiny birds detached itself from the sun-bright cluster. It was a tiny female—and it flew straight down toward the skeleton on the tree. It perched, absurdly, upon the fleshless ribs; as though peering into the bony bars of a cage.

Quong gazed with new interest. He drew himself up on one elbow, painfully. The bird was sitting there—and then—there were two birds!

Was it hallucination, dying delirium? Or had another bird suddenly appeared from *inside* the skeleton? A yellow form, whirring within the ribs where the heart had been?

And now the two winged out, together. Their beady little eyes rested upon the recumbent form of the Mandarin.

He sank back, strange horror tugging at his heart. A female bird—Yu-Li. And a male from the skeleton of the dead bowman? *Psychopomps?*

The two flew upward, to where the yellow cloud hovered in midair. They flew to the forefront, shrilling as though in command. And then they wheeled, swooped down. Quong screamed in utter fear. Dead souls were exacting *their* vengeance. Yellow knives stabbed and struck home; ten thousand fluttering forms tore and clawed at the writhing thing upon the ground.

And so there was no one to hear the final moment when it came—it was in a deserted garden that the last sweet serenade was sung by the canaries of the Mandarin Quong.

# Waxworks

It had been a dull day for Bertrand before his discovery of the waxworks—a dark, foggy day which he had spent in tramping aimlessly about the dingy streets of the quay district he loved. It had been a dull day, but none the less it was of a sort that Bertrand's imaginative nature best loved. He found a morose enjoyment in the feel of the stinging sleet upon his face; liked, too, the sensation of semi-blindness induced by the nebulosity of outline conjured up with the fog. Mist made the dingy buildings and the narrow streets that threaded crookedly between them seem unreal and grotesque; the commonplace stone structures squatted in blueness like vast, inanimate monsters carven from cyclopean stone.

So, at least, thought Bertrand, in his somewhat maudlin fashion. For Bertrand was a poet—a very bad poet, with the sentimentally esoteric nature such beings affect. He lived in a garret in the dock district, ate crusts of bread, and fancied himself very much put upon by the world. In moments of self-pity, which were frequent, he made certain mental comparisons between his estate and that of the late Francois Villon. These estimates were none too flattering to the latter gentleman; for after all, Villon had been a pimp and a thief, whereas Bertrand was neither. Bertrand was just a very honorable young man whom people had not yet learned to appreciate, and if he starved now, posterity would spread him a pretty feast. So his thoughts ran a good part of the time, and days of fog like this were ideal for such personal compassions. It was warm enough in Bertrand's garret, and there was food there; for after all, his parents in Marseilles did send him money regularly, under the impression that he was a student at the college. Yes, the garret was as fine refuge on such a dismal afternoon, and Bertrand could have been hard at work on one of those noble sonnets he was always intending to produce. But no, he must wander about in the fog, and think things out for himself. It was so—romantic—he grudgingly conceded, in his mind, for he hated to use "trite" expressions.

This "romantic" phase was beginning to pall on the young man after an hour's walk about the wharves; sleet and drizzling rain had dampened more than his ardor. Then too, he had just discovered in himself a most unpoetic case of the snuffles.

In consequence, he was more than heartened by the sight of the dim lamp that shone through the murk from a dark basement doorway between two houses on this obscure side street. The lantern served to illuminate a sign proclaiming *Waxworks Within*.

Upon reading this legend, Bertrand felt a faint tinge of disappointment. He had hoped that the beacon ornamented the door of a tavern, for our poet was given to the bottle at those odd times when he found himself in funds. None the less, the light was a symbol of warmth and shelter within, and perhaps the waxworks would be interesting.

He went down the steps, opened the dark door, and stepped, shivering slightly at the sudden change, into a warm, dimly lit hallway.

A fat little man in a greasy cap shuffled out from behind a side door and took his three francs with a shrug of surprise, as if wordlessly indicating his amazement at securing a customer at such a time.

Bertrand glanced down the plain hall as he removed his wet jacket. His fastidious nose wrinkled slightly at the musty odor about the place; this, combined with the peculiar acridity common only to discarded wet garments in a warm room, gave the air a genuine "museum smell."

As he walked down the hall to the wide doorway leading into the exhibit he was conscious of a subtle heightening of his melancholy, which the fog had so visibly augmented. Here in this shabby darkness he felt a profound spiritual depression. Without knowing it, he slipped from self-dramatization into reality. His mind craved morbidity, his thoughts were steeped in umber stillness . . . steeped in umber stillness . . . he must remember that, and write it down.

He was, in point of fact, quite properly in the mood for the waxworks exhibit which he now beheld. It was a carnival of the gruesome and the macabre.

Once, in a moment of temporary affluence, Bertrand and a feminine companion had visited the great Madame Tussaud's. His memories of the occasion were vague, and dealt more fully with the charms of the young lady than with the rather inanimate attractions of the statuary. But as he recalled it, the wax figures had been those of historically prominent and journalistically notorious personages; representations of generals and statesmen and movie stars. This had been Bertrand's sole experience in viewing such objects, save for the odious Punch and Judy displays in the traveling carnival companies he visited during his far-off childhood. (He was twenty-three.)

A casual glance served to show that these waxworks were of a vastly different nature.

A long vast chamber stretched before him—a surprisingly large chamber for such an obscure enterprise, he thought. It was low-ceilinged, and the fog outside the narrow windows lent an effective dimness to the already poor lighting-arrangements; so that the atmosphere was one of profound gloom appropriate to the scene.

An army of still white figures paraded in arrested processional against the dingy walls—an army of stiffly-staring corpses—an army of mummified, embalmed, petrified, ossified . . . he ran out of descriptive terminology, and realized guiltily that his words were pitifully inadequate to describe the impressiveness of these silent wax figures. They held an attitude of arrested motion which in turn captured a peculiar feeling of ominous *waiting.* They seemed to have just died; or rather to have been frozen in some airy, invisible ice that was about to melt and release them once again at any moment.

For they were realistic. And the lighting-effects of the room disguised what crudities and blemishes might exist. Bertrand began to walk along the left wall, and gazed intently at each figure or group of figures.

The subject-matter of these exhibits was harrowing to the extreme. Crime was the theme—perverse and dreadful crime.

The monster Landru crept upon his sleeping wife in the night, and see, the maniac Tolours lurks with bloody knife behind the barrels as his tiny son descends the cellar stairs. Three men sit within an open boat, and one is armless, legless, headless, while the others feast.... Gilles de Retz stands before the altar, and his beard is dabbled red as he holds his basin high; the sacrifice lies broken at his feet ... a woman writhes upon the wheel and the sharp-fanged rats race round and round the dungeon floor ... flayed alive is he that hangs upon the gibbet, and giant Dessalines advances with a leaded whip ... the murderer Vardac stands accused while from his suitcase trickles a red stain ... the fat monk Omelée digs within his crypt amidst the barrels of bones.... Here sleeping Evil rises from hidden depths in men's souls and slyly grins.

Bertrand saw and shuddered. There was a disturbingly artful verisimilitude in the depiction of these frights which made him ill at ease. They were so cunningly, so artfully conceived! The details of background and setting seemed minutely authentic, and the figures themselves seemed to be the products of a master craftsmanship. Their simulation of life was startling; their molder had instilled genuine action into pose and posture, so that each pictured movement was actually portrayed. And the heads, with the expressions on the faces, were astonishingly real. They glared and twisted with rage, lust, anger; contorted and blenched with fear, shock, agony. The eyes stared with a more than glassy reality, the hair hung naturally from bearded cheeks, lips opened as though warm with breath.

So they stood, the waxworks figures, each living eternally the supreme moment of the horror which justified their existence as images and damned their souls as living men.

Bertrand saw them all. Little signs proclaimed the characters in each pictured melodrama in suitably grandiloquent style, and cards recited bloody histories of famous misdeeds.

Bertrand read them self-consciously. He knew that what he saw was cheapest theatricalism, sensational yellow-journal stuff at its worst; the type of lurid gore-parading in which the moron-mind delights. But he fancied that there was something rather grand about this whole insane array of melodramatics; they seemed to have a certain *intensity* which ordinary life shuns to express in daily actions. He wondered as he stared whether or not this feeling of intensity was one of the attractions for the ordinary foolish sensation-hunters; whether or not they felt it, and were vaguely envious of its contrast to their sedulously eventless lives. And he almost chuckled when he realized that the pictured scenes were real; that their counterparts had actually existed—moreover, were still existing today, in a hundred hidden places. Yes, murderers and rapists and mad fiends crouched unknown even now, waiting to strike. Some of them would be exposed, others die in secrecy inviolate; but their deeds went on—their gory, melodramatic deeds.

The young poet walked on. He was all alone in this room, and the sight of the blue fog-fingers still clawing at the window-panes encouraged him to take his leisure. He spent much time in noting the perfections of the figures. Gradually he approached the right wall of the hall, which seemed to be given over to the bloody scenes of actual recorded history; the burnings, pillagings, tortures and massacres of olden times. Here too he was forced to concede admiration for the designers of the displays; historical costuming was splendid throughout. There must be many details to this waxwork-making business, he thought, as he examined a particularly noteworthy figure of the Emperor Tiberius Caesar at sport in the torture chamber.

Then he saw her. She was standing statue-still, straight and poised and lovely. She was girl, woman, goddess; imperially slender, with the delicious curves of a succubus fashioned in dreams.

Bertrand's poet-eyes deigned to notice actual physical details, though his bemused brain must translate them anew into elaborate imagery. Thus her splendid auburn hair was a crimson cloud, her smiling, finely-chiseled face a mask of enchantment, her starry blue eyes twin pools in which a soul must drown. Her parted lips were curved as though in voluptuous delight, and from them her tongue protruded like a little red dagger whose stab was joy. She wore a filmy, bejeweled robe of sorts, which only served to accentuate the white beauty of the body it half revealed beneath.

Actually, she was a very pretty red-headed woman, and she

was wax—common, ordinary wax, very much of the sort which had served to fashion the form of Jack the Ripper. Her pose was commonplace, but arresting; she stood tiptoe with outstretched arms that held a silver salver; stood before King Herod on his throne. For she was Salome, wanton of the seven veils, white witch and wooer of all evil.

Bertrand stared into her wicked oval face, the eyes of which seemed to flicker with amusement in returning his gaze. And he thought that she was the most beautiful creature he had ever beheld, and the most dreadful. Her slim hands held a silver platter, and on it rested the severed head . . . the gory, decapitated head of John the Baptist, lying with stony eyes, death-bright in a pool of blood.

Bertrand didn't move. He simply looked at the woman. A queer impulse to address her came over him. She was mocking his goggle-eyed gazings, she thought him rude. Speak, man! He wanted to tell her—that he loved her.

Bertrand realized this with a thrill of pain that was almost horror. He *did* love her, love her wildly beyond all dreams of love. He wanted her—this woman who was only wax. It was torture to look at her, the ache of her beauty was intolerable when he realized that she was unattainable. What irony! To fall in love with a waxwork!—he must be mad.

But how poetic it was, Bertrand pondered. And not so highly original at that.

He'd read of similar cases, seen some claptrap dramatizations of the theme which was as old as Pygmalion and his statue.

Reason wouldn't help him, he realized with a sort of despair. He loved her beauty and her menace, always would. He was that sort of poet.

It was amazing, finally to glance up and see the sun sullenly shining through the windows from which fog had fled. How long had he been gaping here? Bertrand turned away, after one last soul-wrenching look at the object of his adoration.

"I'll come back," he whispered. Then he blushed guiltily to himself and hurried down the hall to the door.

2.

He came back the next day. And the next. He became familiar with the pudgy gray features of the little fat man who seemed to be the sole attendant at the door; grew to know the dusty museum and its contents. He learned that visitors were scarce these days, and discovered late afternoon was the ideal time for his hours of worship.

For worship it was. He would stand silently before the cryptically smiling statue, and stare enraptured into the maddening cruelty of her eyes. Sometimes he would mumble bits of the verse with which he struggled by night; often he would plead mad lover's entreaties meant for waxen ears. But redhaired Salome only stared back at him in return, and regarded his ravings with a set and cryptic smile.

It was odd that he never inquired about the statue or any of the others until the day he spoke with the little fat attendant.

The squat, gray-haired man approached him one day at twilight and entered into conversation, thus ending a revery in a manner which greatly annoyed the love-sick Bertrand.

"Pretty, eh?" said the gray-haired man, in the coarse, vulgar voice such unfeeling dolts habitually possess. "I modeled her from my wife, y'know."

His *wife! His* wife—this shabby little old fat fool? Bertrand felt that he was really going mad, until the next words of his companion dispelled the notion.

"Years ago, of course."

But she was alive—real—alive! His heart leaped.

"Yes. She's dead a long time now, of course."

Dead! Gone; as far away as ever, only this taunting waxen shell remaining. Bertrand must talk to this little fool, draw him out. There was so much he had to know. But in a moment he found that there was no need to "draw out" his companion; loneliness evidently begot garrulity upon the little man's part. He mumbled on in his gruff, crude fashion.

"Clever work, isn't it?" The gray-haired dolt was surveying the wax figure in a manner which Bertrand found peculiarly repulsive. There was in his eyes no adoration for the being represented; only the unfeeling appraisal of a craftsman commenting on his handiwork. He was admiring the wax, not the woman.

"My best," mused the little man.

And to think that he had once possessed *her!* . . . Bertrand was sickened dreadfully at the fellow's callousness. But the man did not seem to notice. He kept glancing from the statue to Bertrand and back again. Meanwhile keeping up a steady stream of comment and information.

*Monsieur* must be interested in the museum, eh? He seemed to be a frequent visitor. Good work, wasn't it? He, Pierre Jacquelin, had done it all. Yes, he had learned the waxworks business well in the past eight years. It cost money to hire assistants; so save for occasional group-pieces, Jacquelin had fashioned all the figures himself. People had done him the honor of favorably comparing his work to Tussaud's. No doubt he could get a place on the staff there, but he preferred to run a quiet business of his own. Besides, there was less notoriety. But the figures were good, weren't they? That's where his medical knowledge served him. Yes, it had been Doctor Jacquelin in the old days.

*Monsieur* admired his wife, didn't he? Well, that was not strange—there had been others. They too came regularly. No— no need to take offense. It would be silly to be jealous of a wax image. But it was peculiar the way men still came; some of them not even knowing about the crime.

The crime?

Something in the little man's gray face as he mentioned it caused Bertrand to perk up his ears, to ask questions. The old fellow showed no hesitation in answering.

"Can it be that you do not know?" he said. "Ah well, time passes and one forgets the newspapers. It was not a pleasant thing—I wanted to be alone then, and the notoriety caused me to abandon practice. That is how I began here; to get away from it all. She caused it."

He pointed at the statue.

"The Jacquelin case, they called it—because of my wife, you know. I knew nothing until the trial. She was young, alone in Paris when I married her. I knew nothing of her past. I had my practice,

I was busy, away a great deal of the time. I never suspected. She was pathological, *Monsieur.* I had suspected certain things from her conduct, but I loved her and never guessed.

"I brought a patient to the house—an old man. He was quite ill, and she nursed him very devotedly. One night I came in quite late and found him dead. She had cut his throat with a surgical knife—I came upon her silently, you understand—and she was attempting to go further.

"The police took her away. At the trial it all came out; about the young fellow at Brest she had done in, and the two husbands she had disposed of at Lyons and Liège. And she confessed to other crimes; five in all. Decapitation.

"Oh, I was broken up over it, I can tell you! That was years ago, and I was younger then. I loved her, and when she admitted that she had planned to finish me off next I felt—well, never mind. She had been a good wife, you see, quiet and gentle and loving. You can see for yourself how beautiful she was. And to discover that she was mad! A murderess like that . . . it was terrible.

"I did my best. I still wanted her, after all that. It is hard to explain. We tried to plead insanity. But she was convicted, and they sent her to the guillotine."

How badly he tells the story! thought Bertrand. Material for tragedy here, and he bungles it into a farce! When will Life live up to Art?

"My medical practice was ruined, of course. The papers, the publicity, that was fatal. I had lost everything. Then I began this. I'd made plaster busts, medical figures, to earn a little extra through the years. So I took my savings and began the museum. All these misfortunes had upset me, I can tell you, and I was in a bad way when I started. I had become interested in crime, for obvious reasons. That is why I specialized in this sort of thing."

The little man smiled a bit tolerantly, as though in memory of things long dead and forgotten—his emotions. He tapped Bertrand on the chest with a jollity which the latter found hideous.

"What I did was a capital joke, eh? I got permission from the authorities to go down to the morgue. The execution had been delayed, and my business here was well started; I had learned my technique. So I went down to the morgue after the guillotining, understand, and made a model of my wife. From life—or death, rather. Yes, I made the model, and it's a grand joke. She had beheaded, and now she was beheaded. So why not make her Salome? John the Baptist was beheaded, too, wasn't he? Quite a jest!"

The little man's face fell a bit, and his pale gray eyes grew bright. "Perhaps it wasn't such a joke, *Monsieur*. To tell the truth, at the time I did it for revenge. I hated her for the way she had broken my life; hated her because I still loved her in spite of what she had done. And there was more irony than humor in my doings. I wanted her in wax, to stand here and remind me of my life; my love and her crime.

"But that was years ago. The world has forgotten, and I have, too. Now she is just a beautiful figure—my best figure.

"Somehow I have never again approached the art; and I think you will agree with me that it is art. I have never achieved such perfection, though I've learned more mastery with the years. Men come in and stare at her, you know; the way you do. I don't believe many of them know the story, but if they did, they would still come. You will come again, won't you—even though you know?"

Bertrand nodded bruskly as he turned and hurried away. He was playing the fool, rushing out like a child. This he knew, and he cursed himself under his breath even as he ran from the museum and the hateful little old man.

He was a fool. His head throbbed. Why did he hate the man—her husband? Why did he hate her because she had once lived, and killed? If the story were true—and it was. He remembered something of the Jacquelin case; vague headlines dimmed by the passage of years. He'd probably shuddered over the penny-dreadful newspaper versions as a boy. Why did he feel as though he were in torment? A wax statue of a dead murderess, made by her stupid, insensate brute of a husband. Other men came and stared—he hated them, too.

He was losing his mind. This was worse than silly, it was insane. He must never go back there; must forget all about the dead, and the lost that could never be his. Her husband had forgotten, the world had not remembered. Yes. He had made his decision. Never again. . . .

He was very glad that the place was deserted the next day as he prayed before the silent, red-haired beauty of Salome.

3.

A few days later, Colonel Bertroux came to his lodging. An insufferable boor, the colonel; a close friend of his family—a retired officer and a born meddler. It did not take Bertrand long to discover that his worried parents had sent the colonel down to "reason" with him.

It was the sort of thing they would do, and the sort of thing a pompous ass like the old colonel would enjoy doing. He was brusk, dignified, pedantic. He called Bertrand "my dear boy," and wasted no time in coming to the point. He wanted Bertrand to give up his "foolishness" and return home to settle down. The family butcher shop—he belonged there, not in a Paris attic. No, the colonel was not interested in his "poetry scribbling." He came to "reason" with Bertrand.

And more of the same thing, until Bertrand was half frantic with exasperation. He could not insult the old dodderer, try as he may. The man was too stupid to understand his satirical deprecations. He followed Bertrand about the streets when he ate, and took it for granted that he was invited. He "put up" at a near-by hostelry and spent his first night in conversation. He was absurdly confident that "the dear boy" would heed his wisdom.

Bertrand gave up after that evening. The colonel put in his appearance again at noon, just as Bertrand was about to leave for the museum. Despite pointed hints, Colonel Bertroux would be only too glad to accompany him to the waxworks. He did.

Once inside the place, Bertrand sank into the strange mood of mysterious excitement he had now learned to expect—no, to hunger for. The colonel's asinine commentaries on the criminal displays he was able to ignore. His reveries drowned out the conversational background.

They approached *her*. Bertrand said nothing—stood silent on the spot, though his eyes cried out. He gazed, devoured. She mocked. Silently they duelled, as minutes fled down the path of eternity.

Abruptly, Bertrand jerked back to consciousness, blinking like a sleeper just awakened from an enthralling and ecstatic dream. Then he stared.

The colonel was still beside him, and he was gaping at the statue of Salome with utter bemusement. On his face was a look of wonder so alien and somehow *youthful* that Bertrand was amazed. The man was fascinated—as fascinated as he was!

The colonel? It was impossible! He couldn't have—not he. But he had. He was. He felt it, loved her too!

Bertrand wanted to laugh, at first. But as he looked into that utterly absorbed old face once again he felt that tears might be more appropriate. He understood. There was something about this woman that called forth the dreams buried in the soul of every man, old or young. She was so gorgeously aloof, so wickedly wanton.

Bertrand glanced again at her evil tenderness, noted the shapely grace with which she stood holding that horrid head.

That horrid head—it was different, today. Not the black-haired, blue-eyed, glassy-staring head he had seen on previous visits. What was wrong?

A touch on his shoulder. The little gray-haired owner of the waxworks, horribly solicitous.

"Noticed it, eh?" he mumbled. "Deplorable accident; the old head was accidentally broken. One of her—her gentlemen friends tried to poke at it with an umbrella, and it fell. I substituted this, while repairing the original. But it does detract."

Colonel Bertroux had glanced up from his shattered reveries. The little gray-haired man fawned on him.

"Pretty, eh?" he began. "I modeled her from my wife, y'know."

And he proceeded to tell the whole grim story, just as Bertrand had it from him a week before. He told it just as badly, and in practically the same words.

Bertrand watched the sick-hurt look on the colonel's face, and wondered with a start if he had not appeared much the same way when he listened for the first time.

In curious parallel to his own behavior, it was the colonel who turned on his heel and walked away at the conclusion of the narrative. Bertrand followed, feeling the eyes of the little gray man appraising their departing backs in a quizzical fashion.

They reached the street and walked in silence. The colonel's face still wore that dazed expression. At the door of his lodging, the colonel turned to him. His voice was curiously hushed.

"I—I think I'm beginning to understand, my boy. I'll not trouble you again. I'm going back."

He marched up the street, shoulders strangely erect, leaving Bertrand to ponder.

Not a word about the waxworks incident. Nothing! But he loved her too. Strange—the whole affair was strange. Was the colonel going away or *fleeing?*

The little man had retold his story with such curious readiness. It was almost as though he had rehearsed it. Could it be that the entire business was a hoax of some sort? Perhaps it was all a fabrication, a clever ruse on the part of the museum-keeper.

Yes, that must be the explanation. Some artist had sold him the wax figure; he noted that its realistic beauty attracted lonely men, and concocted the story of a notorious murderess to fit the statue's history. The case might be real enough, but the little man did not look as though he had ever been the husband of a murderess. Not *her* husband. The story was just bait, a lure to keep the men coming, keep their money rolling in. With a start, Bertrand computed the amount in francs he had spent visiting the museum these past weeks. It was considerable. Clever schemer!

Still, the real attraction lay in the statue itself. The figure was so beautiful, so *alive* in its loveliness, through which there breathed a sort of alluring wickedness. Salome was a red witch, and there was a mystery in her which Bertrand felt he was soon to penetrate. He had to understand that smile and its spell over him.

So thinking, he retired. And the next few days he wrote. He started an epic poem of surprising promise, and labored without pause. He was thankful the colonel had left; grateful to *her* for helping. Perhaps she did understand; perhaps she was real; mayhap she heard his wild mutterings in the night, his lonely entreaties cast up to the stars. Perchance in some far-off poet's Avalon she waited, or in some flaming poet's Hell. He would find her. . . .

He told her that the next day when he thanked her for removing Colonel Bertroux. He was going to recite to her a stanza of his sonnet when he became aware that the eyes of the museum keeper rested on him from a distance down the hall.

He ceased his mutterings, crimson with shame. Spying on him? How often had he gloated over the anguish of the poor wretches enmeshed in her beauty? Withered little beast!

Bertrand tried to look away. He stared at the new head of John the Baptist. Substitute, eh? He wondered under what circumstances the original had been cracked. Some fool with an umbrella, the little man had said. Trying to touch her—as though such a desire were granted a mere mortal! This substitute head was fine, though; as realistic as the first. The closed eyes of the blond young man lent a rather morbid note lacking in the pallid stare of the other. Still, it was not exactly John the Baptist. Hm.

The little man was still staring. Bertrand cursed under his breath and turned away. No more peace today. He hurried down the hall, trying to appear oblivious. As he neared the door he bent his head and sought to avoid the stare of the keeper. In doing so he almost ran into the oncoming figure of a visitor. He muttered a hasty "Your pardon, please" and left. Turning back he gazed with a shock at the retreating back of the man he had jostled.

Was he mad, or did he perceive the shoulders of Colonel Bertroux?

But Bertroux had left—or had he? Was he lured back to worship in privacy, as Bertrand worshiped; as others did? Would the little old man stare at him? Had Salome ensnared another?

Bertrand wondered. The next few days he came at odd hours, hoping to encounter the colonel. He was interested. He wanted to question the older man; seek to learn if he too were affected by this puzzling infatuation for a waxen image.

Bertrand could have questioned the little gray museum keeper concerning his friend, but he felt a vague dislike for the fellow which restrained him. If the keeper's story were a hoax he hated the imposture; if true, he could not forgive him for having known, for having embraced a beauty Bertrand would have given his life to possess.

The poet left the museum in a state of mental anguish. He hated the place, hated its keeper; hated *her* because his love chained him. Must he come to this dark old dungeon forever, mutely suffering away his life for a glimpse of beauty forever denied him? Must he walk past mocking murderers in gloom to gaze into the eyes of his waxen tormentress? How long? The mystery was unseating his reason. How long?

4.

Wearily he climbed the steps to his room. His key turned the lock, his door opened on lighted brilliance, and he stepped forward in surprise to confront—Colonel Bertroux.

The old man was seated in the easy-chair, his elbows resting on the table as he faced the poet.

"Pardon this intrusion, boy," said the colonel. "I used a skeleton key to enter. I could have waited outside for you, but I prefer remaining some place where I am locked in."

His voice was so grave and his face so serious as he spoke these last words that Bertrand accepted their import without questioning.

He framed a reply; he wanted to inquire why Bertroux had not left town; if it had indeed been he whom the poet had seen leaving the museum a few hours previous. But the older man lifted a hand in a tired gesture and mentioned Bertrand to a seat on the couch. His dim blue eyes stared out from a face lined with exhaustion.

"Let me explain this visit," he began. "But first, a few questions. I beg of you to answer these truthfully, my boy. Much depends on your veracity, as you shall learn."

Bertrand nodded, impressed by the utter gravity of his visitor.

"First," said the colonel, "I want to know just how long you have been visiting that wax museum."

"About a month. In fact, a month ago tomorrow I made my initial visit."

"And just how did you come to go there, of all places?"

Bertrand explained the circumstances of the fog, the chance glimpse of the sign with its hint of shelter. The colonel listened intently.

"Did the keeper speak to you during that first visit?" he asked.

"No."

The old man started, blinked in puzzlement. He mumbled to himself. "Strange ... eliminates hypnosis ... latent force in the statue ... never took that rot about demonology seriously."

He checked himself hastily, and his glance met Bertrand's once again. He spoke very slowly.

"Then it was—*she*—who drew you back?"

There was that in his voice which caused Bertrand to affirm the truth; caused him to pour out his story in a ceaseless rush of words untouched by any attempt at concealment or adornment of the queer tale. At its conclusion the old man sighed, heavily. He stared at the floor for a long time.

"I thought as much, my boy," Colonel Bertroux said. "Your family sent me down suspecting that something—or rather, someone, was holding you here. I had guessed that it was a woman, but I never dreamed that she was a woman of wax. But when you took me to the museum and I saw how you gazed at that statue, I knew. After looking at the image myself, I knew and understood far more. And then I heard the tale of the museum keeper. It started me thinking—if think I could, and with a mind bemused by that damnable beauty of the cursed figure.

"At first, when I bid you good-bye, I intended to go. Not so much for your sake, but for my own. Yes, I shall admit it frankly, I feared for myself. Bertrand, you understand the power that queer image holds over you, and other men as well, if the keeper is to be believed. That power it exercised upon me. I was frightened by the feeling I, an old man long forsaken by thoughts of love, experienced on seeing that red witch."

Bertrand stared at the colonel, who continued without heed.

"But I did not go back. The next day I returned to the museum in the morning, to gaze as you gazed, alone. And after an hour before that strange simulacrum, I left in a daze of wonder commingled with practical alarm. Whatever power that statue possessed, it was not good, or right, or wholly fashioned by sanity.

"I acted on impulse. I recalled the story of the museum keeper, this man Jacquelin. I went down to the newspaper offices to search the files. At last I found the case.

"Jacquelin had stated that the affair occurred many years ago, but he had not said just how many. My dear boy, that case was closed *over thirty years ago!*"

Bertrand's gasp was cut short as Bertroux rushed on.

"It was true, all true. There was a murder, and the wife of Doctor Jacquelin was convicted of it. It did come out that she had perpetrated five similar crimes under various names, and the journals of the day made capital out of certain testimony that was formally disbarred. This testimony spoke of wizardry, and hinted that Madame Jacqueline was a witch, whose mad butcherings were actuated by a sort of sacrificial frenzy. The cult of the ancient goddess Hecate was mentioned, and the prosecution hinted that the red-headed woman was a priestess of some sort whose deeds constituted a monstrous worship. This offering of male blood in honor of a half-forgotten pagan deity was, naturally, disallowed as testimony; but there was enough evidence to convict the woman of actual killings.

"It was fact, remember. And I uncovered things in the old papers of which this Jacquelin did not speak. The witchcraft theory was not formally recognized, but it got the doctor himself banned from the practice of medicine. It was more than substantiated that he was beginning to indulge in certain practices, encouraged by his wife; little pilferings of blood and flesh and sometimes vital organs from corpses in the morgues. That seems to be the real reason why he abandoned his practice after the trial and execution.

"The narrative about obtaining his wife's body from the morgue for sculpturing purposes is not mentioned, but there *is* an item about the body being *stolen*. And Jacquelin left Paris after the execution, thirty-seven years ago!"

The colonel's voice was harsh.

"You can imagine what this discovery did to me. I searched through year after year in the files, trying to trace the path of the man. Never did I find the name of Jacquelin mentioned. But occasionally little disturbing items about traveling waxworks exhibits cropped up. There was a wagon show run under the name of *Pallidi* which toured the Basque provinces in 1916, and after it left one town the bodies of two young men were discovered buried beneath the lot where the exhibition tent had been pitched. They were headless.

"A *George Balto* operated for a time in Antwerp under almost identical conditions about '24. He was called in to testify concerning the case of a mutilated body found in the streets outside his museum one morning, but was exonerated. There are other couplings of disappearance connected with waxworks, but the names and dates vary. In two of the later ones, however, the press reports distinctly describe a 'short, gray-haired proprietor.'

"What does it all mean? I wondered. My first impulse was to communicate with the *Sureté*, but a pause convinced me that wild theories do not concern the police. There was much to be learned. The real mystery was just why men continue to stare at that statue. What is its power? I cast about for an explanation; for a time I guessed that the proprietor might hypnotize his solitary male visitors, using the statue as a medium. But why? For what purpose? And neither you nor myself was so hypnotized. No, there's something about that image alone; some secret power connected with it that smacks of—I must admit it—sorcery. She's like one of those ancient lamias one reads about in fairytales. One can't escape her.

"I couldn't. After leaving the newspaper offices that afternoon I went back. I told myself that I was going to interview the little gray man, clear up the mystery. But in my heart I knew better. I brushed him aside as I entered the place and sought the statue. Once again I stared into her face and that terrible fascination of evil beauty flooded me. I tried to read her secret but she read mine. I felt that she knew my emotion toward her, and that she rejoiced and exercised her cold power to rule my mind.

"I left in a daze. That evening at the hotel, while I tried to reason things out, to plan a course of action, I felt a strange urge to go back. It cut across my thoughts, and before I knew it, I was on the street, walking toward the museum. It was dark, and I returned home. The longing persisted. Before I could sleep I was forced to bolt my door."

The colonel turned a sober face to Bertrand as he whispered.

"You, my friend, went to her willingly every day. Your torment at her aloofness was slight compared to mine, which fought against her enchantment. Because I would not go willingly she compelled. Her anguishing memory haunted me. This morning, as I started here to see you, she forced my footsteps to the museum. That's why men go there—if willing, like you, they worship unbidden. If unwilling, she commands and they come. I went today. When you came I was ashamed and left. Then I came here, to wait, and opened your door so that I might lock it from the inside and fight to keep from leaving until I could see you. I had to tell you this so that we might act together."

"What do you propose?" Bertrand asked. It was strange how earnestly he believed the other's story; he could realize only too easily that his beloved was evil without ceasing to adore her. He knew that he must fight against her siren magic even while his heart cried out to her. The colonel, he understood, shared his feelings. Therefore he asked eagerly.

"We will go to the museum tomorrow," the colonel said. "Together we will be strong enough to fight against that power, suggestion—whatever it is. We can speak frankly to Jacquelin, hear him out. If he refuses to talk, we shall go to the police. I am convinced that there is something unnatural about all this; murder, hypnotism, magic, or just plain imagination, we must get to the bottom of it quickly. I fear for you, and for myself. That cursed statue is chaining me to the spot, and always it seeks to draw me back. Let us clear up this affair tomorrow, before it is too late."

"Yes," Bertrand agreed, dully.

"Good. I will come for you about one in the afternoon. You will be ready?"

Bowing at Bertrand's nod of assent, the colonel withdrew.

5.

The poet worked all that evening on his poem; first to forget the strange tale of Bertroux, and second because he felt that he could not rest until he had completed his epic. In the back of his mind was a puzzling suspicion that he must work fast, that matters were coming to a head in such a fashion as to demand haste.

He was exhausted by daybreak, and somehow thankful that his tired sleep would be dreamless. He wanted to be free of that flame-haired image that haunted him by night, free to forget his terrible bondage to a wax woman.

He slept deeply as the sun crept from window to window of his attic room. When he arose it was with the prescience that noontide had passed, though by this time the sunlight had gradually faded into a mist of yellow fog that grew ever thicker beyond the window-panes.

Glancing at his watch he was startled to note that it was already long past three o'clock.

Where was the colonel? Bertrand was confident that his *concierge* would have awakened him with racket to spare should he have a daytime visitor. No, the colonel had not come. And that meant only one thing. He had been called, lured. Bertrand jumped up, raced to the door.

Hastily he crammed the finished manuscript of his poem into the ulster he donned against the encroaching fog. He took the stairs hastily, then rushed out along the dismal, fog-drowned streets.

This was like that first day, a month ago. And still he was running to the museum to keep his inevitable tryst with torment.

The very moment seemed to make him forgetful of his real errand, the finding of the colonel. Instead he could think only of *her* as he rushed through the gray fog to the gray room, the gray man, and the scarlet glory of her hair. . . .

The building loomed out of the mounting mists ahead. He hurried down the stairs, entered. The place was deserted, the little doorkeeper gone. A strange surmise rose in Bertrand's heart, but it receded before an irresistible urge to commune once more with Salome.

The air was tense with a feeling of impending fury, as though the crystallization of some cosmic dread was near. The murderers leered waxenly within as he paced down the hall. No Bertroux.

Deserted in the darkness, he stood alone before her. Never had she seemed so radiant as today. In the half-light she wavered, slitted eyes shining with wild invitation to forbidden rhapsodies. Her lips hungered.

Bertrand leaned forward, staring into that inscrutable, age-lessly evil face. Something about her knowing smile of appease-ment caused him to glance down—to glance at the silver salver that held the head of John the Baptist. Staring, still, wide-eyed it gaped.

The head of *Colonel Bertroux!*

## 6.

Then he knew as he glanced at the mocking smile of anguish, glanced at the blood flooding forth from the slashed neck. *Realistic art!* The first head a month ago, the second last week, and now the colonel, who felt the flooding desire to return. Young men forever coming to worship her beauty—newspaper accounts of decapitation tragedies. The beauty of a murderess unveiled in a deserted wax museum—she who had beheaded her lovers for witchery. *How often was that head changed?*

The little gray man crouched at his back, his eyes filled with leaden fire. His hand held a surgeon's knife. He smiled—at *her.* And he mumbled.

"Why not? You love her. I love her. She was not like a mortal woman—she was a witch. Yes, she killed when she lived, she liked the blood of men and the sight of eyes forever fixed in wor-ship of her beauty. We worshipped together her mistress Hecate. Then they guillotined her. And so—I stole the body to model this image. I became her priest. Men come and they desire her, and to them I bring the gift I bring to you. Because they love her, I give them what I can—the chance to rest their tortured heads within her hands. Wax hands, perhaps, but her spirit is near. They all feel her spirit, and that is why they come and adore. Her spirit talks to me at night and asks me to bring new lovers. We have traveled together many years, she and I, and now we have returned to Paris for new adorers. They must lie in her hands, bleeding and bright, and stare their stare of love forever into her face. When she tires, I give her a new admirer.

"The colonel came this morning, and when I told him that which I tell you, he consented. They all do. And you shall consent, my friend; I know you will. Think of it; to lie within her pale white hands and stare forever; to die with the benediction of her beauty in your eyes! You will make the sacrifice, won't you? No one will know; they never suspect. You will play John the Baptist? You want me to, now, don't you? You want me to—"

Hypnosis. Hypnosis at the last. Bertrand tried to move as the voice droned, the eyes stared in glorious pleading from above.

And the cold edge of the knife caressed his throat. The blade began to bite. He heard words through the gray fog, through the scarlet fog as he stared into *her* face. She was a witch, a Medusa— to lie within her arms and worship as others had worshipped! A poet's death? In a moment his head would be resting on the salver and he could see her as he sank into the dark. He could never possess her—why live on? Why not die and know her radiance forever? It was easy, her husband knew and he was being kind to Bertrand. Kind. The knife bit.

Bertrand's hand went up. A sudden horror flickered in his soul. He grappled with the screaming little madman and the blade clattered to the floor. They fell in a lashing embrace, as Bertrand tore at the pudgy gray face, clawed deeply in the blazing eyes.

Something deep within him had risen in resurrection. Youth— sanity—the will to live. His fingers pressed as he shoved the gray man's head against the floor. He squeezed, throttled, until time dissolved in the welter of red anger. When his hands finally loosened, the little maniac lay quite still and dead.

Bertrand rose and faced his impassive goddess. Her smile was unchanged. He looked again into her infernal beauty and his soul wavered once more. Then his hands fumbled at the breast of his ulster and he gained courage.

He drew forth the crumpled manuscript that lay there—his finished poem to Salome.

He found matches.

He lit the manuscript. It flamed as he held it forth, held it to her flaming hair. Fire mingled with fire as she continued to stare in the way Bertrand could not yet understand, the terrible way that enchanted him and all men and lured them to doom.

Impulse seized him even at the last. He took Salome in his arms—took her in his arms as she burned, writhing and moving with fiery life. He held her close for a moment as the glowing flames spread, then eased her again to the stand. She was burning horribly fast.

Witches must burn. . . .

And like a witch, her dying features changed. They melted into a hideous mass—her face became a gargoyle horror, a melting, shapeless yellow blob from which two glassy eyes fell like blue tears. Her body wiggled in agony as wax limbs sloughed. She was real then—real, and tortured. Tortured, just as Bertrand was as he beheld her waxen agonies. Tortured by fire; but a fire that purified.

Then it was all over. Bertrand stared at the man on the floor; still and dead he lay as the fire began creeping redly against the fog. It would soon blot the museum out forever; blot out the horror that lured men to a tragic re-enactment of an ancient crime. Fire purified.

Bertrand stared again at the little pile of melted yellow liquid that lay bubbling and seething as though in some hasty process of putrefaction. He stared, and then he prayed that the fire would mount swiftly. For now, with a gasp of horror, he understood, knew the mystery of her allure which had eluded him.

The maniac murderer on the floor—he had fashioned the statue from the morgue-procured body of his wife. This he had told Bertrand. But now Bertrand saw more; knew and guessed the secret of the statue's evil power. There is a miasma of evil about the dead body of a witch. . . .

Bertrand turned and ran sobbing from the redly ravaged room, ran sobbing from the sight of that yellow, bubbling pile of melted wax from which protruded the *charred, bony skeleton of a woman that had served as the statue's frame.*

# The Feast in the Abbey

A CLAP of thunder in the sullen west heralded the approach of night and storm together, and the sky deepened to a sorcerous black. Rain fell, the wind droned dolefully, and the forest pathway through which I rode became a muddy, treacherous bog that threatened momentarily to ensnare both my steed and myself in its unwelcome embrace. A journey under such conditions is most inauspicious; in consequence I was greatly heartened when shortly through the storm-tossed branches I discerned a flicker of hospitable light glimmering through mists of rain.

Five minutes later I drew rein before the massive doors of a goodly-sized, venerable building of gray, moss-covered stone, which, from its extreme size and sanctified aspect, I rightly took to be a monastery. Even as I gazed thus perfunctorily upon it, I could see that it was a place of some importance, for it loomed most imposingly above the crumbled foundations of many smaller buildings which had evidently once surrounded it.

The force of the elements, however, was such as to preclude all further inspection or speculation, and I was only too pleased when, in reply to my continued knocking, the great oaken door was thrown open and I stood face to face with a cowled man who courteously ushered me past the rain-swept portals into a well-lighted and spacious hallway.

My benefactor was short and fat, garbed in voluminous gabardine, and from his ruddy, beaming aspect, seemed a very pleasant and affable host. He introduced himself as the abbot Henricus, head of the monkish fraternity in whose headquarters I now found myself, and begged me to accept the hospitality of the brethren until the inclemencies of the weather had somewhat abated.

In reply I informed him of my name and station, and told him that I was journeying to keep tryst with my brother in Vironne, beyond the forest, but had been arrested in my journey by the storm.

These civilities having been concluded, he ushered me past the paneled ante-chamber to the foot of a great staircase set in stone, hewn out of the very wall itself. Here he called out sharply in an uncomprehended tongue, and in a moment I was startled by the sudden appearance of two blackamoors, who seemed to have materialized out of nowhere, so swiftly silent had been their coming. Their stern ebony faces, kinky hair and rolling eyes, set off by a most outlandish garb—great, baggy trousers of red velvet and waists of cloth-of-gold, in Eastern fashion—intrigued me greatly, though they seemed curiously out of place in a Christian monastery.

The abbot Henricus addressed them now in fluent Latin, bidding one to go without and care for my horse, and ordering the other to show me to an apartment above, where, he informed me, I could change my rain-bedraggled garments for a more suitable raiment, while awaiting the evening meal.

I thanked my courteous host and followed the silent black automaton up the great stone staircase. The flickering torch of the giant servitor cast arabesque shadows upon bare stone walls of great age and advanced decrepitude; clearly the structure was very old. Indeed, the massive walls that rose outside must have been constructed in bygone day, for the other buildings that presumably were contemporaneously erected beside this had long since fallen into irremediable, unrecognizable decay.

Upon reaching the landing, my guide led me along a richly carpeted expanse of tessellated floor, between lofty walls tapestried and bedizened with draperies of black. Such velvet finery was most unseemly for a place of worship, to my mind.

Nor was my opinion shaken by the sight of the chamber which was indicated as my own. It was fully as large as my father's study at Nimes—its walls hung in Spanish velvets of maroon, of an elegance surpassed only by their bad taste in such a place. There was a bed such as would grace the palace of a king; furniture and other appurtenances were of truly regal magnificence. The blackamoor lighted a dozen mammoth candles in the silver candelabra that stood about the room, and then bowed and withdrew.

Upon inspecting the bed I found thereupon the garments the abbot had designated for my use during the evening meal. These consisted of a suit of black velveteen with satin breeches and hose of a corresponding hue, and a sable surplice. Upon doffing my travel-worn apparel I found that they fitted perfectly, albeit most somberly.

During this time I engaged myself in observing the room more closely. I wondered greatly at the lavishness, display and ostentation, and more greatly still at the complete absence of any religious paraphernalia—not even a simple crucifix was visible. Surely this order must be a rich and powerful one; albeit a trifle worldly; perchance akin to those societies of Malta and Cyprus whose licentiousness and extravagance is the scandal of the world.

As I thus mused there fell upon my ears the sounds of sonorous chanting that swelled symphonically from somewhere far below. Its measured cadence rose and fell solemnly as if it were borne from a distance incredible to human ears. It was subtly disturbing; I could distinguish neither words nor phrases that I knew, but the potent rhythm bewildered me. It welled, a malefic rune, fraught with insidious, strange suggestion. Abruptly it ceased, and I breathed unconsciously a sigh of relief. But not an instant during the remainder of my sojourn was I wholly free from the spark of unease generated by the far-distant sound of that nameless, measured chanting from below.

2.

Never have I eaten a stranger meal than that which I partook of at the monastery of the abbot Henricus. The banquet hall was a triumph of ostentatious adornment. The meal took place in a vast chamber whose lofty eminence rose the entire height of the building to the arched and vaulted roof. The walls were hung with tapestries of purple and blood-royal, emblazoned with devices and escutcheons of noble, albeit to me unknown, significance. The banquet table itself extended the length of the chamber—at one end unto the double doors through which I had entered from the stairs; the other end was beneath a hanging balcony under which was the scullery entrance. About this vast festal board were seated some two-score churchmen in cowls and gabardines of black, who were already eagerly assailing the multitudinous array of foodstuffs with which the table was weighted. They scarcely ceased their gorging to nod a greeting when the abbot and I entered to take our place at the head of table, but continued to devour rapaciously the wonderful array of victuals set before them, accomplishing this task in a most unseemly fashion. The abbot neither paused to motion me to my seat nor to intone a blessing, but immediately followed the example of his flock and proceeded directly to stuff his belly with choice titbits before my astounded eyes. It was certain that these Flemish barbarians were far from fastidious in their table habits. The meal was accompanied by uncouth noises from the mouths of the feasters; the food was taken up in fingers and the untasted remains cast upon the floor; the common decencies were often ignored. For a moment I was dumbfounded, but natural politeness came to my rescue, so that I fell to without further ado.

Half a dozen of the black servants glided silently about the board, replenishing the dishes or bearing platters filled with new and still more exotic viands. My eyes beheld marvels of cuisine upon golden platters—verily, but pearls were cast before swine! For these cowled and hooded brethren, monks though they were, behaved like abominable boors. They wallowed in every kind of fruit—great luscious cherries, honeyed melons, pomegranates and grapes, huge plums, exotic apricots, rare figs and dates. There were huge cheeses, fragrant and mellow; tempting soups; raisins, nuts, vegetables, and great smoking trays of fish, all served with ales and cordials that were as potent as the nectar of nepenthe.

During the meal we were regaled with music from unseen lutes, wafted from the balconies above; music that triumphantly swelled in an ultimate crescendo as six servitors marched solemnly in, bearing an enormous platter of massy, beaten gold, in which reposed a single haunch of some smoking meat, garnished with and redolent of aromatic spices. In profound silence they advanced and set down their burden in the center of the board, clearing away the giant candelabra and smaller dishes. Then the abbot rose, knife in hand, and carved the roast, the while muttering a sonorous invocation in an alien tongue. Slices of meat were apportioned to the monks of the assemblage on silver plates. A marked and definite interest was apparent in this ceremony; only politeness restrained me from questioning the abbot as to the significance of the company's behavior. I ate a portion of my meat and said nothing.

To find such barbaric dalliance and kingly pomp in a monastic order was indeed curious, but my curiosity was regrettably dulled by copious imbibing of the potent wines set before me at the table, in beaker, bumper, flask, flagon, and bejeweled cup. There were vintages of every age and distillation; curious fragrant potions of marvelous headiness and giddy sweetness that affected me strangely.

The meat was peculiarly rich and sweet. I washed it down with great drafts from the wine-vessels that were now freely circulating about the table. The music ceased and the candle-glow dimmed imperceptibly into softer luminance. The storm still crashed against the walls without. The liquor sent fire through my veins, and queer fancies ran riot through my addled head.

I sat almost stupefied when, the company's trenchermannish appetites being at last satisfied, they proceeded, under influence of the wine, to break the silence observed during the meal by bursting into the chorus of a ribald song. Their mirth grew, and broad jests and tales were told, adding to the merriment. Lean faces were convulsed in lascivious laughter, fat paunches quivered with jollity. Some gave way to unseemly noise and gross gesture, and several collapsed beneath the table and were carried out by the silent blacks. I could not help but contrast the scene with that in which I would have figured had I reached Vironne to take my meal at the board of my brother, the good curé. There would be no such noisome ribaldry there; I wondered vaguely if he was aware of this monastic order so close to his quiet parish.

Then, abruptly, my thoughts returned to the company before me. The mirth and song had given place to less savory things as the candles dimmed and deepening shadows wove their webs of darkness about the banquet board. Talk turned to vaguely alarming channels, and cowled faces took on a sinister aspect in the wan and flickering light. As I gazed bemused about the board, I was struck by the peculiar pallor of the assembled faces; they shone whitely in the dying light as with a distorted mockery of death. Even the atmosphere of the room seemed changed; the rustling draperies seemed moved by unseen hands; shadows marched along the walls; hobgoblin shapes pranced in weird processional over the groined arches of the ceiling. The festal board looked bare and denuded—dregs of wine besmirched the linen; half-eaten viands covered the table's expanse; the gnawed bones on the plates seemed grim reminders of mortal fate.

The conversation was ill-suited to further my peace of mind— it was far from the pious exhortations expected of such a company. Talk turned to ghosts and enchantments; old tales were told and infused with newer horror; legends recounted in broken whispers; hints of eldritch potency passed from wine-smeared lips in tones sepulchrally muted.

I sat somnolent no longer; I was nervous with an increasing apprehension greater than I had ever known. It was almost as if I *knew* what was about to happen when at last, with a curious smile, the abbot began his tale and the monkish presences hushed their whispers and turned in their places to listen.

At the same time a black entered and deposited a small covered platter before his master, who regarded the dish for a moment before continuing his introductory remarks.

It was fortunate (he began, addressing me) that I had ventured here to stay the evening, for there had been other travelers whose nocturnal sojournings in these woods had not reached so fortunate a termination. There was, for example, the legendary "Devil's Monastery." (Here he paused and coughed abstractedly before continuing.)

According to the accepted folk-lore of the region, this curious place of which he spoke was an abandoned priory, deep in the heart of the woods, in which dwelt a strange company of the Undead, devoted to the service of Asmodeus. Often, upon the coming of darkness, the old ruins took on a preternatural semblance of their vanished glory, and the old walls were reconstructed by demon artistry to beguile the passing traveler. It was indeed fortunate that my brother had not sought me in the woods upon a night like this, for he might have blundered upon this accursed place and been bewitched into entrance; whereupon, according to the ancient chronicles, he would be seized, and his body devoured in triumph by the ghoulish acolytes that they might preserve their unnatural lives with mortal sustenance.

All this was recounted in a whisper of unspeakable dread, as if it were somehow meant to convey a message to my bewildered senses. It did. As I gazed into the leering faces all about me I realized the import of those jesting words, the ghastly mockery that lay behind the abbot's bland and cryptic smile.

The Devil's Monastery ... subterrene chanting of the rites to Lucifer ... blasphemous magnificence, but never the sign of the cross ... an abandoned priory in the deep woods ... wolfish faces glaring into my own. ...

Then, three things happened simultaneously. The abbot slowly lifted the lid of the small tray before him. ("Let us finish the meat," I think he said.) Then I screamed. Lastly came the merciful thunderclap that precipitated me, the laughing monks, the abbot, the platter and the monastery into chaotic oblivion.

When I awoke I lay rain-drenched in a ditch beside the mired pathway, in wet garments of black. My horse grazed in the forest ways near by, but of the abbey I could see no sign.

I staggered into Vironne a half-day later, and already I was quite delirious, and when I reached my brother's home I cursed aloud beneath the windows. But my delirium lapsed into raving madness when he who found me there told me where my brother had gone, and his probable fate, and I swooned away upon the ground.

I can never forget that place, nor the chanting, nor the dreadful brethren, but I pray to God that I can forget one thing before I die; that which I saw before the thunderbolt; the thing that maddens me and torments me all the more in view of what I have since learned in Vironne. I know it is all true, now, and I can bear the knowledge, but I can never bear the menace nor the memory of what I saw when the abbot Henricus lifted up the lid of the small silver platter to disclose the rest of the meat. ...

It was the head of my brother.

# Slave of the Flames

HE HAD ALWAYS loved the sight of flame, ever since he was a boy. There had been the haymow in the barn, the cottage where he spent the night while tramping to the city. Fire made him feel strange inside, as if it were burning there. And it was beautiful to see things burn.

They hadn't understood that when they made him leave the farm after the haymow in the barn had burned; Squire Henslow had beaten him and said he was "touched." People never understood—they didn't realize what he was trying to do. Why, making a fire was like—like painting a picture, or playing music; it was making something beautiful.

They didn't understand. That's why he ran away after staying at the cottage. He hit the farmer over the head with a poker while he slept, because he wouldn't have understood either. Then he had done *it* and hurried off. It looked wonderful in the night. It was beautiful to see things burn. And not only things now—people also.

He had imagined about that all the way to the city. If only the farmer had waked and tried to get out—how would he look?

Would he be all red, like those pictures of Hell in the Bible?

Well, one could find out those things now. Here in the city it would be easier and better. Such tall buildings, so many of them! It was the biggest city he had ever seen—one of the biggest there was, they had said back home.

He walked around for a long time. All day, all night, all the next day. He didn't eat, didn't sleep. He had no place to go. He just walked, and looked at the people and buildings, trying to imagine what it was going to look like.

It would be the biggest thing in the world, what he was going to do. He had to laugh, inside of course, so nobody would suspect. All the carriages going by, and the men hurrying, and just as soon as it was dark the lights in the houses winking so pretty.

Just as soon as it was dark there'd be light enough. . . .

He stopped in front of the stable on the street. It was nearly midnight, and there was nobody around. All over, in all these houses, a million people slept.

He walked around in back. There was a big wooden wall stretching out from the side of the barn. It was dry, thick. It would start things nicely.

His hand had been in his pocket for an hour now, holding the box. He felt that it was almost soaked with sweat, but he took it out. The striking surface was dry enough.

He bent down against the wall and lit a match. One match.

And Chicago burned.

The fire ravaged four city blocks. All that evening of October seventh it raged, and the brigades labored at the hydrant unceasingly. It was a tense situation. The watching crowds gazed silently at the ominous red glare that rose from the razed ruins, but though they felt that curious prescience of warning, they did not conceive the whole truth with all its implications. The firemen did. This blaze was in the nature of a mere hint, a taste of what might befall. This the firemen knew only too well. For Chicago, in that summer of 1871, had felt but little rainfall. All through the year the dry gusty winds from the prairie had swept the city; the hot summer sun had blazed down on frame buildings and wooden sidewalks. Now these sudden flames had taken fifty dwellings and a score of lives in the space of a few hours. It was a grisly example of what might so easily happen. A stray spark, a vagrant breeze, a few minutes time—then there might be no checking of the blasts. The fire department was small, the waterworks inadequate. Chicago was wooden, vulnerable.

But the men had come in time. The watching crowd sighed with relief. Sun rose over smoky ashes.

Somewhere in the crowd he had stood. Men had run past him, throngs pushed and jostled as they strained forward. Of this he knew nothing, for his soul was in his eyes—his eyes that reflected the flames as they gazed at the ghastly glory that streamed in the sky. The Apocalypse in the Bible ... it was like the picture in the book ... this was even better than he had thought it would be.

See how the big building behind the stable caught. Little red tongues were licking at the sides, a monster with many mouths eating its walls and breathing hot sparks. And the people were running out and trying to get away from the monster. There was an old man on the porch, who moved very slowly. And the cunning monster watched him—see, it had coiled its flaming tail to bar his path and now it was swelling up closer to wrap around the old man like a big snake. The man screamed, and the monster roared and hissed as it fed on the wooden boards beneath the old fool's feet. The monster crackled with glee because it was soon going to feed on flesh. It did. Hungry monster!

Greedy, greedy monster! It was creeping toward a second house now—no, it was holding out its arms on both sides to embrace two houses at once. It must keep feeding and growing if it would leap like that; leap swiftly as it now leapt at the other buildings. Then its chuckle would grow louder. It had to eat to grow, and the more it ate the hungrier it got because of its size ... but that was too mixed up to think about.

No, think about how pretty the monster was. All red and glowing and alive against the black sky; beautiful beast eating ugly frame houses. It had put its fingers on the roof-tops now, and tossed a shower of red-hot roses to the sky. Happy monster!

Oh, now the people came. And the horses pulling the fire-wagons. They were going to fight the monster. Fools! They couldn't stop the feast now. Look—the whole block was burning. Roping off the squares wouldn't help. These foolish men—they were going to try and fight the monster with the little black snakes they dragged in their arms, the little black snakes that spit water instead of venom. Water-snakes.

So much noise! Bells clanging and men shouting and horses neighing and people wailing. Well—the monster heard it too, and drowned it out with loud roars, as it crawled over the second block of houses. It was pulling in its tail after it and winding it around new victims, not people now, but whole buildings. How big and fast it was!

Everybody was so excited. Silly! Why didn't they watch this pretty thing while they could?

The fighting men angered the red monster. Roaring, he toppled over the wall of a building. It fell like a flaming wave, and several of the firemen disappeared. Good! But more kept coming, and there were hundreds of little hissing snakes spitting and poisoning the monster's body. But it was cunning. It knew! Now it had broken up into many parts—divided into a dozen smaller monsters. That was wise. A dozen mouths to eat and grow and curl scarlet lips around windows and doors and drag down roof or chimney in flaming fingers. A dozen roaring monsters to fight back as they crawled over the black house-tops and spat embers and ashes on the heads of those puny fools. A dozen dancers, a dozen writhing roarers . . . pull over more walls on the fighters and feast!

Oh . . . it was going! There were too many men, too many snakes. Three of the monsters died. Another was spluttering and fuming, trapped inside a house while stabbing streams of water pierced its bowels so that it belched black smoke and sang in agony. The firemen closed in. They had the biggest monsters trapped in a street-corner. The monsters crawled inside the buildings but the snakes followed them. Some men carried them in to get at the heart of the monsters, and the silver water stabbed them there. They groaned as they died, and pulled down roofs in their death throes. Sometimes their fingers or their tails still moved after they were dead, but the men were now running everywhere and stabbing these fingers or chopping away the tails with axes. Only one monster left now, far away, and it was bleeding. It turned pinker and pinker as it was drained of its life by the water-poison shot by the snakes. Then it turned rose-color; red rose, pink rose, yellow rose, white rose. It was dead.

It was dead. They were all dead, after their feasting. They lay amidst the bones of the buildings on which they had feasted. Dead—poor monsters!

When he realized this he again became conscious of who and where he was. He looked about and saw that he stood against the ropes along the street, in the middle of a great crowd. Now he was suddenly afraid, and all his beautiful thoughts were slipping away; all the beautiful thoughts about monsters and roses and feasts that had surprised him even when he imagined them. These lovely ideas were all gone, and he was standing in a mob alone with his crime.

It was a crime. It was—Sin! He was a sinner, and afraid. Suppose somebody knew? Perhaps one of these people had seen what he had done. Maybe there were men who had watched him while he looked at the fire and guessed why he had such glowing eyes. What if they were looking for him now? They would come for him and take him away because he had given life to the beautiful red monsters and they were angry. Now that the monsters had died they could not protect him any more, and he didn't have fine thoughts to make him brave. No—he must get away quickly.

He jostled his way out of the throng, elbowed through until he was back on the wooden walk, then hurried off into a side street. He walked fast, and he really wanted to run only people would stare. They *were* staring. Here—down this alley, now . . .

Had he been followed? No . . .

Yes.

A man in a cloak was walking down the alley behind him. He walked faster. Perhaps the man would not see him. But the man was hurrying, too.

Where to hide? The cloaked man was approaching. He broke into a run, down the dark alley red-etched in flames from behind. The cloaked man, he saw, was bearing down upon him. He gasped.

A hand fell on his shoulder. A waxen yellow face smiled into his own, as the stranger's bearded lips curled back.

"Come with me," said the man.

And he propelled him back through the alley, pushed him through a gate, entered a yard.

The cloaked man was not a constable or a policeman. He had smiled. He seemed to know, but he didn't act as others would. And he was being hurried into a darkened house, standing back in the yard.

They walked up long stairs until they came to the door of a big room. It opened, and they entered in brilliant candle-light.

There were flaming tapers and torches set on low tables. A sweet smell came from the smoke that curled up out of great urns and pots set on the floor. The room was curtained in velvet, and very barely, though regally, furnished. Only a great divan stood at the opposite end, and through the gray vapor from the urns he saw a man lying upon the couch. He stared as the man sat up.

The occupant of the couch was fat—monstrously so—and his great barrel-body was clothed in a long white robe. He had a peculiar green wreath on his head, and everywhere his flesh was covered with jewels; ear-rings, necklaces, rings, bracelets, medals, ornaments—big rubies that flickered with fire, and yellow flame-opals tinged with smoky hues.

The fat man had a face that was old and awful; his flesh was blue and hung in pulpy folds under his eyes, his cheeks, his chin. His nose was hooked and his curved lips purple and swollen.

He looked like a big blue corpse, like the man they had found drowned in Squire Henslow's creek—all swollen up and bloated. Only his eyes were alive, and they were terrible. They were redder than the rubies and more fiercely flaming. They stared at him, never moving.

The cloaked man dropped his arms and sank to his knees.

"I have found him, Divinity," he murmured.

Fat face bobbed, but the eyes never changed. They kept staring. Then curved purple lips, opened, and a voice—a deep, dead, drowned voice that was oh so old—spoke.

"Good. Good, indeed. This is the one. I dreamt that it would be so. You remember Apius, my friend? And his spirit, that shone again in Roger that time at London? The cycle of incarnation has revolved again—this man has the look of Apius and of Roger about him. Mark the vacant eye, the dwarfed body, the ever-moving fingers. 'Tis Apius to the life, and his deed alone proclaims it. The final omen has been secured. We are ready, then, at last!"

"Yes, Divinity." The cloaked man pushed his garment to one side, revealing a white robe similar to the one worn by the fat man on the couch.

The fat man stared, then spoke again. "What is your name?" he purred.

"Folks call me Abe," said the incendiary.

"You shall be called Apius, as is your right," pronounced the fat man, with a frown of annoyance. Then, in brighter tones, "Did you start the fire?"

Abe stood silent for a moment. Something inside him was clamoring for outlet. Reason—even his twisted reason—told him that he must speak the truth. This was no ordinary man; even city folks didn't live in houses like this or wear such clothes. This man seemed to know about him, seemed to understand in spite of his funny way of talking. He was interested. Nobody had ever understood Abe, and most people laughed at him to hide that they really hated him. Abe knew that; he wanted to tell the truth.

"Yes, I started the fire." The words came easily after that. Before Abe realized it he had told the whole story. And he described for the first time his feeling about flames. He told about the monsters and the fight with the water-snakes, and was reassured by the smile spreading over the puffy countenance of the fat man as he listened carefully. The tale was soon told, and it felt wonderful to be able to show other people that Abe could think up dreams like that out of fire.

"Apius!" exclaimed the man on the couch to the bearded one. "I knew it. He lacks wit, but in his crude way he fumbles to Beauty. And did you mark the tale of the monster—'tis Apius' *Salamander* fancy, and Roger's *Great Dragon!*"

He turned to Abe.

"And now, my friend, I shall tell you why you were brought here; tell you my own story. I think you will understand, and soon I shall furnish proof. Listen, then."

The tale was told; the gross body quivered earnestly, the age-blue lips writhed, and the red eyes stared. Abe listened.

"In ancient days I ruled a throne. I was a poet—I sought the perfect beauty in life. Being Caesar, I knew no manmade law in my search for the sublimities that shine in stars. I tasted all delights, those of the flesh and of the spirit. And Beauty eluded me at the last. In drugs and in wine I found a soaring glory, but it was not true Beauty, for it fled and left only ugliness upon awakening. I abandoned such debauchery early in youth. When I became ruler I builded temples of marble and towers of chrysolite and jade so that my eyes might feast upon their loveliness as they stood straight and clear in the sunlight from the green hills. This delighted me, but there were days when the sun shone not, and then the stone was gray and ugly, and I saw that wind and rain and dust had destroyed the perfection of Beauty I sought. And age would crumble these monuments I knew, so that I builded no longer.

"In women I hoped to find that intangible delight of soul that poets dream of. Their bodies are but mortal clay, I found, and the ecstasies of passion wane. I turned to new and curious pleasures, yet they too palled to imperfectness. I read the literature of the ancients, but though some had glimpsed the Beauty from afar, none had imprisoned it fully in their stropes or sentences. I walked with philosophers and priests, sought jewels and perfumes, searched every avenue where my prize might lurk. I found it not. For Beauty lay only in Life, and Life is—*fire*."

The ancient one paused. There was anguish in his flabby face.

"They called me cruel—they said that Nero was a monster! No one ever understood that I sought only happiness and perfection and the meaning behind all lovely things! Because I burnt those damnable criminals they branded me a beast, a sadist! I dipped them in oil and tallow and placed them upon crosses whilst the flames consumed their worthless lives; only because fire is beautiful, and I had thought perhaps that when it fed on flesh its glory would become transcendent.

"I burnt pyres on altars, beacons in a pharos. I loved to watch the flames rise and dance as they sang their song of life eternal and unchanging. I sought the way to capture the true Beauty I found in those ocher, crimson, orange, violet, multicolored depths—sought a way to prison and prolong it. Then Zarog came."

He indicated the bearded man who had worn the cloak.

"Zarog told me of the Rosicrucians—those Orient worshippers of the Eternal Fire that is Life. He told me of Prometheus and Zoroaster, and of the Phenix Fable. He was a priest of the Rosicrucian sect, and I learned his mystery. He told me of bright Melek Taos, the Peacock god of Evil, and imparted to me the secret weddings of Evil and Beauty.

"But I bore you with these esoterics, which you do not comprehend. Suffice that I learned. Zarog told me how a lover of

Beauty might dedicate himself for ever to its search; of what Melek Taos might grant if given a sufficient sacrifice of fire.

"For a while I was afraid. Rome was in tumult, and the people hated me because they did not understand. They called me a tyrant, a madman—I, the greatest poet of them all! But Zarog pleaded. I must sacrifice my empire for eternal life. I wavered before this decision.

"I had a slave named Apius, who loved me. He too sought Beauty. And it was he, at last, who showed me the way to strength. He knew what Zarog wanted of me, and one night he crept away and performed the deed. He entered the thieves' quarter of the city and fired the houses. The district burned; the work was attributed to the Nazarenes, or Christians, as they called themselves.

"Apius had set the example to give me courage. I would dedicate myself to eternal Beauty, as Zarog wished; sacrifice with fire to Melek Taos. So—I burned Rome."

The red eyes were glazed with reminiscence, the ancient voice mused onward.

"I watched the towers topple one by one, and with my lyre I sounded the paeans of prayer. Day and night the fire raged, and day was night under the sable smoke. The sky was bleeding and I stared at the terrors of Hecate's Hell. Thus I sacrificed an empire to Melek Taos and the Beauty that is Fire. Fire, the eternal life of flames, was now mine.

"When the time came, a harmless dupe—my double, whom I sent in my stead to civil functions—was forced to kill himself to appease the wrath of my deluded people, who did not understand that I had made myself a god. When he died, Nero died. Zarog and I left."

Compassion entered his voice.

"I left Rome, left my poor, foolish people that lacked the wit to understand a god. They found no truth in Beauty, and they hated me until my name became a twisted legend of evil. Irony! But I, a poet, am content that this was so.

"And I have lived on. Zarog and I had sacrificed, and we could not die. Only the flame of Melek Taos can destroy us now; nor shall it descend while yet we worship.

★

"You must know that we have wandered far since those lost days. Their history is too lengthy for repetition here, but they have brought many things. In many lands and under various disguises we have quested. It has been necessary from time to time to renew our bond to Melek Taos, and sacrifice again. Paris, Prague, a thousand cities have burned in the night on one vast altar to Beauty and Fire.

"In London, long centuries ago, we kindled a blaze that delighted the eyes of the Bright God. And it was there that I again lacked courage to carry on. A villein called Roger was my servant, as Apius was in Rome. Once again he led the way and kindled the preliminary flame of sacrifice. His deed gave me the strength, so London burned.

"Centuries of Beauty, my friend. Centuries dedicated to the perpetuation of poetry. But now the time for sacrifice drew near again. Zarog and I were beginning to age once more, a sign that our bond with the Bright God needed renewal. We abandoned our journeys, then, and came to this new world. That was a dozen years ago, and since then we have not prospered aright.

"Ten years ago, during the Draft Riots in New York, our mission failed. The fire we lighted did not spread. And age crept close. So we have wandered here, at last. The city is large enough for our purpose. My money has insured us secrecy until the deed is accomplished. And Zarog's pyromancy has shown the time to be ripe.

"We had planned to act soon. Once again my courage failed at the last—but now you, Apius anew, have come as an omen to lead the way. Tomorrow night we shall set the fire; and it will be a fire to delight your soul, a flame of triumph rising to charm the eyes of the Bright God so that he shall again renew his pledge."

Abe listened. The fat oldster drew a great ruby ring from his finger and presented it to him. The monstrous red stone was set in the beak of a silver bird.

"Here," said Nero. "A gift, my servant. The Phenix-seal is yours by right. Take it, and pledge your support."

Abe glanced dubiously at the man. His head was reeling; this was all so confusing . . .

"It shall be such a fire," purred Nero. His eyes flickered on Abe's, craftily winked as he gloated and coaxed with wicked words.

"Such a fire as you have never dreamed of, it will be. Or, rather, such a fire as you *have* dreamed of. The fire you meant to start tonight. The great fire, when the streets are sheets of flame, and the houses turn to red hells in which little burning devils dance and scream for deliverance. Little burning devils, these stupid people will be, shrieking in their torment—these stupid people that never understood you and your love of Beauty. The Bright God wants such people destroyed; so that then the earth shall be free for you and me and the other poets to whom the secrets of Truth are revealed. And we shall see this wonder, then go away to other lands and worship anew. You will be safe; Zarog, here, is very clever. With aeromancy to control the winds, and divination to aid, we cannot be deterred. And after that, to live for ever—you would like money, women, power, excitement; you long for these things, my friend. You can have them, with moments of scarlet ecstasy as well. Say you will come."

"I—will." Abe placed the ring on his finger.

The Emperor smiled.

"Now I have courage," he asserted. "Zarog, let us prepare that which is to come."

On October the eighth, 1871, one day after the first blaze that had so alarmed citizens everywhere, the catastrophe came. At nine-thirty in the evening, Taylor Street burst into a flood of flame.

And with this, as though the first flaring of the fire were a cosmic signal of disaster, a skirling wind rose. The fire-force faced disaster as the blaze crept onward. Great gusts of sparks swirled across the river, and the South Side and business district were showered with angry embers. Soon a great glare arose and soared over the city. A red hurricane roared, belching smoke and ashes and cinders from a crimson maw that engulfed the city in relentless wrath.

Balls of fire swept the skies and descended to raven at random. On the ground the flames writhed onward more slowly, but they were thorough. Wood and fabric and flesh were food not to be ignored.

Madness stalked the city. Throngs rioted in a stampede of

utter fear; the streets were choked with fleeing figures; drays and vans and carriages trampled the hysterical crowds that swept the streets in utter horror and despair. The roar of the fire drowned out all sound save the screams of the dying and wounded, and the shrieks of insane torture from trapped and burning horses. The gas works exploded with a thunderous detonation that shook the wooden sidewalks along which the flames now flowed in rivulets of doom. The great bell of the Court House fell with a final clang of terror, and its collapse was echoed by the crash of crumbled walls.

A river of melted lead ran from the Federal Building. Frightened pigeons sobbed as they rose against the scarlet skies, then dropped, burning as they flew, like winged comets. Daybreak brought new dread as the flames wheeled and spread again, dividing and subdividing so that they combed each street, each alley-way with fiery teeth. Nightfall again, and new horrors. Thousands fought the blaze in vain fury, while the city roared into red ruin.


Abe saw it all. He and Zarog crept forth, after those curious prayers in the old dark house which they had made at sunset. Zarog wore his cloak, and under it he carried the tarred, oil-soaked ropes. He had chosen a spot in the meaner quarter of the city; a row of ramshackle houses stood close, and a dark alley entered on a stable front. Here, as darkness fell, Zarog knelt. Abe lit the match, after the ropes had been placed so very cunningly by Zarog's long white fingers. Abe lit the match . . .

They ran. The carriage waited around the corner, and they drove back, furiously. Behind them was a faint pinkish flicker in the sky . . .

The wind came, just as Zarog had said it would. He explained about the prayers, and the circle he had made on the floor. He and the fat man who called himself Nero had talked a lot.

Perhaps they spoke the truth; perhaps they were crazy. Abe didn't know. He couldn't understand half of what they had said, at any rate. All he knew was that he had been promised the fire. The ring he wore was pretty, but he wasn't Apius. Zarog told him that he had seen him start his fire the night before and knew that he was a "reincarnation"; Abe didn't know what this meant, but he disliked being called Apius. Still, they were nice men, and they understood about the flames, and now the fire had started. What a great wind!

Back at the house, it was curious to see the fat man wearing a cloak and a tall hat. He was waiting, and when Zarog spoke to him in a funny language he smiled.

"Come," he said to Abe. "Let us roam abroad. We'll find rare sport tonight."

They had driven down the street together. Abe saw it all. After a while they had to get out and walk because the whole way was choked with people and buggies. They were screaming and shouting, so Abe knew that the fire must be spreading fast. Soon he saw the red skies, and then ashes started falling, and he heard the thunder of the blaze.

They struggled through the streets. People were running out of houses carrying bedding and furniture, loading their goods into vans that could not move for lack of space. Women and children cried, dogs raced everywhere as they howled in animal fear. Men on horseback fled through the throngs, trampling and crushing those who barred their way, and lashing out at them with whips.

Now they were in the heart of the fire, and Abe forgot the people as he watched the red walls about him. Fat Nero and lean Zarog stared and smiled.

"We walk through Hell tonight, I think," said the fat man. "And how else, pray, does one reach Heaven? May Melek Taos heed this offering!"

Abe ignored this. Some more of the old man's ravings about Beauty and living forever, he guessed. Better to watch the fire— the glowing, living fire. It was a thousand monsters now, a thousand roaring beautiful beasts lashing tails of sparks and beating great red wings.

Crash! A wall fell from the crimson skeleton that was the building ahead.

"Back," Zarog counseled. "Blade or bullet cannot harm us, Caesar, but beware of flame."

"A poet dies by that he worships," observed the Emperor. "But I have no urge to unduly hasten that demise."

Abe only half heard this nonsense. He stared at the embers over his shoulder as they hustled back along the deserted street. All living here had fled before the onrush of the flames.

They came to the center of the city. Here men rioted in streets, smashing the windows of the stores, plundering them of food, liquor, precious goods. Pickpockets, thieves, drunkards, held high revel as they pillaged unhindered.

"Fools!" sneered Nero. "If these be men, they deserve to die. Behind them is Beauty, and they grovel in trash."

A detonation shook the streets, and waves of liquid horror pulsed down the thoroughfare. Burning oil lapped about the feet of the drunken roisterers. They screamed and fled, or sank into the seething sea to perish. A hostelry with imposing pillars smoldered into flames, and its great iron columns melted like waxen tapers with the heat.

Molten metal sprayed the heads of the retreating crowd.

Abe and his companions were engulfed in the madness; they fought and trampled with the rest. Mad women cackled in hysterical glee as they tore their garments from white bodies made crimson by reflected flames. Idiotic men cursed and fought and clawed one another in raving delirium. And underfoot great startled rats raced and scurried, padding from their holes beneath the sidewalks.

Abe began to laugh and sing, so that Zarog and Nero had to drag him into the side streets. Night merged into day, but darkness remained as the smoke pall shrouded the city. And the roaring of hungry flames obscured all lesser sounds.

The carriage took them to the cemetery high above the city, and here they stood amidst the grassy graves and peered down into the lake of fire. They stood in peace and watched a purgatory, while he who called himself Nero laughed and played upon a curious stringed instrument.

All alone they were, on a hill beneath a sky of blackness, and the strange fat man played a wild sad tune that had no words— nor needed any to aid the voice of mad despair. The man called Nero sang, too, and his voice was singularly sweet. His language was not one Abe could understand, but it too held despair that was a worship. And the bearded Zarog lifted his eyes to the billowing, burning skies and chanted. They were alone with the dead that day, and there was curious wine to drink that somehow made the music easier to understand.

Abe lay back and watched the burning city, and he felt a peace he could never express in thought or word. This was the most beautiful thing of all. And if the man who called himself Nero was mad, his madness was right, and just. Didn't they call Abe mad? People—like those awful ones rioting in the streets—never could understand.

Night again. "It will burn through the evening," said Zarog. "Let us return to the house and arrange for our departure."

He drove the carriage back along the quieter, deserted streets. It was dusk on the drive—a dusk of ashen hue, and through a blackly sooted sky flames redder than sunset mounted in the north.

This section of the city was almost deserted, but here in the quiet, untouched sections, strange figures crept abroad. There were little old men scurrying close to the walls with leaves and faggots. A small boy was lighting matches before a house with opened doors which proclaimed it to be deserted. A laughing woman was dancing before a flaming barn as they passed, and startled neighbors swarmed out of an adjacent building, shouting threats and oaths as she ran, cackling shrilly, down the smoke-filled street.

"You see?" purred the man who called himself Nero. He sank back in the carriage seat and gripped Abe's arm. "There are a few of us, after all. Pyromania, the fools call it. Little do they know of the true beauty these folks serve in their hearts—the true beauty of Fire, pure and pulsing with the elixir of Life."

They came to the house in the alley-way, left tethered horses and entered, proceeded to the curtained room. There Zarog lit the candles and the braziers.

Abe and the fat man sat in the taper-light as the bearded one scurried about, placing incongruous objects and garments in open trunks and suitcases.

The fat man sighed and spoke. "It is over, my friend. The three of us shall leave here before morning—the fire will be dead by then. But it was glorious—a dream of rhythm from the cemetery hilltop—and a tribute to Melek Taos."

Abe listened, uncomprehending.

"You shall have your reward now. Remember what I told you; how our sacrifice is rewarded. Zarog and I are not as you see us now—we shall become young men once more, youthful and vigorous for many years to come. Melek Taos shall again grant us youth.

"I have riches hoarded in many places. We shall seek them and live again for pleasure's sake until the cycle comes upon us and we kindle another flaming tribute. You shall come with us, friend. For your unwitting aid you shall have all that you can desire."

Abe smiled, fingering his ring. These words meant nothing. This old man was crazy—crazier than they had said Abe was.

The fat one saw his smile, and frowned. Then a gasp of pain crossed his face. Looking up, he motioned to Zarog.

"Hasten," he said. His voice had become shrill and cracked these last few moments.

"Hasten. I feel the time approaching. I'm numbing a bit; I can feel age running sluggishly in my veins, cooling the blood. Before we go—rear the altar and conjure Melek Taos to grant us the boon of youth again."

Zarog bowed. Abe saw that his beard was indeed graying almost perceptibly each passing moment; noted that he shuffled away as he crossed to the center of the room and began to heap incense on a great open brazier placed there.

The fat man who called himself Nero turned again to Abe. He wheezed his words painfully.

"You do not yet believe, friend Apius reborn? Then as I promised, here is the proof. Remember what I told you—how Zarog and I long ago dedicated ourselves to eternal life, given by the Bright God in return for the burnt offering we placed before him.

"Now we shall evoke the spirit of Melek Taos once more, and receive youth. For fire is Life; fire gave birth to this earth ages ago, and through fire men have been enabled to live upon it. Always they have worshipped their gods with flame; always they worshipped fire under many names. Moloch, Satan, Ahriman, Melek Taos—the Divine Principle remains the same and shall be served."

Nero turned his head again. "Pour the sacred oils, my friend," he called. "Hasten."

Abe listened. In the dusk he perceived with a start of horror that the bluish tinge of Nero's face had deepened. Great blackened lines now wrinkled the flabby face; it was as though this incredibly old man was slowly putrefying before his eyes.

"Look," croaked the one called Nero. "Here is testament and proof for you. I shall invoke the Fire-God and ask the boon."

Abe saw the old man creep across the floor. Zarog, stooping, cast pungent oil into the brazier; so that it glared up redly and illumined the blackness of the room. The great pot of fire flamed, and heady smoke swirled and filled the air with acrid perfume. Zarog knelt down, tracing lines upon the floor with phosphorescent oils, which he lighted so that a little flaming line formed a pentagon in which the two old men now stood.

The man Nero now produced the curious stringed instrument and held it in trembling hands. Slowly he twanged eery notes that rose above the crackling of brazier-born fires. And Zarog, as though in rhythm to the music, began a measured chanting in an alien tongue.

Abe shifted uneasily. These madmen with their curious ritual unnerved him. The insane story had been bad enough, but now this strangely disturbing ceremony made him feel afraid.

Flames seemed to tower ceilingward. The room became filled with a purple haze through which music and chanting crawled.

And then, as Abe rose and gasped, a Presence formed.

Out of the somber smoke, rising from the brazier on roots of fire, a vast intangible outline was limning.

The music, chanting, figure swelled simultaneously. The fire-shape was blinding in its brilliance, but it slowly resolved into the definite figure of a man, a gigantic Being of Flame who writhed out of the brazier-coals and seemed to peer down at the two ancients in the pentagon.

"Melek Taos," breathed a cracked voice.

Then Abe believed. He knew that somehow the story was all true—this was Nero, and he had made a pact with the Lord of Fire.

Nero was speaking, in a high, quavering voice that came slowly, painfully, from an aging throat. His hideous purpled face was shrunken.

"Quickly, O Lord," he wailed. "You have seen that which we have given you in sacrifice—this mighty city we have kindled that its smoke rise to pleasure you. And now we ask again the boon of renewed youth, in accordance with our pact of old."

Abe listened. In a flash, a thought struck and stunned him.

His voice rose above the crackling flames.

"But *you* didn't start the fire. *I* did."

Nero and Zarog wheeled. Abe proceeded, unwittingly. He would boast before this god.

"Remember? When we set fire to the stable—I lighted the match, not you or Zarog. It's my fire—not yours. Mine!"

The two ancients stared, horrified realization on their faces. It was true! Nero's lyre fell suddenly silent.

Above them the flaming figure pulsed. It seemed to crouch, and out of the fiery depths an angry purring rose. The god was wrathful. Two great reddish tongues of flame swooped out, arm-like.

Abe did not hear the screaming of the stricken men within the burning pentagon. He was watching the great man-flame now, staring as though hypnotized at the pillar of fire which writhed from the brazier and hummed madly.

The idiot's eyes glazed. This was another fire—a beautiful living fire. And *he* had brought it. *He* had burned a city to do this!

A shrill laugh escaped his lips. This Nero and his priest—they were running about in the circle and screaming, and the light fell cruelly upon rotting faces as they lurched about. Then the men were sunken upon all fours, crawling weakly as the fire-arm swooped and descended.

Two great flames seemed to circle the crumbling bodies and lift them high into the air. A single shriek rang out, and then both figures disappeared into the center of the fiery head. The Bright One, Melek Taos, had feasted.

Abe laughed, maddened by the beauty of the mounting red glare—laughed to see what he had wrought. He knew that he should flee the place, for the fire was spreading rapidly; yet he wanted to remain.

Now the figure of fire reached out again. It had seen him—Abe! It was roaring angrily. Abe could not stop it.

Or could he? Nero's lyre still lay upon the floor where it had fallen. The old one had played upon it; perhaps its music would appease the rage of the flames.

Abe crawled toward it, picked up the silver instrument. His fingers strummed, as around him whirled bright butterflies of flame.

But two arms were reaching out. Melek Taos wanted *him!* Abe roared as they descended. The lyre fell; he was lifted in blazing paws that seared with incredible torture. There was a moment of terrific anguish, then engulfment.

\*     \*     \*

Searchers in the ruins of the great Chicago fire of 1871 made many startling discoveries. The freaks of the conflagration had resulted in hideousness. There were many bodies found in the lake, in a condition which can only be described as *cooked*. Evidently some poor unfortunates had been driven into the very water before encroaching flames; here oil-blasts had so heated the lake-shore currents that the dead had been boiled alive.

Fires had also started in isolated sections; single houses had burned in vicinities far from the main path of the holocaust. In one of these dwellings, on the near south side, searchers amidst the debris-filled roof-boards found a curious relic, perhaps the most incongruous object of all the myriads uncovered after the disaster. Its total disassociation with the setting in which it was unearthed caused considerable comment, and the object was finally placed on exhibition in the Art Institute some years later. To this day, the story behind the token is unknown, but visitors are still privileged to stare at the strange instrument discovered in the prosaic ruins of a Chicago house.

It was the battered, tarnished, but unmistakable fragment of an old Roman lyre.

# The Shambler from the Stars

(*Dedicated to H. P. Lovecraft*)

I AM WHAT I profess to be—a writer of weird fiction. Since earliest childhood I have been enthralled by the cryptic fascination of the unknown and the unguessable. The nameless fears, the grotesque dreams, the queer, half-intuitive fancies that haunt our minds have always exercised for me a potent and inexplicable delight.

In literature I have walked the midnight paths with Poe or crept amidst the shadows with Machen; combed the realms of horrific stars with Baudelaire, or steeped myself with earth's inner madness amidst the tales of ancient lore. A meager talent for sketching and crayon work led me to attempt crude picturizations involving the outlandish denizens of my nighted thoughts. The same somber trend of intellect which drew me in my art interested me in obscure realms of musical composition; the symphonic strains of the *Planets Suite* and the like were my favorites. My inner life soon became a ghoulish feast of eldritch, tantalizing horrors.

My outer existence was comparatively dull. As time went on I found myself drifting more and more into the life of a penurious recluse; a tranquil, philosophical existence amidst a world of books and dreams.

A man must live. By nature constitutionally and spiritually unfitted for manual labor, I was at first puzzled about the choice of a suitable vocation. The depression complicated matters to an almost intolerable degree, and for a time I was close to utter economic disaster. It was then that I decided to write.

I procured a battered typewriter, a ream of cheap paper, and few carbons. My subject matter did not bother me. What better field than the boundless realms of a colorful imagination? I would write of horror, fear, and the riddle that is Death. At least, in the callowness of my unsophistication, this was my intention.

My first attempts soon convinced me how utterly I had failed. Sadly, miserably, I fell short of my aspired goal. My vivid dreams became on paper merely meaningless jumbles of ponderous adjectives, and I found no ordinary words to express the wondrous terror of the unknown. My first manuscripts were miserable and futile documents; the few magazines using such material being unanimous in their rejections.

I had to live. Slowly but surely I began to adjust my style to my ideas. Laboriously I experimented with words, phrases, sentence-structure. It was work, and hard work at that. I soon learned to sweat. At last, however, one of my stories met with favor; then a second, a third, a fourth. Soon I had begun to master the more obvious tricks of the trade, and the future looked brighter at last. It was with an easier mind that I returned to my dream-life and my beloved books. My stories afforded me a somewhat meager livelihood, and for a time this sufficed. But not for long. Ambition, ever an illusion, was the cause of my undoing.

I wanted to write a real story; not the stereotyped, ephemeral sort of tale I turned out for the magazines, but a real work of art. The creation of such a masterpiece became my ideal. I was not a good writer, but that was not entirely due to my errors in mechanical style. It was, I felt, the fault of my subject matter. Vampires, werewolves, ghouls, mythological monsters—these things constituted material of little merit. Commonplace imagery, ordinary adjectival treatment, and a prosaically anthropocentric point of view were the chief detriments to the production of a really good weird tale.

I must have new subject matter, truly unusual plot material. If only I could conceive of something that was teratologically incredible!

I longed to learn the songs the demons sing as they swoop between the stars, or hear the voices of the olden gods as they whisper their secrets to the echoing void. I yearned to know the terrors of the grave; the kiss of maggots on my tongue, the cold caress of a rotting shroud upon my body. I thirsted for the knowledge that lies in the pits of mummied eyes, and burned for wisdom known only to the worm. Then I could really write, and my hopes be truly realized.

I sought a way. Quietly I began a correspondence with isolated thinkers and dreamers all over the country. There was a hermit in the western hills, a savant in the northern wilds, a mystic dreamer in New England. It was from the latter that I learned of the ancient books that hold strange lore. He quoted guardedly from the legendary *Necronomicon*, and spoke timidly of a certain *Book of Eibon* that was reputed to surpass it in the utter wildness of its blasphemy. He himself had been a student of these volumes of primal dread, but he did not want me to search too far. He had heard many strange things as a boy in witch-haunted Arkham, where the old shadows still leer and creep, and since then he had wisely shunned the blacker knowledge of the forbidden.

At length, after much pressing on my part, he reluctantly consented to furnish me with the names of certain persons he deemed able to aid me in my quest. He was a writer of notable brilliance and wide reputation among the discriminating few, and I knew he was keenly interested in the outcome of the whole affair.

As soon as his precious list came into my possession, I began a widespread postal campaign in order to obtain access to the desired volumes. My letters went out to universities, private libraries, reputed seers, and the leaders of carefully hidden and obscurely designated cults. But I was foredoomed to disappointment.

The replies I received were definitely unfriendly, almost hostile. Evidently the rumored possessors of such lore were angered that their secret should be thus unveiled by a prying stranger. I was subsequently the recipient of several anonymous threats through the mails, and I had one very alarming phone-call. This did not bother me nearly so much as the disappointing realization that my endeavors had failed. Denials, evasions, refusals, threats—these would not aid me. I must look elsewhere.

The book stores! Perhaps on some musty and forgotten shelf I might discover what I sought.

Then began an interminable crusade. I learned to bear my numerous disappointments with unflinching calm. Nobody in the common run of shops seemed ever to have heard of the frightful *Necronomicon,* the evil *Book of Eibon,* or the disquieting *Cultes des Goules.*

Persistence brings results. In a little old shop on South Dearborn Street, amidst dusty shelves seemingly forgotten by time, I came to the end of my search. There, securely wedged between two century-old editions of Shakespeare, stood a great black volume with iron facings. Upon it, in hand-engraved lettering, was the inscription *De Vermis Mysteriis,* or "Mysteries of the Worm."

The proprietor could not tell how it had come into his possession. Years before, perhaps, it had been included in some second-hand job-lot. He was obviously unaware of its nature, for I purchased it with a dollar bill. He wrapped the ponderous thing for me, well pleased at this unexpected sale, and bade me a very satisfied good-day.

I left hurriedly, the precious prize under my arm. What a find! I had heard of this book before. Ludvig Prinn was its author; he who had perished at the inquisitorial stake in Brussels when the witchcraft trials were at their height. A strange character—alchemist, necromancer, reputed mage—he boasted of having attained a miraculous age when he at last suffered a fiery immolation at the hands of the secular arm. He was said to have proclaimed himself the sole survivor of the ill-fated ninth crusade, exhibiting as proof certain musty documents of attestation. It is true that a certain Ludvig Prinn was numbered among the gentlemen retainers of Montserrat in the olden chronicles, but the incredulous branded Ludvig as a crack-brained imposter, though perchance a lineal descendant of the original warrior.

Ludvig attributed his sorcerous learning to the years he had spent as a captive among the wizards and wonder-workers of Syria, and glibly he spoke of encounters with the djinns and efreets of elder Eastern myth. He is known to have spent some time in Egypt, and there are legends among the Libyan dervishes concerning the old seer's deeds in Alexandria.

At any rate, his declining days were spent in the Flemish

lowland country of his birth, where he resided, appropriately enough, in the ruins of a pre-Roman tomb that stood in the forest near Brussels. Ludvig was reputed to have dwelt there amidst a swarm of familiars and fearsomely invoked conjurations. Manuscripts still extant speak of him guardedly as being attended by "invisible companions" and "Star-sent servants". Peasants shunned the forest by night, for they did not like certain noises that resounded to the moon, and they most certainly were not anxious to see what worshipped at the old pagan altars that stood crumbling in certain of the darker glens.

Be that as it may, these creatures that he commanded were never seen after Prinn's capture by the inquisitorial minions. Searching soldiers found the tomb entirely deserted, though it was thoroughly ransacked before its destruction. The supernatural entities, the unusual instruments and compounds—all had most curiously vanished. A search of the forbidding woods and a timorous examination of the strange altars did not add to the information. There were fresh blood-stains on the altars, and fresh blood-strains on the rack, too, before the questioning of Prinn was finished. A series of particularly atrocious tortures failed to elicit any further disclosures from the silent wizard, and at length the weary interrogators ceased, and cast the aged sorcerer into a dungeon.

It was in prison, while awaiting trial, that he penned the morbid, horror-hinting lines of *De Vermis Mysteriis,* known today as *Mysteries of the Worm.* How it was ever smuggled through the alert guards is a mystery in itself, but a year after his death it saw print in Cologne. It was immediately suppressed, but a few copies had already been privately distributed. These in turn were transcribed, and although there was a later censored and deleted printing, only the Latin original is accepted as genuine. Throughout the centuries a few of the elect have read and pondered on its lore. The secrets of the old archimage are known today only to the initiated, and they discourage all attempts to spread their fame, for certain very definite reasons.

This, in brief, was what I knew of the volume's history at the time it came into my possession. As a collector's item alone the book was a phenomenal find, but on its contents I could pass no judgment. It was in Latin. Since I can speak or translate only a few words of that learned tongue, I was confronted by a barrier as soon as I opened the musty pages. It was maddening to have such a treasure-trove of dark knowledge at my command and yet lack the key to its unearthing.

For a moment I despaired, since I was unwilling to approach any local classical or Latin scholar in connection with so hideous and blasphemous a text. Then came an inspiration. Why not take it east and seek the aid of my friend? He was a student of the classics, and would be less likely to be shocked by the horrors of Prinn's baleful revelations. Accordingly I addressed a hasty letter to him, and shortly thereafter received my reply. He would be glad to assist me—I must by all means come at once.

2.

Providence is a lovely town. My friend's house was ancient, and quaintly Georgian. The first floor was a gem of Colonial atmosphere. The second, beneath antique gables that shadowed the enormous window, served as a workroom for my host.

It was here that we pondered that grim, eventful night last April; here beside the open window that overlooked the azure sea. It was a moonless night; haggard and wan with a fog that filled the darkness with bat-like shadows. In my mind's eye I can see it still—the tiny, lamp-lit room with the big table and the high-backed chairs; the bookcases bordering the walls; the manuscripts stacked in special files.

My friend and I sat at the table, the volume of mystery before us. His lean profile threw a disturbing shadow on the wall, and his waxen face was furtive in the pale light. There was an inexplicable air of portentous revelation quite disturbing in its potency; I sensed the presence of secrets waiting to be revealed.

My companion detected it too. Long years of occult experience had sharpened his intuition to an uncanny degree. It was not cold that made him tremble as he sat there in his chair; it was not fever that caused his eyes to flame like jewel-incarned fires. He knew, even before he opened that accursed tome, that it was evil. The musty scent that rose from those antique pages carried with it the reek of the tomb. The faded leaves were maggoty at the edges, and rats had gnawed the leather; rats which perchance had a ghastlier food for common fare.

I had told my friend the volume's history that afternoon, and had unwrapped it in his presence. Then he had seemed willing and eager to begin an immediate translation. Now he demurred.

It was not wise, he insisted. This was evil knowledge—who could say what demon-dreaded lore these pages might contain, or what ills befall the ignorant one who sought to tamper with their contents? It is not good to learn too much, and men had died for exercising the rotted wisdom that these leaves contained. He begged me to abandon the quest while the book was still unopened and to seek my inspiration in saner things.

I was a fool. Hastily I overruled his objections with vain and empty words. I was not afraid. Let us at least gaze into the contents of our prize. I began to turn the pages.

The result was disappointing. It was an ordinary-looking volume after all—yellow, crumbling leaves set with heavy black-lettered Latin texts. That was all; no illustrations, no alarming designs.

My friend could no longer resist the allurement of such a rare bibliophilic treat. In a moment he was peering intently over my shoulder, occasionally muttering snatches of Latin phrasing. Enthusiasm mastered him at last. Seizing the precious tome in both hands, he seated himself near the window and began reading paragraphs at random, occasionally translating them into English.

His eyes gleamed with a feral light; his cadaverous profile grew intent as he pored over the moldering runes. Sentences thundered in fearsome litany, then faded into tones below a whisper as his voice became as soft as a viper's hiss. I caught only a few phrases now, for in his introspection he seemed to have forgotten me. He was reading of spells and enchantments. I recall allusions to such gods of divination as Father Yig, dark Han, and serpent-bearded Byatis. I shuddered, for I knew these names of old, but I would have shuddered more had I known what was yet to come.

It came quickly. Suddenly he turned to me in great agitation, and his excited voice was shrill. He asked me if I remembered the legends of Prinn's sorcery, and the tales of the invisible servants he commanded from the stars. I assented, little understanding the cause of his sudden frenzy.

Then he told me the reason. Here, under a chapter on familiars, he had found an orison or spell, perhaps the very one Prinn had used to call upon his unseen servitors from beyond the stars! Let me listen while he read.

I sat there dully, like a stupid, uncomprehending fool. Why did I not scream, try to escape, or tear that monstrous manuscript from his hands? Instead I sat there—sat there while my friend, in a voice cracked with unnatural excitement, read in Latin a long and sonorously sinister invocation.

*"Tibi, Magnum Innominandum, signa stellarum nigrarum et bufaniformis Sadoquae sigillum . . ."*

The croaking ritual proceeded, then rose on wings of nighted, hideous horror. The words seemed to writhe like flames in the air, burning into my brain. The thundering tones cast an echo into infinity, beyond the farthermost star. They seemed to pass into primal and undimensioned gates, to seek out a listener there, and summon him to earth. Was it all an illusion? I did not pause to ponder.

For that unwitting summons was answered. Scarcely had my companion's voice died away in that little room before the terror came. The room turned cold. A sudden wind shrieked in through the open window; a wind that was not of earth. It bore an evil bleating from afar, and at the sound my friend's face became a pale white mask of newly awakened fear. Then there was a crunching at the walls, and the window-ledge buckled before my staring eyes. From out of the nothingness beyond that opening came a sudden burst of lubricious laughter—a hysterical cackling born of utter madness. It rose to the grinning quintessence of all horror, without mouth to give it birth.

The rest happened with startling swiftness. All at once my friend began to scream as he stood by the window; scream and claw wildly at empty air. In the lamplight I saw his features contort into a grimace of insane agony. A moment later, his body rose unsupported from the floor, and began to bend outward to a back-breaking degree. A second later came the sickening grind of broken bones. His form now hung in midair, the eyes glazed and the hands clutching convulsively as if at something unseen. Once again there came the sound of maniacal tittering, but this time it came from *within the room!*

The stars rocked in red anguish; the cold wind gibbered in my ears. I crouched in my chair, my eyes riveted on that astounding scene in the corner.

My friend was shrieking now; his screams blended with that gleeful, atrocious laughter from the empty air. His sagging body, dangling in space, bent backward once again as blood spurted from the torn neck, spraying like a ruby fountain.

That blood never reached the floor. It stopped in midair as the laughter ceased, and a loathsome sucking noise took its place. With a new and accelerated horror, I realized that that blood was being drained to feed the invisible entity from beyond! What creature of space had been so suddenly and unwittingly invoked? What was that vampiric monstrosity I could not see?

Even now a hideous metamorphosis was taking place. The body of my companion became shrunken, wizened, lifeless. At length it dropped to the floor and lay nauseatingly still. But in midair another and a ghastlier change occurred.

A reddish glow filled the corner by the window—a *bloody* glow. Slowly but surely the dim outlines of a Presence came into view; the blood-filled outlines of that unseen shambler from the stars. It was red and dripping; an immensity of pulsing, moving jelly; a scarlet blob with myriad tentacular trunks that waved and waved. There were suckers on the tips of the appendages, and these were opening and closing with ghoulish lust. . . . The thing was bloated and obscene; a headless, faceless, eyeless bulk with the ravenous maw and titanic talons of a starborn monster. The human blood on which it had fed revealed the hitherto invisible outlines of the feaster. It was not a sight for sane eyes to see.

Fortunately for my reason, the creature did not linger. Spurning the dead and flabby corpse-like thing on the floor, it purposely seized the dreadful volume with one slimy, sinuous feeler and shambled swiftly to the window; then squeezed its rubbery, viscous body through the opening. There it disappeared, and I heard its far-off, derisive laughter floating on the wings of the wind as it receded into the gulfs from whence it had come.

That was all. I was left alone in the room with the limp and lifeless body at my feet. The book was gone; but there were bloody prints upon the wall, bloody swaths upon the floor, and the face of my poor friend was a bloody death's head, leering up at the stars.

For a long time I sat alone in silence before I set on fire that room and all it contained. After that I went away, laughing, for I knew that the blaze would eradicate all trace of what remained. I had arrived only that afternoon, and there were none who knew, and none to see me go, for I departed ere the glowing flames were detected. I stumbled for hours through the twisted streets, and quaked with renewed and idiotic laughter as I looked up at the burning, ever-gloating stars that eyed me furtively through wreaths of haunted fog.

After a long while I became calm enough to board a train. I have been calm throughout the long journey home, and calm throughout the penning of this screed. I was even calm when I read of my friend's curious accidental death in the fire that destroyed his dwelling.

It is only at nights, when the stars gleam, that dreams return to drive me into a gigantic maze of frantic fears. Then I take to drugs, in a vain attempt to ban those leering memories from my sleep. But I really do not care, for I shall not be here long.

I have a curious suspicion that I shall again see that shambler from the stars. I think it will return soon without being re-summoned, and I know that when it comes it will seek me out and carry me down into the darkness that holds my friend. Sometimes I almost yearn for the advent of that day, for then I too shall learn once and for all, the *Mysteries of the Worm*.

# Mother of Serpents

IT WAS MANY years ago, soon after the slaves had revolted. Toussaint l'Ouverture, Dessalines and King Christophe freed them from their French masters, freed them after uprisings and massacres and set up a kingdom founded on cruelty more fantastic than the despotism that reigned before.

There were no happy blacks in Haiti then. They had known too much of torture and death; the carefree life of their West Indian neighbors was utterly alien to these slaves and descendants of slaves. A strange mixture of races flourished; fierce tribesmen from Ashanti, Damballah, and the Guinea Coast; sullen Caribs; dusky offspring of renegade Frenchmen; bastard admixtures of Spanish, Negro, and Indian blood. Sly, treacherous half-breeds and mulattos ruled the coast, but there were even worse dwellers in the hills behind.

There were jungles in Haiti, impassable jungles, mountain-ringed and swamp-scourged forests filled with poisonous insects and pestilential fevers. White men dared not enter them, for they were worse than death. Blood-sucking plants, venomous reptiles, diseased orchids filled the forests, forests that hid horrors Africa had never known.

For that is where the real voodoo flourished, back there in the hills. Men lived there, it is said, descendants of escaped slaves, and outlaw factions that had been hunted from the coast. Furtive rumors told of isolated villages that practised cannibalism, mixed in with dark religious rites more dreadful and perverted than anything spawned in the Congo itself. Necrophilism, phallic worship, anthropomancy, and distorted versions of the Black Mass were commonplace. The shadow of *obeah* was everywhere. Human sacrifice was common, the offering up of roosters and goats an accepted thing. There were orgies around the voodoo altars, and blood was drunk in honor of *Baron Samedi* and the old black gods brought from ancient lands.

Everybody knew about it. Each night the *ratta*-drums boomed out from the hills, and fires flared over the forests. Many known *papalois* and conjure-doctors resided on the edge of the coast itself, but they were never disturbed. Nearly all the "civilized" blacks still believe in charms and philtres; even the church-goers reverted to talismans and incantations in time of need. So-called "educated" Negroes in Port-au-Prince society were admittedly emissaries from the barbarian tribes of the interior, and despite the outward show of civilization the bloody priests still ruled behind the throne.

Of course there were scandals, mysterious disappearances, and occasional protests from emancipated citizens. But it was not wise to meddle with those who bowed to the Black Mother, or incur the anger of the terrible old men who dwelt in the shadow of the Snake.

Such was the status of sorcery when Haiti became a republic. People often wonder why there is still sorcery existent there today; more secretive, perhaps, but still surviving. They ask why the ghastly *zombies* are not destroyed, and why the Government has not stepped in to stamp out the fiendish blood-cults that still lurk in the jungle gloom.

Perchance this tale will provide an answer; this old, secret tale of the new republic. Officials, remembering the story, are still afraid to interfere too strongly, and the laws that have been passed are very loosely enforced.

Because the Serpent Cult of Obeah will never die in Haiti—in Haiti, that fantastic island whose sinuous shoreline resembles the yawning jaws of a monstrous *snake.*

2.

One of the earliest presidents of Haiti was an educated man. Although born on the island, he was schooled in France, and studied extensively while abroad. His accession to the highest office of the land found him an enlightened, sophisticated cosmopolite of the modern type. Of course he still liked to remove his shoes in the privacy of his office, but he never displayed his naked toes in an official capacity. Don't misunderstand—the man was no Emperor Jones; he was merely a polished ebon gentleman whose natural barbarity occasionally broke through its veneer of civilization.

He was, in fact, a very shrewd man. He had to be in order to become president in those early days; only extremely shrewd men ever attained that dignity. In those times the term "shrewd" was a polite Haitian synonym for "crooked".

In his short reign he was opposed by very few enemies; and those that did work against him usually disappeared. The tall, coal-black man with the physical skull-conformation of a gorilla harbored a remarkably crafty brain beneath his beetling brow.

His ability was phenomenal. He had an insight into finance which profited him greatly; profited him, that is, in both his official and unofficial capacity. Whenever he saw fit to increase the taxes he increased the army as well, and sent it out to escort the state tax-collectors. His treaties with foreign countries were masterpieces of legal lawlessness. This black Machiavelli knew that he must work fast, since presidents had a peculiar way of dying in Haiti. So the president worked very fast indeed, and he did a masterful job.

This was truly remarkable, in view of his humble background. His father was unknown. His mother was a conjure-woman in the hills, and though quite well known, she had been very poor. The president had been born in a log cabin; quite the classic setting for a future distinguished career. His early years had been most uneventful, until his adoption, at thirteen, by a benevolent Protestant minister. For a year he lived with this kind man, serving as house-boy in his home. Suddenly the poor minister died of an obscure ailment; this was most unfortunate, for he had been quite wealthy and his money was alleviating much of the suffering in this particular section. At any rate, this rich minister died, and the poor conjure-woman's son sailed to France for a university education.

As for the conjure-woman, she bought herself a new mule and said nothing. Her skill at herbs had given her son a chance in the world, and she was satisfied.

It was eight years before the boy returned. He had changed a great deal since his departure; he preferred the society of whites and the octoroon society people of Port-au-Prince. It is recorded that he rather ignored his old mother, too. His newly acquired fastidiousness made him painfully aware of the woman's ignorant simplicity. Besides, he was ambitious, and he did not care to publicize his relationship with such a notorious witch.

For she was quite famous in her way. Where she had come from and what her original history was, nobody knew. But for many years her hut in the mountains had been the rendezvous of strange worshippers and even stranger emissaries. The dark powers of *obeah* were evoked in her shadowy altar-place amidst the hills, and a furtive group of acolytes resided there with her. Her ritual fires always flared on moonless nights, and bullocks were given in bloody baptism to the Crawler of Midnight. For she was a Priestess of the Serpent.

The Snake-God is the real deity of the *obeah* cults. The blacks worshipped the Serpent in Dahomey and Senegal from time immemorial. They venerate the reptiles in a curious way, and there is some obscure linkage between the Snake and the crescent moon. Curious, isn't it—this serpent superstition? The Garden of Eden had its tempter, and the Bible tells of Moses and his staff of snakes. The Egyptians revered Set, and the ancient Hindoos had a cobra god. It seems to be general throughout the world—the kindred hatred and reverence of serpents. Always they seem to be worshipped as creatures of evil. Our own American Indians believed in Yig, and Aztec myths follow the pattern. And of course the Hopi ceremonial dances are on the same order.

But the African Serpent legends are particularly dreadful, and the Haitian adaptations of the sacrificial rites are worse.

During the President's reign, some of the voodoo groups were believed to actually breed snakes; they smuggled the reptiles over from the Ivory Coast to use in their secret practices. There were tall tales current about twenty-foot pythons which swallowed infants offered up to them on the Black Altar, and about *sendings* of poisonous serpents which killed enemies of the voodoo-masters. It is a known fact that several anthropoid apes had been smuggled into the country by a peculiar cult that worshipped gorillas; so the serpent legends may have been equally true.

At any rate, the president's mother was a priestess, and equally as famous, in a way, as her distinguished son. He, just after his return, had slowly climbed to power. First he had been a tax-gatherer, then treasurer, and finally president. Several of his rivals died, and those who opposed him soon found it expedient to dissemble their hatred; for he was still a savage at heart, and savages like to torment their enemies. It was rumored that he had constructed a secret torture-chamber beneath the palace, and that its instruments were rusty, though not from disuse.

The breach between the young statesman and his mother began to widen just prior to his presidential incumbency. The immediate cause was his marriage to the daughter of a rich octoroon planter from the coast. Not only was the old woman humiliated because her son contaminated the family stock (she was pure Negro, and descendant of a Niger slave-king), but she was further indignant because she had not been invited to the wedding.

It was held in Port-au-Prince. The foreign consuls were there, and the cream of Haitian society was present. The lovely bride had been convent-bred, and her antecedents were held in the highest esteem. The groom wisely did not deign to desecrate the nuptial celebration by including his rather unsavory parent.

She came, though, and watched the affair through the kitchen entrance-way. It was just as well that she did not make her presence known, as it would have embarrassed not only her son, but several others as well—official dignitaries who sometimes consulted her in their unofficial capacity.

What she saw of her son and his bride was not pleasing. The man was an affected dandy now, and his wife was a silly flirt. The atmosphere of pomp and ostentation did not impress her; behind their debonair masks of polite sophistication she knew that most of those present were superstitious Negroes who would run to her for charms or oracular advice the moment they were in trouble. Nevertheless, she took no action; she merely smiled rather bitterly and hobbled home. After all, she still loved her son.

The next affront, however, she could not overlook. This was

the inauguration of the new president. She was not invited to this affair either, yet she came. And this time she did not skulk in the shadows. After the oath of office was administered she marched boldly up to the new ruler of Haiti and accosted him before the very eyes of the German consul himself. She was a grotesque figure; an ungainly little harridan barely five feet tall, black, bare-foot, and clad in rags.

Her son quite naturally ignored her presence. The withered crone licked her toothless gums in terrible silence. Then, quite calmly, she began to curse him—not in French, but in native *patois* of the hills. She called down the wrath of her bloody gods upon his ungrateful head, and threatened both him and his wife with vengeance for their smug ingratitude. The assembled guests were shocked.

So was the new president. However, he did not forget himself. Calmly he motioned to his guards, who led the now hysterical witch-woman away. He would deal with her later.

The next night when he saw fit to go into the dungeon and reason with his mother, she was gone. Disappeared, the guards told him, rolling their eyes mysteriously. He had the jailer shot, and went back to his official chambers.

He was a little worried about that curse business. He knew what the woman was capable of. He did not like those threats against his wife, either. The next day he had some silver bullets molded, like King Henry in the old days. He also bought an *ouanga* charm from a devil-doctor of his own acquaintance. Magic would fight magic.

That night a serpent came to him in dreams; a serpent with green eyes that whispered in the way of men and hissed at him with shrill and mocking laughter as he struck at it in his sleep. There was a reptilian odor in his bedroom the next morning, and a nauseous slime upon his pillow that gave forth a similar stench. And the president knew that only his charm had saved him.

That afternoon his wife missed one of her Paris frocks, and the president questioned his servants in his private torture-chamber below. He learned some facts he dared not tell his bride, and thereafter he seemed very sad. He had seen his mother work with wax images before—little mannikins resembling men and women, dressed in parts of their stolen garments, Sometimes she stuck pins into them or roasted them over a slow fire. Always the real people sickened and died. This knowledge made the president quite unhappy, and he was still more overwrought when messengers returned and said that his mother was gone from her old hut in the hills.

Three days later his wife died, of a painful wound in her side which no doctor could explain. She was in agony until the end, and just before her passing it was rumored that her body turned blue and bloated up to twice its normal size. Her features were eaten away as if with leprosy, and her swollen limbs looked like those of an elephantiasis victim. Loathsome tropical diseases abound in Haiti, but none of them kill in three days. . . .

After this the president went mad.

Like Cotton Mather of old, he started on a witch-hunting crusade. Soldiers and police were sent out to comb the countryside. Spies rode up to hovels on the mountain-peaks, and armed patrols crouched in far-off fields where the living dead-men work, their glazed and glassy eyes staring ceaselessly at the moon. *Mamalois* were put to the question over slow fires, and possessors of forbidden books were roasted over flames fed by the very tomes they harbored. Blood-hounds yammered in the hills, and priests died on altars where they were wont to sacrifice. Only one order had been specially given: the president's mother was to be captured alive and unharmed.

Meanwhile he sat in the palace with the embers of slow insanity in his eyes—embers that flared into fiendish flame when the guards brought in the withered crone, who had been captured near that awful grove of idols in the swamp.

They took her downstairs, although she fought and clawed like a wildcat, and then the guards went away and left her son with her alone. Alone, in a torture-chamber, with a mother who cursed him from the rack. Alone, with frantic fires in his eyes, and a great silver knife in his hand. . . .

The president spent many hours in his secret torture-chamber during the next few days. He seldom was seen around the palace, and his servants were given orders that he must not be disturbed,

On the fourth day he came up the hidden stairway for the last time, and the flickering madness in his eyes was gone.

Just what occurred in the dungeon below will never be rightly known. No doubt that is for the best. The president was a savage at heart, and to the brute, prolongation of pain always brings ecstasy....

It is recorded, though, that the old witch-woman cursed her son with the Serpent's Curse in her dying breath, and that is the most terrible curse of all.

Some idea of what happened may be gained by the knowledge of the president's revenge; for he had a grim sense of humor, and a barbarian's idea of retribution. His wife had been killed by his mother, who fashioned a waxen image. He decided to do what would be exquisitely appropriate.

When he came up the stairs that last time, his servants saw that he bore with him a great candle, fashioned of corpse-fat. And since nobody ever saw his mother's body again, there were curious surmises as to where the corpse-fat was obtained. But then, the president's mind leaned toward grisly jests....

The rest of the story is very simple. The president went directly to his chambers in the palace, where he placed the candle in a holder on his desk. He had neglected his work in the last few days, and there was much official business for him to transact. For a while he sat in silence, staring at the candle with a curious, satisfied smile. Then he called for his papers and announced that he would attend to them immediately.

He worked all that night, with two guards stationed outside his door. Sitting at his desk, he pored over his task in the candle-light—the candle-light from the corpse-fat taper.

Evidently his mother's dying curse did not bother him at all. Once satisfied, his blood-lust abated, he discounted all possibility of revenge. Even he was not superstitious enough to believe that the sorceress could return from her grave. He was quite calm as he sat there, quite the civilized gentleman. The candle cast ominous shadows over the darkened room, but he did not notice—until it was too late. Then he looked up to see the corpse-fat candle wriggle into a monstrous life.

His mother's curse....

The candle—the corpse-fat candle—was *alive!* It was a sinuous, twisting thing, weaving in its holder with sinister purpose.

The flame-tipped end seemed to glow strongly into a sudden terrible semblance. The president, amazed, saw a fiery face—his mother's; a tiny, wrinkled face of flame, with a corpse-fat body that darted out toward the man with hideous ease. The candle was lengthening as if the tallow were melting; lengthening, and reaching out toward him in a terrible way.

The president of Haiti screamed, but it was too late. The glowing flame on the end snuffed out, breaking the hypnotic spell that had held the man betranced. And at that moment the candle leapt, while the room faded into dreadful darkness. It was a ghastly darkness, filled with moans, and the sound of a thrashing body that grew fainter, and fainter....

It was quite still by the time the guards had entered and turned up the lights once more. They knew about the corpse-fat candle and the witch-mother's curse. That is why they were the first to announce the president's death; the first to fire a bullet into his temple and claim he committed suicide.

They told the president's successor the story, and he gave orders that the crusade against voodoo be abandoned. It was better so, for the new man did not wish to die. The guards had explained why they shot the president and called it suicide, and his successor did not wish to risk the Serpent Curse.

For the president of Haiti had been strangled to death by his mother's corpse-fat candle—*a corpse-fat candle that was wound around his neck like a giant snake.*

# The Secret of Sebek

I SHOULD NEVER have attended Henricus Vanning's costume ball. Even if the tragedy had not occurred, I would be better off had I refused his invitation that night. Now that I have left New Orleans I can view the episode in saner light, and I know that I made a mistake. The remembrance of that final inexplicable moment is a horror that I still cannot face with a rational mind. Had I suspected beforehand, I might now be spared the recurrent nightmares which afflict me.

But at that time of which I speak there was no premonition to guide me. I was a stranger in the Louisiana city, and very lonely. The Mardi Gras season served only to accentuate my feeling of utter isolation. During the first two evenings of celebration, tired from long vigils at the typewriter, I wandered alien and alone along the quaintly twisted streets, and the crowds that hustled by seemed to mock my solitude.

My work at the time was very exhausting—I was doing a series of Egyptian stories for a magazine—and my mental state was a bit odd. During the day I sat in my quiet room and gave my mind over to images of Nyarlathotep, Bubastis, and Anubis; my thoughts were peopled with the priestly pageantries of olden times. And in the evenings I walked unknown amidst thoughtless throngs more unreal than the fanciful figures of the past.

But enough of excuses. To be perfectly frank, when I left the house that third night after a weary day, I expressly intended to get drunk. I entered a café at dusk, dining lavishly with a bottle of peach brandy. The place was hot and crowded; the ribald, costumed masqueraders all seemed to be enjoying the reign of Momus.

After a time this did not disturb me. Four generous goblets of the really excellent *liqueur* had set the blood running like elixir in my veins; bold, reckless dreams cascaded through my head. I now gazed at the impersonal swarms about me with new interest and understanding. They too were trying to escape tonight—escape from maddening monotony and humdrum commonplace. The fat man in the clown costume near by had looked silly an hour ago; now I seemed to sympathize with him. I sensed the frustration behind the masks these strangers wore; appreciated how valiantly they strove to find forgetfulness in the Mardi Gras.

I would forget, too. The bottle was emptied. I left the café and once more walked the streets, but this time I no longer had any feeling of isolation. I strode along like the carnival king himself, and traded gibe for gibe with chance buffeters.

Here memory is temporarily blurred. I went into a club lounge for scotch and soda, then continued on my way. Where my feet led me I cannot say. I seemed to float along effortlessly, but in my mind was crystal-clear.

I was not thinking of mundane things. Through some quirk I recalled work again, and I contemplated ancient Egypt. Through crumbled centuries I moved, in visions of secret splendor.

I lurched down a dim, deserted street.

*I walked through templed Thebes, while sphinxes stared.*

I turned into a lighted thoroughfare where revellers danced.

*I mingled with the white-clad acolytes adoring sacred Apis.*

The carousing mob blew paper trumpets, strewed confetti.

*To the shrill litany of lutes the temple virgins showered me with roses red as the blood of betrayed Osiris.*

Thus I passed through streets of saturnalia, my thoughts still wine-wafted and far away. It was all very much like a dream when at last I entered that obscure thoroughfare in the heart of the Creole district. Tall houses reared deserted on either side; darkened, dingy domiciles deserted by their owners, who mingled with the merrymakers amidst more pleasant surroundings. The buildings were old; in the fashion of ancient days they stood narrowly together, row on row.

*They are like untenanted mummy-cases in some forgotten tomb; they stand deserted by the maggot and the worm.*

From the steeply gabled roofs little black windows yawned.

*They are empty, like the eyeless sockets of a skull, and like a skull they too hide secrets.*

Secrets.

*Secret Egypt.*

It was then that I saw the man. Threading my way down that black and twisted street, I noticed a figure in the shadows before me. It stood silent, as though awaiting my approach. I endeavored to hurry past, but there was something about the motionless man which arrested my attention. He was dressed—unnaturally.

Suddenly, shockingly, my drunken dreams were fused with stark reality.

*This waiting man was dressed like a priest of ancient Egypt!*

Was it hallucination, or did he wear the triple-crowned insignia of Osiris? That long white robe was unmistakable, and in his lean hands was the sceptered diadem of Set, the Serpent.

Overcome with bewilderment, I stood stock-still and stared. He stared back, his thin, tanned face bland and expressionless. With a quick gesture, his right hand darted under his robe. I shrank back, as he withdrew it once more and pulled out—a cigarette.

"Got a match, stranger?" asked the priest of Egypt.

Then I laughed, remembered, and understood. Mardi Gras! What a scare he had given me, though! Smiling, my head suddenly clear once more, I extended my lighter. He used it, and as the flame flared upward, peered curiously into my countenance.

He started, gray eyes evincing sudden recognition. To my astonishment, he spoke my name in interrogation. I nodded my head.

"What a surprise!" he chuckled. "You're the writer, aren't you? I've read some of your recent stuff, but I had no idea that you were here in New Orleans."

I mumbled a few words of explanation. He genially interrupted.

"That's great luck. My name is Vanning—Henricus Vanning. I'm interested in the occult myself; we should have a lot in common."

We stood chatting for several minutes; or rather, he chatted and I listened. I learned that Mr. Vanning was a gentleman of means and leisure. He touched a bit glibly and flippantly on his studies in primitive mythology, but expressed a patently genuine interest in Egyptian lore. There was mention of a social group whose mutual and private researches in metaphysics might interest me.

As if seized with sudden inspiration, he clapped me heartily on the back.

"What are your plans for the evening?" he said.

I confessed my predicament. He smiled.

"Splendid! Just had dinner, myself. I'm on the way back to the house now to play host. Our little group—I told you about them—is holding a costume ball there. Like to come along? Interesting."

"But I'm not in costume," I protested.

"Doesn't matter. I think you'd particularly appreciate this affair. Most unusual. Come on."

He beckoned me to follow and started off down the street. I shrugged, but acquiesced. After all, I had nothing to lose, and my curiosity was aroused.

As we walked, the garrulous Mr. Vanning carried on a smooth and intriguing conversation. He spoke in greater detail of his little "circle" of esoteric friends. I gathered that they rather ostentatiously referred to themselves as *The Coffin Club,* and spent much of their time in pursuit of exotic and macabre phases in art, literature or music.

Tonight, according to my host, the group were celebrating the Mardi Gras in their own unique fashion. Defying the conventional masquerade, all members and invited friends planned to come attired in supernatural garb; instead of the usual clowns, pirates, and Colonial gentlemen, they would represent the more outlandish features of fancy and myth. I would mingle with werewolves, vampires, gods, goddesses, priests and black magicians.

I must confess that this news did not wholly please me. I never could stomach the pseudo-occultist or the quack devotee and metaphysicist. I dislike a bogus interest and a sham knowledge of legendry in others. Petty dabblings in spiritualism, astrology, and "psychic" charlatanry have always been repellent to my tastes.

I feel that it is not good for fools to mock the old faiths and the secret ways of vanished races. If this was to be one of the usual groups of middle-aged neurotics and pallid-purple dilettantes, then I would spend a boring evening.

But Henricus Vanning himself seemed to have more than a surface smattering of erudition. His cultured allusions to various myth-sagas in my stories seemed to hint at deep knowledge and sincere research that peered beyond the blacker veils of human thought. He spoke quite fluently of his delvings into Manicheism and primal cult-ceremonials.

I became so absorbed in his words that I failed to heed the direction in which he led me, though I know we walked for some time. When we drew up at last, it was to turn into a long, shrubbery-bordered walk which led to the doors of a well-lighted and imposing mansion.

In simple truth, I must admit to being so seduced by Vanning's picturesque statements, that I cannot remember a single concrete detail of the house's exterior appearance or the environs in which it stood.

Still bemused, I followed Vanning through the opened door and walked into—nightmare.


When I stated that the house was brilliantly lighted, I meant just that. It was lighted—*in flaming red*.

We stood in a hallway; a hallway of hell. Scarlet scimitars of light scintillated from the surface of mirrored walls. Vermilion drapes cloaked inner entrances, and the crimson ceiling seemed to smolder with the crystalline carmine fires of ruby gas-torches that hung in blood-imbrued braziers. A Luciferean butler took my hat, handed me a goblet of cherry brandy.

Alone in the red room, Vanning faced me, glass in hand.

"Like it?" he inquired. "Gay setting to put my guests in the mood. Little touch I borrowed from Poe."

I thought of the splendid *Masque of the Red Death*, and winced inwardly at this crude and vulgar desecration.

Still, this evidence of the man's eccentricity did intrigue me. He was *trying* for something. I was almost moved when I lifted my glass to the pseudo-priest of Egypt there in that eery anteroom.

The brandy burned.

"Now—on to our guests." He pushed a tapestry aside, and we entered the cavernous chamber to the right.

Green and black were the velvet backgrounds of these walls; silver the candles that lighted the niches. The furniture, however, was modern and conventional enough; but when I first surveyed the throng of guests I felt for a moment as if I were again in dreams.

"Werewolves, gods, and black magicians," Vanning had said. There was more of understatement than exaggeration in that cryptic remark. The occupants of that room constituted a pantheon from all the hells.

I saw an obscene Pan dancing with a withered night-hag; a mad Freya embracing a voodoo priest; a Bacchante clinging lecherously to a wild-eyed dervish from Irem. There were archdruids, dwarfs, nixies and kobolds; lamas, Shamans, priestesses, fauns, ogres, magi, ghouls. It was a sabbat—a resurrection of ancient sin.

Then, as I mingled with the throng and was introduced, the momentary illusion faded. Pan was merely a stout, rather puffy-eyed, middle-aged gentleman with an obvious paunch which no goatskin girdle could obliterate. Freya was a desperately-bright debutante, with the predatory slut-eyes of a common harlot. The voodoo priest was just a nice young man in burnt cork, with a slightly incongruous English lisp.

I met perhaps a dozen guests, and quickly forgot their names. I was a trifle surprised by Vanning's seeming superciliousness; he almost snubbed several of the more talkative.

"Enjoy yourselves," he called over his shoulder as he dragged me across the floor. "Those are the fools," he confided in a lower voice. "But there are a few I want you to meet."

Over in the corner sat a little group of four men. All wore priestly raiment similar to Vanning's own, in that religion dominated.

"Doctor Delvin." An old man, in Babylonian, almost biblical robes.

"Etienne de Marigny." Dark, handsome priest of Adonis.

"Professor Weildan." A bearded gnome in a kalender's turban.

"Richard Royce." A young, bespectacled scholar, monkishly cowled.

The foursome bowed courteously. Upon my being introduced, however, there was an immediate slackening of their reserve. They crowded about Vanning and me in a rather confidential way, while our host spoke softly in my ear.

"These are the real members of the group I spoke about. I saw the way you looked at the others here, and I quite understand and agree with you. Those people are silly fools. We, here, are the initiates. Perhaps, then, you wonder at the reason for their presence. Let me explain. Attack is the best defense."

"Attack is the best defense?" I echoed, puzzled.

"Yes. Suppose, now, that I and my friends here are really deep students of black magic."

There was a subtle suggestion in the way he breathed "suppose."

"Suppose that is true. Don't you think that our society friends would object, gossip, investigate?"

"Yes," I admitted. "That sounds reasonable."

"Of course. That's why we formulated our attack. By publicly proclaiming an eccentric interest in occultism, and showing it by giving these stupid parties, we are left quite unmolested to carry out our serious work by ourselves. Clever, eh?"

I smiled in agreement. Vanning was no fool.

"It might interest you to know that Doctor Delvin, here, is one of this country's foremost ethnologists. De Marigny is a well-known occultist—you may remember his connection with the Randolph Carter case several years ago. Royce is my personal aide, and Professor Weildan is *the* Weildan, Egyptologist."

Funny, how Egypt kept recurring in the course of the evening!

"I promised you something interesting, my friend, and you shall have it. First, though, we must endure these cattle for another half-hour or so. Then we'll go up to my room for a real session. I trust you will be patient."

The four men bowed to me as Vanning again led me into the center of the room. The dancing had stopped now, and the floor was covered by little groups of idle chatterers. Demons drank mint-juleps, and virgin sacrifices to the Magna Mater artfully applied their lipstick. Neptune passed me, with a cigar in his mouth. The gayety was shrill.

*Masque of the Red Death,* I thought. Then I saw—him.

★

It was all Poe, his entrance. The black and green curtains at the end of the room parted, and he glided in as though emerging from the hidden depths of the hangings rather than the door behind them.

Silver candle-light silhouetted his figure, and as he walked a grisly nimbus seemed to cloak each movement. I had the momentary impression of gazing at him through a prism, since the queer lighting made him appear indistinct and sharply-etched in turn.

He was the soul of Egypt.

The long white robe concealed a body whose contours were elusively problematical. Taloned hands hung from swirling sleeves, and the jeweled fingers clasped a rod of gold, set with the seal of the Eye of Horus.

The top of the robe terminated in a cape-collar of black; it stood, a stiffly hooded background for a head of horror.

*The head of a crocodile. The body of an Egyptian priest.*

That head was—awful. A slanted, saurian skull, all green and scaly on top; hairless, slimy, slick and nauseous. Great bony ridges socketed the embered eyes, staring from behind a sickening sweep of long, reptilian snout. A rugose muzzle, with great champing jaws half opened to reveal a lolling pinkish tongue and scummy teeth of stiletto-like sharpness.

What a mask!

I have always prided myself on a certain *sensitivity*. I can *feel* quite strongly. Now, gazing at that triumph of morbid mummery, I received a sensory shock. I felt that this masquer was real—more real than his less grotesque fellows. The very outlandishness of his costume seemed to carry added conviction when contrasted with the makeshift pretenses of those through which he walked.

He seemed to be alone, nor did anyone attempt to converse with him in passing. I reached forward and tapped Vanning on the shoulder. I wanted to meet this man.

Vanning, however, swung ahead to the platform, where he turned and spoke to the orchestra men. I glanced back, half intending to approach the crocodile-man myself.

He was gone.

I searched the crowd with eager eyes. No use. He had vanished.

Vanished? Had he existed? I saw him—or thought I did—only

for a moment. And I was still a little befuddled. Egypt on the brain. Perhaps I had been over-imaginative. But why the queer flooding feeling of reality?

These questions were never answered, for my attention was distracted by the performance on the platform. Vanning had started his half-hour of entertainment for the "guests." He had told me it was a mere sop to conceal his real interests, but I found it more impressive than I expected.

The lights turned blue—haggard, graveyard-misty blue. The shadows darkened to indigo blurs as the celebrants found seats. An organ rose from beneath the orchestra platform, and music throbbed.

It was my favorite number—the superb and sonorously sepulchral Number One scene from *The Swan Lake,* by Tchaikovsky. It droned, mocked, shrilled, blared. It whispered, roared, threatened, frightened. It even impressed and quieted the milling geese about me.

There was a Devil Dance following; a magician, and a final Black Mass ritual with a really terrifying illusion of sacrifice. All very weird, very morbid, and very false. When the lights went up at last and the band resumed their places, I found Vanning, and we hastened across the room. The four fellow-researchers were waiting.

Vanning motioned me to follow them through the curtains near the platform. We made our exits unobtrusively, and I found myself walking down a long, darkened hallway. Vanning halted before an oak-paneled door. A key flashed, grated, turned. We were in a library.

Chairs, cigars, brandy—indicated in turn by our smiling host. The brandy—a fine cognac—momentarily sent my thoughts astray once more. Everything was unreal; Vanning, his friends, this house, the entire evening. Everything but the man in the crocodile mask. I must ask Vanning. . . .

Abruptly, a voice summoned me back to the present. Vanning was speaking, addressing me. His voice was solemn, and held an unusual timbre. It was almost as though I was hearing him speak for the first time; as if this were the real man, and the other genial inhabitant of an open house merely a sham as insubstantial as the Mardi Gras costumes of the guests.

As he spoke, I found myself the focus of five pairs of eyes; Delvin's Celtic blue, Marigny's penetrating Gallic brown, Royce's bespectacled gray, Weildan's deep umber, and the gun-metal pinpoints of Vanning himself. Each seemed to ask a question:

"Do you dare?"

But what Vanning said was much more prosaic.

"I promised you an unusual time. Well, that's what you're here for. But I must admit that my motives are not altruistic alone. I—I need you. I've read your tales. I think you are a sincere student, and I want both knowledge and advice. That is why we five are admitting a comparative stranger to our secret. We trust you— we must trust you."

"You can," I said, quietly. For the first time I realized that Vanning was not only earnest; he was nervous. The hand holding the cigar shook; perspiration gathered beneath the Egyptian hood. Royce, the scholarly student, was twisting the belt of his monkish costume. The other three men still watched me, and their silence was more disturbing than the unnatural earnestness in Vanning's voice.

What was all this? Was I drugged, dreaming? Blue lights, and crocodile masks, and a melodramatic secret. Yet I believed.

I believed, when Vanning pressed the lever in the great library table so that the false drawers beneath swung outward and revealed the gaping space within. I believed when I saw him hoist out the mummy-case, with de Marigny's aid.

I became interested even before I noted the peculiarities of the case itself. For Vanning went over to a shelf and came back with an armful of books. These he handed to me silently. They were his credentials; they confirmed all that he had told me.

Nobody but a recognized occultist and adept could possess these strange tomes. Thin strips of glass protected the crumbling covers of the ill-famed *Book of Eibon*, the original editions of *Cultes des Goules*, and the almost fabulous *De Vermis Mysteriis*.

Vanning managed a smile when he saw the light of recognition in my face.

"We've gone in pretty deep these past few years," he said. "You know what lies in these books."

I knew. I have written of *De Vermis Mysteriis* myself, and there are times when the words of Ludvig Prinn fill me with a vague fright and an indefinable repulsion.

Vanning opened the latter volume. "You are familiar with this, I believe. You've mentioned it in your work."

He pointed to the cryptic chapter that is known as *Saracenic Rituals.*

I nodded. I knew the *Saracenic Rituals* only too well. The account dealt with Prinn's mysterious sojourn in Egypt and the Orient in what he claimed were Crusader days. There is revealed the lore of the *efreet* and the *djinn,* the secrets of the Assassin sects, the myths of Arabian ghoul-tales, and the hidden practices of dervish cults. I had found within it a great wealth of material on the legends of ancient Inner Egypt; indeed, much story material was culled from those tattered pages.

Egypt again! I glanced at the mummy-case.

Vanning and the others watched me intently. At last my host shrugged.

"Listen," he said. "I'll put my cards on the table. I—I must trust you, as I said."

"Go ahead," I rejoined, impatiently. Such mystery of manner was irritating.

"It all started with this book," said Henricus Vanning. "Royce, here, dug it up for me. We got interested in the Bubastis legend, at first. For a while I contemplated some investigations in Cornwall—looking up the Egyptian ruins of England, you know. But then, I found a more fertile field in actual Egyptology. When Professor Weildan, here, went on his expedition last year, I authorized him to obtain anything of interest he might discover, at any price. He returned last week, with this."

Vanning stepped over to the mummy-case. I followed.

He didn't have to explain further. One detailed inspection of that mummy-case, combined with what I knew of the *Saracenic Rituals* chapter, led to an inference that was unmistakable.

The hieroglyphs and markings on the case indicated that it contained the body of an Egyptian priest; a priest of the god Sebek. And *Saracenic Rituals* told its own story.

For a moment I mentally reviewed my knowledge. Sebek,

according to reputable anthropologists, was a lesser deity of Inner Egypt; a fertility god of the Nile. If recognized authorities be correct, only four mummies of his priesthood have ever been found; though numerous statuettes, figurines, and pictures in tombs testify to the veneration accorded this deity. Egyptologists have never fully traced the history of the god, though some unorthodox surmises and wild linkages have been made or hinted at by Wallis-Budge.

Ludvig Prinn, though, had delved further. I recalled his words with an appreciable shudder.

In *Saracenic Rituals,* Prinn spoke of what he had learned from Alexandrian seers; of his journeyings into the deserts and his secret tomb-lootings in hidden valleys of the Nile.

He told a tale, historically authenticated, of the Egyptian priestcraft and its rise to power—how the servants of the dark nature-gods ruled the Pharaohs from behind the throne, and held the land in their grip. For Egyptian gods and religions were based on secret realities. Strange hybrids walked the earth when it was young; gigantic, lumbering creatures—half-beast, half-man. Human imagination alone did not create the gigantic serpent Set, carnivorous Bubastis, and great Osiris. I thought of Thoth, and tales of harpies; thought of jackal-headed Anubis and the legend of werewolves.

No, the ancients trafficked with elemental powers and beasts of the beyond. They could summon their gods, the humans with the heads of animals. And, at times, they did. Hence their power.

In time, they ruled over Egypt; their word was law. The land was filled with rich temples, and every seventh man owed allegiance to the ritual bodies. Incense rose before a thousand shrines—incense, and blood. The beast-mouths of the gods hungered for blood.

Well might the priests adore, for they had made strange and curious bargains with their divine Masters. Unnatural perversions drove the cult of Bubastis out of Egypt, and a never-mentioned abomination caused the symbol and story of Nyarlathotep to be forgotten. But ever the priests waxed stronger and bolder; their sacrifices more outrageous, and their rewards greater.

For the sake of life everlastingly reincarnated, they pleasured the gods and assuaged their curious appetites. To safeguard their mummies with divine curses, they offered up scapegoats filled with blood.

Prinn speaks of the sect of Sebek in particular detail. The priests believed that Sebek, as a fertility deity, controlled the sources of life eternal. He would guard them in their graves until the resurrection-cycle was completed, and he would destroy their enemies who sought to violate their sepulchers. To him they offered virgin maidens, to be torn between the jaws of a golden crocodile. For Sebek, the Crocodile God of the Nile, had the body of a man, the head of a crocodile, and the lustful appetites of both.

The description of these ceremonies is grisly. The priests wore crocodile masks, in emulation of their Lord, for that was his earthly aspect. Once a year, they thought, Sebek himself appeared to the High Priests in the Inner Temple of Memphis, and then he too assumed the form of a man with a crocodile head.

The devout believed that he would guard their graves—and countless screaming virgins died to support their faith.

This I knew, and hurriedly recollected, while glancing at the mummy of the Priest of Sebek.

For now I looked into the case, and saw that the mummy had been unwrapped. It lay under a pane of glass, which Vanning removed.

"You know the story, then," he said, reading my eyes aright. "I've had the mummy here a week; it's been chemically treated, thanks to Weildan, here. On its chest, though, I found this."

He pointed to an amulet of clear jade—a saurian figure, covered with ideographic images.

"What it it?" I asked.

"Secret code of the priesthood. De Marigny thinks it's Nacaal. Translation? A curse—as the Prinn story has it—a curse on the heads of tomb-looters. Threatens them with the vengeance of Sebek himself. Nasty wording."

Vanning's flippancy was forced. I could tell that by the restless stirring of the others in the room. Doctor Devlin was coughing nervously; Royce twisted his robe; de Marigny scowled. The gnome-like Professor Weildan approached us. He glanced at the mummy for some time, as if seeking solution to a secret in those eyeless sockets that blindly brooded in the gloom.

"Tell him what I think, Vanning," he said, softly.

"Weildan, here, has done some investigation. He managed to get this mummy in past the authorities, but it cost him plenty to do it. He told me where he found it, and it's not a pleasant story. Nine of the caravan boys died on the return journey, though it may have been bad water that did that. The professor has gone back on us, I'm afraid."

"I have not," interposed Weildan, sharply. "When I tell you to get rid of the mummy it is because I want to live. We had some notion of using it in ceremonials here, but this is not possible. You see, I believe in the curse of Sebek.

"You know, of course, that only four mummies of his priests have ever been found. That is because the others repose in secret crypts. Well, the four finders are all dead. I knew Partington, who found the third. He was investigating this curse myth quite thoroughly when he returned—but he died before publishing any reports. It was rather curious, his end. Fell off the bridge into a crocodile pit of the London Zoo. When they pulled him out, he was a mess."

Vanning looked at me. "Bogey man," he said, deprecatingly. Then, in more serious tones, he continued. "That's one of the reasons I asked you here to share this secret. I want your own opinion, as a scholar and occultist. Should I get rid of the mummy? Do you believe in this curse story? I don't, but I have felt quite uneasy of late. I know of too many peculiar coincidences, and I have faith in Prinn's veracity. What we intended to use the mummy for does not matter. It would have been a—a desecration great enough to anger any god. And I wouldn't like to have a crocodile-headed creature at my throat. What do you say?"

Abruptly, I remembered. The man in the mask! He had been dressed like a priest of Sebek, in emulation of the god.

I told Vanning what I had seen of him. "Who is he?" I asked. "He should really be here. It makes things—appropriate."

Vanning's horror was not feigned. I regretted having spoken, after observing his terrified reaction.

"I never saw *that!* I swear I didn't! We must find the man at once."

"Perhaps it's a polite form of blackmail," I said. "He may have the goods on you and Weildan, and frighten you into paying hush-money."

"Perhaps." Vanning's voice held no note of sincerity. He turned to the others.

"Quickly," he said. "Go back into the other room and look among the guests. Collar this elusive—stranger; bring him here."

"Police?" suggested Royce, nervously.

"No, you fool. Hurry, all of you!"

The four men left the room, and their footsteps echoed in the outer corridor as they receded.

A moment's silence. Vanning tried to smile. I was in a strange oblivious fog. The Egypt of my dreams—*was it real?* Why had that one glimpse of the mysterious man in the mask so impressed me? The priests of Sebek spilt blood to bind a bargain of vengeance; could they satisfy an ancient curse? Or was Vanning mad?

A soft sound. . . .

I turned. And there in the doorway stood the man in the crocodile mask.

"That's the fellow!" I exclaimed. "That's—"

Vanning leaned against the table, his face the color of wet ash. He just stared at the figure on the threshold, but his tormented eyes telepathically conveyed a dreadful message to me.

The man in the crocodile mask . . . nobody had seen him but myself. And I was dreaming in Egypt. Here, in this room, was the stolen mummy of Sebek's priest.

The god Sebek was—*a crocodile-headed god.* And his priests were dressed in his image—*they wore crocodile masks.*

I had just warned Vanning about the vengeance of the old priests. He himself had believed and was afraid when I told him what I had seen. And now, in the doorway, stood the silent stranger. What was more logical than to believe it was a resurrected priest, come to avenge this insult to his kind?

Yet I could not believe it. Even when the figure entered, sinister and still, I did not guess its purpose. Even when Vanning cowered and moaned against the mummy-case, I was not convinced.

Then, everything happened so swiftly that I had no time to act. Just as I was about to challenge the unnatural intruder, doom was unleashed. With a darting, reptilian movement, the body beneath the white robe *undulated* across the room. In a second it towered above the cringing figure of my host. I saw clawing hands sink into sagging shoulders; then the jaws of the mask descended and *moved*. Moved—in Vanning's quivering throat.

As I leapt, my thoughts seemed sluggishly calm in contrast. "Diabolically clever murder," I mused. "Unique death-weapon. Cunningly contrived tooth-mechanism in a mask. Fanatic."

And my eyes, in a detached fashion, observed that monstrous muzzle biting into Vanning's neck. Moving, the squamous horror of the head loomed like a camera close-up.

It took only a second, understand. Then, with sudden purpose, I had seized a sleeve of the white robe, and with my free hand wrenched at the mask of the murderer.

The killer wheeled, ducked. My hand slipped, and for a moment rested on the crocodile snout, the bloody jaw.

Then, in a flash, the invader wheeled and disappeared, while I was left screaming before the ripped and tattered body on the mummy-case of Sebek.

Vanning was dead. His murderer had disappeared. The house was crowded with revellers; I had but to step to the door and call for aid.

I did not. I stood for one stark second in the center of the room, screaming, while my vision veered. Everything was swimming around and around—the blood-blotched books; the sere mummy, its chest now crushed and crimsoned by the struggle; the red, unmoving thing on the floor. All blurred before my eyes.

Then, and only then, did volition come to me. I turned and ran.

I wish my tale could end there, but it cannot. There is a conclusion to be drawn. It must be revealed so that I can know peace once more.

I'll be frank. I know it would make a better story if I had asked the butler about the man in the crocodile mask and heard him say that no such person entered the place. But this is not a story, but truth.

I *know* he was there, and after I saw Vanning die I did not wait to interview another soul. I made that last desperate clutch at the masked murderer, then screamed and ran from the room. I rushed through the revellers on the floor without even giving an alarm, dashed out of the house and panted up the street. Grinning horror bestrode my shoulders and urged me on, until I lost all consciousness and ran blindly back to the lighted lanes and laughing throngs that dwelt smugly safe from the terrors I knew.

I left New Orleans without investigating any further details. I purposely did not buy a paper, so that I do not even know if the police discovered Vanning's body or investigated his death. I have never attempted to learn anything more, nor dare I. There might be a sane explanation for it all—and then, again . . .

I prefer not to be sure. I desperately try to make myself believe that I was drunk; that the whole incident never happened, or if it did, that part of it was unreal. Even Vanning's death I could bear, but not that legend of Sebek and the mummy-case of Sebek. I told Vanning the truth about that, and my belief has been hideously confirmed.

Knowledge came during that last moment, when I saw the stranger sink his curiously constructed crocodile muzzle in poor Vanning's throat—sink in with saber-teeth slashing. It was then that I grabbed him for a moment before he slipped away; grabbed at him, screamed, and hysterically fled.

I grabbed him, in that horrible moment, by the bloody muzzle of the frighteningly realistic crocodile mask. Just a single moment of horrid contact, before he disappeared. But it was enough.

For when I seized that bloody, reptilian muzzle, I felt beneath my fingers, *not a mask, but living flesh!*

# The Eyes of the Mummy

EGYPT HAS always fascinated me; Egypt, land of antique and mysterious secrets. I had read of pyramids and kings; dreamed of vast, shadowy empires now dead as the empty eyes of the Sphinx. It was of Egypt that I wrote in later years, for to me its weird faiths and cults made the land an avatar of all strangeness.

Not that I believed in the grotesque legends of olden times; I did not credit the faith in anthropomorphic gods with the heads and attributes of beasts. Still, I sensed behind the myths of Bast, Anubis, Set, and Thoth the allegorical implications of forgotten truths. Tales of beast-men are known the world over, in the racial lore of all climes. The werewolf legend is universal and unchanged since the furtive hintings of Pliny's days. Therefore to me, with my interest in the supernatural, Egypt provided a key to ancient knowledge.

But I did not believe in the actual existence of such beings or creatures in the days of Egypt's glory. The most I would admit to myself was that perhaps the legends of those days had come down from much remoter times when primal earth could hold such monstrosities due to evolutionary mutations.

Then, one evening in carnival New Orleans, I encountered a fearful substantiation of my theories. At the home of the eccentric Henricus Vanning I participated in a queer ceremony over the body of a priest of Sebek, the crocodile-headed god. Weildan, the archeologist, had smuggled it into this country, and we examined the mummy despite curse and warning. I was not myself at the time, and to this day I am not sure what occurred, exactly. There was a stranger present, wearing a crocodile mask, and events were precipitated in nightmare-fashion. When I rushed from that house into the streets, Vanning was dead by the priest's hand—or fangs, set in the mask (if mask it was).

I cannot clarify the statement of the above facts; dare not. I told the story once, then determined to abandon writing of Egypt and its ancient ways for ever.

This resolve I have adhered to, until tonight's dreadful experience has caused me to reveal what I feel must be told.

Hence this narrative. The preliminary facts are simple; yet they all seem to imply that I am linked to some awful chain of interlocking experiences, fashioned by a grim Egyptian god of Fate. It is as though the Old Ones are jealous of my pryings into their ways, and are luring me onward to a final horror.

For after my New Orleans experience, after my return home with the resolution to abandon research into Egyptian mythology for ever, I was again enmeshed.


Professor Weildan came to call on me. It was he who had smuggled in the mummy of Sebek's priest which I had seen in New Orleans; he had met me on that inexplicable evening when a jealous god or his emissary had seemed to walk the earth for vengeance. He knew of my interest, and had spoken to me quite seriously of the dangers involved when one pried into the past.

The gnome-like, bearded little man now came and greeted me with understanding eyes. I was reluctant to see him, I own, for his presence brought back memories of the very things I was endeavoring to forget for ever. Despite my attempts to lead the conversation into more wholesome channels, he insisted on speaking of our first meeting. He told me how the death of the recluse Vanning had broken up the little group of occultists that had met over the body of the mummy that evening.

But he, Weildan, had not forsaken his pursuit of the Sebek legend. That, he informed me, was the reason he had taken this trip to see me. None of his former associates would aid him now in the project he had in mind. Perhaps I might be interested.

I flatly refused to have anything more to do with Egyptology. This I told him at once.

Weildan laughed. He understood my reasons for demurring, he said, but I must allow him to explain. This present project of his had nothing to do with sorcery, or mantic arts. It was, as he jovially explained, merely a chance to even the score with the Powers of Darkness, if I was so foolish as to term them such.

He explained. Briefly, he wanted me to go to Egypt with him, on a private expedition of our own. There would be no personal expense involved for me; he needed a young man as an assistant and did not care to trust any professional archeologists who might cause trouble.

His studies had always been directed in recent years toward the legends of the Crocodile Cult, and he had labored steadily in an effort to learn of the secret burial-places of Sebek's priests. Now, from reputable sources—a native guide in his pay abroad— he had stumbled onto a new hiding-place; a subterranean tomb which held a mummy of a Sebekian votary.

He would not waste words in giving me further details; the whole point of his story was that the mummy could be reached easily, with no need of labor or excavation, and there was abso- lutely no danger, no silly truck about curses or vengeance. We could therefore go there alone; the two of us, in utter secrecy. And our visit would be profitable. Not only could he secure the mummy without official intervention, but his source of informa- tion—on the authenticity of which he would stake his personal reputation—revealed that the mummy was interred with a hoard of sacred jewels. It was a safe, sure, secret opportunity for wealth he was offering me.

I must admit that this sounded attractive. Despite my unpleas- ant experience in the past, I would risk a great deal for the sake of suitable compensation. And then, too, although I was deter- mined to eschew all dabblings in mysticism, there was a hint of the adventurous in this undertaking which allured me.

Weildan cunningly played upon my feelings; I realize that now. He talked with me for several hours, and returned the next day, until at last I agreed.

We sailed in March, landed in Cairo three weeks later after a brief stopover in London. The excitement of going abroad obscures my memory of personal contact with the professor; I know that he was very unctuous and reassuring at all times, and doing his best to convince me that our little expedition was entirely harmless. He wholly overrode my scruples as to the dis- honesty of tomb-looting; attended to our visas, and fabricated some trumped-up tale to allow the officials to pass us through to the interior.

From Cairo we went by rail to Khartoum. It was there that Professor Weildan planned to meet his "source of information"—the native guide, who was now admittedly a spy in the archeologist's employ.

This revelation did not bother me nearly as much as it might have if it occurred midst more prosaic settings. The desert atmosphere seemed a fitting background for intrigue and conspiracy, and for the first time I understood the psychology of the wanderer and the adventurer.

It was thrilling to prowl through twisted streets of the Arab quarter on the evening we visited the spy's hovel. Weildan and I entered a dark, noisome courtyard and were admitted to a dim apartment by a tall, hawk-nosed Bedouin. The man greeted the professor warmly. Money changed hands. Then the Arab and my companion retired to an inner chamber. I heard the low whisper of their voices—Weildan's excited, questioning tones mingling with the guttural accented English of the native. I sat in the gloom and waited. The voices rose, as though in altercation. It seemed as though Weildan were attempting to placate or reassure, while the guide's voice assumed a note of warning and hesitant fear. Anger entered, as Weildan made an effort to shout down his companion.

Then I heard footsteps. The door to the inner chamber opened, and the native appeared on the threshold. His face seemed to hold a look of entreaty as he stared at me, and from his lips poured an incoherent babble, as though in his excited efforts to convey his warning to me he had relapsed into familiar Arabic speech. For warning me he was; that was unmistakable.

A second he stood there, and then Weildan's hand fell on his shoulder, wheeling him around. The door slammed shut as the Arab's voice rose high, almost to a scream. Weildan shouted something unintelligible; there was the sound of a scuffle, a muffled report, then silence.

Several minutes elapsed before the door opened and Weildan appeared, mopping his brow. His eyes avoided mine.

"Fellow kicked up a row about payments," he explained, speak-

ing to the floor. "Got the information, though. Then he came out
here to ask you for money. I had to put him out the back entrance,
finally. Fired a shot to scare him off; these natives are so excitable."

I said nothing as we left the place, nor did I comment on
the hurried furtiveness with which Weildan hastened our way
through the black streets.

Nor did I appear to notice when he wiped his hands on his
handkerchief and hastily thrust the cloth back into his pocket.

It might have embarrassed him to explain the presence of
those red stains. . . .

I should have suspected then, should have abandoned the project at once. But I could not know, when Weildan proposed a ride
into the desert the following morning, that our destination was
to be the tomb.

It was so casually arranged. Two horses, bearing a light lunch
in the saddle-bags; a small tent "against the midday heat" Weildan
said—and we cantered off, alone. No more fuss or preparation
about it than if we were planning a picnic. Our hotel rooms were
still engaged, and not a word was said to anyone.

We rode out of the gates into the calm, unrippled sands that
stretched beneath a sky of bucolic blue. For an hour or so we
jogged on through serene, if searing, sunlight. Weildan's manner
was preoccupied, he continually scanned the monotonous horizon as though seeking some expected landmark; but there was
nothing in his bearing to indicate his full intention.

We were almost upon the stones before I saw them; a great
cluster of white boulders outcropping from the sandy sides of a
little hillock. Their form seemed to indicate that the visible rocks
formed an infinitesimal fragment of the stones concealed by the
shifting sands; though there was nothing in the least unusual
about their size, contour, or formation. They rested casually
enough in the hillside, no differently than a dozen other small
clusters we had previously passed.

Weildan said nothing beyond suggesting that we dismount,
pitch the small tent, and lunch. He and I pegged in the stakes,
lugged a few small, flat stones inside to serve as table and chairs;
placing our pack-blankets as padding for the latter.

Then, as we ate, Weildan exploded his bombshell. The rocks before our tent, he averred, concealed the entrance to the tomb. Sand and wind and desert dust had done their work well, hidden the sanctuary from interlopers. His native accomplice, led by hints and rumors, had uncovered the spot in ways he did not seem anxious to mention.

But the tomb was there. Certain manuscripts and screeds bore testimony to the fact it would be unguarded. All we need do would be to roll away the few boulders blocking the entrance and descend. Once again he earnestly emphasized the fact that there would be no danger to me.

I played the fool no longer. I questioned him closely. Why would a priest of Sebek be buried in such a lonely spot?

Because, Weildan affirmed, he and his retinue were probably fleeing south at the time of his death. Perhaps he had been expelled from his temple by a new Pharaoh; then, too, the priests were magic-workers and sorcerers in latter days, and often persecuted or driven out of the cities by irate citizenry. Fleeing, he had died and been interred here.

That, Weildan further explained, was the reason for the scarcity of such mummies. Ordinarily, the perverted cult of Sebek buried its priests only under the secret vaults of its city temples. These shrines had all been long destroyed. Therefore, it was only in rare circumstances like this that an expelled priest was laid away in some obscure spot where his mummy might still be found.

"But the jewels?" I persisted.

The priests were rich. A fleeing wizard would carry his wealth. And at death it would naturally be buried with him. It was a peculiarity of certain renegade sorcerous priests to be mummified with vital organs intact—they had some superstition about earthly resurrection. That was why the mummy would prove an unusual find. Probably the chamber was just a stone-walled hollow housing the mummy-case; there would be no time to invoke or conjure any curses or other outlandish abracadabra such as I seemed to fear. We could enter freely, and secure the spoils. In the following of such a priest there surely were several expert temple craftsmen who would embalm the body properly;

it needed skill to do a good job without removing the vital organs, and religious significance made this final operation imperative. Therefore we need not worry about finding the mummy in good condition.

Weildan was very glib. Too glib. He explained how easily we would smuggle the mummy-case wrapped in our tent-folds; how he would arrange to smuggle both it and the jewels out of the country with the help of a native exporting firm.

He pooh-poohed each objection that I stated; and knowing that whatever his personal character as a man might be he was still a recognized archeologist, I was forced to concede his authority.

There was only one point which vaguely troubled me—his casual reference to some superstition concerning earthly resurrection. The burial of a mummy with organs intact sounded strange. Knowing what I did about the activities of the priests in connection with goety and sorcerous rituals, I was leery of even the faintest possibility of mishap.

Still, he persuaded me at the last, and following lunch we left the tent. We found the boulders no great hindrance. They had been placed artfully, but we discovered their appearance of being firmly imbedded in rock to be deceptive. A few heavings and clearing away of minor debris enabled us to remove four great stones which formed a block before a black opening which slanted down into the earth.

We had found the tomb!

With the realization, with the sight of that gaping, gloomy pit before me, old horrors rose to mock and grin. I remembered all of the dark, perverted faith of Sebek; the minglings of myth, fable, and grimacing reality which should not be.

I thought of underground rites in temples now given to dust; of posturing worship before great idols of gold—manshaped figures bearing the heads of crocodiles. I recalled the tales of darker parallel worships, bearing the same relationship as Satanism now does to Christianity; of priests who invoked animal-headed gods as demons rather than as benignant deities. Sebek was such a dual god, and his priests had given him blood to drink. In some temples there were vaults, and in these vaults were eidolons of the god shaped as a Golden Crocodile. The beast had hinged and barbed jaws, into which maidens were flung. Then the maw was closed, and ivory fangs rended the sacrifice so that blood might trickle down the golden throat and the god be appeased. Strange powers were conferred by these offerings, evil boons granted the priests who thus sated beast-like lusts. It was small wonder that such men were driven from their temples, and that those sanctuaries of sin had been destroyed.

Such a priest had fled here, and died. Now he rested beneath, protected by the wrath of his ancient patron. This was my thought, and it did not comfort me.

Nor was I heartened by the noxious vaporing which now poured out from the opening in the rocks. It was not the reek of decay, but the almost palpable odor of unbelievable antiquity. A musty fetor, choking and biting, welled forth and coiled in strangling gusts about our throats.

Weildan bound a handkerchief over his nose and mouth, and I followed suit.

His pocket flashlight flicked on, and he led the way. His reassuring smile was drowned in the gloom as he descended the sloping rock floor which led into the interior passageway.

I followed. Let him be the first; should there be any falling rock traps, any devices of protection to assail interlopers, he would pay the penalty for temerity, not I. Besides, I could glance back at the reassuring spot of blue limned by the rocky opening.

But not for long. The way turned, wound as it descended. Soon we walked in shadows that clustered about the faint torchbeam which alone broke the nighted dimness of the tomb.

Weildan had been correct in his surmise; the place was merely a long rocky cavern leading to a hastily-burrowed inner room. It was there that we found the slabs covering the mummy-case. His face shone with triumph as he turned to me and pointed excitedly.

It was easy—much too easy, I realize now. But we suspected nothing. Even I was beginning to lose my initial qualms. After all, this was proving to be a very prosaic business; the only unnerving element was the gloom—and one would encounter such in any ordinary mining-shaft.

I lost all fear, finally. Weildan and I tilted the rock slabs to the floor, stared at the handsome mummy-case beneath. We eased it out and stood it against the wall. Eagerly the professor bent to examine the opening in the rocks which had held the sarcophagus. It was empty.

"Strange!" he muttered. "No jewels! Must be in the case."

We laid the heavy wooden covering across the rocks. Then the professor went to work. He proceeded slowly, carefully, breaking the seals, the outer waxing. The design on the mummy-case was very elaborate, inlaid with gold leaf and silver patterns which highlighted the bronze patina of the painted face. There were many minute inscriptions and hieroglyphs which the archeologist did not attempt to begin deciphering.

"That can wait," he said. "We must see what lies within."

It was some time before he succeeded in removing the first covering. Several hours must have elapsed, so delicately and carefully did he proceed. The torch was beginning to lose its power; the battery ran low.

The second layer was a smaller replica of the first, save that its pictured face was more exact as to detail. It seemed to be an attempt to duplicate conscientiously the true features of the priest within.

"Made in the temple," Weildan explained. "It was carried on the flight."

We stooped over, studying the countenance in the failing light. Abruptly, yet simultaneously, we made a strange discovery. The pictured face was eyeless!

"Blind," I commented.

Weildan nodded, then stared more closely. "No," he said. "The priest was not blind, if this portraiture is correct. His eyes were *plucked out!*"

I stared into torn sockets which confirmed this gruesome truth.

Weildan pointed excitedly to a row of hieroglyphic figures which ornamented the side of the case. They showed the priest in the throes of death upon a couch. Two slaves with pincers hovered over him.

A second scene showed the slaves tearing his eyes from his

head. In a third, the slaves were depicted in the act of inserting some shining objects into the now empty sockets. The rest of the series were scenes or funeral ceremonies, with an ominous crocodile-headed figure in the background—the god Sebek.

"Extraordinary," was Weildan's comment. "Do you understand the implication of those pictures? They were made *before* the priest died. They show that he *intended* to have his eyes removed before death, and those objects inserted in their place. Why would he willingly subject himself to such torture? What are those shining things?"

"The answer must be within," I answered.

Without a word, Weildan fell to work. The second covering was removed. The torch was flickering as it died. The third covering confronted us. In almost absolute blackness the professor worked, fingers moving deftly with knife and pryer as he broke the final seals. In the yellow half-light the lid swung up, open.

We saw the mummy.

A wave of vapor rose out of the case—a terrific odor of spice and gases which penetrated the handkerchiefs bound round nose and throat. The preservative power of those gaseous emanations was evidently enormous, for the mummy was not wrapped or shrouded. A naked, shriveled brown body lay before us, in a surprising state of preservation. But this we saw for only an instant. After that, we riveted our attention elsewhere—upon the eyes, or the place where they had been.

Two great yellow disks burned up at us through the darkness. Not diamonds or sapphires or opals were they, or any known stone; their enormous size precluded any thought of inclusion in a common category. They were not cut or faceted, yet they blinded with their brightness—a fierce flashing stabbed our retinas like naked fire.

These were the jewels we sought—and they had been worth seeking. I stooped to remove them, but Weildan's voice restrained me.

"Don't," he warned. "We'll get them later, without harming the mummy."

I heard his voice as though from afar. I was not conscious of again standing erect. Instead I remained stooped over those flaming stones. I stared at them.

They seemed to be growing into two yellow moons. It fascinated me to watch them—all my senses seemed to focus on their beauty. And they in turn focused their fire on me, bathing my brain in heat that soothed and numbed without scorching pain. My head was on fire.

I could not look away, but I did not wish to. These jewels were fascinating.

Dimly came Weildan's voice. I half felt him tugging at my shoulder.

"Don't look." His voice was absurd in its excited tones. "They aren't—natural stones. Gifts of the gods—that's why the priest had them replaced for eyes as he died. They're hypnotic . . . that theory of resurrection. . . ."

I half realized that I brushed the man off. But those jewels commanded my senses, compelled my surrender. Hypnotic? Of course they were—I could feel that warm yellow fire flooding my blood, pulsing at my temples, stealing toward my brain. The torch was out now, I knew, and yet the whole chamber was bathed in flashing yellow radiance from those dazzling eyes. Yellow radiance? No—a glowing red; a bright scarlet luminance in which I read a message.

The jewels were *thinking!* They had mind, or rather, a will—a will that sucked my senses away even as it flooded over me—a will that made me forget body and brain alike in an effort to lose myself in the red ecstasy of their burning beauty. I wanted to drown in the fire; it was leading me out of myself, so that I felt as though I were rushing toward the jewels—into them—into something else—

And then I was free. Free, and blind in darkness. With a start I realized that I must have fainted. At least I had fallen down, for I was now lying on my back against the stone floor of the cavern. Against stone? No—against wood.

That was strange. I could feel wood. The mummy lay in wood. I could not see. The mummy was blind.

I felt my dry, scaly, leprously peeling skin.

My mouth opened. A voice—a dust-choked voice that was my

own but not my own—a voice that came from death shrieked, "Good God! *I'm in the mummy's body!*"

I heard a gasp, the sound of a falling shape striking the rocky floor. Weildan.

But what was that other rustling sound? *What wore my shape?*

That damned priest, enduring torture so that his dying eyes might hold hypnotic jewels god-given for the hope of eternal resurrection; buried with easy access to the tomb! Jeweled eyes had hypnotized me, we had changed forms, and now *he walked*.

The supreme ecstasy of horror was all that saved me. I raised myself blindly on shriveled limbs, and rotting arms clawed madly at my forehead, seeking what I knew must rest there. My dead fingers tore the jewels from my eyes.

Then I fainted.


The awakening was dreadful, for I knew not what I might find. I was afraid to be conscious of myself—of my body. But warm flesh housed my soul again, and my eyes peered through yellowed blackness. The mummy lay in its case, and it was hideous to note the empty eye-sockets staring up; the dreadful confirmation afforded by the changed positions of its scabrous limbs.

Weildan rested where he had fallen, face empurpled in death. The shock had done it, no doubt.

Near him were the sources of the yellow luminance—the evil, flaring fire of the twin jewels.

That was what saved me; tearing those monstrous instruments of transference from my temples. Without the thought of the mummy-mind behind them they evidently did not retain their permanent power. I shuddered to think of such a transference in open air, where the mummy body would immediately crumble into decay without being able to remove the jewels. Then would the soul of the priest of Sebek indeed arise to walk the earth, and resurrection be accomplished. It was a terrible thought.

I scooped up the jewels hastily and bound them into my handkerchief. Then I left, leaving Weildan and the mummy as they lay; groping my way to the surface with the aid of illumination afforded me by matches.

It was very good to see the nighted skies of Egypt, for dusk had fallen by this time.

When I saw this *clean* dark, the full nightmare force of my recent experience in the evil blackness of that tomb struck me anew, and I shrieked wildly as I ran across the sand toward the little tent that stood before the opening.

There was whisky in the saddle-packs; I brought it out, and thanked heaven for the oil lamp I uncovered. I must have been delirious for a while, I fancy. I put a mirror up on the tent wall, and stared into it for a full three minutes to reassure myself as to identity. Then I brought out the portable typewriter and set it up on the table slab.

It was only then that I realized my subconscious intention to set down the truth. For awhile I debated with myself—but sleep was impossible that evening, nor did I intend to return across the desert by night. At last, some elements of composure returned.

I typed this screed.


Now, then, the tale is told. I have returned to my tent to type these lines, and tomorrow I shall leave Egypt for ever behind me—leave that tomb, after sealing it again so that no one shall ever find the accursed entrance to those subterranean halls of horror.

As I write, I am grateful for the light which drives away the memory of noisome darkness and shadowed sound; grateful, too, for the mirror's reassuring image that erases the thought of that terrifying moment when the jeweled eyes of Sebek's priest stared out at me and I *changed*. Thank God I clawed them out in time!

I have a theory about those jewels—they were a definite trap. It is ghastly to think of the hypnosis of a dying brain three thousand years ago; hypnosis willing the urge to live as the suffering priest's eyes were torn out and the jewels placed in the sockets. Then the mind held but one thought—to live, and usurp flesh again. The dying thought, transmitted and held by the jewels, was retained by them through the centuries until the eyes of a discoverer would meet them. Then the thought would flash out, from the dead, rotted brain to the living jewels—the jewels that hypnotized the gazer and forced him into that terrible exchange of personality. The dead priest would assume man's form, and the man's consciousness be forced into the mummy's body. A demoniacally clever scheme—and to think that *I* came near to being that man!

I have the jewels; must examine them. Perhaps the museum authorities at Cairo can classify them; at any rate they're valuable enough. But Weildan's dead; I must never speak of the tomb— how can I explain the matter? Those two stones are so curious that they are bound to cause comment. There is something extraordinary about them, though poor Weildan's tale of the god bestowing them is too utterly preposterous. Still, that color change is most unusual; and the life, the hypnotic glow within them!

I have just made a startling discovery. I unwrapped the gems from my handkerchief just now and looked at them. They seem to be still alive!

Their glow is unchanged—they shine as luminously here under the electric torch as they did in the darkness; as they did in the ruined sockets of that shriveled mummy. Yellow they are, and looking at them I receive that same intuitive prescience of inner, alien life. Yellow? No—now they are reddening—coming to a point. I should not look; it's too reminiscent of that other time. But they are, they must be, hypnotic.

Deep red now, flaming furiously. Watching them I feel warmed, bathed in fire that does not burn so much as it caresses. I don't mind now; it's a pleasant sensation. No need to look away.

No need—unless . . . *Do those jewels retain their power even when they are not in the sockets of the mummy's eyes?*

I feel it again—they must—I don't want to go back into the body of the mummy—I cannot remove the stones and return to my own form now—removing them imprisoned the thought in the jewels.

I must look away. I can type, I can think—but those eyes before me, they swell and grow . . . look away.

I cannot! Redder—redder—I must fight them, keep from going under. Red thought now; I feel nothing—must fight. . . .

I can look away now. I've beaten the jewels. I'm all right.

I can look away—*but I cannot see.* I've gone blind! Blind—the jewels are gone from the sockets—*the mummy is blind.*

What has happened to me? I am sitting in the dark, typing blind. Blind, like the mummy! I feel as though something has happened; it's strange. My body seems lighter.

I know now.

I'm in the body of the mummy. I know it. The jewels—the thought they held—*and now, what is rising to walk from that open tomb?*

It is walking into the world of men. It will wear my body, and it will seek blood and prey for sacrifice in its rejoicing at resurrection.

And I am blind. Blind—and *crumbling!*

The air—it's causing disintegration. Vital organs intact, Weildan said, but I cannot breathe. I can't see. Must type—warn. Whoever sees this must know the truth. Warn.

Body going fast. Can't rise now. Cursed Egyptian magic. Those jewels! Someone must kill thing from the tomb.

Fingers—so hard to strike keys. Don't work properly. Air getting them. Brittle. Blind fumble. Slower. Must warn. Hard to pull carriage back.

Can't strike higher case letters anymore, can't capitalize, fingers going fast, crumbling away in air. in mummy now no air. crumbling to bits. dust fingers going must warn against thing magic sebek fingers grope stumps almost gone hard to strike.

damned sebek sebek sebek mind all dust sebek sebe seb seb seb se s sssssss s s s. . . .

# One Way to Mars

JOE GIBSON was higher than hell and he didn't know where he was and he didn't care as long as the bar was in front of him and he was laughing and somebody was singing in a sad voice very far away and he said sure he'd have another one and then—

There was this character in the brown overcoat.

He was an odd little whack and he kept his pockets and his collar turned up and his hat-brim pulled down low like an extra in a gangster movie.

The whack was talking to him but it took a minute before the words reached him and made sense.

"Trouble with you, friend, you need a little vacation," said the whack. "Sort of get away from it all."

"Sure, sure," said Gibson, trying to find his glass. It was lost down there somewhere in the fog.

"I've been watching you, friend," said the whack. "Said to myself, there's a man with trouble. There's a man who needs to get out of all this. You look lost, friend."

"Sure," said Gibson. "Sure. I'm a lost soul. Will you have a drink or kindly get the hell out of here?"

The little whack didn't pay any attention. He went right on talking in an earnest voice. A Dutch uncle.

"I'm with the Ace Travel Bureau, Buddy. How'd you like to buy a ticket?"

"Where to?" asked Gibson, as if he gave a damn.

The whack in the brown overcoat shrugged.

"How about a ticket to Mars?" he asked.

Gibson let that one sink in for a minute. Then he grinned.

"Mars, eh? How much'll it cost me?"

"Oh, I don't know. Make it cheap for you. Let's say $2.88."

"$2.88 to Mars? Sounds very reasonable." Gibson paused. "Is this a round trip or just one way?"

The whack coughed apologetically.

"Uh—one way. You see, we haven't been able to figure out how to make a return trip yet."

"Bet you don't sell many tickets," said Gibson.

"We have our customers," said the character in the overcoat. "You interested?"

"I don't think so." Gibson found the glass, drew it up through the fog and swallowed the scotch with a shudder.

"You will be interested some other time, perhaps?" coaxed the whack.

"Listen, you—" said Gibson, suddenly.

"I've had you on my list for quite a while, friend," the whack mumbled, not noticing how Gibson's fist closed around the glass in his hand. "I know we'll do business sooner or later."

"How about right now?" said Gibson, softly.

He drew his hand back, intending to smash the whack in the face. He was set for it, his body began to pivot, and he braced himself for the moment when the blow would land solid, hard.

And then he followed his fist and the fist shot out, out past the stars and into the darkness beyond. Joe Gibson went with it and fell through the darkness as it tunnelled down . . . deep down . . .

"Jeez! what a beaut you had last night," said Maxie, stirring the cup before he placed it to Joe Gibson's lips. "Were you stinko—but completely."

"Shut up," said Gibson.

"The face on the bar room floor. Out cold," said Maxie, forcing the contents of the cup down Gibson's unwilling throat.

"Forget it," and Gibson, as soon as he could talk.

Maxie shrugged.

"OK, pal," he said. "I'll forget it. You're riding high. I line you up a five hundred a week deal with the hottest name combo in the business and what do you do? Go out and plaster yourself over half the brass rails in town and pass out in front of the guy who does the pillar for *Billboard*. You tell me to forget it. So I'm willing to forget everything—and that includes you."

Gibson sat up in bed. He moved very quickly for a man with a hangover.

"No, Maxie," he said. "I didn't mean it. Honest I didn't. I'm sorry. And I never would of socked the guy if he hadn't gone and cracked wise about this Mars stuff. I'm just standing and minding my own business when he ups with his wise lip about a trip. So I let him have it and went out on my face."

Maxie stared at him.

"I saw it happen, Joe," he murmured. "You're standing at the bar with nobody within ten feet of you on either side. You start mumbling to yourself, and then you turn around and haul off and go down for the count. Hitting air."

"But the whack in the brown overcoat—" Gibson began.

"I didn't see any whack in a brown overcoat," said Maxie, slowly. "All I see is a whack named Joe Gibson doing a nose-dive with a snootful."

Gibson sighed. "That's how it was?"

"That's how it was."

"I had the snakes," Joe Gibson shuddered.

Maxie sat down on the bed.

"Remember the old days, Joe?" he asked. "You were a punk from K.C. when I picked you out of the Rialto pit. Playing non-union dates at stags. I spotted you, got you the bookings. Made you work. Brought out your style."

"Where's your violin?" asked Gibson. "You need soft music for this line."

"I'm not handing you a line," said Maxie. "I'm just telling you."

"What you telling me?" Joe Gibson sat straight up and brushed Maxie's hand off his shoulder. "So all right. You picked me up in the gutter and you made a big horn out of me. Not a side man, a big horn. Big enough for Goodman, Shaw, Miller, anybody. Like hell you did! It's me, Joe Gibson—I'm the guy who blows his heart out through the tube. You know a good thing when you see it, so all right, you build me up. But you get your ten per cent out of it, don't you? I'm the musician. You're just the flesh peddler."

Maxie didn't move. His smile was low and sad.

"It's not that, Joe," he sighed. "I don't want the credit. You were a good kid. You worked hard. But not any more."

He rose. "I don't figure it," he said. "First there's the lush act you pulled in Scranton, when you got stinko on the stand. And the way you run out on that combo I set for the Rainbow Room, almost. And the time I hauled you out of the jam in Chi when you didn't show for the Decca recordings. Between that wrongo babe of yours and the rotgut you're getting a pretty good reputation for yourself, huh? Joe Gibson, one of the best boys on trumpet in the business. But don't buy him! Because he's also one of the best boys on blondes and bourbon."

Joe Gibson was sitting almost bent double. His head hung in his lap and he sobbed.

"Awright," said Maxie. "I don't know what's got into you. I don't know what you're scared of. Maybe you'll snap out of it all of a sudden. Don't make me promises, though. I'm gonna see what I can do. Maybe I can square that booking. The rest is up to you. Get some rest. Call you tomorrow."

Maxie went out.

Joe Gibson slid back under the covers. His face gradually stopped twitching. He prepared to sleep.

The phone rang.

Joe Gibson slid one hand over to the bedside cradle phone.

"Hello," said a familiar voice. Gibson couldn't place it so he grunted softly.

"I was just wondering," said the voice, "about our little talk last night. Made up your mind yet about that trip to Mars?"

Joe Gibson slammed the receiver down with a bang. His head disappeared under the covers and he lay shuddering and sobbing for a long time.

Opening night was solid.

It had to be. The week before it was just pure hell. Maxie had worked like a dog sewing the contract up again. Joe Gibson sweated the alcohol out of his system in rehearsal.

Now he sat on the bandstand waiting for the downbeat and he had the trumpet poised in his lap. He knew it was all right.

There was just one thing wrong. His eyes. Joe Gibson's eyes hurt him. They hurt him because of all the squinting he'd done for the past week. Squinting at faces in crowds, faces he saw from bus tops or through windows.

Joe Gibson was looking for somebody. A little whack in a

brown overcoat. He was afraid of seeing him. And somehow he was more afraid because he *didn't* see him.

Now he gazed down at the dim dance floor, blinded by the harsh spot from overhead, and he squinted again.

So his eyes hurt, and all the time he kept kidding himself that it was all right, he was all right, this was just another opening—

But he prayed for the moment when he'd put the horn to his lips, and blow out all the fear and the worry, blow out the thought of squinting and the thoughts that lay behind the squinting.

The hands holding the trumpet trembled and little beads of sweat dropped along the sides of the horn.

One last hasty glimpse of the tables bordering the dance floor. No brown overcoat.

Downbeat.

Joe Gibson raised his horn.

Then it *was* all right for sure.

The crowd was dancing. Joe Gibson didn't even bother to look for the whack any more. His eyes were closed. He was out of this world. Riding for the stars on a trumpet, sweeping up with a boogie beat.

It was hot, solid; something to hang onto. He twisted each note, reluctant to let it go. He wanted a solo ride, wanted to play his horn, keep his eyes closed, keep his brain closed to everything except the sending sound. Out of this world.

He was all right at last. Completely grooved through each number until intermission.

Then Joe Gibson sat back after the signature and realized for the first time that his shirt and dickey were wringing wet and his new tux was ripped under the left arm. He had been too solid to notice. And now the other boys were leaving the stand for a smoke and the crowd drifted off the dance floor.

Joe Gibson got up. He saw Maxie waiting for him over behind the bandstand. He tucked his horn into the case and stood up straight, took a quick stride to the steps behind the stand.

He glanced out at the deserted floor. The deserted floor that was not *quite* deserted.

A brown blur spun out there beyond the glare of the lights. A solitary figure weaved into a solo dance of its own. And the figure whirled up to the platform in a strutting glide, and Joe Gibson saw the face under the pulled-down hat brim and then he heard the words rustle up.

"Enjoyed your playing. You're almost ready for your Mars trip now, I believe."

Joe Gibson cleared the bandstand in a leap. He wasn't quite fast enough. The brown overcoat bobbed off between the tables. Nobody seemed to notice it at all.

But almost everybody saw Joe Gibson jump from the bandstand and run screaming out of the room into the streets beyond.


Joe was all right as long as Max stayed in the room with him but then the croaker told him to step outside and he began to talk to Joe alone.

The croaker was a smooth soft-speaking guy and he seemed to know his business. Maxie said he was the best psychiatrist in the racket and Maxie knew about those things.

But now Maxie had stepped out and Joe was lying down on the couch with a light shining in his eyes, and the croaker was telling him to relax, take it easy, stop thinking and just say whatever popped into his head.

It reminded Joe too much of those gangster pictures where they give a guy the third degree. But at that it was better to lie down than to have the croaker tapping him on the knee and making him stretch out his arms with his eyes closed. That was supposed to test your reflexes, but Joe Gibson didn't gave a damn about his reflexes. He was afraid of the man in the brown overcoat. The man he couldn't catch, the man he couldn't even see on the street the night he chased him out of the café and lost his job.

Joe began to explain this to the croaker, choosing his words very carefully, because after all he didn't want this psychiatrist to think there was anything the matter with him *really.*

It wasn't as if he heard voices, or stuff like that. There was nothing wrong with him except seeing that whack.

But the croaker kept asking questions, and pretty soon he had Joe admitting all kinds of stuff—not so much admitting as remembering. Dizzy ideas he had when he was a kid. Screwy things.

Like when he used to sneak off to sit in the coal cellar after his old man had a fight with his old lady. He'd fall asleep down in the basement and dream that he wasn't in a coal cellar at all—that he wasn't really anywhere. There was no coal cellar in those dreams and no upstairs, either. No outside and no people. There was just the dark and Joe Gibson.

Joe told the croaker a lot of dizzy things like that. He could remember more and more as he lay there under the lamp. He told about getting his first horn and practicing indoors all the time so he wouldn't have to play with the gang outside.

He told about getting his first job and the way he'd run off without collecting his dough from the stick, and then he got to telling how he loved music—particularly the kind where you didn't have to read notes but just played it out of your own head and it did something to you, the way liquor did.

Then Joe realized he was getting his story pretty close to *now*, and he would have to tell about the man in the brown overcoat and he didn't want to do that, so he talked louder and faster to keep the thoughts back but it didn't work, and then he was spitting it all out and the croaker was firing questions in a very low voice, and he said, yes, he'd seen the man at the bar and no, he wasn't queer-looking and yes, he did have a face and the skin around the mouth was like crumpled tissue-paper.

Funny ... Joe didn't know he remembered about the skin around the whack's mouth until the croaker asked him.

Now it felt kind of good to get it off his chest. So he told all about it, what he said and what the guy said about the Ace Travel Bureau and the $2.88 ticket to Mars, one way only, and about the other customers the man said they got, and he told about passing out.

Then he explained about the phone call and the dance floor. Only he kept insisting to the croaker that he didn't have anything to drink this last time, and he saw the little whack in the brown overcoat just as plain, and he could hear his voice, so he wasn't nuts.

The croaker smiled and said Joe was all right and then he called Maxie back. They stood talking together for a while in the next room and Joe couldn't catch anything they said.

The croaker came in again and showed him a telephone book. It was the Classified one, and he opened it up to where the travel bureaus were and there was no Ace Travel Bureau in the list.

That made Joe feel a little better until the croaker began to ask him what he knew about the planet Mars. Then he realized what the guy was driving at, and shut up like a clam. The croaker asked him what the number 288 meant to him and Joe played dumb like a fox.

So the croaker smiled and told him to get up and he should come back in a couple days when they checked the physical tests.

Maxie told Joe to run along to the hotel alone, he'd be up in a few minutes after he settled the bill with the psychiatrist.

So Joe got up and walked out.

There was a patient in the waiting room reading a *National Geographic*, but when Joe walked through, the patient put his magazine down and Joe saw the little man in the brown overcoat.

"I've got your ticket all made out," said the whack. "You can leave today if you like."

Joe didn't say anything. He just stood there, staring down at the crinkly crumpled skin around the whack's lips and the little eyes under the shadow of his hat brim. Joe looked at the brown overcoat with the stains on it, and the big ragged moth holes along the collar.

He took a deep breath and he could smell the coat and something else—something old and stale and sour.

So Joe knew he could see and hear and smell this thing and all the while the little guy was grinning up at him and then he reached into his pocket and Joe knew he was fumbling around for his ticket to Mars.

This time Joe was ready. He jumped him in a flash, and he felt his fingers close around something and choke and choke and everything turned red and black and back to red again and somebody was screaming, way off in the distance and it was Joe screaming but he didn't know that any more because he went out cold.

When Joe Gibson woke up he was lying in bed again and he felt good. Very good.

At first he couldn't figure it out and then he remembered why. Because he'd jumped the whack, of course. He wondered if he'd killed him. He couldn't have or he would be in jail now, not in his hotel room.

Still, it was a good feeling. He wanted to celebrate.

Maxie came in. He didn't look as though he felt so good.

Joe began to tell him he was all right now, but Maxie kept mumbling something about the fit he'd thrown in the croaker's office.

Joe proved he wasn't crazy right then and there. He admitted he had thrown a fit and he didn't say anything about choking the whack in the brown overcoat.

"I think I'll get dressed and go out for a walk," Joe said.

He knew Maxie wouldn't like this, but he felt too good to care.

But Maxie didn't try to stop him. He said, "OK," and sat down on the bed and lit a cigar while Joe dressed. He stared at the carpet and frowned when Joe began to whistle.

"Joe," he said.

"Yeah?"

"You aren't gonna take a walk."

"Who says?"

"You got to take things easy."

"Sure. I am taking things easy. I'll be back early."

"No. That's not what I mean, Joe. You're going to rest up in bed. In a sanatorium."

"What the—"

"I been talking to the Doc. They're coming for you in half an hour. It's nothing to get excited about now, you'll be out again in—"

That's the way it was going to be. He understood the setup now.

Joe walked over to the bureau.

"Where are you going?" asked Maxie.

"Got to get my cigarettes. Don't worry. It's all right. I understand everything."

"After all, it's for your own good," said Maxie, still not looking at Joe.

"Of course it is," Joe said. He opened the drawer.

"No hard feelings," said Maxie.

"No hard feelings," said Joe.

He turned away from the bureau and shot Maxie twice through the stomach with the gun he'd pulled from the drawer.

Joe wasn't crazy and he'd never felt better in his life, or else he couldn't have figured it so perfect.

He went downstairs and checked out, paid his bill with the dough he found on Maxie, and grabbed a cab. If he could get over to Jersey in the supper rush, they'd never find him.

So he went to the station and got his ticket and ran for the 5:14 and made it just as the train started to pull out.

He walked down the aisle and laughed because he remembered that the little whack in the brown overcoat was dead. There was nothing to worry about now except this crowd, all these people. He wanted to get away for a while and think out his next move.

So he looked for the washroom at the end of the car and opened the door and walked in. The light wasn't working and it was dark in there, but Joe could see out the window.

It took a minute for his eyes to focus right, but then he saw what was outside. Just a big black emptiness with stars sweeping past, glaring and winking.

Then the door opened, and Joe knew it was the conductor. But the conductor was wearing a brown overcoat and his hat had a pulled-down brim. A hand reached out for Joe's ticket.

He stared at it in the light from the stars, and read his name and the price and the destination—and then there was nothing for Joe Gibson to do but stand there and wait while he rushed on and on, out of this world.

Printed in the USA
CPSIA information can be obtained
at www.ICGtesting.com
JSHW020044181024
71734JS00009B/82

9 781960 241337